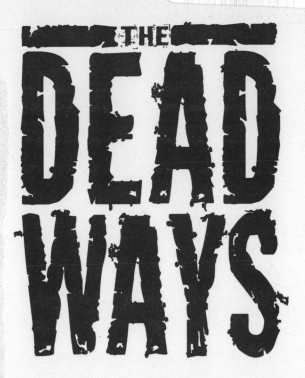

# THE DEAD WAYS

# THE DEAD WAYS

## CHRISTOPHER EDGE

Catnip

*For Chrissie, my inspiration*

CATNIP BOOKS
Published by Catnip Publishing Ltd
14 Greville Street
London EC1N 8SB

First published 2011
1 3 5 7 9 10 8 6 4 2

Text © 2011 Christopher Edge
The moral right of the author has been asserted.

A CIP catalogue record for this book is available from the
British Library.

ISBN 978-1-84647-132-2

Printed in Poland

www.catnippublishing.co.uk
www.christopheredge.co.uk

# 1

As the car sped through the busy London streets, its blacked-out windows glinting in the early summer sunshine, Scott knew that something wasn't right. From the moment the car had pulled up outside his school gates, an uneasy feeling had started to knot in his stomach and right now, as the driver swerved round a right-hand corner and straight through a red light, scattering pedestrians in front of him, the knot was being pulled tight.

Having a driver pick you up from school every day was one of the drawbacks you had to suffer when your dad worked in the heart of government.

'Security precautions,' he had said when Scott complained. 'These are dangerous times.'

It wasn't as though his dad worked for MI5 or anything interesting like that – Alex Williams was only a civil servant at the Department for Transport – but Scott's protests had still fallen on deaf ears.

'Don't worry,' his dad had joked, affectionately ruffling

Scott's tousled mop of blond hair. 'I'll make sure they send a really flash car that'll impress your mates.'

That afternoon, as Scott had waited by the gates of his exclusive private school, his slim arms folded across his athletic frame, the usual government car, a sleek Bentley Continental, had pulled up to the kerb, its black paint gleaming in the sunlight. As the window rolled down, Scott saw yet another driver, this time an unfamiliar weasel-faced man, staring out at him inquisitively.

'Scott Williams?' the man asked, scratching at the fading acne scars on his cheek.

Scott nodded. He was tall for his age and, with his piercing blue eyes and chiselled features, was often mistaken for being older than his thirteen years. Gathering up his school bag, he headed for the passenger door as it swung open to greet him. The drivers changed on almost a weekly basis. There was no time to make any kind of friendly connection as the cars shuttled him from home to school and back again. However, the last driver, an old guy named Max with snow-white hair, had lasted for nearly a fortnight and Scott now found himself disappointed by the change.

'Where's Max?' he asked as he climbed into the back.

A glass screen shielded the driver and as Scott fastened his seat belt he heard the sound of the door lock clicking shut.

'Max? Oh, he's not feeling too well today.' The driver looked over his shoulder as he pulled away from the kerb, a sinister grin spreading across his ferret-like face. 'But don't worry, we're taking care of him.'

The car roared through the city, the familiar streets rapidly giving way to other less known roads as the driver stepped on the accelerator. As they headed south of the river, Scott's unease started to fuse into an ominous sense of dread. Loosening his seat belt, he leaned forward and knocked on the glass screen.

The driver glanced back, his narrow face hardening into an expression of irritation.

'What?' he grunted.

'You're heading the wrong way,' Scott replied. He gestured with his thumb in the direction of the turning they'd just missed. 'My house is—'

'I know where your house is,' the driver cut across him. He leaned forward and pressed a button on the dashboard. Scott suddenly saw his own suspicious face reflected in the glass as the screen turned black. The driver's disembodied voice cut through the partition. 'But you won't be seeing it for a while. Now sit down and shut up.'

Scott's mind reeled in confusion. The car windows through which he'd seen the busy London streets racing by were now an impenetrable black, sealing him inside a dark cocoon. As the car picked up speed, he hammered on the blacked-out screen.

'What do you mean? Look, when my father finds out—'

'Oh, your father will find out soon enough,' the driver

interrupted. 'In fact, I'm taking you to meet somebody who's got a message for him.'

'What message?' Scott shouted through the darkened glass. 'Just tell me and take me home.'

He heard the driver's muffled laugh. 'You don't understand. *You* are the message – well, you will be when we've finished with you.'

A shiver ran down Scott's spine as the driver's chilling words hit home. He heard the echo of his father's voice – *these are dangerous times*. Trapped in the back of the car, Scott's mind raced, frantically searching for answers. Now he wished he'd paid more attention to TV news reports about terrorists, hijackings and kidnappings, although the few details he could remember made him shiver with fear.

One thing though was certain – he needed to start taking his own security precautions and get out of this situation fast. In desperation, he lunged for the door handle, trying to force it open. But the lever just clicked uselessly in his grasp before the car swerved, hurling him sideways.

'Oi, cut that out,' the driver barked, 'unless you want to end up as pavement pizza.'

Sinking back in the leather seat, Scott breathed deeply, trying to control his fear.

'Keep calm,' he murmured. 'Keep it together. You're going to get out of this. You've just got to wait for the right moment.'

The wail of a police siren in the distance momentarily raised his hopes, but then the sound quickly faded into nothingness. They weren't looking for him.

As the driver leaned on the horn, swerving the car around yet another corner, Scott suddenly remembered his mobile phone, nestling in his jacket pocket. It was too risky to try and make a call. The goon up front was probably watching him like a hawk through the one-way glass, but if he could just send a message . . .

Stealthily, he slipped the phone out from his pocket, shielding it in his hand as he feverishly tapped out a text:

*kidnapd in blk car headin sth of river call cops*

Scott quickly found his dad's number and pressed send. The progress bar on his mobile showed the message sending, but then he felt the car suddenly brake and barrel over two speed bumps in quick succession, before heading down a steep slope. His faint hopes of rescue extinguished as he saw the mobile signal disappear.

At the bottom of the ramp, he felt the car pull a sharp turn before heading down another steep slope, then another. *It must be an underground car park*, thought Scott. As the car slowly cruised to a halt, his body tensed. Whatever they had planned, it looked like he was going to be finding out soon enough.

Scott heard the driver's door open, the sound of heavy footsteps and then the low murmur of voices outside. He strained to make out what was being said:

*No problem at all . . . Does Williams know yet? . . .*
*Switch cars now, then we'll finish it . . .*

The lock clicked and Scott saw the door start to open, revealing a gloomy subterranean half-light outside. One chance. He had to make it count. Bracing himself, he kicked out with all the force he could summon. The door swung back with a satisfying crack and he heard a curse escape from the lips of the driver as he staggered backwards. Scott leapt out of the car and dashed into the shadows.

Catching a glimpse of another bulky figure lurking in the gloom, Scott saw huge bear-like arms reach out to grab him. He ducked, diving beneath their grasp, and rolled as he hit the floor, the cold concrete scraping at his skin. Scrambling to his feet Scott looked around, desperate to find a way out.

He was in a cavernous underground car park, barely lit by the rows of flickering sodium lights overhead. The place was deserted except for the car that had brought him there and a dark-blue BMW parked alongside it. Ahead of him, the soft orange glow of an exit sign pointed towards a thin sliver of light. An open door. A way out. Scott ran. Behind him he heard a barrage of curses, the men's voices thick with violence.

'Get after him!'

Scott slammed through the exit door, finding himself at the bottom of a grimy stairwell with endless grey concrete steps stretching up in front of him. He sprinted up the stairs, using the cold metal handrail to catapult himself forward as he cleared every corner. Below him, the door slammed open once more and then the relentless pounding of footsteps came echoing up the stairwell.

Level 3. Level 2. Scott's lungs were burning and his heart thudded in his mouth. Level 1. They were gaining on him but he could hear the sound of traffic on the street outside. At the top of the stairwell, a sign in white flaking paint announced Level 0.

He burst through the door, the sunlight half blinding him as he raced forward into a street alive with people. Scott stumbled out into the path of an oncoming black cab, a squeal of brakes and a blaring horn berating him as the driver leaned out of his window.

'You want to get yourself killed?' the cabbie barked.

Racing around the side of the cab, Scott piled into the back seat. 'Westminster,' he gasped, slamming the passenger door behind him. 'Please hurry.'

As the cab pulled away into the stream of traffic, the driver tutting under his breath at the youth of today, Scott risked a glance through the rear window. He saw his pursuers barge through the door of the car park and look around intently for their prey. A grim-faced scowl scarred the lean, pockmarked face of his abductor while the thick-set heavy slammed his fist into his open palm.

Scott ducked out of sight and when he dared to glance up again, the two men were heading back inside, the weasel-faced driver kicking at the swinging door in frustration as they disappeared from view.

The dark imaginings his brain had been holding at bay came out in a juddering sigh of relief. He'd got away. Suddenly, he felt the insistent buzzing of the mobile in his pocket. He looked down at the caller ID as he flipped open the phone. It was his dad.

'Scott – what's happened?' The voice at the other end of the line was frantic with worry. 'Where are you?'

'Dad – it's OK.' Scott looked out of the window as the Thames rolled into view, with Big Ben and the Houses of Parliament looming on the far side of the river. 'I'm all right. I'll be with you in five minutes.'

Thick tendrils of mist curled around the beams of his headlights as Detective Inspector Jason Dyer hunched forward over the steering wheel, his eyes straining against the gathering gloom. Ahead of him, the thick line of motorway traffic had slowed to a crawl, the red brake lights of the cars ahead squinting through the creeping fog, filling the night with eyes.

Cursing softly, Jason turned the radio on, flicking impatiently through the pre-set stations as he searched for the traffic news. Fifty miles out of London, late on a Sunday night, yet the traffic was worse than a Monday morning rat-run into the city. There must have been an accident. If he could just find out where, then maybe he'd be able to find a way around it and get back home before dawn broke.

Amongst the DJ chatter, Jason's ears snagged on a news bulletin and his finger paused above the button. The traffic report would be on next. The bland tones of the newsreader rolled from the speakers:

'*Our final story tonight – the Minister for Transport, Jerry Daedalus, speaking ahead of a ceremony to launch the government's controversial Greening of the Roads scheme, reassured drivers that the project would mean an end to congestion and pollution on Britain's road and motorway networks. Today, at eight sites across the country, bulldozers moved in to start dismantling the highways that have lain dormant since the opening of the replacement high-speed Maglev rail networks.*'

'Wonderful,' Jason muttered, staring out into the sodium-lit haze of the motorway's clogged artery of concrete and cars.

'*And now here's Stacey with the traffic.*'

'*Thanks, Peter. Well, it's good news for anyone heading back into the city after a weekend away enjoying the summer sunshine, with no reports of any delays and all routes in and out of the capital moving freely.*'

Jason angrily switched off the radio as the report ended with a jingle. He looked out disbelievingly at the gridlocked lines of cars stretching endlessly in front of him, exhaust fumes mixing with the mist to create a nearly impenetrable haze of yellow-tinged fog that gave the night a sickly pallor.

It was then that he saw them.

Shapes shifted in the mist up ahead; a thin, ragged line of upright shadows moving through the traffic. As the line of figures shambled forward, there was a fractional delay and then the cars behind them erupted in a synchronised chorus of shrieking alarms and flashing hazard lights.

Jason's first instinct was to reach for the door handle. If these jokers were the reason he was stuck in this traffic jam, then he was going to sort them out. And if anyone was stupid enough to resist arrest . . . Jason checked his jacket pocket where his police-issue taser nestled in its holster. Well, just let them try.

But as his hand closed around the door handle, he glanced again at the shadowy figures. Traffic carpeted the motorway, cars jammed nose to tail, but the dark shapes in the mist never once deviated from their onward march. Suddenly, with a heart-stopping lurch of realisation, Jason saw that the figures weren't, as he had first thought, threading a path between the lines of traffic. Instead, they were walking straight through the cars as if they weren't even there.

He felt his fingers loosen and drop from the door handle. Through a break in the fog, Jason could just make out the shape of a dark, hooded figure heading straight for his car. A cold shiver of fear ran down his spine, fixing him to his seat. It was less than ten metres away now – arms and legs moving as if human, but its feet were gliding beneath the surface of the tarmac as though it was water.

A sudden rush of adrenalin kick-started Jason into action, flushing the fear from his veins. With one hand he reached again for the door handle, while the fingers of his other hand reached inside his jacket, closing around the reassuring shape of his taser and pulling it from its holster in readiness.

Only five metres away, the looming figure seemed more substantial, more real somehow. *Good*, thought Jason, as he pulled at the door handle, *I can deal with real*. But the door refused to open, the handle clicking uselessly as the crushing weight of the fog outside pushed back, sealing him in.

Three metres now. Jason slammed his shoulder against the door, trying to force it open, but it wouldn't budge. He turned back towards the windscreen, his mouth contorting into a defiant snarl of frustration as he faced the apparition, its dark robes of mist melting into the front of the car. Ice-cold gleams of light emanated from the shadow where its face should have been.

'Come on then,' Jason yelled, brandishing his taser defiantly. 'Let's see what you're made of!'

As the figure stepped forward, a choking fog filled the car. Jason fought hard to breathe as the apparition loomed in front of him. He looked up through wreaths of mist at two pale pinpricks of light surrounded by absolute blackness. They gazed back at him with cold indifference. Then the figure enveloped him in its shadowy robes and Jason felt the pain.

Icy tendrils of mist invaded his mind. He was frozen, trapped in a world of shadows. The breath was crushed from his body as a soul-searing agony rushed through his veins.

Jason didn't know how long he lay there frozen in the darkness. Fragments of thoughts floated free from the fog of pain. Somewhere deep inside him, a memory stirred. He had been holding something before . . .

Jason fought hard to remember, but the pain was slowly devouring everything except itself. The faint shape of something held between his fingers . . . The memory stirred. His taser. He could feel the outline of it in his hand, his finger hovering over the trigger. He knew what he needed to do.

He tried to move his finger, but the freezing paralysis held him tightly in its grasp. With a superhuman effort, he tried again to send the message through the static of pain. He strained, willing himself to move just one tiny muscle. In answer, he felt his finger contract once in spasm, the trigger clicking beneath his touch. Then the taser fired.

50,000 volts of electricity surged through his body, stripping the shadows from his mind in a blinding flash of living fire. It roared through his frozen bones, his dead limbs pulsing back into life. Jason's eyes jolted open and breath flooded into his lungs like a diver resurfacing for air.

He was sitting in the driver's seat of his car, the taser held limply in his burning fingers. Through the windscreen, he could see a forest of flashing hazard lights coming into view as the fog began to clear. People were stepping out of their cars, legs buckling as they touched the tarmac, heads shaking in dazed confusion as the chorus of car alarms filled the cold night air.

Under the sodium lights of the motorway, the wail of a police siren grew louder. Jason buried his head in his hands. He was alive.

'Six months ago, the spot where I am standing was thick with exhaust fumes from the gridlocked traffic below. Tailbacks, ten, twenty, thirty miles long, spewed out carbon dioxide and caused immeasurable damage to the environment.'

Standing behind a lectern on the raised stage that had been constructed on the concourse of the new Maglev train terminal, Jerry Daedalus spread his arms wide. The sun was shining and the Minister for Transport was dressed in a pale-blue open-necked shirt, the gentle summer breeze barely ruffling his carefully coiffured hair as he gazed out over his audience. On the platform below, rows of local dignitaries, business leaders, environmentalists and journalists – the great and the good – listened in respectful silence as TV cameras captured the minister's every word.

'Now, with the opening of the high-speed Maglev rail link, those same frustrated travellers can make their journeys in a fraction of the time.'

He swept his right hand upwards, gesturing towards

the sweeping curve of track behind them. Suspended in the flawless blue sky, a floating Maglev train was waiting on the arc of polished steel, ready to whisk passengers to their destinations at speeds of over 300 miles per hour without ever touching the ground.

'This groundbreaking project is a testament to the government's commitment to the green health of the nation,' Daedalus continued, his features galvanised with passion as he gripped the edge of the lectern. 'Here, and along seven other routes across the country, every trace of the roads scarring the landscape will soon be removed. And this is just the beginning.'

He turned towards the giant video screen at the side of the stage as the strains of the hymn *Jerusalem* swelled over the sound system.

*And did those feet in ancient time*
*Walk upon England's mountains green?*

A series of images flashed across the screen – snaking queues of traffic jamming the motorways; car exhausts pumping out clouds of polluted fumes; overhead motorway signs flashing DELAYS AHEAD. Then a map of Great Britain filled the screen, the blue veins of motorway routes pulsing with congestion.

*And was Jerusalem builded here*
*Among those dark Satanic mills*

On the screen, the blue lines bisecting the country from north to south, east to west, were slowly erased and replaced by green routes – the new Maglev rail network. An image of a sleek Maglev train gliding along the raised track above a lush green landscape filled the screen as the hymn reached its crescendo.

*Till we have built Jerusalem*
*In England's green and pleasant land*

As the screen faded to black, Jerry Daedalus turned back towards his audience.

'This is our commitment to Britain – to build an environmentally friendly transport system for the twenty-first century. The Greening of the Roads is the beginning of a brighter tomorrow.'

As one, the audience erupted into spontaneous applause, rising to their feet to acclaim Daedalus's vision. At the edge of the concourse, Scott was on his feet with them, his heart thumping with pride as he clapped his hands. He knew that the words which had brought them all to their feet weren't Daedalus's own, but had come from the speech that his dad had spent countless nights crafting. As Chief Secretary at the Department for Transport, his father was tasked with making the Greening of the Roads scheme happen.

Scott remembered the passion in his father's voice when he had first told him about the project. *'Finally, we're doing the right thing and protecting the environment for your generation to enjoy.'*

As Jerry Daedalus stood there now in the sunlight, hands raised in false modesty as he soaked up the applause, Scott scanned the stage for a glimpse of his father. Though school had not yet finished for the summer, he'd begged his dad to bring him along today, desperate to see his father's dream finally realised.

He spotted his dad cloistered in the shadows at the back of the stage, flanked by two more civil servants from the department. They watched the minister step down from the lectern and pace the front of the stage. Flashes from the press cameras below captured the scene for the next day's newspapers.

Even though applause was still ringing across the gleaming concourse and ecstatic grins were spread across the faces of the audience, Scott saw that his father's own face was set in a grave expression with anxious lines etched into his brow. He couldn't understand it. This should be his dad's proudest moment, but ever since the attempted kidnapping of Scott two weeks earlier, a cloud of worry seemed to follow his every move.

Scott had answered endless questions from the police and security officers at his father's Whitehall offices, but still they had no idea who had been behind it. No answers. No arrests. Security had been stepped up and, on the surface, his dad was trying to pretend that everything was back to normal, but Scott could tell that some deeper worry was gnawing away at him.

A sudden shout from the back of the audience pulled Scott's attention away from the stage. A jowly middle-aged man brandishing a placard reading *GIVE US BACK OUR ROADS* was being bundled out of his seat by two uniformed police officers. As he was dragged away, the protester twisted his head back to the stage.

'This is all just an environmental con trick!' he yelled, angry spittle speckling his face. 'We need better roads – not toy trains that run on hot air!'

In response to the interruption, Jerry Daedalus had stepped back to the lectern, leaning over the microphone to address the man.

'If you want to crawl along at ten miles an hour and waste your time in tailbacks, I think you'll find there are still plenty of motorways left for you to drive on,' the minister announced with a wry smile. 'But for those of us who have joined the twenty-first century and want to get where we're going in style and comfort, we'll let the new Maglev trains take the strain.'

A chorus of cheers and laughter greeted the minister's remark as the protester was finally bundled off the concourse and out of view. From the lectern, Jerry Daedalus turned towards his team of civil servants, who quickly hurried to his side as he walked towards the steps leading off the stage. Below, local dignitaries and officials were lined up, waiting to greet the minister and give the project their seal of approval.

Scott tried to catch his dad's eye as he accompanied Daedalus down the steps. As his dad glanced across, Scott waved, a proud smile on his face. His dad returned the smile, but there was still a trace of those unnamed troubles lurking in his grey-blue eyes.

As Scott's father tried to shepherd the minister towards the first of the waiting dignitaries, Jerry Daedalus held his hand out to pause him.

'Wait a second, Alex,' Daedalus said, pointing out Scott by the edge of the platform. 'That's your boy over there, isn't it?'

Alex Williams nodded with a frown.

'Yes,' he replied flatly.

'Well bring him over,' the minister said, half turning towards the line of people waiting to greet him. 'Let's see what the next generation thinks about the work we're doing here.'

The middle-aged officials smiled and nodded in agreement.

With a nervous feeling pricking at the lining of his stomach, Scott sloped over to meet the minister.

'It's Scott, isn't it?' Daedalus greeted him, enveloping Scott's hand in a firm handshake. 'Your father's told me all about you.'

Dropping Scott's hand, the minister gestured expansively around the concourse, his sweeping hand taking in the elevators and boarding platforms leading up to the glinting track.

'So what do you think of all this then?'

Scott looked around the station; every surface polished steel and shining glass, like some science-fiction dream.

'I think it's amazing,' he replied simply. 'I mean, everyone's been going on about saving the environment for years – all pretending to care – but this is really doing something. Getting cars off the roads, cutting down on pollution, letting the countryside breathe again.' Scott glanced across at his dad, knowing how hard he'd worked to make all this happen. 'You're making Britain a better place for everyone.'

'You've got a chip off the old block here, Alex,' said Daedalus, a broad smile breaking across his face as he clapped Scott on the shoulder. 'I'm so pleased that you approve. And the best thing is – we're only just getting started.'

# CHAPTER ONE

*Six months later*

Quarter to eight on a Tuesday morning and the Crime Squad operations room was practically deserted; just the dregs of the night shift remained, a handful of bleary-eyed detective constables one-handedly typing up crime reports from the night just gone.

Nobody even acknowledged Jason as he slumped into his chair and surveyed the chaos of his desk. He stared at the untidy stack of papers spilling out from his in-tray and spreading across his desk, where they were eventually held at bay by a rough barricade of empty coffee cups and the remains of a half-eaten sandwich, fresh mould beginning to curl its edges. Shaking his head in disgust, Jason swept the sandwich into the rubbish bin beneath his desk.

Running his fingers through his dark-brown hair, he glanced at his watch. Morning briefing wasn't due to start for another fifteen minutes; he might be able to get at least one of these case reports off his desk first. Cracking his knuckles in preparation, Jason reached up and grabbed the topmost file from the stack of papers, then cursed as the rest of the pile slid further across his desk, demolishing the makeshift barrier of coffee cups.

Taking a deep breath, Jason deposited the coffee cups into the overflowing bin and then, clearing a space on his desk for the chosen file, flipped it open. A pile of witness statements waiting to be typed up stared back at him. He'd been lumbered with investigating a string of minor burglaries, the kind of case usually given to some wet-behind-the-ears detective constable, not a detective inspector with nearly five years' experience on the Crime Squad.

Jason shook his head in frustration, the dark shadows beneath his hazel eyes making him look older than his thirty-one years. His career had been stuck in reverse ever since he'd called for back-up that fateful night on the motorway. He tried to keep his mind from thinking about the horrors lurking in the mist, but he couldn't stop himself from remembering every humiliating detail of what had happened afterwards.

First to arrive had been a squad car of uniformed officers, bemused flickers of disbelief spreading across their faces as Jason recounted what he'd seen and how he'd managed to escape. Forced expressions of concern failed to hide their half smiles that told him that they didn't believe a word he was saying. The other drivers had retreated to their cars, lips sealed and engines running, eager to leave the scene of their nightmares behind. Why risk being arrested for drunk driving by telling some crazy story about the shadows in the fog? As the traffic cops slowly cleared the jam, Jason had driven back home that night with the sound of their mocking sniggers ringing in his ears.

When he'd reported for work the next day, Jason had found himself called into the chief super's office to be told he was suspended from duty with immediate effect. Chief Superintendent Warren had shaken his head sadly as he told Jason that maybe he'd been pushing himself too hard recently and that this break would be a good thing. But the pitying look in his eyes told Jason that really he was finished. The same embarrassed half smiles were plastered across the faces of his colleagues as they watched him clear his desk, the police grapevine already buzzing with reports of what he said he'd seen.

It was only several days later, when other reports from that night on the motorway began to leak out, that they'd started to listen. Witness statements that described an army of grey-hooded ghosts marching down the carriageway as fog swirled around them; half-human figures melting through the traffic as if it wasn't there. A terrified taxi driver recounted how he had cowered helplessly in his cab as a towering apparition loomed out of the night, arms as insubstantial as mist enveloping him in an icy embrace. A dozen similar stories, their details lost in a fog of fear and confusion, but each and every one backed up Jason's account.

Chief Superintendent Warren had had no choice. Reluctantly, he'd reinstated Jason, putting him back on duty but telling Jason's governor, Detective Chief Inspector Eddie Nicholls, the head of the Crime Squad, to keep him safely behind a desk with a stack of dead-end cases to plough through. 'Ease you back in slowly,' DCI Nicholls had said with a dismissive nod when Jason complained.

As for that night on the motorway, the authorities had managed to explain it all away. Mass hallucination was the favoured theory: terrorists seeding the thick fog with psychoactive chemicals, hoping the strange visions they induced would cause carnage on the motorway. They'd pinned the attack on one of those petrol-head protest groups that had sprung up to challenge the government's scheme to close the motorways down. Jason wasn't convinced.

'All right, you lot!'

Jason was shaken from his reverie by the sound of DCI Nicholls's bark reverberating around the operations room. He glanced up to see the governor framed in the doorway.

'Briefing room – two minutes.'

There was a shrill squeaking sound as chairs were pushed back from desks in unison and a stream of plain clothes police officers headed for the briefing room. Sighing, Jason shut the file of witness statements, pushed his chair back from the desk and followed the exodus out of the room.

The briefing room was crowded with bodies as the morning shift arranged themselves on desk corners and chairs, some still looping ties around their necks, while others gingerly sipped at cups of steaming black coffee. DCI Nicholls was waiting impatiently beside the large whiteboard that dominated the front of the room. Jason slipped into a vacant chair next to DC Skinner, the new face on the shift who'd recently transferred from a station south of the river.

'Morning,' Jason nodded briefly in acknowledgement.

Looking up, a frown of recognition clouded the young constable's face. 'Sir,' he replied with a thin-lipped scowl before shifting in his chair to face away.

Jason shook his head. He was still the toxic man as far as the rest of the Crime Squad were concerned, even to this new kid who had barely outgrown his acne.

'Quiet!' DCI Nicholls bellowed.

A sudden hush descended on the briefing room. Nicholls waited for a moment, cocking his head for the slightest sound. When he had their complete attention, he turned to the whiteboard and with a black marker pen scrawled a name in six-inch-high letters across the board:

ALEXANDER WILLIAMS

Next to this he stuck an A4 photograph showing the face of a smiling man with closely cropped dark hair peppered with grey.

The chief turned back to face his assembled officers.

'Alexander Williams. Male, forty-two years old. Divorced with sole custody of his thirteen-year-old son, Scott. Chief

Secretary at the Department for Transport. One of the top civil servants in Whitehall. He was found dead in his government office at 6:30 this morning, his throat cut from ear to ear.'

Nicholls fixed a second photograph to the whiteboard, this picture showing the same man lying prostrate on a carpeted floor. His face was twisted towards the camera in a rictus of pain, a halo of dark blood pooled around his head.

'The office door was locked from the inside. It was only when a cleaner couldn't gain access that the alarm was raised, and when security forced the door open, this is what they discovered. Uniform, who were first on the scene, found a suicide note addressed to his son – the usual stuff. The body's been sent for autopsy to confirm the time of death.'

Nicholls paused for a moment as he surveyed his officers, registering the barely hidden disappointment on the faces of a few of his gung-ho constables who thought life in the force should be a non-stop action film with extra car chases and weren't happy unless they had a juicy murder to investigate.

'I know what you're thinking,' he continued. 'This should be an open-and-shut case. Why is the governor wasting our time? Well, let's get one thing straight.' Nicholls banged his fist against the picture of the grisly crime scene, rattling the whiteboard in its frame. 'The political angle means the press are going to be all over the case. If this is a suicide, I want the evidence to be watertight. Forensics are on the scene at the moment, but we need to be seen to leave no stone unturned.'

Nicholls scanned the room, checking faces to make sure his message had been fully received.

'Uniform are trying to track down Alex Williams's son, Scott. Apparently he's away on a school trip. The ex-wife's been notified and she's travelling back from the US, where she lives with her new partner, to be with her son.

'Now you all know that the first few hours of any investigation are crucial.' Nicholls turned back to the whiteboard, marker pen in hand. 'So this is how we're going to tackle it. Dyer!'

Nicholls's bark snapped Jason to attention.

'Guv,' he replied, quickly straightening in his chair.

'I want you to head back to the crime scene. Take witness statements, interview colleagues, find out all you can about Williams. Make sure this all adds up.'

Jason nodded, barely able to contain his surprise. He'd been stuck investigating minor crimes for months now – dealing with teenage shoplifters and petty thieves – and now here was the DCI assigning him a high-profile case at the heart of Whitehall. What had he finally done right?

As Nicholls reeled off names and responsibilities, his black marker pen filling the whiteboard as he assembled the investigating team, Jason fidgeted in his chair, eager to make a start. For whatever reason, this was it. He was back in the fast lane.

'And when they opened the door, I saw him lying there . . .' The woman's voice tailed off into a whisper before she buried her tear-stained face into Jason's white handkerchief and blew her nose with a honk. 'I mean, I've seen some awful things in my life,' she continued. 'You wouldn't believe some of the messes I've had to clean up. But I've never seen anything as terrible as that.' A shiver rippled her broad shoulders. 'That poor man.'

Jason nodded his head sympathetically as he slipped his notebook back inside his jacket pocket.

'I know, Mrs Brown. I know.' He got to his feet, signalling the end of the interview and held out his hand. 'And I really appreciate you going through it all again for me.'

The cleaner took Jason's hand as she raised herself from the chair. 'Well, if you're sure you've got everything you need.' She gathered up her coat and bag before offering Jason his handkerchief back.

He looked down at the crumpled square of cloth, the white handkerchief now distinctly grey in places. 'Don't worry – you keep hold of it.'

As Mrs Brown bustled out of the wood-panelled outer office, tutting as she waited for the officer at the entrance to lift the police tape and let her past, Jason turned back towards the inner office to take a look at the crime scene. Through the open door he could see Forensics packing away their kit. Every scrap of evidence, from the fibres in the carpet to the prints on the computer keyboard, had been collected in clear Ziploc bags, each and every one precisely labelled. Apart from a single bloody reminder, a dark wine-coloured stain on the carpet, there was nothing to suggest a man had been found dead in this room less than three hours ago. But was it by his own hand or was something else at play here?

'We're finished – it's all yours.'

Jason nodded in thanks as the plastic-suited forensics team slowly trooped out of the office, their arms filled with boxes of evidence. Stepping for the first time into the inner sanctum, he carefully appraised the scene.

The room was lit by a single chandelier and, in the absence of any windows, dark oak bookshelves lined the walls, their shelves filled with thick leather-bound volumes. Jason ran his finger along one of the shelves, reading the titles as he went – *Hansard and Sons: Catalogue of Parliamentary Papers, 1696–1834; House of Commons: Sessional Papers of the Eighteenth Century*. He stifled a yawn.

The far wall of the office was dominated by an imposing desk, its polished walnut surface free from the papers and coffee cups that blighted Jason's own. In one corner, a silver anglepoise lamp was positioned above a single red box file. Jason ran his finger along the edge of the desk, feeling the polished grain beneath his finger. Everything was so ordered. He sank into Alex Williams's leather chair and tried to put himself into the man's mind. What would drive someone like him to take their own life? Jason had read the suicide note – three cryptic sentences that raised more questions than answers:

*Things are getting worse and I don't know what else I can do. I've got to end it all now. Remember the good times and keep the memories safe.*

The chief had dismissed it as the usual stuff, but to Jason something unsettling lurked in these words.

His eyes focused on the red box in front of him. The embossed seal on the lid read *Property of Her Majesty's Government*. Even forensics hadn't been able to carry this off with the rest of their evidence, although Jason knew that they would have been through its contents with meticulous precision. He flipped open the file.

Inside was a stack of official-looking documents, the topmost reading *Cabinet papers – ministers' eyes only*. Jason glanced around him. Leave no stone unturned, the chief had said. Well, he needed to find out what exactly Williams had been working on.

He flicked through the papers, painstakingly scanning the impenetrable sentences for any sign of Williams's presence in the dense lines of text. At the very bottom of the red box lay a slim report entitled *Implementation of the Greening of the Roads project*. With a tired sigh of resignation, Jason began to flick through its pages, eyes half glazing over as he read through endless statistics about environmental impacts, economic targets and ecological renewal rates.

*All this nonsense*, thought Jason, *just so they can dig up a few roads and leave the rest of us stuck in ten-mile tailbacks.*

He was just about to discard the report back to the depths of the red box when his eye snagged on a glimmer of green ink amidst the monochrome paragraphs. In the margin of one of the pages was a single scribbled comment: *The Dead Ways*.

Jason stared hard at the page then pulled a copy of Williams's suicide note from his jacket pocket. There was no mistake. The same hand that had written it had scrawled these three words.

Jason reread the report page, paying close attention to the paragraph next to the scrawled comment. This section of the report described the first stage of motorway demolition, the routes and roads earmarked for environmental renewal – the A303, the M6, the A14, the M23, and many more roads stretching across the country. Jason turned the page to see a map of the United Kingdom, the highlighted routes reaching from north to south, east to west, in the shape of a twisted upside-down cross, every corner of the country touched by the scheme.

So Williams had been working on the Greening of the Roads project. The crowning jewel in the government's transport policy – the so-called end to congestion and pollution. He knew the spiel backwards from the slick TV ads the government had produced to neutralise the howls of protest from outraged car drivers and road haulage firms.

A shadowy sense of unease niggled at the corners of Jason's mind. He recognised the sensation. Instinct, he used to call it until DCI Nicholls had told him that instinct was as much use in the Crime Squad as a pair of chocolate handcuffs. He'd learned to keep his mouth shut after that, but he still trusted the nagging sensation that itched at the back of his skull whenever he turned up an important clue.

There was a connection here. Something that he was missing. Jason's train of thought was derailed by the sound of a raised voice in the corridor outside.

'I don't care if this is a crime scene,' the voice pronounced in frosty tones that sounded like the first smattering of snowflakes preceding an avalanche. 'I'm a minister of Her Majesty's Government and this is my department.'

Jason heard a muttered apology followed by the sound of police tape being pulled to one side. He looked at the ministerial red box open on the desk in front of him and shoved the report back inside, quickly shovelling the stack of briefing papers on top of it and then snapping the lid shut just as the owner of the voice entered the room.

'And what on earth are you doing in here?'

Jason rose from his chair and stepped out from behind the desk, holding out his hand to greet the minister whose daytime-TV friendly features were masked by a scowl of irritation.

'I'm Detective Inspector Dyer, sir, and I'm investigating Alexander Williams's death.' He sized up the Saville Row suit and expensive silk tie and even though he already recognised the face, Jason asked the question anyway in order to maximise the irritation. 'And you are?'

The minister looked down at Jason's open hand and, with a politician's smile spreading across his face, shook it firmly.

'Jerry Daedalus,' he replied. 'Minister for Transport.' He looked around the office as if taking in his surroundings for the first time. 'So it's true then? I heard the news this morning and came as quickly as I could. Poor Alex. What a waste.'

'You knew Alexander Williams well then, sir?' Jason asked.

'Of course I knew him well,' the minister replied. 'He was the Chief Secretary here at the ministry, my right-hand man.' Jerry Daedalus shook his head sadly. 'I should have seen this coming. I should have tried to help him.'

Jason was onto the revelation like a terrier digging for a bone.

'Should have seen what coming, sir?'

'His suicide, Inspector,' the minister replied bluntly. 'Alex had been working under considerable pressure for some time – the whole department has – to draft and implement my government's new transport plan. You've heard of the Greening of the Roads project?'

Jason nodded, his thoughts flicking back to the report inside the ministerial red box.

Daedalus smiled proudly. 'The department's flagship policy. Now as a police officer I needn't tell you about the outside pressures associated with this project – you'll be all too aware of the security threat.'

Jason gave a tight little nod. Everyone in the force was aware of the security threat – the crackpot protesters who were trying to sabotage the new Maglev rail network.

'Quite. Anyway,' Daedalus continued, 'Alex believed in the project passionately, but he took too much onto his own shoulders.' The minister moved his hand to his mouth as though the memory was too painful to recall. 'I tried to get him to delegate more . . .' His voice tailed into nothingness as he stared down at the dark circular stain tainting the cream carpet.

Daedalus stood there for a moment, his eyes closed and his hands clasped in front of him as if in prayer. Jason fidgeted awkwardly at the edge of the silence, waiting for the opportunity to ask his next question.

The minister's eyes snapped back open and he looked down at his wristwatch. 'Now if that's all, Detective Inspector Dyer, I'm due to make a statement to the House in fifteen minutes' time and these,' he reached down to pick up the ministerial file, 'are my briefing papers.' Tucking the red box under his arm, Daedalus turned to leave. 'If there's anything else that your people need, just call my office.'

'There is just one more thing,' said Jason, momentarily wrong-footed by the minister's sudden switch of mood.

He wanted to ask Daedalus about the Dead Ways and see if he could shed some light on Williams's cryptic note, but that same nagging instinct stayed the words on his lips. Instead, he asked, 'Why now, do you think? I mean, wasn't this Roads project coming to an end? What sent Alex Williams over the edge?'

Daedalus turned around, a flicker of irritation evident under his smooth features.

'I really wouldn't like to speculate,' he replied briskly. 'Who can say what's going on in another man's mind.' He fixed Jason with a cold-eyed stare. 'Don't you agree, Inspector?'

Jason shifted uncomfortably under the politician's penetrating gaze. The sudden buzzing of his mobile phone saved him from having to answer. Raising an apologetic hand, he turned away from Daedalus and, reaching inside his jacket, took out his mobile and glanced at the caller ID. Headquarters.

'Dyer.'

He listened to the voice at the other end of the line and then with a terse nod replied, 'I'll be right there.'

Pocketing his phone, Jason turned back to the minister. 'Thanks again for all your help, sir. If we do need anything else, we'll be in touch.'

'Has something more pressing come up?' Daedalus asked, his face carefully crafted into a concerned frown.

'You could say that, sir,' Jason replied. 'I've got to go and tell Scott Williams that his father is dead.'

# CHAPTER TWO

Scott stared down at the desk in front of him, the grain of the wood drifting randomly in front of his eyes as he tried to make sense of it all. The police officer, DI Jason Dyer, pushed a cup of steaming tea towards him.

'Here.' He gestured towards the mug. 'Drink this.'

Unthinking, Scott picked up the tea and lifted it to his lips, the tasteless grey liquid washing down his throat, his fingers numb to the heat of the cup in his hands. His whole body – even his mind – was numbed to the truth.

They hadn't let him see his father's body, tried to convince him it would be too upsetting. But without any proof that this was real, Scott couldn't bring himself to feel what he should be feeling. He hadn't cried a single tear; he just felt empty inside. Maybe this was all just a stupid mistake – they'd got the wrong person. Any moment now, his dad was going to walk through that door.

'Had your dad been acting out of character recently?'

The detective's question jerked Scott back to the present. He stared at the cup in his hands as though it was the first time he had seen it.

'What?'

'Had your dad been acting strangely?' DI Dyer repeated the question. 'Maybe he'd been under pressure at work?'

Scott shook his head.

'No, he's been busy at work – but nothing out of the ordinary.' As Scott sat there, the detective's question seemed to jar and loop in his brain: *Had your dad* . . . He was talking about him in the past tense.

'What happened?' Scott's voice cracked for the first time. DI Dyer shook his head.

'It's really too early to say, but I'm afraid that one theory we're looking at is suicide.'

The prim social worker sitting beside Scott pulled a handkerchief out of her handbag and tried to press it into his hand, but he pushed it away angrily.

'That doesn't make any sense,' he replied, struggling to keep his emotions under control. 'Dad was fine when I left. He was going to take some time off work soon – we were planning a trip.' His words trailed to a mumble. 'He just wouldn't kill himself.'

As Jason was about to ask another question, the social worker flashed him a warning stare.

'Don't you think that's enough, Inspector?' She closed her handbag with a snap. 'Can't you tell the boy's upset?'

But now that Scott had let the emotions in, more memories stirred, providing the answers to the questions the policeman had been asking.

'This can't be suicide.' Scott's words rushed out in a sudden scramble. 'Six months ago, someone tried to kidnap me. They said they wanted to send a message to my father. *They* must have done this – *they've* murdered him.'

His last words came in a choking sob.

Jason's mind whirred. A kidnapping? The file had said nothing about this.

'Wait a minute – did you report this?'

Scott nodded. 'We spoke to the police at the ministry where my dad works. They said it was all under control.' He banged his fists down in frustration on the table. 'But it can't have been – not if this has happened.'

The social worker flashed Jason another warning stare.

'I really think that Scott needs to rest. The boy's just lost his father. Surely there will be time for questions later.'

'No – I want to speak.' Scott's voice cracked again as he angrily wiped his hand beneath his eyes, trying to staunch the tears that lurked there. 'I want to help you find who killed my dad.'

Jason looked at Scott. The boy's shoulders shuddered as he fought to keep his grief from overwhelming him, but a look of fierce determination stared out from his bloodshot eyes. Then Jason's gaze shifted to the sour-faced social worker sitting next to Scott, her tight-lipped frown showing that she thought he'd pushed Scott too far.

'I know you do,' Jason told Scott, 'and I want to make sense of everything too, but Mrs . . .' He faltered as he tried to remember the social worker's name.

'Mrs Grant,' she snapped.

Jason smiled apologetically. 'Mrs Grant's right,' he continued. 'There will be time to answer questions later.' He reached into his pocket and pressed his card into Scott's palm. 'Give me a call tomorrow and we can discuss things then. It'll give you more time to remember.'

Scott looked down at the card. The Metropolitan Police logo sat next to the name Detective Inspector Jason Dyer, Westminster CID – Crime Squad and a mobile phone number.

He closed his fingers around the card as Mrs Grant looked on disapprovingly.

'Thanks. I will.'

⠿

Scott sat alone in the darkness. He was curled up in the old armchair in the corner of his father's study. Downstairs, he could hear the social worker clattering about in the kitchen, clearing away the food he hadn't touched. His mum's flight had been delayed out of Miami and she wasn't due in until late tomorrow. He'd spoken to her briefly on a scratchy phone line across the Atlantic, desperately wishing she was here with him now.

As the kitchen finally fell quiet, Scott heard the TV in the lounge being switched on and the late evening news started to float up the stairs. *'And finally, an undertaker in Brighton received quite a shock today when—'* The click of the living-room door closing cut off the newsreader's voice. Scott flicked on the lamp and, getting out of the chair, looked around his father's study.

When he was younger, he used to come in here while his dad was working, tapping away at his laptop surrounded by government papers. He'd noisily flick through the books on the shelves that lined the far wall until his father switched off his computer and turned to him with a smile to say, *'OK, I get the message. What shall we do now?'* Then the two of them would either head down to the park for a kickabout, go and catch a film, or just sit there and talk – his dad listening intently as Scott poured out stories about the latest events at school.

Now his father's chair sat empty, and behind the desk it was piled high with stacks of papers and folders. At the top of one pile a black stone paperweight, a chunk of demolished motorway, a souvenir from his father's beloved Greening of the Roads project, held the papers in place. Underneath the paperweight, Scott noticed a slender rectangular package addressed to his father. The package was unopened. It must have arrived in the post that morning and been left there by the cleaner. Too late now to ever reach his dad. Scott was about to open it when he caught sight of the framed photograph next to it on the corner of his father's desk.

The picture had been taken on his birthday earlier that year – his dad had arranged a party for Scott and his friends on the London Eye. In the photograph his dad was standing with his arm around Scott, smiles beaming from both their faces as the lights of the city stretched out majestically behind them.

Picking up the picture, Scott retreated to the safety of the old armchair. This was the last photograph he had of his dad. For the first time since he'd heard the news, something broke inside Scott as he realised he'd never see his father's face again. Without warning, tears welled in his eyes. He heard footsteps coming up the stairs and quickly dimmed the lamp, not wanting the social worker to see him like this. As he waited in the darkness, a sudden tiredness crept over him and as the footsteps retreated, he closed his eyes and surrendered to a fitful sleep.

Scott's dreams were dark and hunted. His mind stumbled through the fog of sleep, searching for answers. He saw snatched glimpses of his father's face hidden in the shadows, but they always faded out of sight.

He awoke suddenly into an inky blackness. The faint moonlight from the open window slowly reminded him that he was still curled up in the armchair in his father's study. As his eyes adjusted to the darkness, Scott saw a beam of torchlight and the figure of a man hunched over his father's desk. The word escaped from Scott's lips before he had a chance to realise its impossibility:

'Dad?'

At the sound of Scott's voice, the figure turned and, seeing Scott rising from the chair, let out an oath of surprise. As Scott stepped forward, confusion still crowding his half-asleep mind, the man launched himself at him with a growl of recognition. The torch in the intruder's hand struck Scott a glancing blow, sending him crashing into the bookshelves. He fell to the floor, books cascading down around him as the ringing pain in his head roused him into sudden waking. This was no dream.

Scott scrambled to his feet, desperately searching for an escape route in the darkness. Half glimpsing a shape in front of him, he struck out blindly, but his hands only found the frame of a mirror, sweeping it from the wall in his confusion and sending it crashing to the floor where it shattered into countless pieces. Scott let out a desperate yell for help.

Then the intruder was on him, fingers closing around his throat, choking Scott's cry into sudden silence. Scott staggered backwards, lurching into his father's desk as he struggled to free himself, papers scattering in the melee. The dark silhouette of a face in front of him snarled with satisfaction as long, powerful fingers tightened their grip on his windpipe. Scott could feel the blood pounding in his brain as he struggled in vain to break the death grip. The man was too strong. He was going to kill him.

Scott's head was slammed backwards, cracking with sickening force against his father's desk. Once. Twice. Three times. He could feel a wetness seeping into his eyes, a dull red haze filling his vision. Blood. Then the hands wrapped themselves around his neck once more, squeezing with deadly intent. Scott could feel himself teetering on the edge of unconsciousness and knew that if he slipped, he wouldn't wake again.

His fingers scrabbled desperately amongst the debris on his father's desk and his hand closed around the paperweight. The cool stone was strangely soothing in his grasp. The throttling grip around his throat narrowed, and Scott felt himself falling forwards into the darkness of the abyss. He had to save himself. The fingers squeezed tighter. With sheer force of will, Scott brought his hand upwards, the paperweight still in his fingers, even as oblivion dragged him down. As he slipped towards unconsciousness, he felt the tremor of a distant impact. Moments later, the fingers around his throat loosened as the intruder staggered backwards and fell to the floor.

Scott rubbed his neck, his lungs burning as his breath came in ragged, juddering gasps. Alone in the darkness, he called out again for help, his voice a shredded whisper, but still nobody came. Picking himself up from the desk, Scott staggered to the door and reached for the light switch with shaking hands. As light flooded the room, he looked down in horror at the body lying on the floor, the bulky black bomber jacket and combats motionless amidst the chaos of scattered books and broken glass.

Numbed, Scott skirted around the figure, almost clinging to the wall. He couldn't have killed him. He'd only been trying to protect himself. Then he saw the deadly shard of mirror jutting from the side of the man's head, a dark halo of blood pooling beneath it. As the man's face edged into view, Scott gasped in surprise. Staring back at him with cold, dead eyes, a thin line of blood trickling from his mouth, was the narrow, weasel-like face of a man he'd last seen six months ago. The man who'd tried to kidnap him.

Scott turned away, suddenly retching as a wave of nausea caught hold of him. Choking back the bitter taste of bile, he slumped against the wall. This wasn't happening. This couldn't be real.

He didn't know how long he sat there staring at the body, trapped in a waking nightmare. As the dull grey edges of dawn began to stain the sky, Scott remembered the words of the police officer, DI Dyer: *Give me a call tomorrow and we can discuss things then.* Picking out the card from his pocket with shaking fingers, Scott tapped the number into his mobile.

The phone rang twice and then a bleary voice answered with a hacking cough.

'Dyer.'

'It's me – Scott Williams,' Scott stammered. He paused, struggling to find words that could make sense of the madness. 'Someone just tried to kill me.'

# CHAPTER THREE

DI Dyer looked down at the corpse sprawled on the floor of the study. The face was twisted away from him, but he could see the thin, spear-like sliver of mirrored glass protruding from the wound at the side of the skull. He turned back to Scott, who was standing mutely beside him.

'You did this?'

Scott shook his head, forcing himself to look at the body again. *You did this.* The words echoed around his head.

'What happened then?' Dyer edged his way around the corpse, taking care not to disturb the scene. 'Where's the social worker who's staying here with you?'

'I don't know,' Scott replied. 'I fell asleep in the chair and when I woke up, someone was in the room.' His voice tightened at the memory of the man's hands around his throat. 'He was trying to strangle me. I was trying to fight him off. The mirror smashed. He fell . . .' His voice tailed away as his eyes were drawn again to the man's cold dead eyes.

'It's the man I was telling you about.' Scott forced himself to speak. 'The one who tried to kidnap me. But he wasn't alone then, there was someone else. They must be the ones who killed my father and now they're after me.' He could feel the panic rising in his chest and he fought to keep his fear under control.

Jason crouched down beside the corpse to get a better look at the man's face, then shook his head as he struggled to take in the evidence with his own eyes. He'd seen this face, its features now stiffening, staring back at him less than twenty-four hours earlier. It was Detective Constable Skinner, the new cop on the shift.

'This can't be right,' he murmured.

Skinner wasn't even on the case. And this story about him breaking in and attacking the boy – it didn't make any sense.

'Why not?' Scott gestured at the angry red marks staining the skin around his neck. 'He tried to strangle me.'

Dyer looked up at Scott, whose hair was matted with dried blood, and then stared uncomprehendingly back at DC Skinner's lifeless face. 'Because he's a policeman,' he replied.

'What?'

Scott's mind raced as he watched Jason begin to search the body of the silent corpse. The man who'd tried to kill him – who he was now sure must be behind his father's death – was a policeman? And he'd just invited another copper along to investigate – how could he have been so stupid? What if DI Dyer was mixed up in this too? Scott began to silently edge his way towards the door.

'Do you know what this is?'

Scott froze at the sound of Dyer's voice and turned to see the detective brandishing a slender parcel, the same package he'd seen on his father's desk.

'He had it stashed inside his jacket,' Jason continued. 'It's addressed to your father.'

'I don't know,' Scott replied. 'I saw it yesterday. It's probably work papers – my dad's always—' He stopped and corrected himself. 'I mean, he *was* always bringing work home with him.'

Clearing a space on the desk, Jason carefully opened the seal on the package. Scott peered over the policeman's shoulder, his anxiety slowly being replaced with a desire to find out what was inside. Whatever was in the parcel, he'd almost been killed for it. As Jason tipped the package forward, instead of the government papers Scott had expected to see, a slim book slid out.

The book was bound in ancient leather, dulled by time to a dusky grey hue, and on its cover the barely legible title was picked out in spidery silver letters:

*Albion Unbound*

Jason picked up the time-ravaged tome, fingering the cracked and peeling spine.

'What is this?' he murmured as carefully he began to

leaf through the yellowed pages. Ancient words and letters were barely visible on the crumbling parchment, worn away by time and readers alike. The book was written in some kind of archaic English, the writing dense and impenetrable. Many pages seemed to have been torn out, but on several of the remaining ones there were lavish illustrations which showed druids conducting strange ceremonies. On the final page was a map of Britain, the shape of the country slightly stretched and distorted, but still recognisable underneath ornate gold lettering picking out a single word: *Albion*.

The map showed a network of roads and pathways traversing the country, linking together the scattered towns and cities, but far fewer in number than on modern maps. Each pathway was marked with a spidery trail of green ink, while rivers were etched in twisted, looping spirals of blue. But Jason's eyes were drawn to the shape of the routes picked out in faded green lines: a twisted, upside-down cross laid over the country. He'd seen this before. As his eyes strained at the weathered page, he could just make out three words printed next to the map: *The Deade Wayes*.

Jason stared at the page. The Deade Wayes. The Dead Ways. The same words he'd seen scrawled in the margins of a confidential government report were written in the decaying pages of this old book. His whirring thoughts were distracted by the sound of Scott rooting around inside the empty package.

'What are you doing?' Jason snapped.

Scott looked across at Dyer with defiant eyes. 'It was addressed to my father,' he responded angrily, before slowly pulling his hand out of the package to display a small business card. 'Anyway, if you'd been doing your job properly, you'd have found this.'

Jason snatched the business card out of Scott's hand, his face flushing red at his detective skills being called into question by a kid. The card was emblazoned with a drawing of the sun rising over a stone circle above which ran the words *Mystic Moods – Antiquarian and New Age Booksellers*. At the bottom of the card in gothic print was the name of the proprietor, Tom Moody, and an address in Soho. At last, a lead.

'Look, I'm sorry,' Jason told Scott, his temper mellowing at the prospect of finally finding some answers. 'But did your dad ever mention this place?'

Scott examined the card with a frown. His dad didn't believe in any of that New Age rubbish about psychics, crystals and witchcraft, let alone hang out in bookshops filled with the stuff. He shook his head and placed the card back on the desk.

'No,' he replied. 'I've never heard of it.'

Jason nodded and then pulled out his mobile and slid his finger across the screen.

'What are you doing?' Scott asked. 'We need to go and investigate this bookshop. Find out why they sent this book to my dad. It could be important.'

'I'm sorry, kid,' Jason replied as he held the phone to his ear, 'but you're going to have to leave the investigating to me from now on.' He nodded towards the stiffening corpse lying on the floor. 'This mess needs sorting out and I'm afraid the boys back at the station are going to have a few more questions for you.'

Jason turned away as his call connected. 'It's Dyer here – get me DCI Nicholls.' He paused as he listened to the reply at the other end of the line. 'Look, I don't care if he's in with the chief super, I need to speak to him now.'

Scott looked back at the door. A policeman had tried to kill him and this guy expected him to trot along to the station. He'd be lucky to get out of there alive. No, if anyone was going to find out what was going on here, it was going to be him. Grabbing the book and the business card from the desk, he darted for the door.

Jason turned as he heard the sound of footsteps thudding down the stairs, then cursed as he heard the front door opening.

'Scott, wait!' he called out. 'Don't be stupid.'

But Scott wasn't listening. He just ran.

# CHAPTER FOUR

Scott stooped as he stepped through the doorway and down into the gloom of the shop, the watery daylight struggling to find its way past the stacks of books piled up in the window, their peeling covers dissuading passers-by from venturing inside. His shoulders were still tensed, his body coiled, ready to break into a run at any moment.

All the way across London, he'd felt like someone had been following him: the eyes of random strangers tracking him on the tube, cars slowing as they drove alongside him, policemen talking into their radios as he passed. But nobody had stopped him. He'd managed to clean himself up in a public toilet, washing the dried blood from his face and hair, grim reminders of the night just gone. Now he fingered the slim volume hidden inside his jacket pocket. It was time to get some answers.

Inside, the bookshop was even murkier than it had looked from the street. A maze of towering bookcases stretched to the ceiling with books piled on top of them at every angle:

books in tattered dust jackets, leather-bound hardbacks, spindly paperbacks with lurid covers and broken spines. *Mysteries of the Voynich Manuscript*; *A Witchhunter's Manual*; *The Magic of the Celts*. The smell of incense hung in the air and on top of the nearest shelf, propping up yet another row of books, an ancient skull stared eyelessly back at Scott. He shivered and edged away, moving deeper into the heart of the shop.

At the back of the store, a desk lamp picked out a circle of light amidst the gloom and in this, sitting half hidden behind a long counter, was a girl. She was a couple of years younger than Scott, with dark, lank hair falling over her pale features as she hunched intently over the pages of a book. Scott felt some of the tension seep from his shoulders as he approached the counter. He had nothing to fear from her.

Facing away from the counter, the girl was so engrossed in her book that she didn't even register Scott's presence as he stood there waiting, she just turned the pages, her brow furrowed in concentration. Scott coughed to try and attract her attention, but the girl just shivered as though in response to what she was reading. Leaning into the pool of light, Scott peered over the girl's shoulder at the book that was holding her spellbound.

The page was headed *How to Stop a Zombie Attack* and beneath this was a list of instructions and diagrams showing how to kill the undead. *Bludgeoning*, *Decapitation*, *Immolation* – the list went on.

Shaking his head, Scott tapped the girl lightly on the shoulder.

With a shocked yelp, she leapt out of her chair, spinning to face him. Her arms were raised as if to fend off an intruder and her eyes were wide with fear.

'Whoa,' said Scott, stepping back in surprise. 'Sorry, I didn't mean to scare you.'

Seeing Scott standing there, the girl slowly lowered her arms from their martial arts stance.

'You didn't scare me,' she mumbled, a red tide of embarrassment creeping across her cheeks. 'I just thought you might be one of them.'

'One of them?' Scott asked suspiciously, his own nerves still jangling after the events of last night.

The girl glanced down at the book she was still holding in her hands, its back cover reading *WARNING! ZOMBIES!*

Scott started to laugh, but then quickly changed this to an apologetic cough as he caught a glimpse of the girl's disapproving expression. A long, dark fringe fell across her pale face, but behind this her eyes were narrowed into a deadly serious stare. Scott glanced around at the bookshelves heaving with stories of ghosts and ghouls, vampires and werewolves. The girl actually believed this stuff, he realised.

'Look,' Scott started. 'I need to speak to the owner. It's about a book from here.'

The girl shook her head.

'I'm sorry, but my dad's – I mean, the owner's – kind of busy right now.' She screwed up her face as if she was trying to remember something and when she spoke again, her words had a singsong quality to them, as if they'd been learned off by heart. 'If there's a problem with a book you've purchased, I'm afraid the shop has a very strict returns policy.'

She gestured apologetically to the handwritten notice fixed to the till: NO REFUNDS.

Scott frowned.

'You don't understand,' he explained. 'I didn't buy the book from here – it was sent to me. Well, to my dad.'

Suddenly, there was the swishing sound of a beaded curtain being drawn at the far end of the counter and the bulky figure of a man appeared out of the gloom.

'Avalon – who are you talking to?' The voice was a low rumble, and as the man stepped towards the circle of light, Scott saw that he was dressed entirely in black. A thick, wiry beard hid most of his face and long wild hair that had once been black but was now mainly grey descended down sloping shoulders. He stared at Scott with worried eyes. 'I'm Tom Moody; this is my shop. Who are you?'

Scott shifted uncomfortably under the man's penetrating gaze.

'I'm waiting,' Tom growled impatiently.

Looking up into the bright-green eyes that sparkled under bushy grey eyebrows, Scott put his faith in his instincts and decided to risk the truth.

'I'm Scott Williams,' he replied.

Tom's mouth dropped open in surprise and he rushed forward into the light, seizing hold of Scott's shoulders across the counter as he stared hard into his face.

'Good grief, it is!' he cried. 'I don't believe it!' As Scott struggled to shake off Tom's ring-encrusted hands, the young girl, Avalon, looked on with a shocked expression on her face. 'Scott – I've waited a long time to meet you,' Tom continued. 'Alex has shown me pictures of course, but—'

'Wait, you knew my father?'

Scott's question stopped Tom in mid-flow.

'Knew?' he asked, a note of uncertainty creeping into his question.

Scott reached into his jacket pocket to remove the secret he had hidden there.

'You sent him this.'

Tom glanced down and saw *Albion Unbound*. He looked back up, his deep-set eyes suddenly haunted by the same fear that had shone in Avalon's eyes. 'You shouldn't have this – it's not safe.' He grasped Scott's shoulders again, his fingers shaking. 'Where's your father? Where's Alex?'

Scott looked up into Tom's face, but in his mind he could just see his dad's eyes staring back from the shadows. The face that had haunted his dream. His reply came in a cracked whisper.

'My dad's dead.'

The air was cool in the musty stockroom. Cold December daylight poured in from a skylight and slanted over the narrow bookcases, crammed to bursting, that filled the cramped back room. In the far corner, a mouse darted into the shadows behind a box of old comics. Scott sat on a worn office chair, yellow foam escaping from its torn back rest, next to a desk strewn with papers, bills, invoices and receipts, while Avalon fussed with a kettle, pouring hot water into three chipped mugs.

'Tea OK?' she asked, handing Scott one of the piping-hot mugs. 'No milk I'm afraid, so I hope you don't mind it black.'

Scott shook his head.

'Look,' he began impatiently, turning towards Tom who was standing by the doorway with his arms tightly folded, a grim expression hidden behind his beard. Scott brandished the battered volume. 'You said this book was dangerous.' The sunlight picked out the faint silvery letters on the cover. 'What's this all about?'

Ignoring Scott's question, Tom spoke to Avalon as she handed him his tea. 'Go and shut the place up.'

As Avalon disappeared back into the shop, Tom reached out a hand for the book. 'May I?'

Reluctantly, Scott handed him *Albion Unbound*, watching as Tom carefully studied the cracked cover, as though reassuring himself that the book was real. Enormous hands with ornate rings on every finger turned the ancient parchment pages gingerly as Tom's eyes darted back and forth over the incomprehensible text and cryptic illustrations.

He closed the book decisively.

'You need to forget that you ever saw this book, Scott. Forget that you ever came here. It's not safe.' Tom rested his hand on Scott's shoulder. 'Your mum's in the States now, isn't she? You should go there – be with her. Get as far away from here as you possibly can.'

'Forget it all?' Scott exploded with anger, shrugging Tom's hand away and leaping up from the chair. He snatched the book back. 'Someone broke into my house looking for this! They nearly killed me.'

Scott backed away from Tom, watching warily as Avalon rushed to her father's side. Reaching down, he grabbed a lighter from the edge of the desk where it had been resting on top of a tin of tobacco. With one swift movement, Scott flicked open the lighter's lid and sparked a flame, translucent blue fire curling up from the silver case. He held the ancient book next to the flame, watching their horrorstruck faces. 'I want to know what's going on. Right now.'

'Just put the book down, Scott.' Tom's voice was calm and authoritative. 'I know how upset you are about your dad, but this isn't helping.'

Scott shook his head. The anger inside was now threatening to boil over.

'I'm not joking,' he replied as he waved the fragile book

over the eager flame and noted Avalon's horrified gasp with satisfaction. 'I want answers. I want the truth.'

The flame leapt higher, licking the book's cover as emotions danced across Scott's flashing eyes.

'Dad – we have to tell him.' Avalon's voice was almost pleading. 'He deserves to know.'

There was a lingering moment of silence and then Tom replied with a sigh.

'OK,' he said. 'Get the file.'

As Avalon raced out of the stockroom, Tom held out his hand.

Scott eyed Tom warily, then let the flame die as he snapped the lighter shut. He placed it in Tom's hand, but stashed the battered volume of *Albion Unbound* safely back in his pocket – insurance to make sure he finally got some answers.

'It's funny,' said Tom, shaking his head as he looked down at the silver lighter in his palm. 'Alex was always trying to get me to quit smoking. I should've listened to him.'

'How did you know my dad?' Scott demanded, in no mood now for Tom's evasions.

A smile crept out from behind Tom's thick beard. 'Oh, me and your dad go way back. We roomed together at Cambridge. Alex was reading Ancient History and I was studying Archaeology. The first time we met we ended up having a blazing row about why the pyramids were built. Your dad was right, of course. He always was back then.'

He turned to the chaotic desk and, pulling open the

topmost drawer, started to rifle through its contents. 'I should have a picture here somewhere.' Old newspaper clippings, cheque book stubs and yet more bills stamped *Final Reminder* spilled out onto the floor. 'Here it is.'

He thrust a creased photograph into Scott's hand. In it, a group of fresh-faced university students sat by the curve of a river underneath a flawless summer's sky. Their wooden punt was moored by the side of the riverbank, while a tangle of champagne bottles and empty glasses were strewn on the grass in front of them. In the middle of the group, Scott saw with a jolt of recognition his father, some twenty years younger, with his arm slung around the broad shoulders of his friend beside him. Scott studied the man next to his father then looked back up at Tom's face. The long hair was greying and the clean-shaven face now hidden behind a tangled beard, but the eyes shone just the same. It was Tom.

'He never mentioned you,' said Scott, a trace of suspicion still lingering in his voice.

Tom sighed, wincing slightly as though picking at the scab of a painful memory. He shrugged. 'We had a disagreement – a difference of opinion. Things were never the same after that. I dropped out of university and went travelling. We tried to patch things up but slowly drifted out of touch.' He gestured around him at the dusty stockroom filled with mouldering books. 'Our lives had gone in different directions. I hadn't heard from your dad in nearly ten years until he got back in touch six months ago.' Tom paused as though weighing the words before he spoke. 'When it all started to happen.'

'When what started to happen?' Scott asked.

As if in answer to his question, Avalon appeared in the doorway, a red ring-bound folder in her arms.

'This is what's happening,' she announced as she placed the heavy file reverentially on the desk in front of them. Avalon fixed Scott with a solemn stare as she pushed the folder towards him. 'This is what you need to know.'

Leaning forward, Scott opened the file, eager to find the answers that would help him to track down his father's killers. On the very first page he saw a small newspaper clipping, its headline reading HOSPITAL BLUNDER – 'DEAD' MAN WAKES IN MORTUARY. Next to the clipping, a question was scrawled in strangely familiar handwriting. *Is this the start?*

Scratching his head, Scott slowly turned the pages, his confusion growing with every word he read. The folder was filled with newspaper clippings and printouts from internet news sites, a never-ending cavalcade of outlandish headlines:

SPOOKY LIGHTS SPOTTED OVER AVEBURY

SPEEDING GHOST HAUNTS
ABANDONED MOTORWAY

VANDALS ATTACK STONEHENGE – ANCIENT
STONES COATED IN BLOOD

'What is this?' Scott pushed the folder away in irritation.

'I didn't come here to look through some stupid school project about ghosts and freaky phenomena.' He pushed himself up from the chair and turned to leave. 'I'm going to find out what happened to my dad.'

'Sit down.' Tom's words came out in a growl of authority. Something in his voice stilled Scott and, almost unwillingly, he sank back down into the chair, the springs squeaking beneath him. 'Your dad helped Avalon make this file,' said Tom, speaking in a low voice as though afraid of who would overhear. 'Alex was the one who found out what was happening. He saw the signs and realised the danger we all face. If you want to understand, you need to open your mind.' Tom turned to Avalon. 'Tell him.'

Avalon opened the folder again, her dark hair falling across her face as she flicked through its pages.

'For the past six months paranormal events have been occurring across the country,' she explained. 'Ghostly apparitions, supernatural possession, even the dead returning.' Avalon pulled out a map of Britain from the back of the file and pushed it towards Scott. 'Look.'

The map showed the whole country, with major cities, towns and rivers all marked on, but it was also pitted with small red dots clustered around the roads and motorways traversing the country from east to west, north to south.

'The red dots,' Avalon continued, 'record every one of the paranormal incidents catalogued in here. We checked and verified each and every one.'

The pattern of the dots stretching out across the country stirred something in Scott's memory. 'I've seen this before,' he murmured. Reaching out, he grabbed hold of a red marker pen that was half hidden beneath a coffee-stained electricity bill and then started to draw lines between each of the incidents.

'Wait a minute,' Avalon's voice rose in protest. 'You can't just scrawl all over my map!'

Scott waved Avalon's protest away, his head still bent in concentration over the map. 'I've seen this before,' he repeated, a hard edge of conviction rising in his voice as the marker's red ink snaked across the map.

Avalon glanced up at Tom for support, but her father was studying the map intently as Scott slowly joined the red dots together to form the shape of a cross. The lines stretched from Cornwall to Norfolk, from Sussex to the Highlands of Scotland; two crimson corridors almost crucifying the country.

Discarding the marker pen, Scott reached into his pocket to retrieve *Albion Unbound*. He flicked through its time-worn pages, their edges almost crumbling under his touch, before he finally found what he was looking for – the map of ancient Britain. The same lines stretched across the country in a sinister geometry, but this time etched in green ink. He placed the book next to the map of modern Britain. The lines matched exactly.

'The Dead Ways,' breathed Tom.

Scott looked down again at the overflowing file. The newspaper clipping on the last page stared back up at him:

## MYSTERIOUS DEATHS HAUNT GREENING OF THE ROADS PROJECT

Next to this he recognised the familiar scrawl of his father's handwriting in a single scribbled comment: *The Dead Ways are opening.*

'What are the Dead Ways?' Scott asked, looking up into Tom and Avalon's grave faces.

But before either of them could reply, the sound of another man's voice cut through the musty air. Scott turned to see a shadowy figure framed in the stockroom doorway.

'That's what I'd like to know,' said DI Dyer. 'And I want some answers *now*.'

# CHAPTER FIVE

'Who the hell are you?' said Tom, whirling in surprise at the sound of Dyer's voice. 'The shop's closed. Staff meeting.' He shot an accusing glance at his daughter. 'Avalon, I thought I told you to lock up.'

Avalon grimaced in apology. 'I turned the closed sign around.'

'Detective Inspector Dyer,' the policeman replied, flashing his warrant card as he stepped down into the half-lit stockroom. 'I take it you're the owner – Tom Moody, isn't it?' His eyes darted from Tom to Avalon to Scott as he quickly assessed the situation; the three of them crowded around a cluttered desk, a bulging folder open in front of them.

'You shouldn't have run off on me back there, Scott,' Jason continued. 'Stealing evidence, fleeing the scene of a crime, leaving a policeman lying dead on your floor – it doesn't look good. You've got a lot of explaining to do.'

Scott's heart pounded as DI Dyer drew nearer. Out of

the corner of his eye, he saw Avalon's hand stealing towards *Albion Unbound*. Scott grabbed the book and flashed her a warning glare.

'So there's the missing evidence,' said Jason as he saw Scott snatch up the battered volume. He held out an expectant hand.

Scott shook his head defiantly. 'It belonged to my dad. I'm keeping it.'

'Look, Scott,' Jason sighed, his eyes wearily flicking to his watch. 'Your mum's flying in from Miami as we speak. She's due to land at Heathrow in five hours. We've got time to get you down to the station, clear up this mess and then have you waiting for her at the arrivals gate.' He held his palms open. 'What do you say?'

Tom stepped in front of DI Dyer.

'You're not taking him anywhere.' His voice was a low growl of warning. 'You may have got Alex, but you're not taking his son.'

Jason sized up Tom's imposing bulk. With his wild beard and long hair he looked like some kind of Old Testament prophet, but the only prediction Jason could make was that this case wasn't going to get easier any time soon. He knew he should have brought backup. DCI Nicholls had lost it when he'd called in to report Scott missing, but if he knew he'd tried to track him down on his own . . .

He brandished his warrant card again.

'Perhaps you didn't hear me correctly first time, Mr

Moody – I'm Detective Inspector Jason Dyer, Metropolitan Police.' Jason's voice was laced with a menacing authority. 'I'm investigating the suspicious death of Alexander Williams. Last night there was a break-in at his home; an intruder attempted to steal a parcel addressed to Mr Williams. A package which I believe came from this bookshop.'

Without warning, Jason quickly pushed past Tom and snatched the book out of Scott's hand. He spun back to face Tom, who was still turning in surprise.

The bookseller lunged towards him, his hands grasping wildly for the book. More than ten years younger and several stone lighter, Jason easily sidestepped the desperate lunge as Tom's momentum sent him crashing into a bookshelf.

'Hey,' Jason barked out in warning as a set of hardback encyclopedias rained down on top of Tom. He reached into his jacket and unholstered his taser. 'Behave yourself.'

Avalon hurried to her father's side and helped him to his feet, Tom's bluster now punctured by his first-edition bruises.

Jason turned back to Scott. 'So, are you ready to come down to the station now?'

Scott shook his head, backing away from the detective.

'Not until I find out what's going on.' Reaching down to the table, he shoved the red folder towards Jason. 'They say my dad helped make this. He'd found something out. Something important.'

'Scott, no!' Tom's voice rang out in warning. 'You can't trust him.'

Intrigued, Jason started to leaf through the file, recognising the looping curl of Alex Williams's handwriting in the comments inked next to the newspaper clippings.

'You can't be serious.' Jason looked up, his eyes darting nervously to Scott's face. 'This is just a scrapbook filled with silly season stories – the ones that papers run when there's no real news.' He turned the pages at random. 'I mean, listen to this – ZOMBIE LOLLIPOP LADY STALKS SCHOOL CROSSING. This is just a bunch of kids making stuff up to get their pictures in the paper.'

'Liar!'

Jason and Scott spun around simultaneously at the sound of Avalon's querulous voice, a single word spat in accusation. She shrugged Tom's restraining hand from her arm and stormed towards them, her dark eyes glowering.

'What?' Scott asked, his confusion mirroring Jason's own.

'He's a liar,' repeated Avalon, pushing past Dyer and flicking rapidly through the file. When she found what she was looking for, she stabbed her finger at the page accusingly. 'See for yourself.'

A single newspaper story clipped from a Sunday tabloid adorned the page, its sensational headline emblazoned beneath an exclusive banner:

PSYCHO COP CLAIMS GHOSTS CAUSED
MOTORWAY MAYHEM

Jason saw a creased picture of his own face staring back at him from the article and then winced as he read the caption beneath it: *Detective Inspector Jason Dyer is suspended pending psychiatric reports.*

'I knew I'd heard your name before,' Avalon continued, the indignation rising in her voice. 'How can you say it's just a bunch of kids making stuff up. You've seen these things happening with your own eyes.'

Jason was dumbstruck. The stark newspaper headline instantly thrust his thoughts back to the horror of that night, the memory he'd been running away from all this time – the shadowy figure looming in front of him, its ice-cold hands burning the blood from his veins. Any words of denial dried on his lips.

'I don't know whose side you're on.' Tom stepped forward from the shadows, eyeing Jason's unholstered taser warily. 'But if you've seen it for yourself, then you know the danger we face.' His eyes flicked from Jason to Scott and then back again.

Sweeping the detritus of bills and papers to the floor, Tom cleared a space in the centre of the desk and unfolded the map of Great Britain.

'This is Britain,' he declared, his fingers smoothing the creased edges of the map. 'The towns and the cities, the mountains and the moors, every road, every river. But what it doesn't show you is what lies beneath. Show them, Avalon.'

Scrabbling in the desk drawer, Avalon pulled out a red biro and then, with a studious precision, began to draw a series of lines across the map, crossing the country from north to south, east to west – the lines adding to the cross Scott had already marked there. Some of the lines were scored through existing roads and motorways, while others followed dotted footpaths and bridleways.

'These are the Dead Ways,' Tom announced, spreading his hands as he spoke to display the geometric grid enclosing Britain. 'Ancient lines of power carved into the earth, stretching the length and breadth of this island. The Dead Ways form a barrier protecting the physical world – the world we all live in – from the other side.'

'The other side?'

'The Land of the Dead,' Tom replied, his voice steady and emotionless.

Scott's heartbeat quickened.

'In ancient times,' Tom continued, 'when the first people set foot upon this land, they were not alone. The barrier between this world and the next, the living and the dead, was blurred and broken. Powerful spirits walked the earth and the dead held dominion over the living.'

'Dominion?' Scott asked, frowning in confusion.

'Power,' Tom explained. 'The spirits – the Dead Lords the legends called them – ruled this island with inhuman cruelty. Men were forced to raise great monuments to worship the spirits and offered sacrifices to try and placate them. Women, children, entire families were slaughtered – it was never enough. The wheel of life stopped turning.

Crops withered on the stalk. Corpses rose rotting from their graves, no escape even there from the Dead Lords' tyranny.'

As Tom spoke, his words echoed in Scott's mind, burning with a strange intensity. The nightmarish images for a moment seemed as real as the room they were standing in.

'But eventually,' Tom continued, 'the living rose up in rebellion. Great lines of power – the Dead Ways – were carved into the earth. Across moorland and through forests, over hills and through valleys, from coast to coast, until the Dead Lords were finally caged and the living could walk free. Over time, these lines of power became pathways, the pathways became tracks, the tracks became roads. Each generation strengthening the bars of the cage that held the spirits at bay, even though the reasons why were long forgotten. Until now.' Tom's voice cracked with emotion. 'Alex found out what they were planning to do – that's why they murdered him.'

There was a momentary silence in the stockroom. The small square of sky visible through the skylight was now a slate grey and raindrops began to splatter on the glass.

It was Jason who spoke first. The lines drawn on the map, the scrawled comments in the file, the nagging sensation itching at the back of his neck – suddenly he could see where all this was heading, but he had to ask the question:

'What had Alex Williams found out?'

Tom's eyes flicked up to Jason's face as though searching for a sign he could be trusted.

'The Greening of the Roads project,' he finally replied. 'That's how they're opening the Dead Ways.'

'I don't understand,' Scott interrupted, struggling to make sense of Tom's twisting revelations. 'How can something that's helping to save the environment be so terrible?'

'Look at the map,' Tom replied, gesturing again at the outline of Britain stretching across the desk. 'By dismantling the roads and returning the land to nature, they're erasing the lines of power and weakening the cage.' He jabbed his finger at the dots lining the routes, each one marking a freakish story from the bulging red file. 'The spirits are already starting to break through. And if they finally manage to unlock the Dead Ways . . .'

Tom's voice tailed off into nothingness as though the prospect was too dreadful for him to express.

'Let me get this right,' said Jason. 'You're saying that this Greening of the Roads project is just a front? That really the government is secretly plotting to unlock some mystical cage and unleash hell on earth?' He paused for a moment, a technique he'd honed in countless police interviews. 'It's hardly an election-winning manifesto, is it?'

'The government doesn't know what's going on,' Avalon muttered.

'What do you mean?' asked Scott, desperate to make sense of this madness. 'If it's not the government, then who is behind all this?'

'There is a secret power that runs this country,' Avalon

replied, her dark eyes flashing. 'An ancient society called the Brothers of Albion.'

'Avalon!'

The girl snatched an anxious glance towards her father. Tom shook his greying locks, an exasperated growl warning her that she'd said too much.

'This is ridiculous!' Jason placed a hand on Scott's shoulder. 'I've heard enough. Scott, you're coming to the station with me so we can get this whole thing straightened out.' He turned back towards Tom and thrust an accusing finger in his direction. 'And then I'll be coming back for you.'

'Don't you understand?' Tom replied. 'If you take Scott in now, then you're taking him to his death.'

Scott could feel the vein on the side of his temple throbbing. It was too much to take in. Ghosts and spirits. The Dead Ways and psychic cages. Secret societies and twisted conspiracies. He struggled to shape the questions spiralling around his brain.

'Garbage,' Jason responded, unable to mask his irritation at Tom's wild claims any more. 'Where's your proof for any of this?'

Tom stood silently for a moment, his bear-like arms folded across his broad chest and his face almost expressionless behind his thick beard.

'Alex left proof,' he replied softly.

'What do you mean?' pressed Jason, his words still rolling in suspicion.

'In case anything ever happened to him, Alex told me that he'd hidden evidence in his study. Something that proves what I'm telling you. He told me that if things went wrong, I should get it to the press and show them the truth behind the Greening of the Roads project.'

Scott looked up into Tom's grizzled face, his eyes searching for the truth. He'd come here looking for answers – to find out why his dad had been murdered. And now Tom was offering him proof. He roughly shrugged the detective's hand from his shoulder, twisting to face him.

'If you really want to find my dad's killers, then you should be taking this seriously,' he shouted, his voice ragged with emotion. 'This could be important.'

Shocked, Jason looked into Scott's eyes and saw the raw defiance blazing there. He had to put an end to this.

'If I check this out,' Jason said, choosing his words with deliberation, 'then that's it, OK? I do this and you come back to the station and leave me to investigate your father's death properly.'

Scott didn't want to listen to Dyer's calm voice. His nails pressed down into his palms as he fought to keep his emotions in check. The only person he could trust to find the truth was himself, but he had no choice. He had to do this Dyer's way.

'OK,' he finally nodded in grudging assent as he slowly unclenched his fists. 'But I'm coming with you to find the evidence.'

# CHAPTER SIX

Scott stared through the windscreen as Jason pulled into the side street and parked the car in front of a gate in the railings. Across the square, he could see the tall Georgian house, its white stucco brickwork, the large bay-fronted windows, the red front door. Home. He half expected to see his dad standing there, waiting for him on the doorstep.

Instead, a uniformed police officer stood at the bottom of the steps, his helmet protecting him from the freezing rain that had started to fall. At the bottom of the pathway leading up to the house, a bright-yellow line of police tape was stretched across the gate.

As DI Dyer turned off the ignition and unclipped his seat belt, Scott reached for the passenger door handle.

'Where do you think you're going?'

Dyer's words halted Scott in his tracks.

'It's my house,' Scott replied. 'Whatever evidence my dad stashed away, I'll be able to find it.'

'No way,' said Dyer. 'I've taken enough of a risk already

by agreeing to this. I can't risk you compromising the crime scene as well.'

'You mean where a policeman broke into my house?' Scott laughed hollowly. 'Where he nearly killed me?'

'I'm sorry,' Dyer shook his head decisively. 'But you're staying here while I check this "evidence" story out. That's the deal.' He pushed open the door and stepped out of the car. Resting his arm on the doorframe, he leaned down to meet Scott's dissatisfied glare. 'Stay here, OK. I'll be back soon and then we'll take things from there.'

Scott gave a grudging nod. He had no choice. Satisfied, Dyer shut the car door and set off purposefully across the square. Scott watched as he reached the gate, lifted the line of police tape and walked up the pathway, then flashed his warrant card to the uniform standing sentry there. After a brief exchange of words, Scott saw the police officer hold the door open for Dyer as he stepped inside, disappearing from view as the door closed behind him.

Scott stared out at the raindrops that were running in rivulets down the glass. He felt powerless, stuck in this car while less than fifty metres away the evidence that could help bring his father's killers to justice lay hidden. He reached again for the door handle, half opening it this time, but then slowly pulling it shut again as realisation dawned. There was no way he'd be able to get past the copper standing on the doorstep, and Dyer would go ballistic if he even tried.

It was no good. He'd just have to stick to the deal and trust that Dyer was enough of a detective to find whatever his dad had hidden away in there.

Jason stood at the door to the study, carefully appraising the scene. The uniform at the door had told him that forensics had finished up less than an hour ago and he could see their handiwork all around him. DC Skinner's corpse had been spirited away, only a faint scarlet stain remaining on the polished wooden floorboards. The shards of mirror that had lain shattered in a starburst around the body, the scattered books, files and papers – not a sign of them remained. Each and every scrap of evidence had been meticulously bagged, tagged and collected.

On the desk sat Alex Williams's laptop, waiting for the tech guys to pick it up, but every single file and paper that had littered the desk was gone, leaving just a solitary framed photograph of Scott and his father standing there.

Jason cursed underneath his breath. Even if Alex Williams had concealed evidence somewhere in this room, he was too late to find it. Forensics had stripped the study practically bare. When one of their own was killed, they went the extra mile.

He scratched his head as he walked around the study, trying to fit this case's jigsaw-like pieces together. Ever since he'd started investigating Alex Williams's death, supposedly an open-and-shut suicide, things had been getting steadily stranger. The break-in. Detective Constable Skinner apparently attempting to murder Williams's son. Then Scott's bizarre claim that Skinner was the man who'd tried to kidnap him six months earlier.

Jason didn't know much about Skinner as he'd only been transferred to the nick a few weeks ago. The unsettling thing, although he hadn't mentioned this to Scott, was that when he'd informed Nicholls that DC Skinner was lying dead in Alex Williams's study, the guv hadn't even seemed that surprised. What was going on here? Had Skinner been working undercover? Jason remembered Skinner's glassy eyes staring out at him sightlessly, the shard of mirror piercing his skull. He wasn't going to be able to tell him any time soon.

They'd not even been able to track down the social worker who was supposed to have been staying with Scott. It was as if she'd disappeared off the face of the earth. And the only lead he'd found so far led to some old hippy who had got Scott all fired up with stories of supernatural apparitions, secret societies and an apocalyptic hell waiting just around the corner.

Jason picked up the framed photograph of Alex and Scott Williams from the desk. In the picture, Alex had his arm around his son's shoulder, the two of them smiling happily with the London skyline illuminated behind them. Alex Williams had everything to live for. The last sentence of his 'suicide' note nagged at the back of Jason's brain.

*Remember the good times and keep the memory safe.*

As Jason turned the photo frame over in his hands, examining it closely, his fingers felt the hint of a bulge in the back corner. He prised the back of the frame open and saw with a rush of excitement a sliver-thin memory card hidden behind the picture. Intrigued, Jason carefully picked out the memory card and, firing up the laptop on the desk, slotted it into place. As the new device detected icon flashed up, he clicked on it and saw a single audio file appear on the screen with a one-word file name – Truth.mp3. Jason smiled wryly to himself. That would make a welcome change. Opening the file with a click, he heard a sharp hiss of static and then the unmistakable tones of the Minister for Transport, Jerry Daedalus, oozed out of the speakers.

*'The days are growing shorter; our finest hour is almost at hand. Once the final stages of the Greening of the Roads project are completed, the Dead Ways will be open once more. The Brothers of Albion can step out of the shadows and take our rightful place at the dawn of a great new era.'*

Through the speakers came the sound of fists banging on the table in agreement and a chorus of hear, hears.

Jason listened on in disbelief. Daedalus's voice came through the speakers once more.

*'Let the Halcyon Days begin.'*

'What does this mean?' Jason muttered, bewildered by the enormity of the discovery.

'It means you're not as useless as we hoped.'

At the sound of the voice, Jason turned in alarm. Standing in the doorway, pointing a gun straight at him, was Detective Chief Inspector Nicholls.

'I think we need to have a little talk, don't you?'

Scott fidgeted restlessly in the passenger seat. Through the window, he could still see the policeman standing sentry outside, but when he looked up to the window of his father's study there was no movement. Dyer had been in there for almost half an hour and there was still no sign of him reappearing.

He couldn't wait any longer. Pushing the car door open, Scott stepped out into the street. The only way he was going to get at the truth would be if he found it himself. Opening the gate in the railings, he began to walk across the tree-lined square, drumming his fingers nervously against the outside of his thighs as he walked. He'd think of a way to get past the copper stationed at the front door when he got there.

He was just over twenty metres away when he saw a black Mercedes glide up to the kerb outside his front gate. Quickly, Scott stepped behind a tree, dead leaves crunching under his feet as he peered out to see who this latest visitor was. A tall, broad-shouldered man with thinning black Brylcreemed hair stepped out of the car, pulling the collar of his long, dark overcoat up around his neck.

Scott watched as the man pushed past the police tape

and walked up the path towards his house. The policeman standing on the front step seemed to straighten his stance as the man spoke to him. Scott strained to hear their words, but the sound of the icy rain falling through the branches made this impossible.

Scott was surprised to see the uniformed officer step down from his post and walk towards the squad car that was parked just ahead of the Mercedes. The man in the overcoat watched as the police car pulled away from the kerb and sped off down the road, then he pushed open the door to Scott's house and disappeared inside.

Scott hurried to the gate and, ducking under the yellow line of police tape, cautiously approached the front door. Through the frosted glass window at the top of the door, he could see the tall man's dark shape slowly ascending the stairs, heading straight towards his father's study. As the man turned at the top of the stairs and disappeared from sight, Scott reached into his pocket and pulled out his house key. Turning the key in the lock, Scott pushed the door open a fraction, listening intently for any sound from the interior of the house. The empty silence unnerved him. Where was DI Dyer? He cautiously stepped inside, carefully pushing the door closed behind him.

Stepping lightly on the polished floorboards, Scott listened again at the bottom of the stairs. He could now hear faint voices coming from behind the closed study door at the top of the stairs. Moving as quietly as he could, Scott slowly climbed up the stairs, wincing at every creak the floorboards made beneath his feet. He felt like a burglar in his own home.

Reaching the landing, Scott leaned forward to peer through the crack where the door had been left slightly ajar. He could see DI Dyer sitting in front of his father's desk. Behind him the screen of a laptop was open, but Dyer's attention was turned towards the man in the dark overcoat who was standing just behind the door, half blocking Scott's view. The man began to speak and as Scott craned his neck to try and hear exactly what he was saying, he saw with a jolt of fear that the man had a gun in his hand, its shiny black barrel pointing straight at DI Dyer.

'Why did you have to try and prove yourself, Jason?' the man asked. 'I thought we'd done the right thing assigning you to this case – a dead-end investigator who could be relied upon not to start poking around too much.'

'I'm sorry to be such a disappointment to you, guv,' Dyer retorted, his sarcasm battling the tremor in his voice.

DCI Nicholls waved him into silence with the gun.

'Give me the laptop.' He held out his left hand towards Jason, the gun still held in his right. Nicholls's words dripped with an unrefusable authority. 'And that's an order.'

Jason hesitated for a moment, but the sight of the cold barrel of steel staring straight at him forced his hand. He reached back for the computer, clicking the screen shut, and then held it out towards his superior.

Gun still firmly in his grasp, Nicholls took hold of the laptop and then stepped back towards the door of the study. In a sudden violent movement, he smashed the computer against the wall. The casing splintered and cracked as, with a sickening intensity, he hammered the laptop against the wall again and again and again. The screen shattered and the keyboard peeled away, its exposed circuit boards smashing into fragments. All the time, Nicholls kept his gun firmly trained on Jason.

Hidden behind the door, Scott cringed at the violence. His hope of seeing whatever it was that Dyer had discovered, the evidence that his father had hidden, was now being obliterated before his eyes.

The damage done, Nicholls let go of the laptop and it clattered to the floor. He poked through the wreckage to extract the memory card and then brought the heel of his shoe cracking down on it. Scott could hear the plastic casing disintegrate as Nicholls ground it into tiny pieces beneath his heel.

'That's the evidence taken care of,' Nicholls announced with relish as he turned his full attention back to Jason. 'Now, where's Scott Williams?'

Hearing his name, Scott tensed, stepping backwards in shock. The floorboard beneath his feet creaked dangerously. He froze, his heartbeat racing as he silently prayed that he hadn't been heard.

'What do you mean?' Jason asked.

'The boy – where is he?' repeated DCI Nicholls, a new strain of menace entering his voice. 'Don't try and tell me you worked all this out on your own. You're not *that* good a detective. The boy knows something. Why else would he have disappeared?'

Nicholls pulled the safety off the gun, his finger still poised above the trigger.

'So, where are you hiding him?'

Scott's heartbeat thudded in his throat, hammering so hard he felt like he was going to choke. He was standing a few feet away from a man who wanted him dead. A man who was now pointing a gun straight at DI Dyer. All that separated them was a wooden door.

'He's safe,' Jason spat out the words in defiance. 'That's all you're going to get from me.'

'Too bad,' Nicholls replied, holding the gun so that it was pointing straight at Jason's head. 'It might have bought you a few more hours.'

'Why are you doing this?' Jason asked, his voice shaking with a barely suppressed fear. 'You're a policeman for god's sake!'

'I know what I am,' Nicholls answered coldly. 'But my loyalty lies with a much greater power.'

Jason remembered Daedalus's words crackling out from the laptop that now lay smashed on the floorboards in front of him.

'The Brothers of Albion?' he muttered bitterly.

In response to Jason's words, Nicholls's smile tightened, a frown creasing his forehead. He cocked the pistol, its barrel staring straight at Jason's skull.

'Goodbye, DI Dyer.'

Scott heard the click of the gun being cocked. Through the crack in the door, he saw Dyer grimace in anticipation of what was to come. In Scott's mind, the image of the dead man lying on the floor of his father's office flashed by. Not again. He wouldn't allow it.

Instinct overriding his fear, Scott slammed the study door open. It swung with a whip-crack into DCI Nicholls's back and sent him staggering off balance as the shot rang out. The bullet streaked through the air as Dyer dived to the floor. As the bullet's impact sent him spinning sideways, Jason felt a sudden searing pain blossoming in his shoulder. The bullet tore through his skin and then rifled into the wall in an explosion of plaster.

Cursing, Nicholls scrabbled for the pistol that had fallen from his grasp, but Scott was there first and snatched it up from the floor. Holding the gun in his trembling hands, Scott pointed it down at the face that was snarling back up at him.

'You,' said Nicholls, spitting the word in frustration.

Scott stepped backwards as Dyer appeared at his shoulder. Sweat beaded Jason's face as his hand reached up to the crimson stain spreading across his shoulder. When he pulled his fingers away they were sticky with blood.

'I thought I told you to stay in the car,' he said, breathing heavily as he forced out the words.

'Are you OK?' Scott asked, his finger nervously hovering over the trigger as he kept his gaze fixed on Nicholls, who was slowly pulling himself back to his feet. 'What do we do now?'

'I'm fine,' said Jason as he reached out with shaking hands and took the gun from Scott, all the time keeping the barrel firmly trained on Nicholls. When he spoke next, his words were for his boss.

'It's over. I don't know why you've been doing this, sir, but whatever you and the Brothers of Albion were trying to do – it ends now.'

'And how do you think you're going to stop us?' Nicholls laughed dismissively as he sized up Jason's hunched figure, his breath coming in ragged gasps as droplets of blood soaked the floorboards beneath his feet.

'We'll tell them what you've done!' Scott's voice was thick with rage. 'You killed my father. I won't let you get away with it. We'll tell the newspapers, TV – anyone that will listen – what you've done!'

'And you think they'll believe you?' Nicholls asked in a mocking tone, the same dismissive smile playing across his lips. 'Come on now, I mean, you're obviously sick with grief – anyone can see that. I can't blame you for wanting to believe these ridiculous little fantasies.

'As for you.' He turned his gaze towards Jason, not

even flinching at the sight of the gun pointing straight at him. 'Who do you really think they're going to believe? A fruitcake copper who was suspended after seeing ghosts wandering down the motorway? Or a detective chief inspector with over fifteen years' unblemished service.'

With a sinking realisation, Jason recognised the truth of Nicholls's words. Their only shred of proof had just been ground into dust underneath Nicholls's heel. Nobody would believe them.

'And as for evidence,' Nicholls continued, his smile widening. 'Your fingerprints are all over that gun.'

Jason looked down at the gun he was holding, the metal cold and slippery beneath his bloodstained fingers. He shivered uncontrollably, the pain from the wound in his shoulder making it difficult to think straight.

'Come on,' he said, placing a hand on Scott's shoulder for support. 'We've got to get out of here.'

'What? But he's bluffing,' Scott protested. 'We've got the gun – we can *make* him tell the truth. I'm not letting him get away with what they've done.'

'He won't,' Jason promised, wincing as he tried to catch his breath, 'but we've got no proof.' He gestured towards the smashed-up laptop, the memory card completely obliterated in the wreckage. 'Without that, we can't do anything – not here, not now.'

Scott clenched his fists in frustration, angry that what Dyer was telling him was true.

'Come on,' Jason repeated. 'We have to go now.' Keeping the gun gripped in his hand, he shakily unclipped his handcuffs from his belt and, gesturing with the gun barrel, shepherded Nicholls towards the radiator on the far wall of the office. Forcing him to his knees, Jason kept the gun trained on his chief inspector as he handed the cuffs to Scott.

'Put these on him,' he told Scott.

'Whatever you do, wherever you go – we'll find you,' Nicholls sneered as Scott threaded the cuffs through the metal pipes of the radiator and then snapped them around Nicholls's wrists.

'You'll have to get out of these first,' said Scott.

He turned back towards Jason, who was swaying slightly as he stood there, the gun still held in his shaking hand. Blood was oozing from the bullet wound, a spreading crimson tide soaking through Jason's shirt as the roaring static of pain clouded his mind.

Rushing to his side, Scott slipped his arm around Jason before his legs buckled. Behind him, Nicholls struggled to free himself, cursing as he rattled the handcuffs in impotent fury against the metal pipes.

'Let's go,' said Scott as he dragged Jason's dead weight towards the study door.

The two of them staggered down the stairs, slamming through the front door and down the path. Stumbling across the rain-soaked square, Scott flung open the passenger door as Jason slumped inside, blood pumping freely from the wound with every movement he made. As Scott dived around to the driver's seat, Jason fished the car keys from his bloodstained pocket with shaking fingers.

'Can you drive?' he asked, the question barely a whisper as Scott grabbed hold of the keys.

'Of course,' Scott muttered as he turned the key in the ignition and crunched the car into gear. 'My dad used to take me go-karting all the time.'

As they roared off down the street, Scott swerved to avoid the oncoming traffic before glancing at Jason again. Dyer's eyelids flickered faintly, and blood oozing from the raw wound on his shoulder stained the seat of the car.

'Hang in there,' said Scott as he wrestled the car around a corner, a wail of sirens growing in the distance. His juddering gear change slammed Jason against the passenger door, but the detective didn't even make a sound as the clamour of pain filled his mind and he slipped into oblivion.

# CHAPTER SEVEN

Black velvet filled Jason's mind; a comforting veil of nothingness was drawn across his memories, leaving him cocooned in a blissful oblivion. No light. No sound. No thoughts. No pain. Only emptiness remained.

But something was dragging him back. A nagging, burning sensation, throbbing somewhere in the distance, but growing more insistent with every breath that he took. Jason could hear a dim clatter of footsteps, the low murmur of voices and an insistent machine-like beeping growing ever louder, pulling him out of the void and back to reality.

His eyes flickered open to see Scott, his pale face creased with worry, staring down at him. Jason tried to pull himself upright, but then gasped as a sudden roar of pain blazed in his shoulder and the tangle of tubes and wires hooked up to his arms pulled him back down onto the hospital bed.

Scott quickly leaned forward to free the IV tube snagged under Jason's arm. His face flushed with relief as he helped Jason struggle into a sitting position, wedging the lumpy grey pillows behind his back to prop him upright.

Jason tried to speak, but his tongue was a dried husk in the desert of his mouth and only a choking cough that sent fresh shivers of pain jangling through his shoulder came out.

'It's OK,' said Scott, thrusting a glass of water into Jason's trembling hand and then watching with concern as the detective held it to his parched lips and gulped the liquid down. 'They say you're going to be OK. The bullet only hit soft tissue on its way through – it's going to hurt, but it's going to heal.'

In an instant, Jason remembered everything – finding the evidence hidden in Alex Williams's office; the sound of Jerry Daedalus's voice oozing from the tinny laptop speakers; Detective Chief Inspector Nicholls pointing the gun straight at him. He remembered staring down its barrel and then hearing the click of the safety catch and the squeeze of the trigger.

He shivered uncontrollably and then quickly glanced around in fear, taking in his surroundings for the very first time. A garish plastic curtain was pulled around the bed in which he was lying, and beside him an IV drip hung from a stand, its tube running to the vein in his forearm. Next to the bed, Scott perched on a hard plastic chair and behind him a monitor continued to beep reassuringly.

'Where are we?' asked Jason, the question crackling from his dry lips.

'The Royal Alexandra Hospital,' Scott replied. 'I didn't

know where else to go. I couldn't wake you – you were losing so much blood – it was all over the car. The doctor said that if they hadn't been able to stop the bleeding you'd have been dead within the hour.'

Before Scott had even finished speaking, Jason had swung his legs down out of the bed, grimacing as he pulled the IV drip from his arm with a shaking hand.

'What are you doing?' said Scott, leaping up from his chair in alarm as Jason tried to stand.

Jason looked down at the pale-blue hospital gown covering his body. He could see the starched white bandages strapped around his shoulder and beneath these he felt the molten ache of the gunshot wound half hidden behind the anaesthetic haze that lingered in his bloodstream.

'We've got to get out of here,' he told Scott. From behind the curtain, he could hear a nurse checking on the patient in the next bed and the low murmur of his reply. 'Where are my clothes?'

In response to Jason's hissed question, Scott reached into the cabinet beside the hospital bed and pulled out a clear plastic bag filled with clothing.

'Here,' he said, handing it to Jason.

Beneath the plastic, Jason could see his crumpled white shirt splattered with burgundy bloodstains.

'But can't you wait to see the doctor?' Scott continued, concern still etched on his face. 'He said he'd be back once you came round.'

'That's why we've got to go now,' Jason replied, a snarl of pain fixed to his lips as he struggled to dress himself. 'The hospital has to report any patients with gunshot wounds to the Metropolitan Police as soon as they're admitted. Uniform will be on their way to interview me right now.' He pulled his jacket tight to hide his bloodstained shirt. 'Nicholls won't be far behind them.'

Fear flashed in Scott's eyes as realisation dawned. He remembered the triumphant sneer of the sinister man in the overcoat, even as he'd been cuffed to the radiator. *Whatever you do, wherever you go – we'll find you*. Dyer was right. They weren't safe. Not here. Not anywhere.

'Let's get out of here.'

Scott stepped towards the curtain that sealed off the cubicle from the rest of the ward. Jason followed closely behind, breathing sharply through clenched teeth as he tried to control the pain. Then they both froze as the curtain was suddenly drawn back by a white-coated doctor. Stepping into the cramped confines of the cubicle, the doctor looked from Scott to Jason in surprise, a disapproving look hardening on his face.

'And where do you think you're going?' he asked Jason, glancing down at the notes on the clipboard he was holding. 'You only came out of surgery a couple of hours ago – I think it's a little early to be getting back on your feet.'

'I'm discharging myself,' Jason replied, a pained expression creasing his face as he took another step forward.

The doctor ran a hand through his greasy brown hair in frustration, dark circles ringing his eyes as the end of his twelve-hour shift approached.

'As your doctor, I can't allow you to do that. We've stabilised the gunshot wound, but I need to run further X-rays and scans to make sure there are no bullet fragments still in there. You lost a lot of blood and we need to monitor you for any signs of infection.'

Shaking his head, Jason reached inside his jacket pocket and pulled out his police warrant card with trembling fingers.

'As a police officer, I'm telling you that I'm discharging myself – right now.'

The doctor stared at Jason as he stood there, the detective's body swaying slightly from the effort of keeping itself upright. His bloodstained jacket was marked with a charred bullet hole where the left sleeve met his shoulder. Scott stood alongside Jason, nervously shifting his weight from one foot to the other as he watched the doctor's expression quickly change from shock to resignation.

'I do wish you'd at least talk to your colleagues before you go ahead and discharge yourself,' the doctor replied with a sigh. 'See if they can talk some sense into you.'

He gestured past the rows of identical beds towards the reception desk at the entrance to the ward. There, standing with their backs towards them, two uniformed police officers were quizzing the nurse manning the desk.

At the sight of the two policemen, Jason and Scott exchanged an anxious glance, both instantly sharing the same unspoken fear – Nicholls had found them. Sweat beading his forehead, Jason sank back down onto the bed, desperate to buy them some time.

'Don't worry,' he sighed, the raw ache in his shoulder still fogging his mind. 'I'll talk to them – I just need a minute here.'

The doctor stared at Jason, raising a quizzical eyebrow at this sudden change of heart. But before he could speak, he was interrupted by a frantic clatter of footsteps behind him and the simultaneous buzzing of his pager. A red-haired nurse appeared at his shoulder, her freckled face scrunched into an anxious frown.

'Doctor, you're needed in A&E right away,' she told him, her words rushing out. 'There's been a major road traffic accident out on the North Circular. The ambulances won't stop coming – they say that hundreds are injured.' She paused to take a breath, looking for a moment as though she was on the verge of tears. 'It's chaos down there. They need all available medical staff in A&E right now.'

Nodding his head, the doctor turned and strode briskly down the ward at the nurse's side, their footsteps slapping in unison across the worn floor tiles. At the reception desk, the two policemen were still hunched deep in consultation with the receptionist. As the curtain fell back around the bed, screening them from view, Scott turned to Jason.

'They've found us,' he groaned, the fear already pumping adrenalin through his veins. 'We've got to move – now!'

With a painful nod of agreement, Jason pushed himself up from the bed, but then sank back almost immediately with a sharp gasp. His right hand reached up to his bandaged shoulder, the wound a ragged knot of agony.

'I don't know if I can make it,' Jason said, his words coming in short staccato gasps. 'Get out of here. Go back to the bookshop. Tell them what happened . . .'

Shaking his head, Scott cut Jason's instructions short.

'Wait here,' he told him. Pulling the curtain back a fraction, Scott quickly scanned the ward before silently slipping outside and leaving Jason alone on the bed. Then the curtain twitched back as Scott pushed a wheelchair into the cubicle.

'Can you get into this?' he asked, leaning towards Jason's hunched figure with an outstretched hand.

'I can walk,' Jason replied through gritted teeth, an angry flush momentarily colouring his pale features.

'I know,' Scott replied, 'but we've got a better chance of getting past them with you in this.' He stretched out his hand again to help him.

Ignoring Scott's hand, Jason shifted his weight from the edge of the bed and, with a groan of exertion, lowered himself into the wheelchair. Its hard metal lines dug into his body, pressing against his bandaged shoulder until he slumped forward to ease the pressure.

'Here,' said Scott, quickly pulling the sheet from the bed and draping it around Jason's hunched shoulders. 'Cover yourself up and keep your head down.'

As Jason pulled the sheet more tightly around him, its antiseptic odour filling his nostrils, Scott pushed the wheelchair past the garish curtains and out into the ward.

Glancing over his shoulder, Scott could see three nurses clustered around the coffee machine at the far end of the ward, oblivious to the squeak of the wheelchair. Ahead of them, past the line of hospital beds echoing with low moans and spluttering coughs, he could see their way out: two double doors beneath an exit sign. In their path, though, was the reception desk; the nurse's light-blue uniform contrasting with the police officers' dark blue as they leant across the desk to scrutinise a computer screen.

They were less than twenty paces away. Scott gripped the handles of the wheelchair tightly, his heart thumping with every sound that its wheels made across the tiled floor. Fifteen paces now. Ten. The policemen still had their backs towards Scott and Jason, but their hard voices carried across the ward as they interrogated the nurse.

'Look, your patient confidentiality rules don't apply to us,' said the shorter of the two policemen, the three parallel lines on his shoulder asserting his sergeant's rank. 'I want you to check all the admissions in the last twelve hours. Anyone admitted with gunshot wounds – I need to know where they are.'

Scott's knuckles whitened as the sergeant's words confirmed his very worst fear. If the policeman turned around right now, he'd have his answer. Hunched in the wheelchair, Jason tried to shade his face in the folds of the sheet draped across him.

The double doors were just beyond the reception desk; the chance to escape tantalisingly close. Five paces. Keeping his head down and gritting his teeth, Scott steered the wheelchair past the reception desk, the nurse there barely glancing up as he passed. Only another few steps. Jason reached out from under the sheet to push the double doors open as Scott wheeled him through.

'Hey!' the indignant sound of the nurse's voice rang out behind the closing doors. 'Where do you think you're going with that wheelchair?'

Scott glanced back, his face framed in the shrinking gap. 'That's the boy,' the burly sergeant shouted. The two policemen scrambled around the reception desk as the double doors swung shut. 'Get after them!'

Panicking, Scott quickly glanced around the shabby entrance lobby, desperately searching for an escape route as the thunder of police boots rumbled down the ward. Ahead of them, a set of lift doors slid open to reveal a porter pushing out a patient on a trolley.

As the policemen crashed through the double doors, Scott swerved the wheelchair past the trolley, barrelled into the lift and pounded on the control panel to close the doors.

'Come on,' he urged as the doors glided together with agonising slowness. He could see the policemen battling their way past the shocked porter, the unconscious patient spinning on his trolley as they forced their way through.

Just before the lift doors closed, the taller of their pursuers thrust his hand through the sliver of space remaining. The narrow gap slowly began to widen, the policeman's scowling face now visible as he tried to prise the doors open. Another few seconds and he'd be in.

From the wheelchair came a groan of effort and Scott saw Jason's leg kick out, connecting with the policeman's clawing hands with a sickening crunch. The officer let out a shrill yelp of pain and his splayed fingers disappeared through the gap as the doors finally snapped shut.

As the lift began to descend, Scott looked down at Jason. The detective had sunk back into the wheelchair, his grey face a mask of pain.

'They'll be waiting for us,' he told Scott, his words coming in labouring gasps as he shrugged the sheet that had been wrapped around him to the floor. He rose unsteadily to his feet and leaned heavily against the side of the lift, staring at the control panel as the floors ticked by. 'They'll have the exits covered.'

'So what do we do?' asked Scott, frustration flushing his face as his sense of helplessness grew.

The lift juddered to a halt, the reading on the control panel showing that they had reached the basement.

The doors slowly slid open to reveal an empty white corridor. Stark overhead strip lights illuminated a maze of signs branching off to the left and right: Immunology; Microbiology; Haematology; Diagnostic Imaging. At the end of the corridor though, emblazoned in large red letters across white-frosted glass, was the sign they were looking for: EMERGENCY EXIT.

'We get out of here,' said Jason through gritted teeth, draping his left arm around Scott's shoulders for support. They lurched forward, the detective wincing with every step, while Scott struggled to bear his weight.

As they edged along the corridor in short shuffling steps, Scott anxiously glanced over his shoulder as the lift doors closed again with a click. The whirr of hydraulics as the lift rose again told him they didn't have much time.

'Come on,' he told Jason as the detective leant against the wall to catch his breath. 'We need to hurry.'

For the moment, the long corridor was empty – no white-coated doctors, officious nurses or haggard patients blocking their path. It was as though the hospital had ceased to operate below the ground floor, but Scott knew it couldn't last.

As if to prove him right, he heard the sound of voices approaching from a corridor that branched off to the left behind them. Two male voices and the sound of heavy footsteps growing louder, getting nearer.

The exit sign was still an age away at the end of the

corridor. Jason hung like a dead weight on his shoulder and Scott knew they wouldn't make it. A couple of paces ahead on the right was a large door, its surface a polished steel that almost glittered beneath the stark artificial lights. Somewhere to hide.

Hauling Jason towards the door, Scott pulled down on the handle and exhaled in relief as the heavy door slowly opened. As the approaching footsteps grew louder, he dragged Jason through the narrow gap, neither of them looking up to read the sign above the door before it swung closed behind them with a click:

## MORTUARY

The first thing that struck Scott was the chill; the air inside the cavernous room was several degrees cooler than the corridor they had just stepped in from. Then he saw the bodies.

Silhouetted against the stark white expanse of refrigerated storage units lining the walls, a multitude of dark-blue body bags lay on every available surface. In the middle of the room, a row of six autopsy tables, their metallic surfaces gleaming under the bright lights, were draped with the dark shapes of a dozen corpses. Around these corpses were dozens more, the bodies strewn on gurneys littering the room like abandoned shopping trolleys. In some cases, they were only covered with a sheet. Scott shuddered as he saw an exposed arm dangling lifelessly from the nearest trolley.

'What's been happening here?' breathed Jason.

Before Scott could even think of replying, a clattering sound in the corridor outside hijacked his attention. Glancing back, he saw the door handle beginning to turn and then felt Jason tugging at his arm. Without a word, the detective pulled Scott behind the nearest trolley, the sheet draped across the corpse offering them a hiding place as they crouched there silently. Scott heard the mortuary door swing open, followed by another rhythmic clatter and the sound of wheels squeaking across the polished tiles.

'I've already told them that they've filled the place up. I've run out of body bags down here and there's no room left in the freezers. If they don't start diverting them to other hospitals we're soon going to be in trouble.'

Ignoring Jason's warning hand on his shoulder, Scott peered around the edge of the trolley, his eyes darting past the hanging sheet to the two white-coated porters pushing yet another loaded gurney into the crowded mortuary.

'They say the mist came out of nowhere,' the porter continued, his gruff voice echoing around the room. 'One minute sunshine, the next the entire road's carpeted in fog. Right in the middle of rush hour – those poor drivers never stood a chance.'

He wheeled the trolley into one of the few remaining spaces, right next to where Scott and Jason were hiding. Ducking behind the folds of the dangling sheet, Scott saw the trolley wheels jar to a halt in front of him.

'Makes you think the blimmin' government's got the

right idea after all,' the other porter replied, sucking his teeth in resignation. 'Get everyone off the roads and onto them new trains. It's got to be safer that way, ain't it?'

The overhead lights snapped off as the two men exited the mortuary, their voices and footsteps fading as the doors closed behind them with a click. Crouching in the darkness, Scott felt Jason's hand tighten around his shoulder.

'Stay here,' Dyer's voice rasped through the chill air, a strained whisper rising above the constant drone of the refrigeration units. 'We need to make sure they've really gone.'

Scott nodded, his eyes slowly adjusting to the darkness. In front of him, he could make out the dark shape of a hand dangling from the trolley, its splayed fingers faintly silhouetted against the pale sheet. He stared at the hand with a strange fascination, his eyes straining against the dark as they flicked upwards to trace the shrouded shape of the body it belonged to.

He shook his head. It seemed almost impossible that only an hour or so ago, this discarded bundle had been a living, breathing person. Somebody's father maybe. Someone's son.

Scott couldn't stop thoughts of his own father filling his head. Had he been brought somewhere like this? His body shoved on some trolley and left to fester there? He felt his eyes prickle with tears but then angrily wiped them away.

Without thinking, Scott reached out into the darkness,

his fingers brushing against the dead man's cold, lifeless hand. In some strange way he wanted to reassure him that he wasn't alone.

There was a faint rustling sound somewhere on the far side of the room. Then Scott felt the dead man's hand closing around his own, the stiffening fingers cracking as they tightened their ice-cold grasp.

Scott flung himself backwards in fear, his feet scrabbling on the polished floor as he tried to free himself from the dead man's grip.

'What's wrong?' Jason's voice cut through the frigid air in a startled hiss.

Scott clattered against another discarded trolley, his back pressed against the metal frame. He could still feel the touch of the dead man's fingers, even though he'd pulled himself free. Shoulders shaking, he stared up at the shrouded shape looming above him on the trolley. All around he could hear a rustling sound slowly growing louder, interspersed with creaks coming from the heavily laden trolleys.

'He's alive,' Scott murmured, the words falling from his lips in disbelief. He watched the pale sheet slide slowly to the floor as the dark outline of the dead man rose up in front of him. Behind this ominous silhouette, Scott could see the rows of trolleys and tables filling the mortuary, their surfaces a squirming mass of dark shapes and shadows. The scratching, rustling sound now filled the room like the beating of a thousand tiny wings. 'They're all alive.'

He yelped as he felt another hand closing around his arm, then saw Jason's face pulled close to him in the blackness.

'Come on,' the detective hissed through gritted teeth as he dragged Scott up onto his feet. 'We've got to get out of here *now.*'

Scott scrambled after Jason as they blundered through the maze of discarded trolleys. The blinking lights of the refrigerated storage units gave the darkness an eerie green glow and Scott stumbled in the gloom. Throwing his hands out to save himself, he felt them sink into the yielding plastic of a body bag. Beneath this, he could feel cold flesh writhing underneath his fingers. Pulling his hands away in disgust, he saw the body bag thrash from side to side, rocking the trolley as it fought to free itself.

Scott staggered past, clasping his hand to his mouth as he fought back the bilious taste of revulsion in his throat. He was trapped in a nightmare as all around him, in the darkness, the dead continued to rise.

From the far end of the mortuary there was a sudden discordant clanging, the sound of metal striking against metal. Scott glanced back and with a lurch of terror he saw the doors of the freezer units begin to open one by one and the shadowy shapes of the corpses inside burst forward into the gloom.

'Scott!'

At the sound of Jason's shout, Scott swung back to see the detective framed in the doorway, the stark light flooding in from the corridor revealing the full horror of the grotesque scene. He raced towards the light, his eyes half shut against the hideous sight of thrashing body bags, writhing on top of the rattling gurneys like giant maggots. And worse than this, the twisted limbs and torsos rising like spectres from the shining tables, with cold dead eyes gazing sightlessly out from horribly disfigured faces.

Scott burst free from the mortuary into the sanitised sanctuary of the corridor and Jason slammed the heavy steel door behind him with a rifle-shot crack. Catching his breath in sharp juddering gasps, he turned towards Jason. The detective was leaning heavily against the brushed steel of the door, sealing inside the unnatural horrors within.

'What's happening?' Scott asked, the panicked question stuttering from his lips. 'Those people in there – they were dead.'

There was a thud on the other side of the mortuary door, followed by another, then another.

Jason shook his head, wincing from the effort of holding the door shut.

'Not any more,' he replied, sweat dripping from his ashen-grey face.

His eyes flicked up the corridor, fixing on the vivid green of the letters reading: EMERGENCY EXIT.

'This way,' grunted Jason, gesturing towards the sign. He took a stumbling step forward and then grabbed hold of Scott for support as another jagged wave of pain ripped through the fading anaesthetic haze. Scott quickly looped a supporting arm beneath Jason's uninjured shoulder and then the two of them hobbled towards the doors.

As they edged forward, the thudding sound behind them grew louder. Scott felt as though he was treading water against some invisible tide while Jason's dead weight hung heavy on his shoulders. Only a few more metres to go.

'Stop! Police!'

The shout rang out down the corridor.

Glancing back, Scott saw the two policemen advancing towards them. The taller of the two officers had his taser drawn and trained in their direction, his hard-edged stare telling them that this time they wouldn't get away.

'Turn around nice and slow.'

The burly sergeant barked out the order, raising his voice to a shout as the thudding sound echoing down the corridor reached a crescendo. They had almost reached the mortuary now, the first of the policemen nervously eyeing the heavy steel door that was reverberating with every hammer-like blow.

'Sarge, do you think we need to—'

With a shriek, the door to the mortuary exploded outwards. The shambling corpses lurched forward, spilling out of the darkness and into the light. For a split second, Scott saw the two policemen, their faces frozen in horror, and then they disappeared beneath a flurry of broken bodies and twisted limbs.

Scott's legs were frozen, his brain unable to process reality. Then a sudden rush of adrenalin flooded through his veins and he staggered forward again, flinging open the emergency doors to a chorus of alarms.

Behind him, he heard an agonised scream suddenly choked into silence, but Scott didn't look back. With Jason leaning heavily on his shoulder, he stumbled through the emergency exit and out into the freezing gloom. In the distance, a wail of sirens was growing louder as they hobbled across the car park, slowly leaving the nightmare behind.

# CHAPTER EIGHT

'We have to do something. You saw what was happening there – those people, the bodies . . .'

Scott's voice tailed off in frustration as he paced the peeling lino that ran in front of the overflowing bookshelves.

Slumped on a chair, surrounded by the detritus of scattered bills and teetering stacks of books, Jason shook his head, a grim look of resignation haunting his face.

'What can we do?'

After fleeing the hospital, they had staggered through London's twisting side streets, dodging furtively into the shadows at the sound of sirens, heading for the one place they had left to go. The one place where they would be believed.

Now in the cramped stockroom at the back of the bookshop, Scott continued to pace, trying to shake himself free from the cloud of fear still fogging his mind. Tom looked on, stroking his beard with anxious fingers, while Jason sat hunched, waiting for the painkillers he'd just been given to take hold. From the front of the shop, Scott could hear the tinny blare of music from the radio that was resting on the counter where Avalon had stationed herself, ready to fend off any unexpected police enquiries.

'But the dead were walking!' Scott exclaimed, frustration battling the fear in his voice. 'They killed those policemen – God knows what's happening to the patients in there.' His eyes darted from Jason to Tom. 'People will have seen what's happening,' he continued. 'They'll have to believe us.'

Tom shook his head. He pointed to the table and Scott saw the red ring-bound folder lying open there, spilling out its newspaper clippings filled with outlandish stories of supernatural events.

'Nobody believed any of those people,' he replied with a weary sigh. 'Whatever's happened in that hospital, the Brothers of Albion will hush it up.'

At the mention of their name, Scott finally asked the question that had been burning in his brain.

'Who are the Brothers of Albion?'

In response to Scott's question, Tom ran his fingers nervously through his beard. The straggly curtains of hair framing his face twitched as he began to speak.

'The Brothers of Albion are an ancient secret society whose tentacles control every lever of power in this country. Throughout the ages, the very destiny of this island has been shaped by their hands.'

'How do you know this?' Scott asked, a trace of suspicion in his voice. 'I mean, if they are so secretive and powerful, then how come you know all about them?'

'I wish I didn't,' replied Tom bitterly, his frown carving new lines across his brow. 'I curse the day I first heard their name.'

'But how *do* you know?' persisted Scott.

Scratching nervously at his beard, Tom's eyes flicked from Scott to Jason and then back again. When he finally spoke, his words were for Scott alone.

'Your father told me,' he stated simply. 'Alex was one of the Brothers of Albion.'

Scott shook his head.

'That doesn't make any sense,' he stammered. 'You said my dad was trying to stop this – that they murdered him. How could he be one of them?'

'It was when we were at Cambridge,' Tom replied. 'The Brothers of Albion were recruiting the next generation. They tried to lure us in with promises of knowledge and power, showing us the glittering futures that would be ours if we joined them.'

Tom looked across at Scott and saw that his eyes were filled with confusion.

'You've got to understand,' he continued, 'they were offering us the keys to the kingdom. Money. Power. Influence. Alex and I argued about it. He decided to take that path, but I turned away. Your dad told me I was being a fool, but I didn't like the price that had to be paid.'

He lapsed into a brooding silence.

'What happened then?' pressed Scott.

'The Brothers of Albion didn't take too kindly to being rejected.' Tom chose his words deliberately as though picking his way through a minefield of memories. 'They made things difficult for me. I dropped out of university and went travelling – Guatamala, Cambodia, Laos – anywhere off the beaten track and out of their reach. Finally I thought enough time had passed for me to come home. I'd met Avalon's mother by then – gods rest her soul – and she wanted to settle down.'

'What about my dad?'

Tom shook his head.

'Alex joined them,' he explained. 'He thought that with the power they wielded, the Brothers of Albion could help build a better Britain. That's what your dad really cared about. When the plans for the Greening of the Roads project were first laid out, Alex told me he thought they were the answer to his prayers. A scheme to leave your generation a brighter future.'

Scott heard the echo of his father's voice in Tom's words.

'But when he found out what really lay behind the plans,' Tom continued, 'that's when Alex came to me. I was the only person he could trust. He thought that together, with what we knew, we could stop the Brothers of Albion from opening the Dead Ways.'

'That's why we need the evidence – the proof that Alex had hidden.' Tom turned to Jason, a faint flicker of hope sparking in his eyes. 'Did you find it?'

'I found it,' Jason replied, shaking his head bitterly, 'but Nicholls completely destroyed it.'

Tom's shoulders sagged.

'What was the evidence?' he asked.

'It was a recording of some kind of meeting. That government minister – Daedalus – was speaking.' Jason frowned as if he couldn't believe his own words. 'They're going to open the Dead Ways.'

Scott's heart tightened in his chest. Jerry Daedalus – his dad's boss at the Department for Transport. The black knot of bile that had been sitting in the pit of his stomach ever since he'd heard the news about his father tightened. He'd make Daedalus pay. He'd make them all pay.

Scott's dark thoughts of revenge were interrupted by the sight of Avalon standing in the doorway holding the squawking radio in her hand.

'Listen,' she told them, her face flushed with worry. 'You need to hear this.'

'. . . and at a press conference held moments ago, Detective Chief Superintendent Charles Warren who is leading the enquiry made the following statement.'

The newsreader's soft voice was replaced by the superintendent's clipped tones.

'Detective Inspector Jason Dyer is now being sought in connection with the recent suspicious death of Alexander Williams, the Chief Secretary at the Department for

*Transport, and the abduction of his thirteen-year-old son. Members of the public are warned that DI Dyer is thought to be armed and dangerous and under no circumstances should be approached, but any sightings should be reported to the police immediately.'*

Superintendent Warren's voice faded out to be replaced by the newsreader's.

*'In other news, there has been a sudden outbreak of the norovirus, more commonly known as the winter vomiting bug, at London's Royal Alexandra Hospital. Health chiefs have placed the hospital in quarantine while the infection is treated . . .'*

'Turn it off,' Jason growled as he straightened in his chair. The raw ache of pain in his shoulder was slowly dulling, but he could feel the blood pulsing in his veins. He knew that they'd try to smear his name – he just didn't realise how quickly.

'How can they say that?' Scott exploded. 'They're trying to make out you're a killer – that you've abducted me!'

'They must think you can stop them,' Tom muttered darkly.

'What do you mean?' asked Scott.

Jason twisted in his chair to hear Tom's answer.

'Whatever you heard, whatever they think you know – it must be enough to worry them,' Tom replied. 'What else was in that recording?'

Jason held his fingers against his temples, pressing down

hard as though trying to push together the fragments of memory that Nicholls had ground beneath his heel. It was no use.

'It was like I told you. Daedalus was talking about the Greening of the Roads project – how their plans were nearly complete and the Dead Ways could finally be opened.' Jason scratched the base of his neck. 'He said it would be the start of a new era – the Halcyon Days.'

Tom stiffened at the sound of these words.

'Are you sure that's what Daedalus said?' he asked in a low rumble.

Puzzled, Jason nodded his head.

'I think so. Why? What does it mean?'

Scott looked up to hear Tom's resigned reply.

'It means that it's almost too late to stop them.' He reached out his ring-encrusted hand towards Scott. 'Have you got the book?'

Scott nodded, pulling out the ancient tome from where he had stashed it in the folds of his jacket, its dusky leather binding now speckled with droplets of blood.

'What is this?' he asked as Tom's fingers closed around the battered volume, the spidery silver letters of the title dancing across the cover.

'*Albion Unbound*,' Tom replied, his fingers caressing the cracked pages. 'This book tells how the Dead Ways were created and warns what will happen if they are ever opened again. It contains the revelations of the ancient druids, recorded before the Romans even reached the shores of Britain.'

Even though his face was grave, Tom's eyes glinted with a Messianic gleam. He thrust the open book towards Scott.

The tattered page had a faded illustration of a sweeping stone circle, with druids huddled together before a great stone altar. The ancient figures were crouching beneath a terrible gateway, a hole torn in the sky through which grim ghost-like spectres poured forth.

'When the ancients built the Dead Ways, they left a gateway through to the other side. Two gates, the First and the Last, are embedded somewhere in the great stone circles and monuments stretching across the country.'

Tom's fingers trembled as he pointed at the illustration and Scott noticed for the first time the crack of light emanating from the depths of the stone circle and reaching up into the blackened sky.

'It's not enough for the Brothers of Albion to destroy the motorways,' Tom continued. 'This just weakens the lines of power. To open the Dead Ways and keep them open, they need to unlock the gates.' Tom ran his fingers through his long straggly hair. 'Alex and I were trying to find out where the gates were hidden. We thought that if we could find them, we might have a chance of stopping the Brothers of Albion from opening the Dead Ways.'

'But surely *we* can still find them,' Scott interrupted, his words fierce and determined. 'What else do you know?'

Tom frowned.

'According to the book, the gates can only be unlocked on one day in every year. The First Gate must be unlocked on the winter solstice – the longest night. That's when this world and the next are separated by the shortest thread.' Tom's head was slumped in his hands, a grim look of dread staring out from his bloodshot eyes. 'This will herald the beginning of the Halcyon Days – a time of slow dying as the land prepares for the return of the Dead Lords. The Last Gate must then be unlocked exactly one year later. This will open the Dead Ways forever and unleash the Dead Lords who are waiting there.'

Scott glanced up at the calendar pinned to the wall: December 18.

'When is the winter solstice?' he asked, anxiety already creeping into his voice.

'Three days' time,' Tom murmured.

A chilling silence fell upon the room as the full meaning of Tom's words hit home. The charcoal sky visible through the skylight window seemed to darken as the dead of night approached.

# CHAPTER NINE

Avalon lay stretched out across her threadbare single bed as Scott unrolled his sleeping bag onto the floor. The walls of the dingy bedroom were lined with yet more books, the garish covers of graphic novels and horror stories stacked on top of each other. From downstairs in the shop, the faint sounds of Tom and Jason's conversation could just be heard through the bedroom door.

Reaching into her back pocket, Avalon pulled out the battered edition of *Albion Unbound* that she'd liberated from her father's hands. As she started to leaf through its pages, Scott sat slumped on the floor with his back against the wall. He wished he could speak to his mum and tell her what was happening. But Jason had warned him that the Brothers of Albion would have her under close surveillance – it was too dangerous even to risk a phone call to let her know he was still alive. It wouldn't be safe until they'd finally put a stop to the Brothers of Albion's plans.

He held his head in his hands, desperately trying to make

sense of everything that he'd learned. As he closed his eyes, he saw again the shambling corpses lurching towards him, their arms flailing in a flurry of twisted limbs as the eerie power of the Dead Ways ran through their veins. Scott rubbed his fingers against his forehead, hoping to wipe the horrific memory from his brain.

Dark hair fell across Avalon's face as her eyes darted up from the book.

'Are you OK?' she asked, pulling herself up into a sitting position on the edge of the bed.

Scott lifted his head from his hands. He looked up at Avalon, the dark circles beneath his eyes giving his face a hunted look.

'There's got to be a way we can stop them,' he said, his voice grim with determination.

Avalon frowned, her fingers still absent-mindedly flicking through the pages of *Albion Unbound*.

'My dad thought he could find the answers in this.' She held up the book so that Scott could see where pages had been torn from the spine and where those remaining were burnt and blackened, the text illegible beneath the scorch marks. 'But they weren't here.'

Scott felt a familiar surge of frustration, his hands unconsciously clenching into fists.

'Someone must know something.'

'That's why your dad stayed with the Brothers of Albion,' Avalon replied. 'Even after he found out what they were planning. He thought that if he kept close to Daedalus, he could find out what we needed to know – a way to stop them. In fact, the night before he . . .'

Her voice faltered and she lowered her eyes as if fearful to see Scott's reaction.

'Go on,' Scott pressed her. He had to find out the truth.

'The night before Alex died,' Avalon continued, 'he sent my dad a message. Told him that he'd found something out – something important – but we never got the chance to discover what it was.'

She glanced back up at Scott.

'I think that's why the Brothers of Albion killed him. Your dad must have found out where the First Gate is.'

Scott stared up at Avalon, still holding the battered edition of *Albion Unbound*. The book that his father had kept secret from him, along with everything else.

'He never told me.' Scott's words tumbled from his lips in a ragged burst of hurt. 'He never told me any of this.'

Outside, a howl of wind rattled the windowpane. Avalon stared at Scott from beneath her dark fringe, watching his shoulders silently shake as he fought back the bitter tide of blame rising inside.

'Why didn't he trust me?' asked Scott, his red-rimmed eyes filled with pain. 'I could've helped him – maybe he'd still be here if I'd known.'

'Alex wanted to tell you what was happening,' Avalon replied, 'but my dad told him that it was too much of a risk.

He said that it would be safer if you didn't know.'

'Safer for who?' Scott broke in, a harsh edge returning to his voice. 'My dad's dead and anything he found out that could stop the Brothers of Albion died with him.'

Scott held Avalon's gaze for a heartbeat then dropped his eyes.

'I'll never get the chance to talk to him again.'

A brooding silence filled the room as outside the wind howled again, the dark curtains drawn across the window shivering in the breeze.

'What if you could?' said Avalon, finally breaking the silence.

Scott looked up at the sound of her question.

'What do you mean?'

'What if you could speak to your dad now?' Avalon asked.

'Are you trying to be funny?' Scott snapped, a flash of temper flushing his cheeks.

Ignoring Scott's challenge, Avalon leaned over the edge of the bed. Her hands scrabbled beneath the overhanging bedspread as she searched for something hidden there. With a grunt of satisfaction, she pulled out a rectangular wooden board, its polished surface covered with letters and numbers. Sitting with her back against the bed, Avalon placed the board on the floor between them.

'I'm not trying to be funny,' she told Scott, her eyes fixed in an unblinking stare. 'We can talk to your dad using this.'

Scott stared down at the board. The arc of the alphabet was carved across its surface above a straight line of numbers running from zero to nine. In the four corners of the board were the words YES, NO, MAYBE and FAREWELL.

'Is that a Ouija board?'

Avalon nodded. 'It's a spirit board – a gateway to the other side. We'll be able to contact your dad and ask him where the First Gate is.' She looked up with a confident smile. 'It'll just be like getting a text from him.'

Scott shook his head doubtfully. The idea seemed so ridiculous. Then he remembered the sight of the dead marching out of the mortuary, a grisly reminder that anything was possible. Deep inside, the pain in his heart ached at the promise of Avalon's words – the chance to speak to his dad again.

'How can you be sure we'll be able to contact my dad?' he asked, finally daring to believe the impossible. 'What if something goes wrong?'

'It's not going to go wrong. I've done this before.' Glancing around, Avalon reached for an empty glass and, turning it over, placed it beneath the curve of letters and numbers on the polished board.

'Come on.' She grabbed a notepad and looked up into Scott's eyes, the spirit board between them. 'Place your left hand on the edge of the glass,' she instructed. 'We need to connect to the spirit world.'

Scott followed the instructions as Avalon did the same

in turn, the upturned glass quivering slightly as their fingers touched the edge.

'I need you to make contact with your dad,' Avalon continued in a hushed tone. 'Talk to him – find out what we need to know. I'll write down the messages we get back.'

She glanced up at Scott, her eyes sparkling with anticipation.

'Are you ready?'

Scott nodded, but a sense of unease was creeping slowly up his spine even as he began to speak.

'Dad, can you hear us?'

Outside the wind hammered against the glass as Avalon's hushed voice repeated the question.

'Alex, are you there?'

Beneath their fingers the glass stayed silent.

'Please, Dad,' said Scott, willing his words to be heard. 'We need your help. Are you there?'

The glass trembled slightly and Scott glanced up in suspicion, but the surprised expression on Avalon's face mirrored his own.

'Dad, is that you?' Scott breathed the words as though he was scared to break the spell.

The light bulb overhead flickered in reply, then Scott felt the glass begin to edge across the board, dragging their fingers to the top-left corner.

YES

Avalon grinned in triumph.

'I told you it would work,' she whispered.

Keeping his fingers pressed against the glass, Scott looked down at the board as Avalon waited, the tension thickening the air between them. All the questions he wanted to ask; all the things left unsaid.

'Ask him about the gate,' Avalon murmured.

'Dad, we're trying to find a way to stop the Brothers of Albion,' Scott explained. 'There's less than three days until the solstice – we need to stop them from unlocking the First Gate.'

Scott could feel the glass vibrating under his fingers as though waiting to give its answer.

'Please,' he leaned forward over the board, almost willing the glass to move. 'We can't find the First Gate without your help.'

With a shiver, the glass slowly began to circle around the board, gliding across the blank expanse surrounding the printed letters and numbers. Then the glass began to travel in ever-quickening circles, Scott's fingers following unwillingly, almost fighting to keep control of the glass.

'Where is the gate hidden?' Avalon whispered.

Without warning, the glass shot across the board and hovered for a second over the letter A before then shooting forward and selecting the numbers 5 – 0 – 1 in rapid succession.

'It's going too fast,' Avalon hissed, scrabbling to write down the message as the glass skittered forward, racing between the letters and numbers on the board.

A – 4 – 1 – M – 1 – M – 1 – 8

'I don't understand, Dad,' Scott frowned as the glass slid back and forth. 'What do you mean?'

He stared down at the lengthening list of letters and numbers that Avalon was frantically scribbling. Was it some kind of code?

A – 1 – A – 6 – 1 – 0 – 8 – A – 6 – 6

Suddenly, the realisation hit him. 'They're roads,' he exclaimed. 'He's giving us directions!'

The glass skittered forwards, hovering over each letter for a fraction of a second before darting forwards again. Spelling out, letter by letter, their destination.

R – E – Y – C – R – O – S – S

'The First Gate,' Avalon breathed. 'It's a place – Rey Cross.'

The glass jagged backwards and forwards, repeating the same pattern of letters.

R – E – Y – C – R – O – S – S – R – E – Y – C – R – O – S – S – R – E – Y – C – R – O – S – S

'Dad, what do we do when we get there?' Scott pleaded, desperate to keep hold of this fragile connection. 'How do we stop them from opening the gate?'

His fingers fought to keep control, the edge of the glass now hot to the touch. He looked up, his gaze meeting Avalon's as their hands were dragged in rapid jerks across the board, the same two words repeated over and over again.

'Why won't he answer?' he whispered, his fingers burning as they stayed glued to the glass. He could see the reflection of pain in Avalon's eyes, her look of triumph replaced by fear as the glass frantically weaved its way across the board.

It was too much. Avalon wrenched her hand from the glass sending it spinning sideways, shooting off the board and smashing against the wall. The glass shattered in a whip-crack of sound, sending Scott and Avalon ducking as the shards rained down on top of them.

The heavy sound of footsteps thundered up the stairs and then Jason yanked open the bedroom door, Tom's anxious face framed in the doorway behind him.

'What happened?' Jason demanded, his eyes darting around the room searching for danger. He looked down at the smashed fragments of glass strewn across the Ouija board as both Scott and Avalon cautiously raised their heads. 'What were you two doing?'

Brushing the shards of glass from his hair, Scott was the first to reply.

'We've found the First Gate,' he told him, a triumphant grin spreading across his face. 'My dad told us where we need to go – Rey Cross.'

Scott stared out of the mud-splattered window of the VW camper van, the desolate moors stretching out into the distance as the road climbed through the darkness. Next to him, Avalon dozed, a book entitled *The Hidden Stone*

*Circles of Britain* open in her lap. In the front, Tom hunched over the steering wheel while in the passenger seat Jason anxiously scanned the road ahead for any sign of the authorities.

They had been driving for most of the day. It had taken Scott and Avalon a long time to convince Jason that they had contacted Alex Williams from beyond the astral plane – and that he'd told them the location of the First Gate. They had argued into the early hours. Jason had been reluctant to believe something that he hadn't seen with his own eyes, but in the end, he'd had no choice. There were only two days left until the solstice.

They had left London early that morning. Following the directions dictated by the Ouija board, Tom had driven north – heading for Rey Cross on the Pennine Moors.

In her book, Avalon had found a description of the forgotten stone circle that lay there.

'Check this out: *Rey Cross occupies a commanding position, 400 metres above sea level, on a prehistoric route, which is now the A66. This desolate circle of stones is the point where east meets west, and north meets south, at the heart of Albion.*'

Scott had listened in silence. It all seemed to fit, but somehow a nagging doubt lingered in the back of his brain. He remembered the glass skittering across the polished surface of the Ouija board in a cavalcade of letters and numbers. His last chance to talk to his dad, but all he'd got was a list of road names. He could feel his fingers burning against the glass before it shattered into a thousand pieces. Why wouldn't his dad speak to him? When Scott opened his eyes, he could see the shadow of his father's face reflected in the glass. He tightened his hands into two clenched fists, the fire in his heart burning with the desire for revenge. Somehow he was going to put an end to all of this and stop the Brothers of Albion. For his dad. For everyone.

The indicator's constant clicking brought Scott's thoughts back to the present. Tom was steering the van towards a darkened slip road, the crooked Y on the broken road sign signalling the turning for the westbound A66. Rey Cross could only be a few miles away now. The road curved upwards, and the van hugged the blind bend as its headlights cut through the gloom. The darkness was thickening as evening edged into night, although the day had never really taken hold with charcoal grey skies tracking their journey north.

As the road straightened, Jason swore and Tom slammed on the brakes, the van skidding to a sudden halt. Scott was thrown forwards and there was an indignant yelp as Avalon was jolted from her sleep.

In front of them, a tall steel fence sealed off the four-lane carriageway, the shining beams of the van's headlights illuminating the abandoned A66. A sign high on the chain-link fence announced:

A GREENING OF THE ROADS SCHEME
RESTORING YOUR GREEN AND PLEASANT LAND

# CHAPTER TEN

Leaving the engine running, Tom stepped outside closely followed by Jason, Scott and Avalon. The four of them walked towards the high chain-link fence. The glare from the headlights threw a quartet of wraith-like shadows across the highway. The A66 stretched into the distance as it climbed across the bleak Pennine Moors caged behind the security fence. An eerie stillness permeated the scene, the worn tarmac of the abandoned road frozen in desolation.

Rey Cross was less than twenty miles ahead as the A66 bent westwards, but as they reached the solid steel links of the high-security fence, it might as well have been another two thousand miles away. There was no way past.

Threading his fingers through the woven metal web, Scott shook the fence in frustration, the Greening of the Roads sign clanging mockingly as the barrier held firm. He turned towards Jason who had taken a step back from the fence, his head swivelling as he scanned the perimeter, which stretched over the horizon in either direction.

'How do we get past this?'

Jason squinted back towards the camper van, the throaty rattle of its engine cutting through the silence of the night. He turned to Tom whose wild, white-flecked hair shone in the glare of its headlights.

'Have you got a tow rope or chain in that thing?'

Glancing across, Tom nodded.

'What do you want to do?' he asked.

'Back the van up to the fence,' Jason replied. 'I think there might be a way through.'

Scott and Avalon watched as Tom climbed into the driver's seat, shifted the van into reverse and then backed up until it was only a metre or so away from the security fence. He jumped from his seat and then hauled a greasy metal chain out from the boot, its thick metal links clanking ominously as it spilled onto the tarmac in front of Jason.

'Here,' Jason grunted as he bent down, struggling to fix one end of the chain to the tow bar. 'We need to secure this to the fence.'

Scott and Tom helped Jason to weave the heavy links of the chain through the fence's web of reinforced steel.

Wincing as he got back to his feet, Jason turned back to Tom.

'I think it would be best if I drove,' he told him.

Glancing back at the towering fence, Tom shuddered and with a sigh dropped the keys into Jason's outstretched hand.

'Get in,' Jason told them as he climbed behind the wheel.

They scrambled back inside the van. Releasing the handbrake, Jason inched the vehicle forward, the clanking sound of the chain unravelling behind them could just be heard over the engine's rumble. Then the van jerked to a stop as the chain pulled tight. Checking in his rear-view mirror, Jason saw the fence bathed in the red glow of the brake lights and the taut chain quivering at the point of maximum tension.

'Are you sure this is going to work?' Tom asked, his face creased into a worried frown.

In reply, Jason revved the engine, a guttural growl that almost drowned out his next order as he glanced back over his shoulder to Scott and Avalon.

'Keep your heads down.'

He pushed his foot down hard on the accelerator, the engine noise rising in a throaty whine of frustration as the chain bit into the fence. The tyres spun uselessly, frozen in motion. Jason gritted his teeth, his right foot almost flat to the floor as the van strained against its steel leash.

Then everything happened at once. With a scream of splitting steel, the fence exploded outwards, the woven metal links shearing away as the van surged forwards. Instinctively, Scott and Avalon glanced back through the rear window to see the heavy chain whipping back through the air towards them. Scott ducked, dragging Avalon down too, bracing himself for an explosion of shattering glass.

Jason gunned the accelerator, the tyres squealing as the

van shot from nought to fifty. The snaking links of the chain fell short, rattling against the tarmac as they were dragged wildly behind the van. Now pressing down on the brake, Jason brought the VW round, churning through the muddy verge at the edge of the slip road, until finally they were facing back the way they'd came.

Ahead, a huge hole had been ripped in the fence, the shredded steel revealing the dark highway beyond. No roadworks. No delays. The A66 was open again.

Tom jumped down from the van, gathered up the heavy metal chain and threw it into the boot. Scott's spirits soared as Tom climbed back inside, adrenalin pumping new hope through his veins. The van accelerated forwards, punching its way through the hole in the fence and out onto the abandoned road. For the first time, it seemed like they were one step ahead of the Brothers of Albion. It was two days until the solstice and here they were, heading towards the First Gate. All they needed to do was find a way to seal it shut for ever, before the Brothers of Albion could even attempt to unlock it.

Scott peered through the windscreen out into the darkness. Wintry winds buffeted the van as the twin beams of its headlights followed the white line in the centre of the road, climbing up across the bleak moorland. He strained his eyes, searching for any sign of the circle. Avalon's book had said that the ruined monument was at the head of the Stainmore Pass, the highest point of the A66, but as they neared the summit, all Scott could see was a dusting of snow on the ground.

On the road ahead, a lay-by branched off to the left and just before this a broken pillar of stone was set back from the road. A broken cross. Rey Cross. They were here.

'Pull over,' Scott called out, gesturing towards the stump of stone. 'This must be it.'

Jason steered the van into the lay-by and cut the engine, the darkness crowding around them as he turned the headlights off. Reaching into the glove compartment, Tom pulled out the torches they had picked up at the service station earlier that day and handed one to Jason, Scott and Avalon in turn.

'The stone circle is out there on the moor,' he told them, gesturing with his torch into the blackness beyond the glass. 'Twenty metres south of the broken cross.'

Scott reached for the door handle, eager to start looking for the First Gate.

'Wait.' Jason twisted in his seat to face Scott. 'We don't know who could be waiting. I'm not putting you at risk – any of you. First, I'm going to check this out on my own – that's my call.'

'No chance,' Scott snapped in reply, keeping his hand closed around the door handle. 'We've tried that before – remember? You ended up getting shot.'

'And the Brothers of Albion won't be anywhere near here,' said Avalon, cutting across Scott. 'The solstice isn't for another forty-eight hours. This time we've beaten them.'

'And you don't know what you're looking for,' Tom concluded with a low rumble. 'The gate could be hidden anywhere in the circle. We'll all go together – we've got more chance of finding it that way.'

There was a moment of silence and then Jason gave an almost imperceptible sigh.

'OK,' he relented, 'but the first sign of danger and I want you to leave.'

They stepped out of the van, their narrow torch beams scratching at the darkness as howling winds whipped around them. The broken pillar lay a dozen car lengths behind, sheltering in the lee of a low fence that marked the boundary between the road and the moorland beyond. Nearby, the hulking silhouettes of earth-moving equipment – bulldozers, excavators, dumper trucks – sheltered beneath darkened banks of construction lights, waiting for the dawn when they could start to tear this road apart. Tracing his hand along the low wire fence for guidance, Jason led the way along the ragged verge, the frost-bitten earth crunching under their feet as they approached the ruined cross. Scanning the pitch-black landscape penned behind the fence, Jason shivered, less from the biting cold and more from a sense of foreboding about what could be waiting out there in the darkness. A handful of steps from the broken stump of stone, his hand snagged against something fixed to the fence post.

Jason swung his torch upwards, its pale beam illuminating a scrappy bunch of plastic flowers tied with a length of wire to the fence post. Next to this, a crumpled plastic envelope held a single sheet of paper.

'Wait a second,' said Jason, leaning into the wind to inspect his discovery as Tom led Scott and Avalon past him towards the broken cross. A photograph of a little girl in a red coat stared out from the crumpled page with a faded smile. Beneath this Jason read the scrawled message, the letters blotched and splattered by the rain: IN LOVING MEMORY OF CHLOE – IN OUR THOUGHTS FOREVER. LOVE, MUMMY & DADDY. Then the date, the third of March this year.

He shook his head sadly. Just another roadside memorial, the greening of this road coming too late for this small child.

Ahead of him, Scott's sudden yell cut through the night, jolting Jason's gaze up from the crumpled memorial. He could see the three of them, maybe twenty paces ahead, their torch beams darting past the broken stump of stone.

'Scott thought he saw something,' Tom called out. 'Someone out there on the road.'

Jason hurried to catch them, his nerves jangling as he reached for the taser hidden in the folds of his jacket.

'Where?' he asked.

Scott gestured into the darkness, the pale beam of his torch sweeping across the carriageway.

'I'm not sure,' he replied through gritted teeth. 'I just caught a glimpse of something.'

Jason strained his eyes against the blackness, the road

silent under a starless sky. His torch beam joined Scott's as they skimmed over the tarmac.

'There!'

A flash of red was caught in their criss-crossing beams. Scott's torch doubled back to illuminate the small figure of a child stepping towards them out of the darkness.

'It's a girl,' he exclaimed in disbelief as he saw the fringe of long blond hair emerging from the hood of a red coat.

'What are you doing here?' Scott called out as he rushed towards the girl. 'Where are your parents?'

Tom and Avalon hung back, bewildered, still trying to work out how this girl had appeared out of nowhere on an abandoned road that had been closed for months.

But Jason knew. He recognised the neatly buttoned red duffel coat and the faded fringe of golden hair. It was the child from the photograph. The girl who had been killed on this road nine months earlier. The realisation hit him like a ten-ton truck.

'No!' Jason's voice rang out in warning as Scott reached the young girl's side, resting a hand on her shoulder.

'Hey,' said Scott gently. 'Are you OK?'

The girl lifted her face and stared up at Scott through cold, dead eyes. Her neck was twisted at an unnatural angle, as though it could barely support the weight of her head and, as her hood fell back, Scott noticed for the first time the gaping wound in the side of her skull, where her long blond hair was matted with dried blood.

Scott stepped back in shock as Jason finally reached him.

'What's up with her?' Avalon asked, the ruined side of the young girl's head still hidden from her view.

'She's dead,' Jason replied, taking hold of Scott's shoulders as he pulled him away from the silent child. She was still staring up at them through lifeless eyes.

As they took another step backwards to where Tom and Avalon were waiting, the girl raised her left arm in a ragged, jerking motion, like a puppet twisted on a string.

Overhead, the banks of construction lights suddenly flickered into life, flooding the scene with a dirty yellow glow. Night was turned instantly into day and Scott saw with a shudder that the girl wasn't alone.

Behind her, stretching out down the highway, a ragged line of people were shuffling silently towards them. Scott scanned the figures at the front of the crowd. A motorcyclist in black racing leathers staggered forwards, the visor on his helmet reflecting the sodium glare of the lights. All the way up his left side, torn leather hung in patches from his shredded skin.

Next to him, a young woman with long black hair falling across her grey pockmarked face wandered down the middle of the road, her arms raised in front of her. Scott's eyes tracked downwards to see jagged edges of bone stabbing through her faded black top with the slogan 'Babe' picked out in diamanté studs.

There were more of them coming – some were walking, some were crawling – dragging themselves along on torn and twisted bodies, spilling over the barriers of the central reservation.

Scott felt Jason's hand tighten on his shoulder.

'Come on.'

They turned back towards the van to see with horror another wave of walking dead swarming past the vehicle, heading straight towards them.

Avalon moaned in dismay.

'Where are they coming from?'

Deep down, Jason knew, but as the massed ranks of joyriders, drunk drivers, crash victims and hit-and-runs lurched towards them, he only had time to shout one word in reply.

'Run!'

They turned in the one direction they could go. It was their only chance of escape – to flee past the broken stump of stone and out into the blackness of the moors.

'This way,' Tom called out, a desperate voice in the darkness, as they scrambled over the fence and down the embankment. 'It's the power of the Dead Ways that's bringing them here. If we can seal off the First Gate, we can stop them coming through.'

Scott swung his torch in search of the stones, the pale beam arcing wildly against the midnight sky as they stumbled across the rough moorland. The boggy ground sucked at his feet as behind them the low moan of the walkers was carried on the wind.

Suddenly he felt his footing slip as he stumbled over

a small boulder sunk fast in the earth. Catching himself before he fell, Scott swept his torch across the ground to reveal a rough circle of small stones, barely visible amongst the tussocks of grass.

'Over here,' he called out. 'I think I've found it.'

A trinity of torch beams rose behind him.

'It can't be,' growled Tom as his torch swept the darkness of the circle. 'Where's the gate?'

'I don't know,' Avalon stammered. 'The spirit board said . . .' Her voice trailed into a whisper, the words almost lost in the darkness as the realisation dawned. 'The Dead Lords must have sent that message. They're trying to stop us from sealing the Dead Ways forever.'

Scott stayed silent, his worst fears now confirmed. The directions hadn't been from his dad. This was a trap. They had to get out of there. Alive.

The low moan was growing louder, carried on the wind whipping around them.

Jason turned towards him.

'Look, we've got to—'

His sentence was snapped into silence as a skeletal hand suddenly thrust through the earth in front of him. Bleached fingers clutched at his ankle, tightening their grip as a forest of bones erupted around them.

Jason stamped on the grasping fingers, the bones splintering into dust as Tom bellowed out a warning. Next to him, Scott and Avalon kicked out wildly at the corpses, which were dragging themselves out, bone by bone, from the boggy ground. Their torches illuminated hideous grins beaming from mud-stained skulls, and clumps of earth still clinging to bones as the bodies clawed their way free.

The curve of the road was behind them, the construction lights still blazing with a sickly yellow glow. Jason could see the waves of walking roadkill crashing over the barrier that separated the road from the moors. They tumbled down the steep embankment before rising again in the gloom, arms outstretched, their low moans rising on the wind. But back on the road, the camper van stood free.

'We've got to get back to the van,' he yelled.

Glancing up, Tom nodded in agreement before smashing his torch against a flailing shape that leapt towards him out of the darkness.

Kicking his way through the forest of corpses, stamping one grinning skull into splinters before volleying another into the darkness, Jason reached Scott and Avalon. He pushed them ahead of him as he urged them to, 'Move!'

Scott didn't need telling twice. The First Gate wasn't here. All thoughts of revenge were replaced with the desperate desire to survive. Dragging Avalon beside him, he ran.

His eyes fixed on the camper van, waiting under the harsh neon glare, he doubled back in a sweeping arc, scrambling over the ankle-wrenching earth. Their torch beams skittered over the wild moorland, the hungry moans of the dead closer now as they neared the road.

'Hurry,' he urged Avalon as they scrambled up the embankment.

Scott crashed into the low wire fence, its cables tensing as Avalon started to scramble over. The van was only a few metres away. Further along the road, the ragged line of walking dead slowly turned, grey faces swivelling as sunken eyes locked onto their location.

Glancing down, Scott yelled out a desperate warning as he saw disembodied hands reach out from the darkness and grab hold of Avalon's ankles. A strangled cry slipped from her lips as the hands, imbued with a supernatural strength, dragged her from the fence and sent her tumbling back down the embankment into the darkness.

Avalon felt the bony fingers tightening their grasp as she careered down the bank. She crashed to a halt, sprawling in a heap in the half-light at the edge of the moors. Frantically, she kicked out to try and free herself, but her kicks only found empty air as the bony fingers clawed their way up her aching body.

She looked down to see a legless ghoul hauling itself forward. It was the corpse of a biker, a shredded leather jacket hanging from a skeletal frame, broken in two at the waist. Two sunken eyes lit by a predatory spark stared out from a face of rotting flesh webbed with blackened veins. The ghoul's jaw hung open in a slavering snarl as it snapped forward in search of her neck.

Avalon twisted away, desperately trying to free herself

as the corpse lunged forward with a guttural growl. She felt a sudden onrush of air and then a metal bar swept out of the darkness, connecting with a sickening crack against the dead man's skull and sending the corpse flailing into the darkness with a disappointed howl.

Scott threw the remnants of the road sign pole to the ground and then reached down to help Avalon to her feet. Next to him, Jason emerged from the darkness, scrambling down the bank.

'There's more of them coming,' he warned. 'We've got to hurry.'

The three of them raced back up the embankment. Tom was waiting for them at the top, his strong arms reaching up to help Avalon and Scott as they hauled themselves over the fence. Under the glare of the construction lights, the shadows were shortening as the walking dead closed in on the camper van, their low moans rising in recognition.

'Go! Go!' yelled Jason.

Dragging Avalon beside him, Scott dived for the rear door as the shambling corpse of a middle-aged man, his business suit splattered with blood, lurched out of the shadows. Darting past his outstretched arms, Scott bundled Avalon into the back of the van and then clambered in behind her, slamming the door shut as bloodstained fingers scratched at the window. In front of them, Tom scrambled into the driver's seat, his shaking fingers clawing at the ignition as he turned the key and the engine spluttered into life. As the line of zombie roadkill relentlessly closed in, Jason yanked open the passenger door and slammed into the seat next to Tom. They stared out of the windscreen at the horror that lay ahead.

The road was filled with a long line of walking dead. Their ragged bodies shuffled relentlessly forward, arms outstretched as if ordering them to stop in a zombie roadblock.

Tom wrenched at the gear stick and then stamped hard on the accelerator, gunning the van forward, its tyres screeching against the tarmac. The dead didn't flinch at the sight of the oncoming vehicle but just kept on advancing.

'Get down!' yelled Tom as, still picking up speed, the van ploughed into the first of the shambling figures.

THUD. THUD. THUD.

The corpses smacked off the chassis, spinning out under the wheels in a rumble of bones. One walker flew across the bonnet, her fingers clawing at the windscreen before Tom tugged at the wheel and the corpse flipped out across the central reservation.

Then the road was clear. Not daring to glance back in the rear-view mirror, Tom kept his foot down hard as the camper van sped along the road. The neon lights slowly faded to blackness as they left the dead behind.

# CHAPTER ELEVEN

'We've tried it your way,' said Jason, his pale face drawn as he glanced from Scott to Avalon and then to Tom in turn. 'It didn't work. Now we do things my way.'

The four of them were slumped around the scuffed table in the stockroom, the last grey fingers of daylight barely reaching through the skylight as the bookshelves surrounding them loomed in the gloom.

The journey back south from Rey Cross had been filled with bickered recriminations – how they had been fooled, the mistakes they had made – their voices raised to keep the silence at bay. For in the silence, the horror returned – visions of the shambling corpses staggering towards them, the skeletal figures rising from the earth and shaking the dirt from their bones.

Scott looked back at Jason across the darkening table. It had taken them the best part of a day to get back; the motorways were in chaos as the Christmas getaway began, all thanks to the government's Greening of the Roads project. The winter solstice fell tomorrow. Just over twenty-four hours left to find the First Gate.

'What do you mean do things your way?' he asked. 'How are *you* going to find the First Gate?'

'By doing what I was trained to do,' Jason replied. 'Following leads, tracking down suspects – good old-fashioned detective work.'

Scott nodded, his blue eyes set in a determined stare.

'Count me in.'

* * *

Scott peered out of the van, the morning drizzle running in rivulets down the windscreen. Beside him, Jason sat hunched in the driver's seat, the upturned collar on his borrowed jacket pulled high to hide his face from the CCTV cameras that swivelled overhead.

They had left the bookshop early that morning, Tom pressing the keys to the VW into Jason's hand.

'Avalon and I will stay here,' he had told them. 'We'll search through every page of *Albion Unbound* again. There might be some hidden clue that we've missed – something that can help us lock the Dead Ways for good. But if you can't find out where the First Gate is, then the Brothers of Albion will have already won.'

Now, as Jason and Scott sat waiting, the van parked opposite the police station, Tom's words hung in the air between them. They had been waiting there for nearly three hours. A stakeout Jason had called it. Waiting to catch a glimpse of one of the only leads they had – Detective Chief Inspector Eddie Nicholls.

'When did you say his shift finishes?' Scott asked, rubbing his hands together for warmth as he turned towards Jason. The cold outside seemed to have seeped into the van as the rain turned to sleet on the windscreen. 'I don't know why we couldn't have gone straight after Daedalus.'

'Daedalus is a government minister,' Jason replied, keeping his eyes fixed on the station. 'There's no way we could get close enough to find out what we need to know. Nicholls is a known quantity. His shift should have finished fifteen minutes ago, all we have to do is . . .'

Jason's words suddenly fell away. DCI Nicholls was heading down the stone steps of the police station, the ice-cold sleet flattening his thinning hair as he wrapped his black overcoat more closely around him.

'There he is,' breathed Jason, leaning forward and then wincing as pain flared in his tightly strapped shoulder.

At the bottom of the steps, Nicholls looked to his left and then right, as if deciding which way to go. As his eyes flicked past the van, Scott and Jason slumped in their seats, hoping that the quickening sleet would keep them hidden from view. Nicholls glanced at his wristwatch, his foot tapping out an impatient rhythm against the pavement.

'What's he waiting for?' said Scott, trying to see past the whirls of sleet now obscuring the windscreen.

As if in reply, a sleek black Bentley Continental drove

silently down the tree-lined street and cruised to a halt in front of the DCI, its windscreen wipers beating furiously against the thickening flurries. The rear passenger door swung open and, without a word to the driver, Nicholls ducked inside, disappearing from sight behind the blacked-out windows. The passenger door closed and as its tyres sent a dirty-grey slurry of sleet spinning up its black paintwork, the limousine sped away.

Jason fumbled the key in the ignition, the van choking asthmatically into life. The limousine was at the top of the street now, its right-side indicator flashing as it waited at the junction.

'Hurry up,' said Scott as Jason crunched the van into gear. 'You're going to lose him.'

The VW lurched forward through the sleet as the limousine turned out into the junction and disappeared from view.

'Come on,' Jason muttered, wincing as he worked through the gears and then sharply braking when he came to the junction. Craning his head to the right, he glimpsed the blacked-out glass of the limousine seven cars ahead. As the traffic lights began to change, the row of waiting cars to the left started to edge forward, but Jason stamped down on the accelerator, pulling the van out ahead of the oncoming traffic. Ignoring the vexed chorus of horns behind him, he tried to keep the Bentley in view as the van's single working wiper moved the sleet from one side of the windscreen to the other.

The traffic was picking up speed now, the road widening as they left North Kensington behind and headed east. As the limousine moved out into the right-hand lane, Jason slowed down.

'What are you doing?' asked Scott, glancing across in alarm. 'He's getting away.'

Jason shook his head, keeping the limousine in sight as he let another car pass them before pulling out into the outside lane.

'We're tailing him, not racing him,' he told Scott. 'It's bad enough that we're stuck in this thing,' he said, banging his hand against the dashboard, 'without driving it right up his exhaust pipe as well.'

'I know we're tailing him,' Scott muttered, his face flushing as he sank back into the passenger seat, 'but what are we going to do when they get to where they're going?'

Turning away, he glanced at the streets they were passing, the shops and cafés now giving way to offices and government buildings as they headed towards Westminster. In the driver's seat, Jason was also watching the street signs. His pulse quickened with every turn the black limousine took. Tom had told them that the Brothers of Albion controlled every lever of power in the country. It looked as if they were heading into the belly of the beast.

They had slowed to a crawl in the thickening traffic, creeping past the grand entrance to another government ministry. Jason glanced anxiously at the uniformed police officers manning the security scanners just inside its tall glass doors. A cluster of CCTV cameras were fixed above the entrance and he flinched as one of the cameras swivelled towards the van.

The limousine was only three cars ahead of them now, turning right at the junction onto Victoria Street.

'Where is he going?' asked Scott, his voice muffled as he anxiously chewed at his fingernails.

Jason stayed silent as he pulled out into the road directly behind the Bentley's blacked-out windows. Hunching forward over the wheel, he hoped the swirling flurries of snow now tumbling out of the sky would keep them screened from Nicholls's view if he glanced behind him. As they edged forward, his eyes scanned the road ahead.

He knew this road so well – the sleek glass building of New Scotland Yard on the left and, in the distance, the clock tower of Big Ben and the Houses of Parliament, protected by a ring of steel – CCTV cameras, road blocks, armed patrols. If that was where Nicholls was heading, they'd have no chance of following him – not with the whole of the Met searching for them.

'We're going to have to call this off,' he told Scott as the limousine pulled out into the right-hand lane. 'That car's taking him to the Houses of Parliament – there's no way we can get in there.'

Scott's eyes jerked from the road back to Jason.

'But we have to!' he begged. 'You said it yourself –

Nicholls is our only lead; if we lose him then we lose our chance of finding the First Gate.'

'It's not safe,' Jason replied, shaking his head as he flicked the indicator down to signal that they were turning left at the upcoming junction. 'We'll have to find another way.'

Ahead of them, the traffic lights changed, but instead of going straight across the junction towards Parliament Square, the black limousine waited in the outside lane, its own right-hand indicator flashing as it waited for a gap in the oncoming traffic. To their right, the gothic grandeur of Westminster Abbey rose up into the heavy sky, its soaring spires and arched windows dusted with snow.

'He's not going to Parliament,' said Scott, grabbing at Jason's arm as the limousine turned right into the triangular courtyard directly in front of the Abbey. It slowly navigated its way through the clusters of duvet-jacketed tourists, their faces and cameras held up towards the snow-clad martyrs and saints sheltering among the carved arches. The car stopped in front of an archway flanked by two wooden security cabins. From the fogged-up windows of the van, Scott and Jason watched as Nicholls emerged from the rear of the limousine, flashing a pass at the security guard stationed inside the cabin and then disappearing through the archway.

Scott reached for the door handle, pushing the passenger door open even as the van trundled forward towards the junction.

'What are you doing?' Jason yelled, stepping on the brake

as Scott swung himself down from the van. Scott stumbled as his trainers slipped in the blackened slush gathered in the gutter, but quickly pulled himself upright.

'This is our chance,' he told Jason, a reckless grin flashing across his face. 'I'm going after him.'

'Wait a second,' Jason spluttered, gesturing back at the impatient line of traffic now queuing behind them. 'I can't just leave the van here.'

Scott glanced across the road, his eyes searching for the archway Nicholls had just disappeared through. If he didn't move now, they'd lose him. As the driver of the black cab stuck directly behind them leaned on his horn, Scott swung the passenger door shut.

'I'll call you,' he mouthed, holding up his clenched hand with his little finger and thumb outstretched. Then he darted out in front of the van, dodging past the cars now edging forward again as he sprinted towards the abbey.

Cursing, Jason banged his fist against the steering wheel, but as the chorus of horns rose up in anger behind him, he shoved the van into gear and, stepping on the accelerator, lurched forward towards the junction, twisting his neck to try and keep Scott in sight.

Weaving his way through the crowds of sightseers, Scott skirted past the front of the abbey, its ornate twin towers reaching up into the alabaster sky – a place of sanctuary, a place of peace. Scott's mind, though, was filled with thoughts of revenge. His heart thudded in his chest as he approached the high archway flanked by the two guardhouses. The barrier was down, but through the archway he could see Nicholls, his black overcoat flapping behind him, striding across the snowy expanse of a large quadrangle flanked on all sides by ancient buildings. He had to follow him.

The security guard stationed inside the right-hand cabin glanced up from his newspaper, but Scott swerved to avoid his gaze, quickly tagging behind a group of schoolboys in matching grey uniforms as they walked laughing through the archway towards the quad beyond. As the chimes of Big Ben rang out, the students melted away into the leafy buildings on the right, scurrying up stone steps and disappearing through timeworn doorways.

Keeping to the shadows, Scott hurried to try to catch Nicholls as he headed towards the grand red-brick building at the far end of the quad. Ahead of Nicholls, Scott could see more dark-suited figures walking up the building's sweeping stone steps that led to three arched doorways, the central one of which was held open by a uniformed usher who greeted each visitor with a respectful bow of the head.

As Nicholls hurried up the stairs and stepped inside the meeting house, the usher manning the door glanced around the deserted quadrangle causing Scott to quickly duck down behind a low wall for cover. The usher then pulled the double doors closed with a hollow thud that echoed across the snowy quad.

As the snow fell in ever-thickening flurries, Scott shivered. The adrenalin that had been pumping through his veins from the moment he had slammed the van door shut suddenly faded and was replaced with doubt. He stared up at the imposing building, the rows of leaded windows ascending for three stories. Even as he crouched in the shadow of the wall, Scott felt exposed, wondering who could be looking down on him and tracking his every move.

His hand reached for the mobile phone in his jacket pocket. He could phone Jason now – tell him where he was, what he'd seen. Wait for him to get here and work out their next move. His freezing fingers hovered over his mobile's touch-screen, trembling in hesitation. Whatever was happening in there was happening now. There was no time to wait. He had to get inside.

The creak of a door opening followed by the sound of footsteps jerked Scott's head to the right. A line of schoolboys were filing out of the building from a side exit. Each of the students carried an instrument case and from inside the open door, the faint sound of discordant music could be heard. At the rear of the group, a red-haired boy bent down to tie his shoelace, leaving his violin case on the wall beside him.

Scott started forward. As he walked he quickly zipped his jacket right up to his throat to disguise his lack of uniform. Brushing past the departing line of younger boys, Scott grabbed the pristine violin case from its perch on the wall. Beneath this, the violin's owner was still bent forward over his laces, mumbling an apology as he shifted sideways to let Scott pass.

Quickly slipping through the door before it swung shut, Scott entered a wide hallway. To his right, three rooms branched off the hall, their doors closed with printed signs cautioning QUIET PLEASE – EXAMINATION IN PROGRESS fixed to the wood-panelled walls between them. From behind the doors the muffled sounds of scraping violin bows and tortured trumpet parps tried to escape.

Outside, behind the door he'd just stepped through, Scott heard an exasperated shout.

'Hey! Who's taken my violin?'

Hurrying forward, the instrument case still tucked under his arm, Scott reached the end of the corridor. Here, the hallway opened out into a wide reception area. A regal staircase led up to the next floor, but two more uniformed ushers were standing guard at the bottom of the stairs. As Scott stepped forward, the shorter of the two ushers blocked his path.

'Where are you going?' the man snapped in irritation. 'We told the school – there's a conference taking place today. Apart from the music rooms, the rest of this building is out of bounds.'

'Forgot my bow,' Scott stammered. He held out the violin case as proof. 'I think I left it in the toilets.'

The usher looked at Scott suspiciously. Then with a

grudging nod of his head, he gestured towards another corridor branching off to the left.

'Be quick,' he told him.

With a sigh of relief, Scott walked down the corridor. He could feel the usher's eyes on his back, tracking his every move. As he reached the men's toilets, Scott pushed open the door with a nod of thanks directed back at the watchful usher. Stepping inside, he placed the violin case on the tiled surface next to the sinks and stared up at his reflection in the mirror facing him. There had to be a way he could get past them.

In the reflection, amongst the gleaming porcelain and tiled surfaces, he caught sight of a grubby-looking door with the sign 'STAFF ONLY' hanging from it. Turning round, Scott walked towards the door and tried the handle. It didn't budge. Scowling, he pushed hard against the door, hearing a protesting squeak as it slowly shifted backwards to reveal a mop and bucket leaning against a towering stack of toilet rolls. As the bright light spilled into the dark supply room, Scott's eyes followed the exposed pipes running across the wall and extending into the shadows.

His fingers scrabbled against the wall in search of a light switch. Finding it, a light bulb overhead flickered into life illuminating a low-level sink below shelves of cleaning products, brushes and bright-yellow buckets. A pair of overalls hung next to the light switch, but at the far end of the room Scott saw another door, this time open, leading out onto a grey-carpeted stairwell. Of course – there had to be a way for the cleaners to get around the building without clattering up the grand staircase with their mops and buckets. And if they could . . .

Grabbing the overalls from their hanger, Scott quickly pulled these on over his clothes. He smiled with grim satisfaction. It was perfect. Like this, he could go anywhere he wanted.

Pulling the door shut behind him, Scott stepped out into the stairwell, peering up the flights of stairs as they twisted upwards. The coast was clear. Moving with stealthy footsteps, he climbed the staircase, pausing at each landing to peer out of the small glass porthole fixed in the door.

At the first floor, Scott could see more uniformed ushers hurrying back and forth, clearing away empty wine glasses and platters of food, but as he looked out of the tiny glass circle onto the second floor, he saw something that made him press back against the wall in fear.

Striding down the long corridor towards him was Jerry Daedalus, his face fixed in a troubled frown. Flanking him was Detective Chief Inspector Nicholls. The policeman was talking to Daedalus in a state of agitation, but from behind the glass the words were lost to Scott. Ducking down, he leant against the door, breathing heavily. Did they know he was here? He found his eyes drawn back to the small round window. He had to know.

Daedalus was now standing in profile halfway down the

corridor, but the broad-shouldered figure of DCI Nicholls was no longer in sight. As Scott watched, he saw the minister straighten his tie and with a sweep of his hand brush his hair into place. Then, Daedalus disappeared through a set of double doors, leaving the corridor empty.

Scott stood frozen, his right hand pressed against the door frame, paralysed by the volley of questions flashing through his mind. Should he call Jason? Should he follow Daedalus? Should he run? And where had Nicholls disappeared to?

For a heartbeat, a heavy silence hung in the corridor and then a resounding tumult of applause erupted from the doors through which Daedalus had stepped.

Scott pushed the landing door open and hurried down the long corridor. He had to get inside and find out what was going on. As he reached the double doors, he peered furtively through the arched glass window at the top.

Inside he could see a grand circular hall lined with oak-panelled walls. The room was filled with rows of seats and hundreds of people sat facing a raised stage at the far end of the hall. There, standing tall behind a red lectern, was Jerry Daedalus. The hall's ceiling was dominated by a huge stained-glass dome that shed a strange light on the stage below, gilding Daedalus in a golden glow.

As Daedalus began to speak, Scott slipped noiselessly inside the hall, trusting that everyone's attention was fixed on the stage. To his left, he saw a narrow staircase leading up to a gallery that encircled the room beneath and Scott began to climb as Daedalus's commanding voice echoed around the hall.

'Brethren,' he intoned. 'Guardians and shapers, destiny-makers, custodians of this island's sacred flame. Brothers of Albion, I welcome you all.'

Reaching the gallery level, Scott crawled forward on his hands and knees until he could peer out through the railings down onto the stage below. Daedalus was gripping the lectern with both hands, his eyes blazing with a fierce intensity as he continued to speak.

'We stand on the threshold of a new age. Tonight, we will finally realise our dream. Our greatest achievement awaits us on the other side of midnight.'

Stepping out from the lectern, Daedalus walked confidently to the front of the stage. Scott's flesh crept at the memory of the last time he'd seen Daedalus – the minister standing by his father's side at the ceremony to open the Greening of the Roads project. Now, as Daedalus looked down from the stage onto the assembled Brothers of Albion, this seemed like a cruel mockery of that moment.

'As we have worked to restore the great lines of power across this broken land, there have been reports of strange happenings. Some of you have expressed concerns about these incidents. But let me assure you, these events are not to be feared,' Daedalus told them, his voice ringing out confidently across the cavernous hall. 'This is the land readying itself for the dawning of the Halcyon Days.'

Half hidden in the gallery above him, Scott shook his head in confusion. *Restoring* the great lines of power? Tom and Avalon had said that the Brothers of Albion were destroying them. A sudden frantic buzzing from his jacket pocket had Scott scrabbling inside the overalls he was wearing as he grabbed at his mobile. Jabbing at the screen, he heard Jason's voice crackle from the phone.

'Scott! Where are you?'

On the stage below, Daedalus's voice was rising to a crescendo.

'When we open the First Gate at Avebury, a new Albion will rise from the ashes of the old – a promised land of unfading splendour and bliss.'

'I can't talk,' Scott hissed, cupping the mobile close to his mouth, but before he could hear Jason's reply, the phone was snatched out of his hand.

Looking up in alarm, he saw DCI Nicholls staring down at him, a cruel grin slashed across the policeman's face as he disconnected the call. From behind Scott, hands seized hold of him and dragged him backwards down the narrow staircase. As he struggled to free himself, his head banged against the oak-panelled walls and then the men hauled him out into the open space of the hall.

Dazed, Scott looked out at the countless faces turning towards him, every one fixed in a venomous scowl. From the stage, Daedalus spread his arms wide in a gesture of welcome.

'And here we have the boy who will help us to open the Dead Ways. Scott Williams, we salute you.'

Dropped to his knees, Scott felt a rough hand press a soaking cloth to his mouth. He gagged as the sweet-smelling fumes filled his throat. A void seemed to be opening up in front of him. As he slipped into the blackness, he heard a distant chorus of voices echoing in unison. A single word repeated into infinity.

*Albion! Albion! Albion!*

# CHAPTER TWELVE

'They've taken him!'

Jason gripped the edge of the table as he looked at Tom. The bookseller was sitting mute at the paper-strewn table, his heavy fingers tapping out an anxious rhythm against its surface. In the next chair, Avalon hunched dejectedly, her legs drawn up with her chin resting on her knees. They looked defeated, still in shock at the news Jason had brought them when he stumbled back into the bookshop.

It was only three in the afternoon but the faint specks of daylight still visible through the skylight window were fading fast. It was the winter solstice. The end of everything. For a moment, the darkening stockroom was silent and then Tom spoke.

'Where?' he asked in a low growl. 'Where have they taken him?'

Jason frowned, scratching his head in frustration.

'Scott couldn't talk. I could hear Daedalus in the background but I could barely make out what he was saying. I think he mentioned a place – Avebury.'

Avalon reached forward in a sudden movement, sweeping away the stray papers crowding the table. She jabbed her finger at the map that still lay open there and looked up in triumph.

'Of course,' she exclaimed, her voice shaking with excitement. 'That's where the First Gate is!'

Jason looked where she was pointing, seeing Avebury lay off the M4, a tiny village just south of Swindon, bisected by the map's red lines.

'What's at Avebury?' he asked.

Avalon stared at Jason in disbelief.

'Only the largest stone circle in the world,' she replied. 'Avebury's over a thousand years older and a hundred times bigger than Stonehenge.'

Tom pushed back his chair, its metal legs scraping against the wooden floor. Rising to his feet, he picked up the set of car keys from the table and threw them to Jason.

'Get the van,' he said, cracking the knuckles on his ring-encrusted hands. 'We're going to Avebury.'

The VW barrelled down the inside lane of the dimly lit motorway, the sickly yellow glare of the road lights struggling to fight its way through the fog that was slowly descending in misty spirals. Looking through the windscreen, Jason gave a shiver and his hand reached unthinkingly to his chest and the crescent shape of the taser burn.

The clock on the dashboard read 22:57. Glancing across, Jason could see Tom bent forward over the steering wheel, his eyes straining against the gathering mist, but his foot still firmly planted on the accelerator as a road sign reading SWINDON 5 flashed by. They had already spent hours trying to find their way around countless roadblocks and diversions on the route to Avebury. They didn't have any more time to waste.

In the back of the van, Avalon poured over the battered edition of *Albion Unbound*, the narrow white beam of her torch flickering across illustrations of black-robed druids and ancient stones, her face pale and anxious in the torchlight.

The van slowed as it left the motorway; Tom ground through the gears as he followed the curving slip road down to a roundabout and then took the exit signposted Avebury. Jason glanced at his watch – 23:09. The motorway lights were gone now and the waxing moon illuminated the winding country roads with a ghostly glow. The roads seemed strangely silent and, as the miles slipped by, the only indication that anyone still stirred was the occasional light from a country cottage as they drove past.

As the van turned a sharp corner, sweeping past a high hedgerow, the figure of a man suddenly appeared in the road in front of them, his bearded face caught frozen in the headlights. Tom swore as he slammed his foot on the brakes, the van screeching in protest as it slowed to a juddering halt less than a foot away. The man on the road blinked in surprise, his long straggly hair swirling in the mists and then slowly faded into nothingness.

'What the . . .'

Jason swung open the door and jumped down from the van. The road was empty. Cold, curling fronds of mist stretched into the desolate countryside. Not a single movement or sound. He turned back to Tom, whose hands were trembling as he gripped the wheel, his eyes staring bleakly ahead.

'Where did he go?'

As if coming out of a dream, Tom shook his head. He shifted the van into gear again as Jason climbed back up into the passenger seat.

'It was nothing. This is the countryside. Probably some old farmer on his way home from the pub.'

Tom's voice was unsteady as though he was still shaken by the near crash. He pressed his foot down on the accelerator and the van lurched into motion again, the road straightening as they left the puzzling scene behind. The fog was returning, a dense cloak of mist that muffled the sound of the engine and shrouded the road ahead in mystery. A broken road sign half hidden in a hedgerow read AVEBURY 1.

Tom slowed the van to a crawl, cursing softly under his breath as he tried to keep it from wandering into the ditches that lined the sides of the narrow road. In the passenger seat next to him, Jason was breathing heavily, forcing air into his lungs as the fog outside the window seemed to press down on his chest.

Then, looming out of the mist, they saw a huge, towering shadow by the roadside. A rough diamond-shaped spike of stone nearly ten feet tall jutted upwards like some huge arrowhead fired into the earth. A second great monolith, a narrow pillar of stone, crept into view on the other side of the road. Straining his eyes against the murk, Jason could see an avenue of stones stretching out ahead of them. At the end of the road sat the black outline of a village, a church tower surrounded by huddling houses, silhouetted by the pale moonlight.

Avebury.

Tom killed the engine and the van trundled to a halt on the deserted road. The thick fingers of mist seemed to scratch at the windows as the headlights cut out and the darkness surrounded them. Silence reigned.

In the front of the van, Jason turned to Tom.

'Whatever Daedalus and the Brothers of Albion are planning to do here, I'm going to stop them,' he told him, his low voice laced with certainty. 'I'm going to find Scott and I'm going to bring him back. But I need you both to stay here.'

'Wait a minute,' Avalon's voice erupted from the back of the van. 'You can't stop us coming too. We can help you.'

Jason shook his head, the lines of his face drawn in a mask of worry.

'You can help me by staying put,' he replied. 'If I'm not back with Scott in half an hour, get out of here and raise the alarm.'

Tom's grizzled face was half hidden in the shadows. There was a heartbeat of silence and then he nodded his head.

'Take care,' he growled.

Jason opened the passenger door and stepped out onto the road. Breathing deeply, he could taste the silvery mist as it crackled in his throat. Resting his hand against the cold towering stone he could see the village nestling in the darkness, but the sight that chilled his blood was the eerie sweep of standing stones that curved around the silent houses, great stone fingers encircling the dwellings in their grasp. His own fingers trembled as the chill of the stone seeped into his skin.

From inside the van, he could hear the muffled sound of Avalon's voice still raised in protest, but as he walked down the narrow road, the fog quickly swallowed up the van and the sound faded into silence. Overhead, the gibbous moon bathed the village in a faint silvery light as the swirling mists flowed and eddied around the pitch-black houses. Not a light could be seen, and even the windows of the village pub, its sign swinging ominously, lay in darkness.

Jason could feel an oppressive silence stalking him as he walked through the village, the thud of his footsteps devoured by the night. The place was deserted. Not a single sign of life.

The church tower loomed in front of him and beyond this he could see the eerie circle of stones standing sentry in a field, waiting silently in the darkness. Suddenly, he glimpsed a movement beyond the stones. A snaking line of shadowy black figures was marching towards the circle.

Dodging through the fog and shadows, Jason set off towards them in a crouching run. The serpentine line of black-clad figures, maybe a hundred strong, was nearing the circle now. Faces hidden by hooded cowls, their chanting filled the air, rising and falling as they endlessly repeated a single word.

*Albion.*

Jason dived for cover in a deep ditch that lay at the edge of the circle. Hoping the shadows of the stones would conceal him, he peered over the top of the ditch as the first in the line of black-robed figures entered the circle. Next, another hooded figure was pushed forward into the ring of stones. His hands were bound in front of him and as he tripped and fell sprawling onto the frostbitten ground, the hood fell back to reveal Scott's deathly pale features.

Crouching in the ditch, Jason watched as an endless line of black-robed Brothers of Albion marched into the circle, surrounding Scott and shielding him from view. The dark figures approached the largest of the stones, a huge megalith pointing to the sky. A single tall figure stepped forward and knelt before the great stone. As he rested his hands on its worn and weather-beaten surface, the chanting intensified. The voices rang out in a chorus across the circle.

*Albion. Albion. Albion.*

As the chanting rose and fell, Jason counted the dozen black-robed figures standing guard over Scott, their shadows flanking the stones. There had to be a way to get him out of there. The beginnings of a plan started to take shape in his mind, but his thoughts were suddenly interrupted as the sound of two protesting voices rose above the chanting.

'This is ridiculous – I demand that you let us go!'

'Get off me! Leave us alone!'

Tom's voice booming in outrage followed by Avalon's indignant yell cut through the night air as the chanting first faltered and then faded into a resentful silence. Twisting his head towards the sound, Jason watched in horror as Tom and Avalon were frogmarched into the heart of the stone circle by another phalanx of black-robed figures.

'Oh God,' he breathed. 'I told them to stay put.'

Tom and Avalon struggled to try and free themselves as their captors led them to the monolith. The hooded figure who knelt before the great stone slowly rose to his feet and inspected the two interlopers. Jason could see Avalon squirming in the arms of one of the black-robed Brothers, while Tom's bulky frame was motionless, his arms pinned behind his back. Then Tom began to speak and Jason strained to hear the words.

'Look,' said Tom, his words a low rumble of anger. 'I don't know what you're playing at here and I don't care either. It's like I told your mates – we've broken down. Just let us go and call the RAC and we'll leave you alone so you can film your spooky movie or do whatever it is you're doing here.'

The voice of one of the figures guarding Tom and Avalon cut through the thickening mist.

'We picked them up in a van on the edge of the village when we were doing a final sweep of the perimeter. They say they've broken down, but the girl had this.'

One of the figures guarding Tom and Avalon handed a small, rectangular object to the tall hooded man standing impassively by the towering pillar of stone. Even though the mist was blurring his view, Jason knew with a sinking feeling of realisation what the object had to be – *Albion Unbound*.

'It's just a book,' blustered Tom as the hooded figure carefully turned the object over in his hands.

'Do you remember me, Tom?' asked the hooded man. He reached up to pull back the hood from his face, revealing the features of the Minister for Transport, his politician's smile twisted into a sinister grin.

'Have you finally decided to join us?' Daedalus asked, his words laced with a mocking tone.

'Never!' Tom spat in defiance. With a growl of anger, he caught sight of Scott's slumped figure at the far edge of the circle. 'And if you've hurt him . . .'

Tom's voice shook as he struggled to free himself, but the black-robed Brothers guarding him held firm. He roared in frustration, his spittle-flecked beard shuddering as with a swift nod of his head Daedalus gestured for the figures to drag Scott to his feet.

'We welcomed him,' said Daedalus, as Scott was marched into the centre of the circle. Scott's head lolled on his shoulder, his eyes half open, the pupils fixed in a thousand-yard stare. 'We welcome you all.'

'In fact,' Daedalus continued, raising his voice to a shout that swirled around the circle, 'we're still waiting for our final guest. Where's Detective Inspector Dyer?' He turned back towards Tom. 'What was the plan? You stay in the getaway car while he comes sneaking around here?'

'I don't know what you're talking about,' said Tom.

'Don't you?' Daedalus turned and looked out across the circle, his eyes piercing through the thickening mists. 'Show yourself, Dyer!'

In the damp and muddy ditch, Jason froze as Daedalus's glare seemed to sweep through the shadows where he was hidden.

'Oh, come on now,' Daedalus's mocking laughter rang out. 'I don't want to have to start this without you.'

In one effortless movement, he reached inside his flowing black robes and extracted a long, ceremonial dagger, its narrow silver blade glinting in the moonlight. Seizing hold of Scott, he pressed the sharp edge of the blade against his neck.

Jason watched the sickening scene unfold as if in slow motion. Scott blinked, his eyes half focusing as he felt the sharp edge of the blade jut menacingly beneath his jugular.

'Leave him alone!' Avalon cried out.

Jason started to scramble up the bank of the ditch. He couldn't let this happen.

'I'm here,' he shouted, clambering to his feet. 'Let him go.'

His eyes dancing with delight, Daedalus released Scott, flinging him back into the arms of the waiting Brothers of Albion. More shadowy figures quickly surrounded Jason, pinning his arms behind his back and dragging him towards the towering monolith in the centre of the circle where Daedalus stood waiting.

'Detective Inspector Dyer – I'm so glad you could finally join us,' he said, his smile widening as he watched the policeman struggle. 'Welcome to the Halcyon Days. Welcome to eternity.'

# CHAPTER THIRTEEN

Thick fingers of mist caressed the stones as the Brothers of Albion, almost invisible in their long black robes, sank a series of burning brands around the perimeter of the circle. But the flickering fire from the torches failed to keep the fog at bay.

At the edge of the circle, Scott shivered. The fog was slowly clearing from his mind as the hard stone bit into his back, the creeping cold seeping into his spine. He was bound to a rough-hewn stone that faced the monolith, which was towering with a brooding menace in the centre of the circle. Next to him, Avalon struggled against the tight bindings that held them trapped there.

'We're going to die,' said Avalon, her voice shaking with cold and fear.

Scott craned his neck but all he could see out of the corner of his eye was Avalon's skinny wrist, bound like his own to the stone.

'It'll be all right,' he said, but as he watched the pack of dark-robed thugs brutally clubbing Tom and Jason to the ground, the lie tasted like ashes in his mouth. As Tom raised his arms in surrender to try and ward off the blows that were raining down, Daedalus approached and with a single gesture stopped the violence.

'Why did you come here, Tom?' he asked, watching in grisly fascination as the two men tentatively examined their injuries – Jason touching his fingers to the cut on the side of his forehead, while Tom spat a broken tooth at Daedalus's feet.

'Had to try and stop you,' he replied, each word accompanied by a blood-flecked shower of spittle as he crouched, breathing heavily, in the shadow of the stones. 'Don't you realise what you're doing? If you open up the Dead Ways, you're going to destroy us all.'

'Nonsense!' Daedalus snorted, shaking his head dismissively. 'Why would we want to do that? Britain is ours to protect.'

He turned his attention towards Jason.

'Is this what he's got you all believing?' Daedalus brandished *Albion Unbound*. 'Is that why you're here?'

Jason stared up at the minister through cold, wary eyes, their roles hideously altered from the last time they had met. He had managed to staunch the bleeding and dried blood matted his eyebrow in a blotchy red crescent. He shook his head.

'I'm here because I'm investigating the murder of

Alexander Williams.' Jason picked his words with a deliberate calm. 'I'm here to bring you to justice.'

Daedalus laughed with delight. 'Wonderful, DI Dyer! Do you always get your man? We obviously underestimated you.' The mists gathered around Daedalus as he began to walk towards the stone where Scott and Avalon were tied. 'But this time I'm afraid you're mistaken,' he called out over his shoulder. 'The only justice here is us.'

Scott fixed Daedalus with an unforgiving glare as he approached, the strange, unsettling sight of the minister's face emerging from the flowing monk-like robes finally convincing him of the truth of his fears. This was the man who had killed his father. He struggled against his bindings as Daedalus drew near, but the ties held firm.

'I'm sorry about all this, Scott,' Daedalus began, his face fixed in an expression of sympathy, 'but our work here is of the utmost importance. We cannot tolerate any more misguided interruptions.'

'Is that what my dad did?' Scott asked, the raw taste of anger almost choking him. 'Interrupt your plans? Is that why you killed him?'

'I'm sorry about what happened to your father,' Daedalus replied, shaking his head almost sorrowfully. 'Alex was a good man, but he gave us no choice. He betrayed the Brotherhood and tried to wreck our finest cause.'

'And what's that?' asked Scott. 'To close down a few motorways and unlock the gates of Hell? My dad worked so hard for you – and you murdered him.'

'That, you will learn, is only a temporary inconvenience,' Daedalus replied. 'And as for opening the gates of Hell, you'd do better than listening to that washed-up old fool.' He jerked his head dismissively towards Tom and Scott felt the binding around his wrist tighten as Avalon clenched her fists. 'The only gate we open here tonight will be the gate to the promised land.'

'What do you mean?'

'A new phase in the evolution of mankind.' Daedalus's eyes glittered with a fiery conviction as he spoke. 'We will finally conquer death itself.'

He glanced back at the preparations that were continuing amongst the stones, at the countless black-robed figures scurrying back and forth.

'By harnessing the power of the Dead Ways, the Brothers of Albion will wrest control of life and death from the eternals. Death will be abolished and more than that, we will be able to bring the dead back to life once more.' He fixed Scott with a knowing glance. 'Even your father.'

The words hung heavy in the cool night air.

'We will take this broken-down nation and raise her up once again to her rightful place in the world,' Daedalus continued, his voice becoming steadily more strident. 'Imagine the Britain we will build with the finest minds from history at our service. William Shakespeare, Sir Isaac Newton, Isambard Kingdom Brunel – the greatest of Britons will be raised from the grave to serve the Brothers of Albion. Other countries will marvel in envy at the utopia we create.'

As he ended his speech, Daedalus clutched his hands together in an impassioned gesture as though he was addressing the crowd at a political rally rather than Scott's cold and fearful figure in the desolate stone circle. There was a moment of silence and then Jason's voice cut through the gloom.

'And what gives you the right?'

'What?' Daedalus spun round at Dyer's question.

'Nobody's voted for any of this madness,' Jason continued, his face bloodied but his voice calm and rational. 'Raising the dead, living forever – if any of it's really true, then why didn't you put it in your election manifesto? I might not have voted for the other lot if you had.'

Daedalus's eyes flashed in irritation.

'Decisions of such importance cannot be left to the fickle finger of democracy,' he snapped. 'Through the centuries it has been the Brothers of Albion's sacred duty to protect this great nation and now as Grand Master I have the chance to banish the darkness forever. I will not shirk from that task.'

He turned back towards Scott and Avalon. Avalon shivered under Daedalus's predatory gaze, but Scott stood stock-still. Daedalus's words had driven the creeping cold from his bones and replaced it with a faint spark of hope. '*We will be able to bring the dead back to life once more – even your father.*'

The chanting had started again, low and insistent around the circle.

'And you can help us, Scott.' Daedalus's words cut through the rhythmic murmur of voices. 'Help us open the Dead Ways and we will give your father back to you.'

'Don't trust him!' Avalon's voice hissed in his ear, but Scott ignored it. The black knot of pain that he'd been holding inside ever since he'd been told that his father was dead now felt as though it was ready to burst. He couldn't stand the agony any longer.

'Can you really do that?' he asked, scarcely believing the words as they passed his lips.

'Yes,' Daedalus nodded, his eyes shining with the promise. 'And you won't ever have to risk losing him again.'

'It's a lie,' Tom's voice rang out in warning. 'If the Dead Ways are opened—'

His sentence was brutally cut short as, with a nod from Daedalus, the Brothers of Albion surrounding Tom rained down an avalanche of blows, their weapons rising and falling in a sudden flurry of violence.

'Dad!' Avalon called out in anguish, but Tom couldn't answer as he lay unconscious on the cold ground. Jason bent over him, desperately trying to revive Tom as a red line of blood trickled from the corner of his mouth.

'Don't listen to him,' Daedalus told Scott. 'Think about your father.'

He held out his hand in invitation.

'We'll let your friends go free – all this unfortunate inconvenience can be forgotten. Will you help us, Scott?'

The words tumbled through Scott's fogged mind. He thought about Tom's apocalyptic warnings – the dark spirits lurking, waiting for the Dead Ways to be opened so that they could resume their reign of tyranny. And Daedalus's vision of an earthly paradise where life stretched blissfully into eternity. Heaven or Hell. Paradise or damnation. Who to trust?

The answer should be a simple one. The Brothers of Albion had killed his father, beaten, threatened and imprisoned them. But what if they were right? The impossible hope of seeing his dad's face again – a chance to put an end to this soul-searing misery . . .

Then he remembered the darkness he'd already seen – the thrashing body bags writhing like maggots in the hospital mortuary; the ragged line of walking dead shuffling down the highway at Rey Cross; the skeletal corpses clawing their way free from the earth. This was what opening the Dead Ways would bring.

'I won't help you,' Scott replied with a decisive shake of his head. He stared up into Daedalus's face, meeting his eyes with a gaze of defiance. 'This is madness.'

'A pity,' said Daedalus, a wry smile playing across his lips. 'It would have been so much easier if you were willing.'

With a sweeping gesture, he signalled for Scott to be freed. The Brothers of Albion standing guard quickly untied

Scott and Avalon's bindings. Then they seized Avalon and marched her to the circle of guards who stood sentry over Jason and Tom's fallen form. More black-robed figures surrounded Scott, roughly forcing him forward as Daedalus held out his hand like a circus showman and led them into the heart of the circle of stones.

Scott stumbled towards the towering monolith. The ebony rock glittered with menace in the pale moonlight. Behind him, the chorus of voices rose up again in triumph. *Albion! Albion! Albion!* As the chanting intensified it seemed to set off a low vibration in the stones, an expectant tremor that hung in the shadows.

Reaching the great stone, Scott shivered.

'What are you going to do?' he asked, his throat dry with fear as Daedalus stood silently by his side.

Daedalus drew out the ceremonial dagger, its long blade glinting hungrily in the silvery light.

'The stones need blood,' he replied.

Scott stepped back in horror, but Daedalus was too quick for him. Reaching out, he grabbed hold of Scott's right arm and with a sigh of pleasure drew the blade across his open palm. Scott gasped as blood welled from the wound and a sickening wave of pain sent him swaying in shock. Daedalus raised Scott's mutilated hand in triumph.

'For Albion!' he roared as the chanting reached a crescendo. He thrust Scott's hand forward, blood dripping through his fingers, until the flesh met the stone. The dark monolith seemed to shiver with delight as Scott's blood ran down its surface.

Daedalus stepped back, his face exultant as he raised his arms aloft.

'Let the Halcyon Days begin!' he cried as the gathering winds swirled thick fingers of fog across the sky, obliterating the pale moon overhead.

Gasping with fear, his breath coming in sharp shuddering gulps, Scott tried to pull his hand away. The wound burned where it touched the smooth surface of the monolith, but some invisible force seemed to be holding it there, fusing his mutilated hand to the stone.

Tiny cracks began to appear on the surface of the pillar and Scott watched with growing horror as questing fingers of light began to poke their way out. When the blood from his wound reached the widening cracks in the stone, Scott saw the fingers of light curl questioningly and then dart with delight towards the source. As the freezing tendrils embraced him, Scott let out an agonised scream.

Icy rivulets of pain flooded through his veins, coursing through his body in a whiplash of agony. His limbs jerked in uncontrollable spasms, the suffering impossible to contain. Scott felt as though he was being eaten away from within. As the stigmata on his palm pulsed through the stone, he screamed again in wordless agony. In some distant corner of his mind, he knew that this wasn't eternal life – this was eternal death.

Jason watched in horror as the grey fingers of light snaked out from the stone pillar. He saw them seize hold of Scott, making him dance like a marionette. The air in the circle crackled with electricity and the taser burn on Jason's chest throbbed in sympathy. *It's happening again*, he thought with a sickening lurch of realisation.

The Brothers of Albion guarding them had turned towards the monolith, their arms raised aloft as they watched their Golden Age begin to dawn. Avalon knelt beside Tom's unconscious body, the slow rise and fall of his chest reassuring her that somehow he was still alive.

'Rejoice!' proclaimed Daedalus as the light emanating from the monolith began to illuminate the sky. 'Rejoice!'

Behind him, Scott continued his pulsating dance of death, his hand still scorched to the stone. The questing searchlights of energy reached out above him into the black night sky like an outstretched hand. As the sound of the chanting redoubled in response to Daedalus's exhortation, the fingers of light curled outwards towards the edge of the circle. Then in one dizzying movement they struck.

The beams raked through the circle. Twisting kaleidoscopes of cold light cut through the swathes of mist and ranks of dark-robed figures. As they struck each standing figure, there came a shrill shriek of pain and then the body crumpled to the floor.

'Keep down,' yelled Jason as Avalon began to rise in confusion. A snaking beam lashed above them, striking down the guards that surrounded them. Jason grabbed hold of Avalon's arm, dragging her down until they were both crouched protectively over Tom's prone body.

'Stay here,' Jason told Avalon as he fixed his gaze on the pulsing pillar of stone, which now radiated an unearthly light. Silhouetted in front of the monument, Scott's body jerked in increasingly frantic movements, his arm still raised as if pleading for help. Whatever was happening, Jason knew Scott couldn't survive it much longer.

As Tom's eyelids slowly fluttered open, staring out in blank horror at the chaos engulfing them, Jason set off on a crouching run towards the great stone. In front of him, the Brothers of Albion were scattering like a murder of startled crows disturbed by a farmer's sudden arrival. One of them was crawling towards him, his hood fallen back to reveal the sweating face of a frightened old man.

'Oh God, please help me,' he repeated in a frantic prayer.

A churning shaft of light ricocheted above him, curdling the words into a sudden shriek of pain as the old man collapsed in a heap on the cold, hard ground. Jason threw himself to the right as the beam raked past him, then he crawled towards Scott, who was framed in the pulsating light. Above the monolith, Jason could see a new darkness in the night sky, a black void waiting beyond the mist and the fog and the shadows. A place where, for the first time in millennia, something was stirring. There was a crack in the sky and something was coming through.

A rotting stench filled the air, making Jason retch as he forced himself forward. He was almost there, but as the shimmering tower of stone loomed in front of him, he didn't know if it was too late.

'Hold on, Scott,' he called out, forcing the words through gritted teeth, the air rank with the stench of death. 'I'm coming to get you.'

Then with a sudden crack of impact, a dark figure barrelled into Jason, knocking the breath from his body and sending him sprawling in the shadow of the great stone. Then the figure was on top of him, pinning him down to the rumbling ground.

'You're not going to stop us now,' snarled Daedalus, his breath hot and heavy on Jason's face. Above Daedalus's head, the snaking tentacles of light fanned out in a twisted halo and behind these, Jason could see Scott's writhing form, almost worn through by the light.

'You're killing him,' Jason gasped as Daedalus's fingers closed around his throat.

'He's saving us all,' Daedalus replied, a demonic smile of certainty splitting his face.

A raking claw of light scratched the stars, tearing its way from another world into this. The sky was opening up above them and the faint outlines of hideous faces peered down into the world that had been denied to them for so long.

As the breath ebbed from his lungs, Jason caught a

glimpse of movement at the periphery of his vision. Then huge bear-like arms tore Daedalus's fingers from his throat and threw the Grand Master through the air with an animal roar of defiance. With his robes flapping like wings, Daedalus crashed against one of the outlying stones, where he slumped, dazed and senseless.

Jason looked up in relief to see Tom, his grey beard matted with blood and his long hair swept out behind him, stumble towards the illuminated monument where Scott's lifeless body hung by one outstretched arm. Reaching up with both hands, Tom grabbed hold of Scott's wrist as his wounded palm pulsed against the stone. His pale skin was icy to the touch and as Tom looked into Scott's eyes he felt as though he was staring into the abyss.

The slick black stone was cracked in a thousand places with every twisting tentacle of light slowly turning towards this new intruder. He only had a fraction of a second until they found him. Bracing himself against the towering monument and with every sinew straining, Tom tried to drag Scott's hand away from the stone.

In the darkness, Scott felt a distant pull, a faint reminder that there was something else beyond this suffering. His thoughts were shattering into fragments, crushed beneath the grinding glaciers of pain consuming him from within. But somewhere amidst the agony, he heard the faint sound of his father's voice.

*Scott, you need to stop them.* The words were almost lost

as Scott started to slip into the void. *Close the gate.*

He didn't know if the voice was real or just a distant memory, but suddenly, he knew what he had to do. Drawing on his last ounce of resistance, Scott wrenched his hand free from the stone.

With a deafening crack, the sudden recoil of pressure sent Scott stumbling backwards and only Jason's quick hands saved him from falling to the ground. Sagging in Jason's arms, Scott took huge juddering lungfuls of air as he tried to flush the choking fog from his veins. From out of the mist, Avalon appeared by Jason's side and then took an anxious step towards her father, now framed in the pulsing light cascading from the monolith.

The monument gave a hideous creaking sound, a grinding gurgle that shook the ground beneath their feet. Tom turned towards them, his eyes wide with terror and his words almost lost in the tumult.

'Get out of here!' he yelled.

The crack in the sky began to close and the flickering faces gathered there let out thwarted howls of despair. Snaking tentacles of light flailed wildly across the circle as they were snapped back, the twisting talons of energy whiplashing into the stone as the cracks began to close.

Avalon held out a desperate hand towards her father.

'Come on!'

Tom started forward, a look of hope flickering across his bruised and bloodied face, then the light surrounded him.

His body was haloed in a blazing supernova and then consumed entirely. The last throbbing tentacles of energy recoiled into the great stone and the myriad cracks criss-crossing its surface sealed shut as though they had never been there.

A deathly silence fell on the circle, broken only by low moans and whimpers of fear. The monolith stood brooding at the heart of the stones, its smooth surface now whole again. Tom was gone.

Avalon twisted back towards Jason, her face frozen in disbelief.

'He can't have . . .'

Her words petered out into a despairing silence.

Jason looked around. In the shadows of the stones, the fallen figures of the Brothers of Albion lay motionless. In this brief moment, they had the faint chance of escape.

Bending his head towards Scott, who was leaning heavily on his shoulder, Jason looked into the boy's haunted eyes.

'Can you walk?' he asked.

Scott nodded, his breath still coming in ragged gasps. The gaping wound on his hand pulsed with hot rivulets of pain, but this was nothing compared to the icy agonies of the stone.

'I can walk,' he gasped.

Jason turned and grabbed hold of Avalon's arm, pulling her back from the shadow of the great stone.

'We've got to get out of here now,' he said, his words laced with urgency.

Avalon shook her head.

'But we need to—'

Jason cut her off with a sweeping gesture towards the black-robed figures slowly rising from the shadows.

'We need to get out of here alive.'

Stifling a sob, Avalon nodded and the three of them stumbled out from the ruins of the circle. With every faltering step, they left behind the dazed ranks of the Brothers of Albion, the cloying fog shielding their escape as they fled from the village down the broad avenue of stones.

Reaching the abandoned van, Scott and Avalon sat shivering in the passenger seat as Jason scrabbled to hotwire the ignition and then gunned the engine into life. Headlights off, the van sped away down the lane, leaving the black silhouette of Avebury behind them, but the despair that had been unleashed at the circle followed them.

'He's not dead.'

Avalon endlessly repeated these words on their journey down the twisting country lanes – a mantra to keep desperation at bay. She'd only lapsed into silence as the darkened roads gave way to the straight lines of the motorway, stained yellow by the overhead lights. Jason hunched over the steering wheel as he urged the van forwards, its whirring heater failing to drive the ice from Scott's bones.

'Did we stop them?' Scott asked, shivering as he slumped in the passenger seat, the bloodied mess of his right hand held in front of him.

'I don't know,' Jason replied. 'That light – those things in the sky . . .'

His voice trailed into silence as on the other side of the crash barrier two police cars, their lights flashing, swept by. Jason tensed as the sirens slowly faded and then stamped down hard on the accelerator, trying to put as much distance as he could between them and the disaster they'd left behind.

'We closed the First Gate, but that light came out of the Dead Ways,' Avalon told them, her dark eyes shining with fear. 'The Halcyon Days are coming.'

## END OF BOOK ONE

# Acknowledgements

Many thanks to my agent Lucy Juckes for keeping the faith, my editors, Anne Marie Ryan and Susila Baybars, Non Pratt at Catnip, and my friends and family for all their support along the way, especially my mum for taking me to the library and my brother Nick for letting me read his comics when I was growing up. Most of all, my thanks and love to Chrissie, Alex and Josie for everything.

# Hotel On
# Shadow Lake

## Daniela Tully

Legend Press Ltd, 107-111 Fleet Street, London, EC4A 2AB
info@legend-paperbooks.co.uk | www.legendpress.co.uk

First published by Thomas Dunne Books, an imprint of St. Martin's Press, Flatiron Building, New York City, New York, United States

Print ISBN 978-1-7871988-9-0
Ebook ISBN 978-1-7871988-8-3
Set in Times. Printed in Bulgaria by Multiprint
Cover design by Simon Levy www.simonlevyassociates.co.uk

**Daniela Tully** was born in Germany, but has lived all over the world, including Mexico, New York and Dubai. As a film-maker she has been involved in projects such as the critically-acclaimed *Fair Game*, box-office hits *Contagion* and *The Best Exotic Marigold Hotel*, as well as the Oscar-winning *The Help*.

*Hotel On Shadow Lake* is her first novel and the rights have already been sold in North America, Denmark, France, Italy and Serbia.

*To my parents,*

*my husband,*

*and my newest love, my daughter Mae*

# Prologue

The fall of the wall in Germany freed people, minds—and also long-lost secrets. Secrets that otherwise would have remained buried. One came in the form of a letter that arrived only a couple of weeks after sixteen-year-old Maya Wiesberg had departed on her year abroad. The year Maya's and her grandmother's life would change forever. "Do for me what I couldn't," Maya's grandmother had whispered in her ear when they parted ways at Munich Airport in 1990.

Maya never saw her grandmother again.

# Martha
# 1990

Martha Wiesberg was a woman of strict routine: Sunday, church; Monday, lunch with her neighbor; Tuesday, book club; Wednesday, laundry press; Thursday, aerobics—all at exactly the same time each week. Even a slight deviation was destructive to people like Martha. She needed routine like air to breathe. Only those who knew her very well—and they were far and few—knew why: it was her way of numbing her mind, of silencing the past and calming the voices that would remind her that life could have been so different, *if only*...

It was four thirty in the afternoon. The sunlight was fading slowly, the way it does when the cold of early autumn starts to creep in. Martha had just fixed herself her daily afternoon cup of coffee (decaf), sat down with her daily crossword puzzle, and put on the television to watch her daily show. But her show wasn't on. Instead, a special program in honor of Germany's recently created *Tag der Deutschen Einheit,* "German Unity Day," was airing. Martha immediately switched off the TV.

The silence in the room engulfed her like a dark blanket, allowing the voices in her head to become louder. This time it wasn't simply the interruption of routine that got to her; it was the most recent milestone in Germany's history: the reunification. Most of the population seemed happy about it, chatting about it in interviews on the TV, about what had caused the separation in the first place: the war, a dark chapter.

For her part, Martha had moved on, or so she liked to think. But of course, there were the memories. Her mind was just about to dive deeper into that muddy lake of painful remembrances when the doorbell rang and jolted her from her thoughts.

Martha opened the door and stared into the face of her postman, who had been delivering the mail to her for over ten years. The setting sun was breaking through the heavy clouds one last time, providing a backlight that gave him an almost ethereal appearance.

"*Grüß Gott*, Frau Wiesberg," he said with a nervous smile. Martha had never liked that salutation. *Greet God? Okay!* She sang to herself, *I will when I see him!* She had always felt a bit out of place in Munich. She was a *Zugereiste*, after all, an "outsider" not born there.

"This is for you," the postman said with outstretched arms. Martha had never been too fond of him, partly because she suspected that he was reading her mail, as letters would often arrive torn open on the side. His curiosity, too, had become a staple in her diet of routine.

Martha took the letter, wondering why the man had bothered to ring the doorbell rather than simply leave the letter in her mailbox. She was about to close the door when he gently tugged her back.

"Yes?"

"Well, in the name of the German Federal Postal Services, we would like to apologize very much for the delay."

Confused, Martha studied the envelope, which had been — or appeared to have been — ripped open by the transport, the letter sticking out one side. Adolf's face in the upper right corner looked out at her sternly. She brought the envelope closer to her eyes. The postmark read December 27, 1944.

"Are you joking?" she asked, and looked up at him.

"No, Frau Wiesberg, believe me, you are not the only one. There are a couple of others who have also been affected."

She gazed down again at the envelope, chills running up her arms. "Affected by what?"

"The wall?" he said, surprised. "This letter was held up, and," he started to explain, "now that the wall has come down, it finally found its way to you."

Martha was still staring at the letter when it slowly began to dawn on her.

"The German Post will of course not charge you any delivery fee." He giggled, and Martha glared at him.

"I mean the German Post stopped charging so little postage a long time ago," he went on.

"I understood that the first time. I just don't find it at all funny," she told him.

The grin on his face died suddenly, and he shuffled his feet nervously. "Is there anything else I can do for you?" Martha asked impatiently.

"No, no. Have a great day."

He was about to turn around when Martha heard him mumble something else.

"What now?" she barked.

"Who is Wolfgang Wiesberg?" Martha slammed the door.

Leaning against the inside of the door, she shut her eyes. She felt like a huge wave was breaking over her. Memories were flowing back into her mind, making her dizzy.

She stared at the handwriting on the envelope. Wolfgang Wiesberg. Her twin brother. How she had suffered when she and Mother had been informed of his death, when the war had ended. Yet she and Wolfgang hadn't been close at the end. In fact, she had probably wished his death at some point. What was there to say, forty-six years later? Whatever was in that letter couldn't turn back time, couldn't bring back the love that life had held in store for her only to have cruelly snatched it away.

*I don't want to remember, I don't want to remember, I don't want to remember,* she told herself over and over again, like a mantra. Martha started to tremble uncontrollably. She had always known that the secrets were only sleeping. Now they had finally woken up and come back to haunt her.

# 1938

Up and down, open and close, they were moving in unison in the summer heat.

"Martha, you are always a little too fast." The rebuke came from the beautiful long-legged Else, her blond hair done into two thick braids. She was sitting next to Martha on the floor, performing the same leg movements. From above, the circle of young women was supposed to resemble a flower that opened and closed as it reacted to sunlight. A gymnastic practice.

"Sorry," Martha mumbled, her skin itchy under the shorts that barely covered her upper thighs, and the white shirt of her uniform.

Else shook her head. "What are you always thinking about?"

Before Martha could respond, Else got up and stopped the music, then waited for the other girls to gather around her. "We still have the chance to be selected to perform for our Führer at the Party Day in Nuremberg in September! Clementine zu Castell herself will soon come and assess us!" Else's words were met with great enthusiasm. Clementine zu Castell was the new Führerin of the organization Faith and Beauty, which Hitler had initiated in January for all working women between the ages of seventeen and twenty-one. Martha was the only one in the group who didn't join in on the cheers. Else's eyes lingered on hers, just long enough. But by the time Martha had forced herself to bring the palms of her hands together, it was too late, and her clapping got lost in the midst of the departing girls.

As she walked over to her bike, Else caught up with her. "I ask myself every time why you keep coming to these meetings," she hissed at Martha. "You know you don't have to."

"I know," Martha said to Else as she mounted her bike. "I'll see you at Traudl's."

She sensed Else's eyes following her as she drove out of the park.

Else was right: participation in Faith and Beauty was optional, unlike membership in the BDM, the League of German Girls. But unlike when she was in the BDM, which was for girls between the ages of ten and seventeen, Martha no longer had to attend events where girls were indoctrinated with twisted historical facts and endless stories about martyrs in the Hitler Youth, and had to sing the anthem of the Nazi Party, the "Horst Wessel Song." She still knew the lyrics by heart, that and the prayer for the Führer they had to recite at the beginning of each BDM session.

Faith and Beauty was ostensibly apolitical, and the uniform did not contain swastikas. Yet still she despised the seemingly never-ending Faith and Beauty sessions in which she learned about pottery, weaving, and interior decorating. These sessions, like the so-called "home evenings" she had attended in the BDM, were meant to prepare the working woman for her future role as wife, mother, and homemaker, while at the same time help her identify and shape her unique skills and individuality.

"Individuality"—a word that was as misplaced in Fascism as Martha was misplaced in this world.

Martha had perfected the skill of letting her mind wander in unpleasant situations. During the incessant chatter about the duties of the German woman, she traveled to the faraway places she had read about in her novels. She loved Goethe, Schiller, Lessing, and Fontane. But what most fascinated her were some of those novels that had appeared on the *schwarzen Listen*, the blacklists, in 1933, many of them written by Jewish authors, titles that were considered "un-German," novels by Bertolt Brecht, Thomas Mann, all of Erich Kästner's books, which she had grown up with, Hemingway's "In Another Country," London's *Martin Eden*. She had read them all over and over, until the pages had begun to fall out. This was her way of getting to know the world outside of her own. With Brecht's *The Threepenny Opera*, she had visited London; with Hesse's *Siddhartha*, India. Hesse had not been on the blacklist, but evil tongues claimed that he was no different and that he helped Mann and Brecht escape the Reich and betray their country. Reading also brought Martha closer to her own world. Mann's *Buddenbrooks* taught her that all families in some way share the same dysfunctional dynamics, regardless of social class or history. She sometimes would find her own hunger for a world beyond her deadening reality mirrored in the protagonist's ongoing struggle in Hesse's *Steppenwolf*.

Daydreaming was the only way for her to endure Faith and Beauty. She, unlike the other girls in her group, had been forced, yes, even threatened, to join by her twin brother, Wolfgang. And saying no to her brother was not a possibility. Not anymore.

Even the slightest form of resistance was no longer an option.

Mother had asked Martha to get some groceries on her way back from the meeting, and Martha was in no hurry to get home. It would be the same sight that awaited her every evening: Mother sitting in the kitchen, staring out of the window, waiting for Wolfgang and her to return. Martha's older sister, Irene, had died of an appendix rupture the year before. Irene had been the fourth child Mother had lost over the years, and Father had died of a heart attack five years before Irene. Martha and Wolfgang were all she had left.

The family lived in a suburb of Munich called Perlach. Their house sat right at the border of the city line, at the edge of a forest as dark as the mood in the house. But tonight, when Martha entered the main hallway, she sensed something was different. It was palpable, the presence of another person. They never had visitors. Mother didn't like to host strangers in the house.

The unfamiliar laughter from the kitchen confirmed her suspicion. From the hallway, she could see Mother, Wolfgang, and a strange man sitting around the table. The bottles at the center betrayed that they were likely not sober.

From the doorway, Martha studied Wolfgang. He was always a nice-looking boy, but today he looked especially handsome, his face glowing.

Martha entered the room, and the stranger immediately rose from his seat. He easily measured over six feet. The short sleeves of his white shirt revealed strong arms, his shorts showed equally strong legs, with knee-long socks bulging over the calves. His athletic body and height made him appear a couple of years older than the twins.

"This is my other child, Martha," Mother explained to the man.

"Heil Hitler, *gnädiges Fräulein*," he said.

Martha had to look up at him to see his face, as she returned the greeting. He was very blond, and his eyes were blue, piercing.

Martha couldn't help but think that he must pass as Hitler's model for the Aryan race.

The man promptly sat back down and turned to Wolfgang, resuming their lively conversation. Mother silently motioned to Martha to take the groceries to the storage room at the back of the kitchen. Normally, Wolfgang would have gotten up and helped her carry the heavy bags, but he appeared too engrossed in his conversation to even notice her.

While unpacking, she listened in on their conversation. As usual these days, the conversation revolved around the Führer's plans to annex the Sudetenland, a region of Czechoslovakia, and its German-speaking population.

"Hänschel keeps me informed about our Führer's recent armament actions," she heard Wolfgang say, referring to the Führer's reactions to the "Czech terror against the Sudeten Germans," as Goebbels kept referring to it on the radio. Hänschel was Wolfgang's boss at the Gestapo.

"The army?" the stranger asked.

"And the air force. He also executed his plans to expand on the fortifications in the west. The Führer wants it to be the biggest of all time!" Wolfgang paused theatrically before continuing. "He had spoken about it for a while, Hänschel says, but we had to execute those strengthening plans immediately after all the lies the Czech regiment spread about us! All the acts of violence against our helpless *Volksgenossen* over there!" Martha, however, had her doubts that all of those 3.5 million Sudeten Germans wanted to become a part of the Third Reich.

"Yes, a great power like ours shouldn't be fooled twice!" the stranger replied, his voice rising in absolute agreement.

After unpacking, Martha joined them at the table. The two men were still in deep discussion, and Mother was hanging on every word coming from Wolfgang's lips. Martha wondered how she could be so supportive of the idea of another war when she had lost most of her family in the first war. But Martha chose not to comment on it. In general, she had stopped saying too much at home. As in the Faith and Beauty meetings, here, too, her mind usually started to drift whenever Wolfgang would drone on and on about the amazing transformation the German Reich was undergoing thanks to Hitler.

"What do you think? Should we go to the pub around the corner, Siegfried?" Wolfgang asked his friend.

The man got up from the table. Again, Martha couldn't help but notice his height. Wolfgang grinned at him, the way that he had once smiled at her when they were about to do something mischievous together, to embark on a new adventure.

She had grown curious about Wolfgang's new friend, whom she noticed didn't speak the regional dialect. "Are you from Munich?"

Wolfgang and Mother seemed surprised to hear words escaping her lips. Siegfried turned around, seemingly annoyed that she'd held them up with her question.

"No, I'm from Hanover. I came here to study."

"What are you studying?"

"Sister, nothing that the blow-dried brains of your gray-haired clients will ever understand," her brother chimed in, accompanied by a nasty cackle.

Martha stared at Wolfgang, her mouth wide open. Mother had not permitted Martha to continue with her education. When she finished school two years ago, at the age of fifteen, she completed an apprenticeship at the local hair salon, where she constantly daydreamed of studying literature instead of doing a decent job. Meanwhile, Wolf-gang had been allowed to attend the *Gymnasium*, where he had even skipped a grade, and received a prestigious grant to study mathematics and engineering at Ludwig-Maximilians University, while undergoing training at the Gestapo. He was well aware that she'd hated the job, but now he suddenly had no problem using it as a cheap joke in front of his new friend, who laughed heartily. She despised Wolfgang's friend instantly.

As they put on their jackets, Mother jumped up from the table. "Wolfgang, no more pub for you tonight."

Wolfgang blushed a deep red before throwing Mother an almost menacing look. "Don't you think I'm old enough to decide this for myself?"

"I always wake up when you come home late. You know how squeaky the mattress is in our room."

If at all possible, Wolfgang blushed even more. "Mother, I am not asking for your permission." Then, he turned and walked out.

"Heil Hitler," Siegfried said as he followed Wolfgang outside.

Mother and Martha cleaned the dishes in silence. Martha was shocked. This was the first time since Irene's death that Mother raised her voice against Wolfgang's.

"I have good news," Mother finally said. "The Schinken-hubers accepted you. Your brother put in a good word for you at the Gestapo!" Poor Mother obviously felt the need to say something nice after the unpleasant incident. "Herr Dr. Schinkenhuber is a highly respected party member."

In less than two months, Martha would start the obligatory year that the Führer had recently introduced for all unmarried and unemployed women under the age of twenty-five. Many girls were sent to farms outside the city for hard labor. But Martha, she would be in Munich, in Schwabing, father's favorite part of the city! "The heart of Munich's artistic and bohemian life," he had always called it. And she would be living right in the center of it!

"Does that mean I don't have to go to Else's meetings anymore?" Martha asked, hopeful.

"Of course it doesn't!" Martha's question had wiped the earlier attempt at a smile from Mother's face. "You'll still go some evenings and on Saturdays. And on Sundays you will need to do the neighbors' hair and help out a little with our income."

The injustice of Mother's words had always made her sad, but anger started to creep in. There was her brother, who once upon a time was the best friend she had, frolicking around in a pub with this new friend of his. Why was it her responsibility alone, and not also Wolfgang's, to help with the income?

"What about Wolfgang?"

"What about Wolfgang? Don't be silly; he can't contribute! He won't have the time. And he wouldn't be going to the university if that grant didn't pay for all his books!"

"What about the Gestapo? Shouldn't they pay him some-thing?" Martha asked.

"What is wrong with you tonight? They pay for his studies!"

With his entry into the Hitler Youth, Wolfgang had begun to pursue a "storybook" career. Wolfgang had discovered his physical strength, excelling in all the Hitler Youth sporting events. His technical skills had received special attention from the Gestapo, and it was Baldur von Schirach himself, head of the Hitler Youth, who had singled out Wolfgang as a valuable asset to the Nazi regime on one of his visits to Munich. For Wolfgang, this had been a life-changing moment.

"Irene studied without a grant," Martha said into the silence that had spread in the room. She had never felt a grudge toward her sister. On the contrary, Martha had loved her big sister with all her heart.

She knew she had just overstepped her boundaries when she saw Mother's eyes narrow. "Irene, she had a God-given talent for music, and someone like her *needed* to study music. It would have been a crime not to let her!"

"I, too, received high grades for the essays I wrote in school."

"So what is it that you would have liked to study, then?" Mother asked.

"Literature," Martha whispered.

Mother laughed out loud. "Literature? What? To become a writer? Your head is filled with crazy daydreams! And your father, God bless his soul, is to be blamed for planting thoughts like that!"

It was the first time she heard Mother talk about Father in that tone, and if at all possible she missed him more than ever in that moment. As she got up and ran out of the kitchen, Mother's comment painfully ringing in her ears, she fled the worst form of loneliness that one could ever feel: feeling lonely at home.

She had difficulty falling asleep that night. Every time she closed her eyes, she saw this intimidating shape get up from the table to greet her: Siegfried, his nasty laughter echoing in the dark bedroom that she had once shared with her brother. That was before he moved over to Mother's bedroom and into the room Mother had once shared with Irene. After Irene's death, Mother pleaded with Wolfgang that she could not be alone at night, forced to face the darkness that the loss of so many of her loved ones had left behind.

She hadn't asked Martha to make that move.

Martha finally gave up and turned on the tiny light on her nightstand. Her father's warm eyes looked out at her from a framed picture, silently reassuring her that everything would be all right.

The last thing Martha heard before finally falling asleep was Wolfgang returning home at dawn. She listened as Mother reprimanded him softly, and Wolfgang gave her a much softer answer than earlier in the kitchen in front of Siegfried.

Martha hoped Wolfgang would not bring him around again.

A couple of evenings later, Martha and Mother were cooking marmalade in one of the big pots in the kitchen when Martha heard two sets of boots in the main hall. Wolfgang hadn't come alone, and the atmosphere in the room changed instantly. A side glance at Mother told her that she was as unhappy about the visitor as Martha.

Mother dried her hands on her apron and turned around. "Heil Hitler," she said to Siegfried. "Would you like to stay for dinner?"

"Yes, Mother, that's why we're here," Wolfgang said, and offered Siegfried a chair.

Martha was glad he was sitting down. His seemed less intimidating that way.

"We just heard the Führer speak," Wolfgang explained

excitedly. He seemed electrified as he recounted the essence of Hitler's speech: the 3.5 million suppressed *Volksgenossen* in Czechoslovakia. "They have a right of self-determination, he said." Wolfgang's voice was as electrified as he looked. Siegfried nodded his head, eagerly. "Father would have been happy to hear what our Führer had to say today," Wolfgang added.

Martha felt like laughing out loud, if what was coming out of her brother's mouth wasn't so sad. "Self-determination"? Yet another word that was completely misplaced in Fascism. And no, Father would not have been happy!

Mother, however, smiled warmly at Wolfgang. "Did you know that your Father, may his soul rest in peace, was present during our Führer's first speech at Circus Krone? Six thousand people were present! That was Munich's biggest venue at the time. I even remember the title of the speech: 'Future or Ruin.' Our Führer was against payment of the reparations to the Allies."

Martha felt the growing pit in her stomach. *Why couldn't she leave Father out of this? He would have never attended a speech by Hitler.*

Then she saw Mother's alarmed stare and realized that she had not just thought these words.

"Well, why wouldn't he have?" Mother smiled apologetically at Siegfried.

"Please, sister, politics is something you really don't have an understanding of at all." Wolfgang laughed at Martha. "You know it; I know it."

It was his nasty, mocking laughter that kindled her fire.

"Well, I am perfectly suited to distinguish between common sense and Fascism."

"But he also attended the following one," Mother was quick to add. "It was at the Hofbräuhaus that same year."

It was the false pride in Mother's words that made Martha snap. Mother was exploiting Father's name to give the pretense of an intact household. In reality, Father had been the only loyal family member to Martha. Wolfgang had turned his back on her after Father's death. Father, she had come to realize, had been the only one who had always truly understood Martha. He had always been there for her, supported her, encouraged her to pursue her dreams. To hear him and Hitler mentioned in the same sentence made her nauseous. So instead of simply letting it rest there, she felt the rage overtake her, as if she were the poor man's equivalent to Anna Karenina and her true opinion was her affair.

"Yes, and that was one of his last big speeches for a while, because it turned into a riot. Numerous political opponents of Hitler attended as well. And in 1925 he was banned from speaking for two years by the Bavarian government, no less!" Martha's voice had risen to a sharp pitch. She turned to Wolfgang. "See, your sister isn't that stupid. Father would have never attended a speech by Hitler. If anything, he was among the opponents, hopefully causing the brawl!"

There was silence in the room. Mother had turned pale. Wolfgang was bright red in the face. She felt herself blush.

"I doubt this is what they taught you at the BDM meetings," Wolfgang said between clenched teeth. Then he turned to Siegfried. "My sister doesn't know what she's talking about. You must not take her seriously."

She felt Siegfried's eyes scrutinizing her.

"Speaking of Hofbräuhaus, should we go and have a last beer?" Wolfgang broke through the tension.

This time, Mother did not object but smiled forcefully at the two men. Siegfried nodded, not taking his eyes off Martha. She was still in a daze when she heard the sounds of their heavy boots marching down the hallway.

This time, even Mother was at a loss for words.


It wasn't until she was in bed that Martha truly comprehended what she'd done. She shouldn't have said anything. Had she not learned that thinking it was one thing, mouthing it another? She, who had reduced her verbal output to a minimum, knew words had become dangerous. Mother's sobs next door only made that point clearer. And she couldn't shake Siegfried's glare from her mind.

At the same time, though, Martha realized that this was the first time she had spoken up in front of a stranger, releasing those words that had wanted out for so long. She should have felt petrified, but to her surprise it also felt cleansing. Was this the sensation her favorite authors had felt when they brought their thoughts out and put them down onto the page?

Martha walked over to the bookshelf in the corner of her room. In 1932, shortly before his sudden death, Father had secretly built the shelf with a hidden chamber for Martha. She carefully removed the books from the first shelf, which carried titles by Goethe and Schiller, "German" literature, and then gently pressed against the wooden backboard. The space behind it revealed the treasure of forbidden novels Father had given her.

Some of the titles had been burned in May 1933 for being Marxist or pacifist, organized by the Student Union. It had been way past their bedtime and was pouring rain when Mother had dragged Wolfgang and Martha to the Königsplatz, which was packed with fifty thousand people, to witness the so-called "purge" of "un-German" literature. That day was the first time Martha had seen Mother with a smile on her face since Father's death eight months before. "Everything will get better now," she had said, staring at the blazing fire, which seemed to mock the rain. Irene had declared earlier that she was sick, and after the fact, Martha wondered whether she had just faked her illness.

Martha hadn't wanted to look at the books. Instead she saw the dancing flames of the fire reflected in Mother's eyes as Mother cheered along with the others each time a new pile had kindled the fire: "Germany wake up! Jews croak! Heil Hitler!" Wolfgang hadn't been looking at the books, either, but for different reasons; when Martha studied his face she noticed that he was looking adoringly at the members of the Hitler

Youth who had organized another book burning just days before and had also come to participate in tonight's spectacle.

"Contra decadence and moral decay. Pro discipline and tradition, I herewith surrender the writings of Heinrich Mann, Ernst Glaeser, und Erich Kästner," the announcer bellowed. Martha's breath caught. Kästner's *The Flying Classroom* was her favorite novel, a children's story about a running feud between two school classes, which always made her laugh out loud. Kästner had a great sense of humor. She had no idea why his books were subjected to the purge. More piles followed—Freud, Tucholsky. More ecstatic cheers. People around the fire screamed: "More books, more books, or the fire will go out!" And as more and more books were thrown into the fire, everyone present seemed to band together tighter—except Martha. With every book that had been surrendered, her sense of belonging had diminished.

Martha often thought back to that day. And with her recurring memories she came to understand more and more that the day had marked the start of a change. From that moment onward, her strong bond with her twin brother had gradually weakened. When he felt his sister's eyes on him that night, Wolfgang looked up, and there was confusion—not compassion—in his eyes. "What's wrong?" he asked her. And only in hindsight did Martha understand that instinctively she had known to withhold her feelings, to keep those thoughts to herself. Until today.

Martha lovingly caressed one of the secret novels. Books were her only companions now. The only ones who managed to numb this feeling of disconnect. She had never found a kindred spirit outside the characters in her novels after Father's death. Else used to be her best friend at school, but then she, like Wolfgang, had climbed the ladder in the BDM and Martha had to start taking orders from her. She had even dragged Martha out of the house when Martha hoped to skip a BDM session unnoticed. Else was one of many who embraced the ideologies of the Führer, and Martha was simply unable to comprehend their dedication to the Third Reich. To her, Adolf Hitler was a sickly dwarf better suited for the sanatorium in Mann's *Magic Mountain* than running a country.

*The Magic Mountain* had been Father's favorite book of them all, and shortly before his death he added it to Martha's collection with a dedication on the first page. She took out the book and opened it: *To my beloved daughter, Martha, the most avid reader and the most beautiful mind that no fiction could ever create. I love you, Father.* Reading those words now filled Martha's eyes with tears, making the page dance before her. She clutched the book to her chest and went over to her bed. Under the blanket she found much-needed warmth and began to read, feeling connected to Father through time and space.

A piercing shriek tore her away from the sanatorium in the Alps. "Dear God, Martha! Have you gone insane?"

Mother was holding Mann's novel gingerly above Martha's head, and before she could react, Mother turned and left. Martha must have fallen asleep with the open book in her hand. Slowly she got out of bed and entered the hallway outside her room, fearful of what would happen next.

"Mother? Mother?"

Mother was nowhere to be seen.

Then she heard a weak voice above her. "How can you do this to me?"

Martha detected her mother on the stairs leading to the attic. Upon seeing her daughter, she walked up the steps, entered the attic, and shut the door. Martha raced up after her and heard the *click* of the door lock.

"Mother, please!"

A muffled voice from inside. "That's it, Martha. I cannot live with this."

Martha was banging against the door. "Please, I'm sorry. Mother, I'm so sorry."

There was silence on the other side for a long, long time. And then the fatal sound of a chair toppling over. Martha cried, screamed, tried to kick the door open with her bare feet. Then she broke down crying, sinking onto the floor. What had she done?

After a few minutes that seemed like an eternity, she heard the key turn in the lock, and her mother appeared in the doorframe. Martha jumped up and dove into her arms, thanking God that her mother was alive. Mother allowed this rare affectionate gesture but without giving anything in return.

"Next time I *will* do it. Do I make myself clear?" she said. Mother waved the forbidden book in Martha's face. "You know what we have to do."

Martha followed her mother downstairs and into the kitchen, where she watched her fire up the oven.

"You are so lucky that Wolfgang isn't here," she told her as she motioned for Martha to come and stand next to her. She held the novel out to Martha.

"Mother, please, this is one of the few presents I have left from Father!" Martha opened the first page, showing Mother the inscription.

"Your father was a mistaken idealist!" The fire was hot enough now.

"Say it." Mother watched her.

Martha couldn't bring herself to comply with her mother's demand.

Mother threw her an impatient look. "Hurry up, before Wolfgang gets back." She suddenly grabbed Martha's hand, forcing her to toss the beloved novel into the flames.

"Heil Hitler," Mother whispered. She threw Martha an expectant look. "Say it!"

Her hand rose to slap her cheek. Martha's eyes filled with tears. She was mourning the loss of Father more than ever. To see the book go up in flames felt a bit like seeing Father die in front of her eyes once more.

Mother's hands sank. "You are your own worst enemy, Martha."

Mother placed Martha under house arrest for the next twenty-four hours, during which she locked herself in her room, refusing to eat or drink. She used that time to hide her novels in a different place. She wasn't sure if Mother had spotted the compartment that she had carelessly left open the previous night. After scouting her room, she decided that a loose floorboard under the bed would be a better hiding place.

Night after night Martha slept on top of the forbidden goods, dreaming of the heroes in her novels, longing to be with them, to be them. And when the night demons came, she thought of Mother and her book. "You are your own worst enemy," Mother had said to her. But wasn't Mother her own worst enemy? So fueled by her belief that she had burned a personal note from her deceased husband? How blinding was this power that the regime held over its followers?

The atmosphere in the house had darkened even more, and Martha couldn't wait to be living in Schwabing. She had started to count the days until she would finally leave. In Schwabing, she would be able to free her mind! She would be close to a history that dated back to times long before this terrible era. And she would be surrounded by different people—hopefully more like-minded people. The only thought that panicked her was that she wouldn't be able to bring any of her books along. Without them she might feel even lonelier than she did at home.

When Martha's house arrest ended, Mother asked her to go to the laundry press in Berg am Laim to pick up sheets Mother had dropped off. One of the poorer areas of Munich, Berg am Laim was mostly inhabited and visited by the lower class. The laundry press was cheap but good, and their family had been using it for years. When Martha arrived, however, it was closed. A note on the door informed her that the owner was in the bar next door due to an emergency, and customers should go there to pick up or drop off orders. When Martha entered the bar, she was immediately engulfed in a cloud of smoke. There was no one tending the bar. Several men at the bar eyed her suspiciously, so she sat down near the entrance and waited.

A deep male voice wafted over to her from a dark corner at the other end of the bar. Through the smoke, she could make out the silhouettes of a man and woman. Martha didn't know what language they were speaking, but she knew it wasn't German. She tapped her fingers along the edge of the bar and scanned the room, wondering whether the laundry press owner would ever show.

After a while, the woman broke through the smoke and walked in Martha's direction. She was gorgeous; her dress was draped over her voluptuous body like a second skin, a daring outfit considering the Führer's rules for women, and it took Martha's breath away. As the figure came closer, Martha looked away, as if merely seeing the woman's dress made her complicit in the act of wearing it.

A few minutes later, the man stood from his seat. Martha gasped when she realized who it was: Siegfried. She quickly ducked behind the bar and only reappeared when she was sure he had left.

The atmosphere at home was so tense that Martha looked forward to being able to escape the house again that night, even if it was for just another Faith and Beauty meeting in the west of Munich. She arrived early but wished she hadn't when she caught sight of Else's sour face. Else ignored her, and when all the other women showed, she announced that they had not been accepted to perform at the upcoming Party Day in Nuremberg. "One of us here always seems to feel the need to march to a different drummer." Her eyes met Martha's.

Martha left the meeting ahead of everyone else, fleeing

their scrutinizing looks. But she was in no rush to get home. It was still light outside and the air was charged with an approaching thunderstorm. She decided to cycle the streets around the Marienplatz. Cycling seemed to be the only activity left that she could do without being given instructions or following guidelines. She had always loved cycling; that and diving into her books were the only ways to feel freedom. She lifted her head and briefly closed her eyes, letting the wind catch her hair and cleanse her mind, only to be harshly brought back to reality as she almost collided with a passerby, yelling "Heil Hitler!" at her when she made eye contact.

It was then she heard them through a window of a beer hall around the corner from the Marienplatz. She stopped her bike, leaning it against the wall, and peered through the window. Her brother was next to his friend, standing on top of wooden benches in a sea of men, all united in screaming Hitler slogans at the top of their lungs. Their feet stamped in the rhythm of the slogans, their bodies swung from left to right, their blood intoxicated with the alcohol and the hypnotizing power of repeating the slogans. Wolfgang looked just like he did the first time he'd brought Siegfried home. His friend shouted something into his ear, and they doubled over with laughter. A long time ago it had been Martha who'd made Wolfgang laugh like that.

As she walked over to her bike, the music suddenly stopped. She heard voices coming from the exit around the corner and realized that it was too late to escape unnoticed. She couldn't risk having Wolfgang and Siegfried spot her. She quickly hunkered down behind a nearby bush. Nobody would dare steal her bike with the regime hovering overhead at all times.

Several people left, and then she heard Siegfried's voice, whispering. She couldn't make out what he was saying, but she heard Wolfgang laugh. They were giggling like little boys. She heard them salute their comrades, bidding farewell to each other, and the sound of Wolfgang's bicycle until it was swallowed by the night.

After that there was a long silence. Martha wasn't sure if Siegfried had left, but she didn't dare peak around the bush.

A voice very close to her rang out. "You can come out."

Martha stayed put, not moving an inch.

"Fräulein Wiesberg, I know you're hiding back there."

Still, she wouldn't move.

"I recognized your bike, Fräulein Wiesberg."

She finally stepped out of her hiding place.

"Why are you hiding?" Siegfried asked, scrutinizing her as always.

"I should get going." She turned toward her bike.

"You didn't answer my question."

Martha shuffled her feet, looking down. "I didn't want my brother to see me here. I—I really should get going. I want to be home before him."

"I'll drive you."

She eyed her bike nervously, trying to find a way out of the situation.

Driving home with this man was the last thing she wanted to do.

"Your bike will fit, no problem," he said, as if reading her mind. And with that he grabbed the bike and pushed it toward his car. "I'm parked around the corner."

They walked through the Marienplatz, accompanied only by the sound of rolling thunder. He loaded the bike in the back and held the passenger door open before getting in himself. Siegfried produced a pack of cigarettes from his pocket and offered one to Martha. Martha was sure he was testing her. She declined.

He started the engine.

"When did your father die?" he asked.

"Six years ago."

"Do you share his views?"

This time she wanted to contemplate her answer before

voicing it, but her heart started beating faster when she noticed that he was driving in the opposite direction of Perlach.

"You didn't answer my question," he said with a side glare at her.

"My father was a good man. And I am not very political. He was. And he suffered for it."

She saw with shock that he was turning toward Königsplatz, the same place Mother had taken them for the book burnings and a place she had avoided ever since. She wasn't sure if she was just imagining it or if he slowed down a bit when they drove by the Nazi Party's headquarters in the Brienner Straße, and then again when passing the Wittelsbacher Palais—the Gestapo headquarters, with its prison cells in the basement. What if he was taking her to an interrogation? What if...worse? She thought of all the other people she knew of, other than her favorite writers: ordinary people; one of Father's closest friends; a science teacher, who had been taken from his home in Perlach; or a client at the hairdresser's shop, whom some officers from the SiPo, the "Security Police," had picked up at the salon. They had disappeared without a trace after voicing their opposing views. Was this how they had felt? She started breathing faster. He noticed, she was sure. She tried to shift less on her seat but had a hard time staying still.

He hadn't commented on her response. Instead he kept quiet as they cruised around the Königsplatz again. She was practically mad with fear.

"Why are you so nervous?" He finally broke the silence.

Martha swallowed. "Are you taking me home?"

He nodded his head and turned right into Gabelsbergerstraße in the direction of the Isar River.

Martha's fear subsided, and as the first raindrops landed on the windshield, she studied his profile. The wind from the cracked-open window played with his blond locks while he puffed on his cigarette. Earlier that morning in the bar, he had looked so different, normal, almost pleasant. She was curious. What had he been doing in Berg am Laim? What was his business with that stunning woman? And what language had he been using? His head suddenly turned in her direction, and she quickly turned to look outside, embarrassed to have been caught staring.

It felt luxurious to be driven by car and not get soaked outside in the rain. She was sure Wolfgang had been having a great time with Siegfried, going to all these places that were difficult to get to by bike or public transport. He could have taken her with him—and would have in the old times.

They entered Perlach and stopped at a place in the forest that would allow her to get to the house unnoticed by Wolfgang. By now it was raining heavily.

"Thank you for the ride." She threw open the door and jumped out of the car, walking around to the back. But he was faster and had already opened the trunk and reached for her bike. He held it in his hands, as if it were as light as a feather, and Martha reached for it. But he didn't release it and just stood there, lingering, as the rain soaked them to the bones.

"You should watch what you say," he simply said, his blue eyes boring into her.

As a form of punishment for having failed the Führerin's assessment, Else made Martha attend as many Faith and Beauty sessions as possible, bringing the invites home to Mother, delivering them straight into her hands.

Now that they had failed the assessment, the group had time on their hands to devote to fashion, which Else never grew tired of pointing out to the others. In a new intense summer course, the women concentrated on sewing. Members of Faith and Beauty were encouraged to design their own dresses, which had to follow the strict guidelines of the Deutsches Modeamt, the German Fashion Institute, and were invited to showcase their creations at fashion shows.

Martha despised this course less, as at least now they were

allowed to exercise a certain degree of creativity. Else had laughed when she had first seen Martha's cut.

"A dress for a ball? Why would you not do something more functional?"

Because she was so tired of being *functional*. Everything seemed to be reduced to that, to *function* for the Führer. And also to spite her old friend, so she stuck to it. After all, the German fashion guidelines didn't forbid ball gowns, as long as they weren't too revealing.

Mother had come out of her gloom a tiny bit more, and she had given Martha a fabric that was supposed to have been turned into a dress for Irene for a piano concert. It was deep blue, like the night. And Martha knew it would suit her red hair and green eyes. They had no machine at home, so outside the sessions, Martha took her dress home and sewed by hand. At first Mother had experienced grief over never being able to see Irene in the dress, but she eventually started to help Martha.

Overall, it was a plain dress, a straight cut, no buttons or pearls, no patterns, but Martha had applied special touches here and there, not conforming 100 percent to the guidelines but enough so that it would pass. Her dress was long and covered not only her knees, one of the guidelines; no, it also covered the ankles, reaching well to the floor. The sleeves covered her wrists, and the high neck took care of any cleavage. But the silken fabric on the sides and half of the sleeves was covered by a slightly transparent chiffon that was supposed to be the undergown, had it been tailored for Irene. And instead of using a zipper on the side, Martha had opted for a long trail of buttons down the back.

"You will look beautiful in it," were Mother's first words after her initial shock. She carefully folded the dress and wrapped it in brown paper, then handed it to Martha with trembling hands. "Be careful not to drop it when you are on the bike."

That night the women met at Else's house. It was the

final session of the sewing course, and the time had come to decide which dresses made the cut for the fashion show. Most of the other women had long forgiven Martha for the group not having been selected for Party Day. But not Else. While Martha changed into her dress in the room next door, she could hear Else praise the other dresses she had seen that night. When Martha entered the room in her gown, the other women gasped in admiration. But she didn't even need to look at her former friend to know that Else wouldn't have liked Martha's dress, no matter its style.

At the end of the night, Else simply announced the names of the three ladies who would not participate. The first two hadn't finished their dresses on time. Martha's name came last.

But Martha didn't care, and seeing the unflinching look on Martha's face seemed to make Else all the more furious. Martha felt strengthened by having created something of her own. How satisfying to see an idea materialize in front of your eyes, to become an artist, even if it was only for a fleeting moment, like authors watching their stories come to life on the pages—and sometimes even on the silver screen. She swore to herself that during her coming year in Schwabing she would take every opportunity she had to soak up the artistic energy there. In her mind, Schwabing was a city within a city where the horrible rules of this world didn't apply.

It was one week until her move to Schwabing when her brother showed up at the end of a Faith and Beauty gymnastic session in the park, with Siegfried in tow. Else had told Martha to stay behind to practice a synchronized dance routine, a dance that only Else knew, making the perspiring Martha look clumsy and incompetent. When Else noticed the two men, her movements became even more graceful, her legs seemingly longer. Martha again felt itchy in her sports outfit the second she saw Siegfried. His eyes silently reminded her of the warning he had given her after the drive in August. She avoided his gaze and shifted her eyes to her brother. It had been a long while since she had seen Wolfgang outside home. He came straight up to her and Else.

"Sister, I need you tonight," he simply said. She could tell from the way he was saying it that he had no other choice but to ask her for this favor. "My boss, Hänschel, invited us to his birthday party. There will be some dancing. He asked me to bring my sister along and another German *Fräulein* for my friend Siegfried here."

She noticed Else eyeing Siegfried greedily. "I'm free," Else said, smiling modestly at Siegfried from underneath her long lashes. She reached his shoulder in height thanks to her long legs.

"I'm very pleased to hear that," Siegfried answered, "but I'm afraid I will need to ask this lovely lady out tonight." He looked at Martha and then back at Else. "It would be a bit awkward if Wolfgang took his own sister to a ball, wouldn't it?" He winked at Wolfgang. Then he addressed Martha again. "What time shall I pick you up, *gnädiges Fräulein*?"

They were sitting in the kitchen, waiting for Siegfried to arrive. Initially Martha had despised the prospect of spending a whole evening in the company of her brother and his friend. Now, however, she felt weirdly excited, also thanks to the dress whose blue fabric seemed to boost her self-confidence as it caressed her skin. It would be nice to leave the house for something other than Faith and Beauty meetings or running errands for Mother.

Wolfgang, on the other hand, seemed displeased that he had to take her along. "Martha, I warn you. You need to keep your mouth shut tonight. You'll already stick out of the crowd like a sore thumb with that dress of yours."

Martha smiled at him; she couldn't help herself. She knew she looked quite different in this dress. Certainly nothing like she had ever looked before. As hoped, the midnight-blue dress complemented the red of her hair and the light green of her eyes. The sun and fresh air of her bike rides had created a healthy glow to accentuate her cheekbones in the absence of makeup.

"I think it's modest enough," Mother jumped in, and Martha smiled gratefully at her.

Right on time, Siegfried entered, and everyone stood. She could hear the fabric of her dress rustle as she attempted to brush it down. Siegfried looked at Martha as if he had never seen her before. And then he smiled at her, for the first time ever. "You look quite beautiful tonight, Fräulein Wiesberg," he said, and offered his arm in gentlemanly fashion.

Just one night, she told herself, she would be someone else. She accepted his arm and was guided out of the kitchen and out of the house.

"I want you to change before we go," Wolfgang said from behind. "Wear that brown dress of yours. Hänschel will not appreciate a daring dress like that."

Martha stopped in her tracks. She felt her eyes filling with tears. She looked down at the floor, not wanting Siegfried to see them. She felt childish. Small. And then she felt Siegfried squeezing her arm ever so slightly. But it was over so quickly that she wasn't able to say if he had meant to show compassion, empathy, or if he had meant to reassure her of Wolfgang's intention, that she shouldn't wear something that would call attention to herself.

When she returned in her brown dress, Siegfried and Wolfgang were already waiting in the car. Mother accompanied her outside. In the car, Wolfgang happily conversed with Siegfried in the front seat, and the previous incident seemed forgotten. Only mother cast her a short look filled with pity before the car drove off.

Every time they stopped at a traffic light, Martha wished she could jump out of the car and run into the night. And each time, she glimpsed Siegfried studying her in the rearview mirror, those piercing eyes lingering on hers.

Hänschel's birthday festivities were held in the Imperial Hall of the Munich Residenz, once home to the Bavarian monarchs. A generous staircase led up to what was probably the biggest room Martha had ever entered in her life; she had always imagined the czarist salon in Tolstoy's *War and Peace* to be a room this size. Here, the gold framing the oil paintings and on the stucco-embellished ceiling was so thick that it seemed to make the room glow. Walls were adorned with large tapestries that depicted scenes from the Old Testament.

Hänschel didn't need to be pointed out to Martha. She knew instantly which of the many people in the room he was: fat, red-nosed, with the demeanor of an emperor ruling over his minions. Needless to say, Martha would have fit in just fine in her blue dress. She had known exactly what dress Wolfgang had been referring to, and in protest, she had chosen her oldest one that also happened to be brown. Mothers words came back to her: "You're your own worst enemy." Yes, she was in many ways. To make Wolfgang look bad in front of his boss, she had put on her shabbiest dress, which made her stick out of the crowd even more than her blue dress would have.

"That wasn't the dress I meant," Wolfgang said, once he finally acknowledged her.

Hänschel walked over to the trio, his arm raised to his swollen face.

"Heil Hitler," he said, and Martha had to brace herself against the stench of alcohol wafting over to her.

Hänschel was all smiles and praise for Wolfgang, who beamed as his boss showered him with compliments. Martha realized she had seen this expression on Wolfgang's face before—whenever Father paid him a compliment.

They hadn't picked up Else en route to the festivities, and neither Wolfgang nor Siegfried had brought her up in the car on the ride there. Else, however, was all smiles when she entered, unbothered by the fact that she had to come on her own. As was to be expected, she was dressed impeccably in white, a chaste color that was encouraged in the guidelines of the German Fashion Institute, and far more becoming than Martha's brown dress. She looked triumphantly over at Martha and was about to make her way to them when Siegfried asked Martha for a dance.

Martha shook her head. "Thank you. I cannot dance." Which was a lie—the BDM had taught her how. Siegfried must have known this and pulled her to the dance floor anyway.

It was a waltz, one of the Führer's favorites. Martha only reached Siegfried's torso as he took her waist with one hand and her arm with the other. He made her feel like a feather swirled over the dance floor, with his hand firmly placed on the spot between her back and behind. He guided her so well that she wouldn't have needed to know the dance as well as she did.

"Blue is your color," he whispered softly enough so only she could hear. "But you still look very nice, my *Fräulein*."

She briefly raised her eyes; he was smiling at her, and they both looked away at the same time. How she wished she was still wearing *her* dress. That he could be the prince she had imagined, that this could have been a pleasant night. But when she looked up at him again, his eyes were cast elsewhere. And when the song ended, he released her abruptly to join Wolfgang and Hänschel at the bar, over on the other side of the cathedral-size hall.

She quickly walked from the center of the dance floor toward the row of sofas against the wall. With a short nod of her head, she passed by a group of ladies, many of whom she had gone to school with, and sat down on the farthest sofa. From her vantage point, she observed as Wolfgang, Siegfried, and Hänschel engaged in lively conversation. Siegfried gave Hänschel a friendly slap on the back while laughing heartily. She had just been dancing with the enemy.

She watched Else walk over and Hänschel greet her with

respect. And again, Hänschel said something that made everyone laugh and Else blush. Then she offered her hand to Siegfried and they walked onto the dance floor. As he danced with Else, Martha observed the same smile that he had regaled Martha with earlier. And the longer she watched that smile, the more venom gathered in her. She got up from her seat and exited the hall, suddenly in need of fresh air.

Outside, she leaned against the wall, exhaling into the fresh air, as if trying to expel the bile that felt like a lump sitting on her lungs. They were all the same. He was just like them. The warnings Siegfried had constantly been given her, those scrutinizing looks of his, this arrogance. Who was he to tell her off? She rushed back inside—and almost ran into him, nursing a beer at a smaller bar by the entrance, alone. A longing expression on his face. Martha had hoped for another moment alone with him, but hadn't expected the situation to present itself so quickly. Sweat was showing on Siegfried's forehead, likely from dancing numerous waltzes with Else. He smiled.

"I saw you the other day," Martha whispered, imitating Siegfried's scrutinizing tone. He should know she saw him.

"Where?"

"In that pub, in Berg am Laim."

His smile died and he glanced around the room, nervously. As he came very close to her, the smile reappeared on his face. He opened his mouth but closed it again. He took her arm, his hand pushing deeply into her flesh, but didn't say a word. She squinted in pain, and he released her before walking over to the bar where Wolfgang was still conversing with Hänschel.

Still in shock, she again observed the trio as they talked. Siegfried was his cool self again, laughing at Hänschel's jokes; the plastered-on smile had found its way back to his face. When Hänschel left the group to talk to some late arrivals, Siegfried leaned closer into Wolfgang and whispered something into his ear. She couldn't see Wolfgang's reaction, as he stood with his back toward her, but his body language said enough. It was as if an electrical shock had shot through his body. He stood taller, rigid, his shoulders broad and intimidating. She was consumed with fear, not knowing what Siegfried had told him. Was it about her? Both men walked over to Hänschel to say their goodbyes, and then turned around toward the exit. Martha was nervous as she looked at Wolfgang as he approached her, expecting to find anger in his expression. But as he came closer, she saw a smile on his face.

"Let's go," he said, brushing past her. She followed, eager to get home as quickly as possible, but again she felt Siegfried's hand on her arm, holding her back. The pressure was less forceful than before, but strong enough to make her shudder under his touch. Maybe she really had imagined his gesture in Perlach earlier, the light, almost airy feel of his palm on her arm.

His blue eyes were piercing. He again came closer, and out of Wolfgang's earshot, he whispered between clenched teeth, "I am telling you for the last time: you should watch what you say." Then he let her go.

She had never felt more tired in the car on the way back to Perlach. Tired of being careful, tired of keeping quiet, tired of playing along. *Soon*, she thought to herself, *I am going to explode*.

The day had finally arrived. Today she would depart for the Schinkenhubers. Martha was standing by the door with her two small suitcases.

"Be careful, Martha! I wouldn't survive if anything happened to you or Wolfgang," her mother said. "You're all I have left." Though she didn't hug her, the tears in Mother's eyes were enough to move Martha. "I'll see you next Saturday evening. I'll make you your favorite meal," Mother added with a smile on her face.

Martha turned to Wolfgang. "Goodbye."

He shook his head. "No. We'll drive you—and make sure you get there safe and sound." He fetched the two valises and headed out the door.

Martha followed obediently.

Outside, Siegfried was leaning against his car in the early sunlight. "Heil Hitler, Fräulein Wiesberg." Siegfried flashed his biggest smile, as if nothing had transpired at the dance the week before. She obliged and returned the Hitler salute. Siegfried loaded Martha's bike in the trunk and threw the two suitcases in the backseat.

"Ready to become a woman?" he asked her as she settled in next to the suitcases, and Wolfgang laughed heartily.

In the car, the two discussed Chamberlain, Britain's prime minister. Siegfried was very agreeable with everything that Wolfgang had to say. Martha's mind wandered elsewhere, but when she heard Siegfried ask Wolfgang about the "progress" Hänschel was making against opposition movements in Schwabing, she suddenly snapped to attention. Wolfgang readily volunteered information about a recent case in which they had found a couple of students who had spread pamphlets all over the city center in the middle of the night. They were immediately taken into custody.

"What will happen to them?" Siegfried asked.

Wolfgang shrugged his shoulder. "I trust Hänschel knows what they deserve."

Siegfried nodded in agreement. "Were you able to find all of the group members?"

"No, but Hänschel will beat it out of them, I'm sure."

Martha felt Siegfried's eyes on her in the rearview mirror. She shivered.

They drove along the Isar, which brought back many happy memories from her childhood: Wolfgang and her playing in the water with Father, Wolfgang buying her ice cream with his pocket money, Wolfgang drawing equations into the ground and Father's admiring looks. Martha's pleas to God to allow for him to grow into a genius and to make them rich.

There never had been envy between them. Wolfgang, too, was looking outside the window, a slight smile on his face. She hoped he was reliving the same memories.

"I am so proud we live in the cradle of the Nazi regime. This"—and with that he motioned to the Isar—"this is where it was born. And I can feel it everywhere." He smiled proudly. Martha's smile slipped away.

They turned into Theresienstraße and then Agnesstraße, where Martha would live for the next year. Lined with oak trees, the street was bathed in shade despite the sunny day. The buildings on both sides were three stories high, each harboring several apartments. They passed number 61, another building with a beautiful ornate facade. A plaque on the wall read: *DR. ELMAR SCHINKENHUBER, FIRST FLOOR*. Martha spotted a haggard woman in her late thirties waiting impatiently at the top of the wide staircase that led up to the entrance. When Siegfried found a parking spot a little farther up the street, Martha was glad to get out of the car. Siegfried lifted her bike out of the trunk, and Wolfgang motioned for her to push it while he carried the suitcases.

"I'll be right back," he said to Siegfried, and followed Martha to the entrance.

"Heil Hitler. We've been waiting for you," Frau Schinkenhuber greeted them. Martha knew they hadn't arrived late; they had left Perlach well on time. She had the sinking feeling that she would be in for a stressful year.

At the bottom of the staircase, Wolfgang held the two suitcases out to her.

"Enjoy the start of university," Martha said, flashing him a sad smile and was surprised to catch a glimpse of the old Wolfgang, the soft, soothing glow of his eyes when he'd consoled her in their childhood.

"Send her to the kitchen already!" Siegfried bellowed from the car.

Wolfgang turned toward him. "Just teaching her one last good lesson!"

When Wolfgang faced Martha again, she could see that Siegfried had successfully destroyed their moment. The hint of sadness in his eyes had been replaced by something harsher. "The Führer knows what he's doing. We need women elsewhere, not at the university."

"Come, we have work to do," she heard Frau Schinkenhuber say from behind. Wolfgang nodded to the woman and turned back without another word to Martha.

"You can leave your bike here in the entrance," Frau Schinkenhuber added.

As they passed the entrance to Dr. Schinkenhuber's practice, one of his patients exited. The boy was about six years old but seemed to have the mind of a one-year-old. His mother was crying.

Through another tall door, they arrived at a big oak staircase leading up to the flats. Here the sunlight managed to enter through the stained-glass windows, creating colorful patterns all around Martha. The old wooden steps squeaked as she followed Frau Schinkenhuber.

"We live on the third floor," she said, and continued ascending fast.

Martha had a tough time keeping up with her, with her suitcases in hand. On the third floor, the woman entered through a large door into the hallway of their flat. When Martha followed her inside, she was in awe. This place reminded her more of the Imperial Hall in the Residenz than a residential flat. Unlike their little dark house in Perlach, this home had high ceilings with sunlight pouring into the hallway through the tall windows in the adjacent rooms. The walls were adorned with portraits and oil paintings, featuring stills and landscapes. A lingering scent of lilac and roses came from a vase of flowers on a side table.

Martha followed Frau Schinkenhuber to the end of the hallway. In the doorframe, six children eyed her curiously.

"This is Martha. She will help your mother with the household," Frau Schinkenhuber said, introducing her. "This is my oldest, Norbert, twelve years old. Then there is six-year-old Sophie, three-year-old Maria two-year-old Gerda, and my youngest, the twins Emma and Hanna, eleven months old."

"Do you play games?" Maria broke the silence.

"Yes, of course I do." Martha tried to smile.

"And can you tell us stories?" Norbert asked.

"Oh, yes, definitely. I'm filled with them."

Sophie came up to her, tugging at her skirt. "And will you stop Mama from crying all the time?"

"Sophie, stop it!" Frau Schinkenhuber interrupted. She looked at Martha, who only then noticed the red-rimmed eyes. "I have a bad allergy, that's all," she said. She motioned to Martha's suitcase. "You'll share a room with our three youngest."

Martha was worked hard. Her feet, her hands, every bone in her body ached each night when she went to bed. Every four hours she was woken up by the twins screaming for their bottles—Frau Schinkenhuber had long ago run out of breast milk.

During the day, Frau Schinkenhuber sent her all over town for errands. At first Martha enjoyed getting out of the house. She would take little detours on her way to and from the Viktualienmarkt, a farmer's market Mother would have never shopped at because of its high prices. She cycled along Sendlinger Straße for a quick stop at the Asam Church, where she marveled at the baroque interior and the high ceilings. She paused at the Marienplatz, briefly closing her eyes and imagining the people who had crossed this square in the nineteenth century. She fed the birds in the Englischer Garten, the "English Garden," with breadcrumbs from the farmer's market, asking herself what these places must have felt like before Hitler had come to power. The more errands she had to run the less she enjoyed them, the less she lingered in the city. When she had errands to run around the Odeonsplatz, she chose the Viscardigasse, avoiding the memorial that Hitler had erected in front of the Feldherrnhalle to the martyrs of the 1923 Beer Hall Putsch, dodging the compulsory Hitler salute, which had gained the tiny alley the name of Drückebergergasse, "Dodger's Alley." The atmosphere in the city, the presence of the regime, the swastikas—it was too overpowering for her, and she'd be glad to return to the flat. Schwabing, once the Bohemian hub that her father had raved about, had also turned oppressive.

In the Schinkenhubers' household, too, Martha was taken aback at first. This year was supposed to be a learning experience, a time to grow and better herself away from her family. Instead, she was more like cheap help.

But in those rare moments when she got a chance to study Frau Schinkenhuber's face, Martha noticed that this woman, too, had been worked hard by the regime and truly needed help. From certain angles she looked more like the children's grandmother than mother. The wrinkles and deep bags under her eyes were a testimony to the lonely, tear-filled nights when Herr Schinkenhuber entered the bedroom, his heavy boots still on, often very drunk, ignoring her pleas to skip "it." As an awarded party member, he enjoyed special privileges, and the more children one gave to the German Reich, the higher the esteem. Frau Schinkenhuber, it seemed, lived in constant fear of becoming pregnant again. Norbert had told Martha that his mother had nearly died during the delivery of the twins. She was nothing more than an empty shell, barely functioning as wife and mother, as she had been forced to simply give too much. Martha wondered what this woman must have been like before they'd used her up.

When the weekends came around, Martha's feet would feel like they were about to fall off by the time she'd finally reach home on her bike. She'd spend her weekends helping Mother manage the household, cutting the neighbors' hair on Sundays. She always had to be back at the Schinkenhubers by Monday morning at seven, and it took her over an hour to get there by bike, so she had to leave Perlach before six.

The only time of the week that promised her a bit of relief was Wednesday afternoon. On Wednesdays, the doctor's practice closed early, and Herr and Frau Schinkenhuber traveled to the countryside to a clinic that held many of his former patients.

It was the end of September and autumn was approaching. The enthusiasm Martha had felt before moving to Schwabing had died down as quickly as the warmth of the last summer sun, now replaced by a cold, biting wind from the Alps. Martha felt lonelier than ever. Her expectations for life in Schwabing had not been met; she neither had the time nor the opportunity to meet like-minded people. It seemed they had all been brainwashed or taken somewhere else. Martha was riding along Schleißheimer Straße with a parcel of winter clothes that had been altered for the thinning Frau Schinkenhuber, when she suddenly stopped in her tracks, braking so hard that she dropped the parcel. It was Siegfried who crossed the street in front of her and entered a small café on the opposite side of the street. He hadn't caught sight of her. Martha got off her bike and gathered the clothes, cursing herself, as one jacket had gotten dirty. The work at the Schinkenhubers had kept her busy, physically and mentally, but had also helped to suppress unpleasant memories, of her brother — and him. Why did she feel so uncomfortable every time she saw him? She shook her head in anger at herself and drove on. And then, in front of a small supermarket a few doors down, he suddenly stepped in front of the bike. Martha screamed, her bike swerved, and she landed hard on the pavement in front of him. He held a hand out to her.

"How did you do that?" she asked instead of accepting his help. "I just saw you enter the café and then..."

He looked at her suspiciously but didn't answer, his arm still outstretched. She grabbed it, and he pulled her up — with the same ease that he had demonstrated during the dance at Hänschel's birthday. Only this time he stood closer; she had never been that close to him, not even at the ball. She could feel the ends of his blond locks on her face, but this time he didn't squeeze her arm the way he had done at the ball; the touch was lighter, still as electrifying. She looked up at this man who had come around out of nowhere and had pulled Wolfgang away from her and even further into this ugly mass of narcissistic men. He was just like the Gestapo: appearing at any time, anywhere, omnipresent.

Siegfried lingered silently with those scrutinizing eyes.

"This can't be a coincidence. I see you in Berg am Laim, and now here." Again, the words were out before she could help it. Something about him triggered her impulsive reactions. "Are you following me? Did my brother put you up to this?" she said, without breaking from the uncomfortable closeness. She was certain that she'd only get to the truth with a close view of his eyes.

A puzzled look crossed them for an instance, but he didn't say anything.

"I apologize," he finally whispered. And only then did he step back, ending the intimacy of the situation. His eyes looked friendlier now. "I hope the Schinkenhubers treat you well?" It struck Martha that the smile on his face was different from the one he had carried at the ball. His lower lip shook ever so slightly.

"Yes, all is well."

He still hadn't answered any of her questions.

"Heil Hitler," he said, and turned around.

"Were you following me?" She heard the tremble in her voice as it broke out of her again.

He stopped. And turned back to her. "Would I have any reason to follow you?" He answered her question with a counterquestion.

She simply shook her head. Then he walked back in the direction of the café.

Her skin still seemed to burn where he had touched her; her legs were trembling so hard that she had to push her bike as she continued on her way.

The recent encounter with Siegfried gnawed at her; she felt controlled on all sides. And she didn't even have her books to escape to. She missed them, her stories, unable to expand her world beyond the tiny one around her. The weeks had begun to crawl by.

"Norbert!" Martha called him over one afternoon a couple of days later. She was standing in the kitchen, trying to come up with another dish for the family.

Martha had grown quite fond of Norbert, who had an insatiable hunger for stories. And once he realized that Martha's promise had not been empty and that she indeed was filled with them, he used every opportunity to ask her for one. At night, when he couldn't sleep, he snuck into the babies' bedroom and snuggled up to her, requesting yet another fairy tale—just like Wolfgang had done when they were little.

"We have many secrets, don't we?" she asked, bending to his level.

Norbert nodded proudly.

"Can we add one to the list?"

Norbert looked at her with wide eyes. "What is it?"

"I want to go to the university on Wednesdays when your parents are away. I'm running out of stories to tell you, so I want to attend a lecture about German literature so I can collect more for you."

Norbert agreed to keep her secret.

"Will you promise me to take good care of your sisters?" The twins always slept from three to five anyway, and the older girls were easy to look after.

"Only if you keep telling me stories." He grinned.

On Wednesday, Martha's heart was beating fast when she arrived at Ludwig-Maximilians University. Hoping that nobody would ask her for identification papers, she had tried to dress as inconspicuously as possible. She had borrowed a mix of Herr Schinkenhuber's and Norbert's clothes: from Norbert a pair of shoes and some pants, which were still too big for him, and a hat from the father. She might even have been able to pass for a male student.

She entered the building through its tall arches and pushed by the students passing in and out. Even though she knew the place was rich in history, she hadn't quite expected such a building. It was hard not to marvel at the entrance hall that was just as ostentatious as the ballroom where Hänschel had celebrated his birthday. Every surface was embellished with marble. Two lions guarding the entrance eyed her curiously from pedestals on each side of a generous staircase as she crossed the expansive hallway with echoing footsteps and ascended the stairs leading up to the lecture halls. She bumped into several students on her way up simply because she couldn't keep her head down when her eyes caught the high, ornate ceiling. She felt jealous, jealous of the students she ran into for being entitled to enter this building every day; of her brother, who could soak up the atmosphere whenever he wanted to, officially, proudly, his head carried high as if to say he had earned it; and not like her, with her hair stuffed under a hat, her breasts hidden under a wide jumper, trying to remain unseen.

She walked into the wing for fine arts and noticed the board that listed the semester's lectures. She quickly found a *Germanistik* lecture and headed for the lecture halls on the eastern end of the hallway, trying to appear as if she knew where she was going. She ran into a flow of students entering a theater, and when she got closer she realized to her relief that this was the lecture she was looking for. She joined the stream and sat down in one of the last rows of the equally impressive lecture hall, an airy, light-flooded space that could easily host several hundred students in their rows of dark wooden benches that were a stark contrast to the natural light flooding in through the ceiling. Only the huge swastikas on the impeccably white walls were a sore spot for her eyes.

She glanced around the room. Nobody seemed to look twice at her. Most of the students were male, as was to be expected. She relaxed, settling into the wooden bench. She had made it. This could work. She would not have to be without stories, without books any longer. She had found a way to connect with the outside world again. In the same moment that she felt consumed by the joy of anticipation, she recognized Wolfgang in the first row. She nearly jumped. Why was he here? His studies were located in a different wing of the building. She felt the anger rise in her. Why did he have to be here? Why did he have to compromise everything that made her happy?

The chatter of the students suddenly died down. Martha was still staring at her twin brother in the front, shocked, when Wolfgang turned around to watch the arriving professor, who had already passed Martha in the last row. She recognized an expression on his face not dissimilar to the way he had looked at her a long time ago, a mix of adoration, admiration, and awe, but his eyes were clearly trained at something or someone farther up in the hall. She followed Wolfgang's gaze, almost mechanically, not thinking twice—and met Siegfried's eyes as he was descending the stairs in the middle of the lecture hall, only a couple of feet behind the professor. She noticed with concern that Siegfried had stopped in his tracks on the stairs, staring at her, his forehead deeply furrowed. Martha felt her body freeze in fear. And then he turned his head and looked ahead, and without glancing at her again, started to descend the stairs, following the professor. Before Siegfried would have the chance to betray her, she quickly jumped up from her chair and ran out of the hall and out the building.

That Saturday when she came home to Perlach, she was afraid she'd find Wolfgang and Mother in the kitchen, scowling at her. But that didn't happen. Still, she was driven by the fear that Siegfried would report her any day now. Had she done something wrong? Yes, she had smuggled herself into the university, with a false identity, under a wrong pretext, while leaving Norbert alone with five small children. She had acted recklessly. But in her heart, she felt a stronger call. It had felt so good to enter the building, to be among students, to be among people other than Frau Schinkenhuber, Herr Schinkenhuber, or the neighbors she passed on the street when running errands for the family. She was well aware that it had been students from that very same university who had been among the 1933 crowd cheerfully throwing her favorite books into the flames. Still, she had felt a different aura inside the building as she glanced into the eyes of the students she accidentally bumped into. She had felt liberated. So the next Wednesday, she returned to the university, to the same lecture. It was worth the risk. Surely Wolfgang wouldn't miss two weeks of his real studies just to go to another literature lecture. She made sure to sit in the last row again, in the center aisle close to the stairs, so that she could escape quickly if she had to.

She scanned the room. To her relief, neither Wolfgang nor Siegfried was in attendance this time. But something else caught Martha's attention: across the aisle just on the other side of the steps, two men and one woman sat closely together, whispering intensely. There was a certain determination in their body language, in their eyes, that made it impossible for Martha to look away. She knew she shouldn't draw attention to herself like that, but she felt pulled toward them, like Bluebeard's wife and the forbidden door in the French folktale.

Minutes later the lecture began, and Martha turned her eyes toward the front. She hadn't checked the board again after last week's lecture, and she couldn't remember today's title, but anything would do, she thought. Just being close to stories, getting into someone else's head. And then the lecturer announced today's topic—"World Views"—and she had a sinking feeling in her stomach.

He opened his speech with a quote from Hans Grimm's novel *People without Space,* "The Germans: the cleanest, most honest people, most efficient and most industrious." She looked around the room as most students proudly nodded their heads in consent. This was no worldview but a perverted way of putting one's own race above everyone else's! She blinked away the tears gathering in her eyes. She had risked so much to come here only to realize that the poison had seeped even into the walls of this building. She got up from her seat, quietly, and noticed that the group of three students also had risen from their seats and were now slipping out of the room. Maybe they felt the same as she did? Martha decided to follow them.

She saw them disappear into the basement. The entrance hall was deserted, and she was about to follow them when a group of students entered from outside. Almost instinctively, she turned around and studied the program on the board next to the lecture hall. She waited for more people to pass behind her, and only turned around once the entrance hall was deserted again. She hurried down the staircase and into a maze of dark hallways. She didn't know her way and had to trust her hearing for guidance, following the faint tiptoes and breathing she could just barely make out in the distance. The farther she descended into the basement, the darker it became. A few times, she lost them and had to stop and strain her ears for any movement. She'd give her eyes time to adjust to the increasing darkness and force herself to listen more carefully, to be more patient, to choose her next steps wisely. After many twists and turns, she felt the distance between them shrinking, the sounds growing louder. She heard the rattle of a key and a door unlocking.

When she turned another corner she was bathed in bright light coming from a nearby room. The students had entered the last room at the end of the hallway, less than ninety feet ahead of her. Martha quickly withdrew behind the corner she had just turned. And that is when she caught a whiff of something in the air. A familiar scent. Her brother. She looked behind her, heart pacing quickly. Had he seen her in the entrance hall and followed her down here? She felt trapped, knowing she wouldn't be able to get away if he was behind her. Considering her options, she carefully peered around the corner again and gasped when she realized, this time, after her eyes had adjusted to the sudden light, that he was hovering between two pipes just sixty feet in front of her, his eyes trained carefully on the room. Next to him squatted Hänschel. She held her breath and slowly retreated back behind the corner.

"Did you hear that?" she heard Wolfgang ask Hänschel. Her heart was beating so fast and loud in her head that she was sure they must hear it.

"Probably mice. Let's not lose focus here, Wiesberg."

Martha was dizzy with fear. The men were quiet for a moment longer, and then she heard their heavy boots run toward the end of the hallway. She heard them burst into the room, and screams coming from inside. Martha used the time to move farther down into the dark part of the tunnel, the direction she had come from. With the light from the room illuminating the hall, she was alarmed to learn that there were no other hallways branching off to the side where she could have hidden.

She hurried on as fast as she could, but after only fifty feet she heard the group coming her way, a mix of angry footsteps from the "hunters" and muffled screams from the "hunted." She broke into a sweat, frantically surveying the hallway in front of her for a way out, tiptoeing as fast as she could. She heard them approach the corner. If they turned now, she would be seen immediately. Then she discovered a small nook in the wall, the end of an old coal chute, right above the floor, small enough for one person on all fours. She squatted down into it just as the group came into view. She waited, shaking, hoping that they hadn't seen her.

And then they marched down the hallway. She was terrified that they would spot her any second now. And they did. But it wasn't Hänschel or her brother who saw her. It was the students who passed Martha at eye level, only inches away from her face as they were dragged over the floor by Hänschel, their knees and noses bloody. The female student caught sight of Martha and looked her straight in the eyes. Martha inhaled, afraid she would betray her. But she didn't. Hänschel kicked her in the side, and she screamed again; her eyes filled with tears and her body convulsed in pain while Hänschel continued with her friends. She kept Martha's gaze until she was pulled out of sight and replaced by one of the two male students. The student held on to the stone wall as Martha's brother dragged him by his hair, and she could see his nails breaking off, leaving a bloody trail.

"Please, let us go," he managed to say to Wolfgang. "I can tell you're not like them."

Wolfgang dropped him, and the group came to a sudden halt. Now the boy, too, was eye to eye with Martha, his eyes bulging in fear. Martha held her breath, shivering, hoping that he wouldn't blow her cover.

"You know what they deserve," she heard Hänschel say expectantly to Wolfgang, his voice wafting over to her hiding place.

The male student looked at her one last time, then closed his eyes, knowing what was coming. Her brother's boots appeared in her field of vision, and for the next few minutes all she saw were those heavy boots kicking the student over and over again, with such a fierce determination, such an ugly passion for violence that Martha wanted to vomit. Her brother kept kicking even after the student had stopped moving. Martha wanted to scream, "Stop it, Wolfgang. Stop it. What are you doing? This is not you!" But she couldn't. She realized that any feeling of affection for him had evaporated and made space for a new feeling: fear. She was afraid of her own brother—and disgusted with him. This creature had

54

nothing in common with her once-so-loving twin. He had been wholly consumed by the evil of the regime. What she had just witnessed was the ultimate proof.

"Well done," Hänschel praised him. "Let's get the scum out of here."

Martha waited until the sounds of the boots and the bodies had been swallowed by the hallway. And then some more. She was trembling uncontrollably. Her thoughts went to Mother. Did she know what her own son was capable of? She had followed him and his transformation almost blindly. But would she be able to tolerate an act of such violence? Or had she, too, been consumed by the evil? She crawled out of her hiding place and lingered for a moment, plotting her next move. What crime had these students committed that they deserved such inhumane treatment?

She decided to go back to the room where they had been caught.

The door was still open. Cautiously, she entered. Except for a makeshift printing machine, it was empty. She walked over to the machine and saw a tiny corner of a sheet sticking out. Four more were stuck to the back of the paper. Without thinking, she folded them and stuffed them in her bag. She knew what they were: she had recently stumbled upon one of those pamphlets on the Marienplatz. Then she had decided to ignore it. This time she couldn't.

When she reached the corner she had first hidden behind, the light suddenly went off, bathing the hallway in complete darkness. Martha froze. What if they had come with a third man and she hadn't noticed?

For a while nothing happened, so she advanced farther into the darkness, away from the room, trying to recall the number of steps she had taken. When her fingers finally found the corners of the old coal chute, she thought she heard someone breathing, and stopped again. The sound slowly grew stronger, closer. She could almost feel it. She made a sudden turn, her hands stretched out in front of her, determined to grab the person behind her. But there was nothing. Nobody. The breathing had stopped.

She waited, engulfed in darkness, lingering at the same spot. But she was alone.

When she arrived at the Schinkenhubers, Norbert was trying to soothe his wailing twin sisters in the living room. He jumped up when she entered the flat.

"Have your parents returned yet?" she quickly asked.

He shook his head. "No, they're still gone."

Martha hurried to pick up the bag that she had dropped on the floor. She was about to run to her room, when she heard Norbert call after her again. "Are you coming back?" he asked fearfully.

She turned and noticed the tear stains on his cheeks. Looking into the swollen eyes of the boy, she felt a pang of guilt in her chest.

"I'll be back in a second, I promise," she said.

In her room, she carefully removed the pamphlets and pushed them under the mattress. Then she rushed back to the boy, who sank into her arms with relief.

When it was time to put the children to bed, she told them a long story to make up for her absence. This night, she told them the legend of the monster that lived in the big maze of dark hallways underneath Ludwig-Maximilians University, then kissed the children good night and headed to her own bed.

An hour later, she felt Norbert enter the room. She sat up and invited him next to her.

"I was so afraid you wouldn't come back," he whispered to her, and then started to cry. She embraced him and stroked his hair, and he relaxed in her arms. When his cries faded away, Martha noticed that she, too, had been tearing up. She meant security to the boy; he needed her. She hadn't felt needed in a long time. The last person who had given her this feeling was Wolfgang, all those times he had been bullied at school, but that was a very long time ago. Now she was overcome with love for this boy in her arms. But what did she have to offer him? In what kind of world would Norbert and his sisters grow up? And what about herself? Was this worth living for?

When she heard Norbert breathing deeply next to her, Martha gently untangled herself from his tiny arms and tucked him under the blanket. Then she reached under the mattress for the pamphlets. She opened the curtains just enough so she could read them with the help of the full moon. The pamphlets told her everything she always felt. The Nazi regime was evil. Only people with a voice could create a community worth living in. Fascism wasn't the solution, but the end to everything. Martha's mind flickered to the eyes of the students as they were dragged by. Had the male student survived? Where were they now? Were they being tortured? She had felt so helpless. There was nothing she could have done. But was that true? Maybe she could have intervened! She could have pleaded to Wolfgang, to her own flesh and blood, to let them go! But if she had, wouldn't that have meant the end for all of them? That version of Wolfgang would have never helped her! How could Martha possibly pretend that nothing had happened? How could she un-see the bodies, un-hear the whimpers?

She pushed the pamphlets under the mattress again, telling herself that she needed to find a new hiding place for them tomorrow, and got back into bed with Norbert. The boy took her hand in his sleep, squeezing it, reassuring himself that she was still there. But whenever Martha closed her eyes, the pleading eyes of the girl appeared in front of her. And when she finally fell into a restless sleep, they were screaming for Martha's help. And this time she wanted to help, but as much as she tried, her legs wouldn't move. And as hard as she tried to scream at her brother to let them go, no words would come out of her mouth.

Martha woke up with a jolt. What if she was wrong?

Maybe the look in the girl's eyes had not been a plea to save her but a plea for Martha to finish what they'd started. To make their actions count. Someone who had gone that far, taken that kind of risk, would put the well-being of the mission over their own.

She carefully released Norbert's hand, placed a kiss on his cheek, and took out the papers. She snuck out of the room and fetched her jacket before entering the cold night.

As she started to walk in the direction of the university, the cold wind stung her eyes. She closed her jacket tighter, driven by one purpose only: to distribute the papers. She would find the other members of the group and join them.

It was past midnight and the streets were deserted. Martha walked faster, her head down to keep in any heat her body managed to create. She should have kept on the warm trousers she had borrowed from the Schinkenhubers, she thought with regret. Instead, the freezing night now entered through the fabric of her stockings below the coat, numbing them, slowing her down. She had walked little more than half a mile when the bang of a closing door made her look up; she spotted an SS officer who had just exited the pub across the street with other officers.

"Hey, you, what are you doing out here this late at night?" he yelled over at her.

Martha hurried on, pretending she hadn't heard.

"Come over here!" one shouted. Another said something to the group, and they laughed. "Yeah, not too bad."

"Carrying your papers?" one yelled.

She glanced up, nervous. They were like a pack of wolves. Now they crossed the street to their prey. As they came closer, Martha slowly retreated back to the entrance to one of the apartment buildings along the street. She felt behind her for the door, not taking her eyes off them. She wanted to be ready to fight back. And then a hand grabbed her from behind, tightly covering her mouth, and she was quickly pulled through the door. The hand tugged her back farther and eventually let go. Her head made a dull sound as it hit the hard stones of the ground. She tasted blood. She saw Siegfried's threatening face above her.

And then came darkness.

# Maya

## 2017

Maya finally arrived 'at her destination: Bangkok's Khao San Road. She hurried in the direction of the river, greedily taking in Bangkok's infamous street, with its tuk-tuks, shops, restaurants, and nightclubs. Her eyes soaked up the colors, her nose the smells; she imagined the taste of a delicious pad thai being prepared in the busy food stalls on both sides of the road. Everyone seemed to be hurrying away from the river, locals and foreigners. As she brushed past all of them, one woman suddenly caught her attention: she was a traveler, like herself. But while everyone else buzzed around her in a mad rush, hungry for much more than just food, that woman sat still, at a table at one of those stalls, with her backpack resting on the floor against her chair. Maya took a closer look: next to the woman's plate was an open book she seemed to be engrossed in. Maya's heart became heavy. How much she wished she had that liberty, how much she longed to share that woman's experience! She wanted to study her face, see the happiness in it, the type of ecstasy only traveling can gift you with. But she was faceless, like all the others she passed on her journeys.

And then the ground started to shake. Three times in short succession.

She snapped out of it and was instantly teleported back to Germany, to her bookstore in the tiny suburb of Bielefeld, the Google Earth street view of Bangkok spread across her laptop. She hadn't heard the call. Her cell phone was on top of the keyboard; someone had left a voice mail, causing the vibration. She checked and saw that it'd been her father. He never called.

She dialed her voice mail with trembling hands.

"Hello, Maya," her father said. His voice sounded different, not as muffled as usual, not as sedated by his medication. He sounded alert, awake. "I just got a call from the police. They found her."

She was back, knocking at the door that Maya had kept shut so tightly for all those years; Bluebeard's forbidden door, as the folktale goes. It had been the only way to cope with the disappearance of her grandmother: locking her out of her mind—and out of her life. *They found her*, her father's words echoed in her head, triggering the most painful memory, the one she had tried to bury the deepest, sending her back to that rainy day in late summer 1990 when Maya departed for her year abroad—that last moment she had seen her grandmother alive.

At the airport in Munich Maya had been filled with nothing but anger. She despised her grandmother for having pushed her to spend the school year abroad. Maya was too shy, too introverted, her grandmother and father had said. She would make new friends, learn about another culture. It would do her well, they had assured her over and over again, ignoring Maya's pleas to spare her, to let her stay home. Maya had ignored her grandmother on the way to the airport, but when it came time to say goodbye, she was forced to acknowledge her. Maya looked up into those eyes, glistening in a million shades of green, inviting the beholder to linger in them, to search for something hidden beneath their surface. Her grandmother's normally composed face held something different. It seemed as if she were looking straight through Maya, as if miles away, in a different time or place. Then she took a step toward Maya and engulfed her in a tight embrace. "Do for me what I couldn't," she whispered into her ear.

Had Maya known this would be the last time to feel those rough, yet loving hands on her hair, she would not have given in to her anger. After the security check and before they could be swallowed by the bustling crowd hurrying to their gates, her classmates turned around to wave a last goodbye to their loved ones. All except Maya. If she had known, she would have looked back, signaling her grandmother with her eyes that she forgave her.

But that message would never be passed on.

"Maya?"

"Yes."

He sounded relieved to hear her voice. "Her remains have been found."

Maya's hands started to shake, her eyes watered. "Where did they find her?"

"They didn't say."

Her head was spinning.

"Maya, the police want to talk to us."

"When?"

"Tomorrow."

She paused. "I'll be there."

On her way home, Maya passed Michael's house, as she did after every unsuccessful day in her bookstore, which was becoming more frequent than she cared to admit. When Maya first learned of Grandmother's disappearance upon her return from her year in the United States, she was tortured by nightmares of guilt and remorse. It was Michael who had been there for her—when she called him after waking from a bad dream—who had cycled through the dark forest in Perlach in the middle of the night to console her. He'd helped her to move on.

She noticed the light coming from inside the house they

had once shared, and was tempted to stop. Michael had been there for her always, every day, until six months ago.

But she knew she had to learn to live without him.

Maya hadn't been back to Munich in twenty-four years, since she and Michael had moved to Bielefeld—after they had finished their senior year together.

The unusually warm September air filled the cabin as the train door opened upon her arrival in the station. Maya spotted her father standing on the platform and made out relief in his face when he saw her. They hugged quickly and then drove to the police station in silence. Maya had dreaded coming back to the place of her childhood, and the pit in her stomach grew with every corner they turned. Every sight, every smell triggered a different memory: the ice cream parlor next to the Munich Residenz, where Grandmother had taken her on hot summer days, or when the Föhn wind from the Alps had regaled the city with an unexpected raise in temperature, like today; the smell of freshly baked pretzels that wafted over from the bakery into the open car window teleported her back to Grandmother's favorite beer garden, where she had taken Maya for buttered pretzels and Obatzda, Grandmother's favorite Bavarian cheese; Maya's favorite shop where Grandmother, despite her meager salary, had gifted her with expensive dirndl shoes for Oktoberfest.

Maya's eyes filled with tears as the memories played in her mind, and she stared out the window, not wanting her father to share in her grief.

The police chief was a stout man, looking as sober and plain as the gray walls of a German police station. He got up from his chair to shake first Maya's hand and then her father's.

"Thank you for coming in."

He invited them to sit down on the two chairs opposite the desk in his tiny office, and then he plopped down behind it. Maya felt unprepared for what would come next. Until this moment her thoughts had been consumed entirely by the returning memories of Grandmother in life, not leaving any room for the realities of her death. Was she truly ready to learn the truth?

"First of all I'd like to offer my deepest condolences," the police chief said in a consoling voice, the look in his eyes not matching the warm tone of his voice. "I have a couple of questions for you."

He glanced at his screen and placed his hands on the keyboard, ready to type.

"You reported your mother, Martha Wiesberg, missing in October of 1990." He looked to Maya's father, who nodded.

The police officer addressed Maya. "Where were you when your grandmother disappeared?"

Maya shifted uncomfortably. "Can you please tell us first where my grandmother was found? What did she die of? When did she die?"

"I know this is not easy for you. We will get to all of that. But it's important to answer my questions first."

Maya's reluctance to be transported back to that year of her life was almost physical. She pushed her chair as far away from her father's as possible. "I was abroad, on an exchange year in the United States."

"Where in the United States?"

"Tarrytown, in Upstate New York."

He typed again and then studied his screen closely. There was silence in the room. After a while that seemed like an eternity to Maya, he looked up at her. "Your grandmother's remains were found seventy miles north of there."

"In the United States?" Maya almost shouted. The room started to spin; the police officer's mouth opened and closed as he continued to talk, but she didn't hear a word. A thought too painful to bear flickered in her mind: Had she come after Maya?

"A landslide revealed her remains. The northerneastern

64

United States received a lot of rain in early spring, way above average," he added, studying Maya's pale face closely.

"She had already been found in the spring?" This was the second time she was asking a question, and she could feel him already starting to lose patience with her.

He sighed. "This is a rather unusual case. The body was found in a crevice. Stones and mud shut it almost airtight. As a result, more of the body remained than what you'd usually find from one that has been dead for over twenty-five years."

"So she might have died the same year she disappeared?" Maya asked. She barely saw the police officer nodding. The pain in her chest momentarily paralyzed her. Grandmother *had* come after her.

"The police in the United States investigated whether the human body matched any person reported missing within their jurisdiction around the time of death. This can take a while. Simultaneously, the results from the autopsy brought new insights." His voice droned on in Maya's ears. "And among them a small, seemingly insignificant detail was discovered: the label that had survived in a piece of cloth from the underwear. It was from Schiesser. So they traced the brand to Germany, and then the local police most certainly would have already sent the case to ViCAP, and..."

"What is ViCAP?" She heard her father speak for the first time at the station.

"ViCAP is short for Violent Criminal Apprehension Program." He stressed the first letter of each word. "It was created by the FBI. The program is a database of the biggest violent-crimes cases."

"FBI? Violent-crime cases?" Maya heard her father call out next to her, aghast.

"Including those cases that involve unidentified human remains" the officer continued, ignoring her father's comment. "So when the local results came in negative, it was sent on to INTERPOL. And INTERPOL found in their records that your grandmother had been reported missing.

And that is when we called you and asked you for a swab—and the laboratory called me yesterday to confirm that it was positive."

Maya sat upright. She spun her head toward her father.

"You knew already?"

Her father looked away.

"Why didn't you call me?" She was shaking, trying hard to suppress her anger.

"I didn't want to bother you."

"You didn't want to *bother* me?" She was shouting now. "Just like you didn't want to bother me back then?"

"Maya, we both know you would have come back home immediately if I had told you. It was for your own good."

Maya jumped up from her chair. She wanted to be out of there, away from her father. She had never forgiven him since the day in 1991 when she'd returned to Germany to find out that Grandmother had disappeared more than eleven months before.

"Of course, I would have come back if you had told me! She was like a mother to me!"

"Please, Maya, I did apologize several times."

"At least this time you should have told it to me straight!"

"It could have been a false alarm. It was a long shot! For Christ sake!" He looked over at the officer, silently asking him for help.

Maya glanced back and forth between the two. The officer was holding up his hand.

"Please, I know this is extremely difficult for both of you. Can you please sit down again, Miss Wiesberg?"

Maya lowered herself back into the chair. The police officer returned to his screen. The only noise that filled the tiny office space was the *clack-clack* of the keyboard as he typed away.

"Where exactly was she found?" Maya finally asked.

He looked at Maya, somewhat puzzled. "I don't know how this information would be of any use to you."

Maya caught sight of a frame on the desk showing a beautiful family of six on the first day of Oktoberfest, all smiling merrily into the camera. "I have this funny hobby, I..." She stuttered, having a hard time finding the right words. "I'm scared of flying — aviophobia. So instead, I go on virtual journeys, so to speak. On Google Earth, and if you told me the name," the tears she had been trying to hold back erupted, "if you told me where she went, I could follow her last footsteps virtually, maybe understand better why she abandoned me. Please?"

He eyed her for a second too long. "Then how did you get to the United States in 1990?"

"I only developed my aviophobia afterward."

He leaned back in his chair, appearing to be contemplating her explanation, and she was pleasantly surprised when he continued.

"It's called Montgomery Preserve. It's a popular weekend getaway for people from New York City."

He rose from his chair. Maya and her father followed. "This should be all for now."

"You didn't mention how she died." Maya took one of the cards that he handed them and looked up.

"We don't know yet." He pointed to the card. "We should know as soon as the investigation has been completed, and we'll notify you then."


Her father still lived in the forest in Perlach. She saw Grandmother everywhere in the house: in the doorway greeting Maya after school, on the sofa reading books to Maya, in the armchair looking up from her crossword puzzle, smiling at her in the kitchen while cooking Maya dinner. She had always been there for her — until she'd left forever.

Maya excused herself and went up to her childhood bedroom, the same room that Grandmother had once shared with her twin brother. Her father hadn't changed anything in the room since Maya had left home, the moment she was old enough to do so. The same *Wizard of Oz* poster still hung on the wall. L. Frank Baum's work always held a special place in Grandmother's heart, so special that Maya's middle name was Dorothy. She fell onto the four-poster bed and remembered Grandmother sitting down at the bed one night when she had found Maya crying.

"What ails you, *mein Engel*?" she had asked.

It was her classmates at school, Maya had told Grandmother, choking out the words between sobs.

Grandmother gently took Maya's chin and moved her face toward hers. "They don't like me," Maya explained.

"I know that feeling," Grandmother said. "But sometimes not being like them is better than to be liked by them. That is what makes you so special."

Then she rocked Maya to sleep.

Maya snapped out of the memory as she became aware of something she hadn't realized in all these years: she didn't feel much differently now. There was a disconnect—with her father, with Michael, with Michael's friends. She had never felt that way with Grandmother. *How much I wish you were still here, with me.* She let her eyes glide through a room that she hadn't entered in over twenty years, and they caught a photo of Grandmother on one of the empty bookshelves. Maya had left it behind when she'd moved out, like so many other reminders of Grandmother.

She walked over and picked up the frame. Grandmother was around Maya's age, and the resemblance was striking, as if she were looking at a photo of herself in a different time. Grandmother too had been a woman trapped, in the past, in a secret that weighed her down.

Except when she was in the dark forest.

Maya tiptoed down the stairs but realized there was no need. Her father had already gone to bed. She grabbed her jacket and left the house.

The dark forest greeted her like a long lost friend, welcoming her back into its midst, and she started to walk with confidence. As if guided by invisible hands, she left the main path and stopped to take off her shoes—something Grandmother and she had always done when entering the dense part of the forest, feeling the soft ground under their soles. She had to slow down as she hiked up an incline, squeezing past newly grown branches, breathing in the scent of the needles around her. She recognized those trees that had served as points of orientation.

She still knew the way to the "happy spot," even all these years later. When she arrived at her destination Maya took a big breath. The clearing almost looked the same as it had twenty-seven years ago. Seeing the two birches on one side of the clearing triggered the memory of Grandmother tying a hammock between the trees. On the opposite side stood an old oak tree, with a stump—once another oak tree—in front of it. They had used it as a table when they brought a picnic to the clearing. And each time they had come here, Grandmother had told her stories. She had been a composed person, rational, practical, controlled, never showing emotions too openly, but whenever they had come here for story time, Grandmother would become a different person. Watching Grandmother's face transform, seeing her let go, was all Maya needed to be embraced by that same glow of happiness.

"I spent the best hours of my life here at this spot. It's magical, isn't it?" she had once told Maya. "You can always come here, *mein Engel*, when you're sad."

And Maya had. Until Grandmother had disappeared.

Maya sat down by the big oak tree on one corner of the clearing, and let her fingers glide over the bark. Then she remembered something, and reached farther behind it, continuing with her hands on the wooden surface. She smiled. The initials that someone had carved into the tree a long time ago were still there, as if no time had gone by at all.

"Today I will tell you a fairy tale, *mein Engel*," Grandmother had said, pointing out the initials to her for the first time.

Maya lay down on the forest soil, imagining she was in Grandmother's lap again, looking up into the treetops. The wind rattled the trees around her, tussling her hair, and it felt as if Grandmother's hands were caressing Maya's head. Maya became the nine-year-old girl again, and she couldn't help but feel excited.

"Once upon a time there were two people who knew this fairy tale. Now there is only me, Maya. And I will pass it on to you. It will be yours, and yours alone, to treasure. It is called 'The War Fairy.'"

# THE WAR FAIRY

In a different world, far away from ours, exists a parallel world in which our times are realms: the Past, the Present, and the Future. These three realms coexist in perfect harmony: every realm needs the other to live, to maintain balance.

Of the three realms, the Present is the only one inhabited by humans. Tiny beings called the "memories," good and bad memories, dwell in the Past. The balance between the good and the bad memories is shifting constantly: sometimes the bad memories prevail over the good ones, and then the humans become angry, bitter, and sad. When the good ones triumph, the humans are happy, serene, and joyful. And this greatly afects the realm of the Future, where the angels and the demons live. When the bad memories prevail, then the humans produce something called "fear," which the demons in the Future feed upon. If the good memories prevail, the humans produce the angel's life elixir, hope. This helps the angels keep the demons at bay.

Of all the three realms, the Present is the strongest, and the humans are the only creatures who can produce LOVE. And the more LOVE they produce, the more light and beauty there will be in the realm.

And as long as everyone remains in their realm, the balance is held and all is well in the world.

But one day, a shift happens in the Present. A young and beautiful woman named Floda starts feeding the humans new thoughts: Why not go for a bigger territory, more land that we can fill with the riches we produce with LOVE? The good memories are all the humans need to produce LOVE! Let's invade and take over the Past's territory, she preaches to them. Let's kill the bad memories and enslave the good ones so we will produce more LOVE, and we will have more territory to fill with our riches that we produce with LOVE!

The initially suspicious humans get increasingly excited and declare Floda their new leader. But Lila, the teacher of LOVE, warns everyone: you are mistaking greed for LOVE. When Floda finds out about her actions, she is furious and imprisons Lila in the new prison, where Lila now waits for her trial for high treason.

The Imaginations are tiny elflike messengers who are the only beings that can move between the realms without upsetting the balance. They are the only ones besides Lila who see the impending doom for the humans. So they offer to help Lila escape to the Past, where she can be safe for now. Lila is grateful for their offer, and they leave immediately. The Imaginations and Lila have barely made it out of the Present when Floda declares war on the Past.

But the memories come prepared: they create a deep swamp running alongside the border in the Past. It swallows the first row of brave soldiers from the Present who fall into the deadly swamp—and to their death.

Floda watches from the Present, a devilish smile on her face. Then she leaves for the Past—but not without checking on Lila first. And when she sees her gone, her smile gets broader. Yes, everything goes according to plan.

While the Present wages a losing war with the Past, the humans in the Present stop being happy—the warfare keeps the memories busy—and they stop producing LOVE.

At first the humans become very sick, and then they start to lose their senses and, last but not least, their faces. The oncesopowerful Present becomes a place of darkness filled with faceless, mindless humans.

In the Future, Floda goes up to the demon king. He is

shocked to see a human in his realm and threatens to kill her. But then she shares her master plan with him: the only human to survive with a pure soul, a face, all senses, and a working mind, is Lila—who has fled to the Past. With a human in their midst, the balance in the Past has gotten out of control, and the memories will soon start waging war with each other. The humans have lost their power, so they can be enslaved and forced to produce the demon's life elixir: fear. Then the alreadyweakened angels will all die. So, if the demon king and Floda join forces, they can rule over all three realms. He nods. "True, but you will cause an imbalance if you stay here," he says to her. Now her moment has arrived. She has always despised the humans and admired the demons. "Not if you make me one of yours," she says, with her devilish grin. And he readily agrees.

Lila is hiding in a clearing at the lake in the sky, a place sacred to the memories. She feels defeated in her mission to spread LOVE and cries herself to sleep every night. One day a young creature—a bad memory—follows the unfamiliar smell of tears, all the way to the clearing. It discovers the teacher of LOVE, and Lila then fears that the little creature will tell on her. But it doesn't. Instead, it comes back every day and Lila starts teaching it lessons of LOVE. And after a while, it starts to feel lonely—something it has never felt before. So one day, on its way to Lila's secret hiding place, it finds another creature, one from the other tribe: a good memory. They aren't supposed to mingle. But it turns out that the good memory is as sad as the bad one, because it, too, feels lonely. So the bad memory tells the good one to join it. As predicted by Floda, the good and bad memories start waging war after winning the war with the Present. So one day the two creatures decide to tell Lila about the war in their realm and for her advice. How can they end it? Lila is shocked to hear this news, for she knows she is the one causing the imbalance. At the end of this session, Lila bids them goodbye, with the promise that a change for the better will come very soon...

When the creatures return the next morning to the clearing for their LOVE lessons with Lila, they find her drowned in the lake! The two memories are devastated and comfort each other in their grief. This is when they realize that they have fallen in LOVE. And they start practicing something that Lila had often spoken about: the act of making LOVE. And in doing so, they create a product of LOVE. What to call it? They look at the tiny creature, a mixture of the two; they cannot name it after either of their tribes. So they call the little one LOVE.

They alert the Imaginations and they come immediately. They are shocked to hear about Lila's death, but they are ecstatic about LOVE: this is the sign they have hoped for! So together they decide to spread the word of LOVE, the parents in the Past and the Imaginations in the Present and Future.

Mother and Father memories go to their respective tribes with the good news. But instead of welcoming the news, the news kindles the war between the tribes even further, because each side wants LOVE to be one of theirs.

When the Imaginations enter the Present, they realize that it is now in the hands of the demons and that the mindless humans pose a serious threat to the Imaginations. Once, the Imaginations were their best friends; now, the humans seek to kill them. So the Imaginations decide to journey onward to the Future and are equally shocked: thousands of enslaved humans are subjected to fear-inducing treatments, feeding their rulers, the demons, with an endless stream of fear. Quickly the Imaginations decide to retreat—but too late. They are captured and thrown into a dark tower, for all eternity.

After many failed attempts, the demon queen Floda finally gives birth to a healthy son, after numerous ofspring were stillborn. But instead of a celebration, the child is added to the mix of prisoners in the dark tower, accompanied by the angry screams of the demon king: the child is a creature, half demon, half human, with no face. Floda appears at the prison door, trying to save her child. But she is dragged away by her hair, back to the castle, to produce an ofspring that the demon king will consider fit for an heir.

The Imaginations care for the newborn prince — a difficult task, for he combines the elements of a demon and a human of impure heart. He has no face, but feels emotions, constantly battling between good and evil. As he grows up, they teach him all about the time when the realms were perfectly in balance. And then the day has arrived to finally tell him about LOVE, who lives in a realm far, far away, in a secret hiding place. "What is LOVE? Is it a beautiful princess?" he asks the Imaginations. The Imaginations smile. "It is whatever you want it to be." They teach him to feed as much as he can on the fear of his demonic side, without giving in to the dark side of his mind. "But how will I see? I have no face!" he exclaims. "We will be your face," the Imaginations assure him.

So one night, when the demon king rapes the now heart-broken Floda again, hoping to produce a healthy demon child, the Imaginations manage to escape, smuggling the unwanted prince out of the Future.

When they cross the Present on their way back to the Past, the prince shivers. "What is this place?" "This is the Present!" the Imaginations explain, "the place your mother is from." "It feels so cold, so sad" the blind prince says. "You described it so diferently to me!" "It was your mother who changed it into this." "Why would she do this?" The Imaginations smile, knowing that their teachings bore fruit in their foster son. At that moment, someone appears from the darkness: an angel of hope, approaching them cautiously. "Who is this creature?" the angel asks the Imaginations. "I am the child of the demon king and Queen Floda!" The boy exclaims. Hearing this frightens the angel of hope, and it is about to return to the darkness, when the Imaginations call the angel back. "Don't be afraid," they say. And they tell the angel about LOVE. "But don't you know LOVE has been imprisoned by DEATH and taken to his cemetery of dead memories and broken dreams?" it asks fearfully. The Imaginations shake their heads. "No, but this doesn't change the plan," they comment. "Can you go into the cemetery with me?" the boy asks the Imaginations. But the Imaginations decline, sadly. "Then I cannot do this, for you are all that I have left!" the boy shouts. They take the boy softly under their wings, consoling him: "If our realms remain like this, then we have no reason to exist. This is the price we have been destined to pay. Let us guide you to your final destination," they plead with him. "Let me accompany you!" the angel of hope declares. It almost starved itself to death by storing as much hope in it as possible, but it now knows the day has arrived that it saved it for!

The war between the memories has worsened; the Past is hardly recognizable. Here, as in the Present, darkness has descended over the oncesobeautiful sphere. While traveling through the warring land, many Imaginations have died, giving their life for the prince. The angel of hope grows weaker and weaker. And there are moments when the demonic side of the child resurfaces, and it engages in the war, enjoying the killing. In these moments, the angel feeds him a bit of hope, carefully keeping enough for later.

When they finally arrive at the cemetery of dead memories and broken dreams, the size of the group has dwindled to nearly nothing.

DEATH guards the cemetery more fiercely than ever. But the remaining Imaginations trick DEATH, offering them-selves to him, distracting him with their generous offer. This gives the angel and the prince a moment to enter unnoticed. All of the remaining Imaginations die. The boy is devastated; tears are running down the place where his face should be. This is the moment when the angel does its work: with the hope stored in it, the angel creates a beautiful face; it gives the prince the most stunning eyes the realms have ever seen. Their warmth glows brightly, lighting their way through the dark cemetery, so brightly that it blinds DEATH, who has come after them and who now wanders aimlessly out in to the Past. The angel holds the boy back by the arm. It is hardly breathing. "From this point on, I cannot go," it says. "But without you, I am all alone!" he screams, the tears glistening in his beautiful eyes. "You are the one who carries the burden that will restore the balance in this world," the angel explains. "How?" The boy feels helpless. "You must learn to let go of everything else and focus on finding LOVE!" the angel explains to him. "But why can't you come with me?" The boy asks desperately. The angel smiles: "Though I am dying, hope itself always dies last."

And then the angel closes its angelic eyes forever.

For the first time in his life, the boy understands what loneliness means. So the boy begins his search for LOVE. And when he finally finds her, he forgets about loneliness, about his grief, about his demonic side. And all he sees is LOVE, the most beautiful and real thing he has ever seen in his entire life.

Together they travel to the Present, to restore what his mother destroyed. And so begins a new era: the war suddenly ends in the Past. With LOVE gone they have no more reason to fight. It is as if both sides suddenly come to their senses. "Why are we doing this? Why are we harming ourselves?" they cry. In the Present, the faces magically reappear on the humans, and the humans are once again happy, content, and joyful, producing a neverending stream of hope, which creates a new breed of angels in the Future, a species so strong that it will never, ever be able to be harmed by anyone. And the demons, along with the king and his ugly queen, are locked away in the Past, in the cemetery of lost memories and broken dreams, where they still live today, their only music the screams of the oncesobeautiful Floda, as she is raped by the demon king, trying to produce a new ruler. And when you are very, very still, late at night, you can hear her screams—an everlasting testament that greed will not bring you to the promised land. And that fear is not stronger than LOVE.

And last of all: the boy and LOVE decide to once and for all reunite Past, Present, and Future, to ensure something like this will never happen again—and all, save for the demons, live happily ever after.

Maya woke up with a horrible pain in her back. The cold soil of the clearing had replaced Grandmother's warm lap, and she had trouble sitting up. The harsh smell of skunk had replaced the sweet pine scent in the forest. It was time to go.

She returned to her childhood room and took her iPad to the bed. In Google Earth, she typed in "Montgomery Preserve Resort." For the first time since she developed her habit, she felt tense. She was about to enter the place, albeit virtually, where Grandmother had spent the last days of her life. She clicked on "street view," and several blue dots popped up. She noticed her hand shaking when she clicked on the first one, a 360-degree view of the hotel at the heart of the Montgomery Preserve. She was sure that J. K. Rowling had pictured something similar for Hogwarts. The hotel was embedded in a high plateau, called the Shawangunk Ridge, of a mountain range that stretched for about twelve miles. The hotel wasn't tall but wide, and was an eclectic potpourri of different architectural styles, seemingly applied and added to the core building over the years, a mix of wood, stone, and dark mahogany. Toward one side, the building loomed proudly over the valley; toward its other side, it threw long shadows over a lake framed by high crevices and rock formations. The water was of the deepest grey, only a couple of shades shy of black, hinting at an immense depth. Maya felt faces behind the opaque windows of the hotel, studying her, unsettling her. She quickly clicked on one of the other dots, which took her into the heart of the woods. Maya shifted nervously on her chair. The forest was dark, foreboding. She remembered the officer's words: *A landslide revealed her remains... in early spring*. Grandmother had not been particularly fond of hiking. In fact, she'd spent her whole life living at the foot of the Alps, yet had never visited. *What were you doing there? Did you come for me?* Maya squinted, looking closer at the dense foliage, half expecting to find the answer there. She felt goose bumps on her arms. There was something magical yet sinister about this place. *Why here?* She again looked at Grandmother in the photo. But Grandmother remained silent.

The house was still when she came down in the morning. Her father hardly ever left, and she knew where she'd find him: in the basement, dwarfed against mountains of papers. He had developed certain neuroses in his life; becoming a compulsive hoarder was one of them. He was incapable of parting ways with certain objects, mostly papers. He gathered and picked up papers of all kinds, such as receipts, wrappers, bills, bank forms.

"I'm not hungry," he said while reluctantly following Maya up the stairs for the breakfast she had prepared.

"You know what Grandma said to me when she took me to the airport back then?" Maya said after a while. "'Do for me what I couldn't' — that's what she said. For the longest time I thought she had been referring to traveling, but now it turns out she herself had left, so she couldn't have meant that. What do you think she meant?"

Surprise showed on his face. "I don't know, Maya. Why brood over that now?" He sounded slightly irritated.

She furrowed her eyebrows. "I'm not."

A painful silence followed.

"Grandma always told me this fairy tale, in which past, present, and future aren't times, but actual places. And..."

Her father looked up from his plate. "'The War Fairy.'"

"You know it?"

He nodded his head.

Maya's disappointment momentarily overshadowed all

other sensations she had experienced in the past couple of days. She felt a sense of entitlement over this story. Grandmother had said it was theirs, and theirs alone. Because Maya was special! How could Grandmother have lied? "I was such a troubled child, Maya." Her father studied her face, carefully choosing his next words. "I... was mad at her. Often. For leaving me alone with your great-grandmother all the time. Mother had no other choice, I know that now, but as a child... And on those rare occasions that she had time to spend with me, she went with me to the clearing. And turned into a different person. She became... I don't know—happy, I guess. But I didn't want her to be happy. I wanted her to be sad, like me."

"This is the first time you've told me about your childhood," Maya said, more to herself than to him.

He shrugged his shoulders. "You never asked." He got up and started gathering the plates but paused abruptly as if trying to convince himself of his next step. "Listen, Maya, I just try not to think too much about the past, that's all."

"Well, that's done wonders for you, hasn't it?" She regretted the words the second they were out.

He put the plates down on the table with a bang and turned to her. "What about you, then?"

"What about me?" she said defensively.

"Where is this sudden interest coming from?"

Maya shook her head. She started picking nervously at a paper napkin, not used to the personal nature of their conversation.

"Do you think it was easy for me when she disappeared?" he said. "And whenever I wanted to talk to you about her, you shut off. You did everything to forget the past, to erase it completely!" His voice had risen to an angry shout that seemed to surprise even him. "Maya, you cannot erase nor change the past. I've learned this the hard way. And I know you well, even though you think I don't. When you bite your teeth into something, you are like a dog with a bone.

Since she disappeared you did everything to ignore she ever existed. Why?"

"I'm so afraid that she..." — Maya swallowed and took a deep breath — "...that she came after me."

Back at home in Bielefeld the next morning, her bookstore greeted her like a long lost friend. Maya inhaled the smell of books. A new delivery had come in, but instead of unpacking, she walked over to the children's section and picked out an annotated copy of *The Wizard of Oz*, with beautiful illustrations inside. She opened it randomly and flipped through for the page where Dorothy says her famous line: *There's no place like home.* She had never felt the ambiguity of this sentence before. What if a place like home didn't exist? What if that cheesy saying was true, *Home is where the heart is?* And if it was, then hadn't she lost her home the minute Michael had left? His final words during the break up still echoed in her ears.

"I am not making you happy, Maya. You always seem dissatisfied, like, like..." He seemed to have searched so hard for the right words. "Like you feel you don't fit here. Like you don't fit in our life." She had thought about Grandmother that moment, that even in all her years she had never felt like she fit.

She looked outside the window, at the people passing by under a gray sky. What was she still doing in a city that no longer meant the safe haven it once did, sheltered from Munich, her father, the memories of Grandmother? Her bookstore was her only link to a place that suddenly seemed as strange to her as the first day she set foot here.

She scanned the long rows of books, all the stories about faraway places that she had surrounded herself with for so long. The wanderlust. That had been something else Maya and Grandmother had in common — in addition to their insatiable lust for stories. And neither she nor Grandmother had been able to still that yearning. "Reading, *mein Engel,* is the closest to traveling out there," Grandmother had always said to Maya.

Maya spent more and more time in her store. Back in Munich she had dug up Grandmother's books and brought them here, where she was rereading them now. She tried to feel as close to her as in the clearing in Perlach, but the novels, too, kept quiet. Grandmother had never volunteered any information about her life before the birth of Maya's father, and only little about the time when her father was a child.

Frustrated, Maya opened her laptop and revisited the Montgomery Preserve, looking for a clue, an answer to the question that was replaying in her head, again and again: *Did you come after me?*

There was a knock at the door. Maya checked her watch and was surprised to note that it was almost ten o'clock. When she came out of the stacks she saw his blond head and broad shoulders through the glass. Michael. Her heart skipped a beat. She hurried over to open the door for him.

"I heard the news from your father," he said. "I'm so sorry."

He stepped closer and welcomed her into his arms. The scent of his aftershave was as familiar as the smell of the books in her store. She felt the muscle under the sleeves of his shirt, the tips of his freshly washed hair on her bare shoulders.

"I went and looked for you at your place every evening this week after my training sessions," he said after they ended the embrace.

"I stay here late," she said and looked around her store.

Michael's eyes caught the open novels behind her on the desk. A love for books had never been something they had in common.

He smiled warmly at her. "I thought I could take your mind off things and take you to L'Osteria?"

Their Italian restaurant for special occasions. Maya

paused. She had driven by his place every night since her trip to Munich, longing to be with him. Now he had come to her when she needed him more than ever.

And yet there was something holding her back.

"Or somewhere else? What would make you happy?" he asked, noticing her hesitation.

*What* would *make me happy?* Maya thought. Again, Michael's words during the breakup came back to her. *You always seem dissatisfied, like you don't fit here.* She asked herself for the first time: *What if he'd been right?* And then it came to her.

"I think I need to go there." "To L'Osteria?"

"To the place where she died."

"And how will you get there? By boat?"

"No, by plane. I know I can beat my aviophobia. I need to see, smell, touch the place my grandmother spent the last days of her life, Michael. Find out why she went there. Seventy miles north from where I spent my year abroad! What if she followed me, maybe..."

"Let me come with you," he interrupted her, his voice strong and steady. She was momentarily taken aback by his offer. Michael had never expressed any desire to travel. He'd barely missed a single training session or tournament and stuck to his schedule religiously. To break out of this routine was big for Michael.

The way he looked at her—she suddenly realized that he had invited her to much more than just dinner at their special restaurant: he was inviting her back into his life.

"You'll see everything in a new light. You'll gain distance. And when you come back, you'll be able to concentrate on your store again, on your life here. You won't need to go on these virtual trips anymore." He smiled weakly at his attempt at a joke. When he started to speak again, his voice broke off and he had to swallow before continuing. "And everything can be the way it used to be. You can have your old life back, knowing what's out there."

Did she want her old life back with him? The thought struck her hard. His eyes didn't leave hers. Try it, accept it, she told herself, give him—and yourself—a second chance.

"Thank you," she finally said, and smiled back for the first time. "But I can't go with you, Michael. I need to do this myself."

# Maya

## Day 1

Maya was completely and utterly lost, cursing herself under her breath. The battery of her smartphone had let her down shortly after exiting the highway in New Paltz. Now she was driving with no sense of direction or clue about how to get to her final destination. She was tired—from the trip and the time difference—but more than anything else from her battle with aviophobia. Ultimately, she had won, otherwise she wouldn't be here, and still she felt anything but a winner. She had panicked on the runway, but the flight attendant and a good dose of red wine had helped her—and Grandmother, she smiled sadly. The rolling hills in front of Maya accepted her in their midst, proudly flaunting their colorful Indian-summer dress, then disorienting her as they closed in around her. How had Grandmother arrived here? Maya had passed a bus stop when she'd left the highway, but as far as she could tell there was no public transport beyond the station. Grandmother didn't have a driver's license. Or was that something else that she had kept secret from Maya?

She passed an old deserted gateway house with a beautiful alley of trees leading up to the hills in the distance. There wasn't a single soul in sight whom she could ask for directions, and she wouldn't even know how to get back to the village she had passed through after exiting the highway. So she kept on driving aimlessly along the country roads. There was something serene to this part of the world, cut off from the present. After miles she finally arrived at a T-junction, and turned left. A sign told her that she had arrived in Stone Ridge. The tiny town, or more of a hamlet judging from its size, consisted of a handful of establishments scattered along the main thoroughfare for two blocks. She passed a petrol station, an antique store, a bagel place, an Asian restaurant, a real estate office—and a library. She stopped the car abruptly and made a sharp turn into the parking lot.

A sign over the entrance of the old stone building read "Stone Ridge Library." She had to push hard to open the door, which seemed to be slightly stuck against the stone ground. A familiar scent began to drift through the crack of the door: the smell of old books. Once the door gave way, the scent completely enveloped her, welcoming her home the same way her bookstore always did, even halfway across the world, on the other side of the ocean.

The counter was unattended, so Maya ventured farther into the building. "Hello?" she called into the library. She started to wander around. The low ceilings lent the place a cozy feeling. The old wooden planks squeaked under her weight as she walked from room to room. Each room had a fireplace and a set of comfortable wing chairs. She looked at the rows of books in front of her, and a smile spread over her face. For the first time since she'd arrived in the United States, she felt at ease.

"We're about to close for the day," a voice behind her said, making her jump. She turned as a short, red-haired librarian emerged from one of the stacks.

"I'm so sorry to disturb you. I won't keep you long. I got completely lost. Could you tell me the way to Montgomery Preserve?"

A smile showed on the woman's face. "Sure, come with me. I'll draw you a map."

Maya followed her back to the counter.

"You don't get these questions often anymore, for directions, in times of iPhones and the like," she was saying as she strutted through the rooms.

"I know. I just flew in from Germany, but my phone died."

"From Germany? We get a lot of international tourists here, especially during the Indian summer. All on tour through the States. Where are you going after this?"

"No, just here," Maya half-whispered.

The librarian stopped and turned around. Maya had focused so hard on finding her way to the resort that she hadn't thought about Grandmother's death for a while. Now she was overcome with sadness again.

The librarian studied her, as if inviting her to say more. "I came here for my grandmother. She died here."

"I'm so sorry to hear that. A funeral is never a nice reason to travel."

"No, she actually died here a long time ago. But her remains were found this spring. In the Montgomery Preserve."

The woman's eyebrows shot up. "The remains they found in the landslide were your grandmother's?"

Maya had to swallow a lump in her throat, and simply nodded instead. The woman's eyes lingered on Maya. "I'll grab you a pen and paper. Maybe you'd like to familiarize yourself with the area?" She pointed at a table in the corner where several books were on display.

Maya followed her suggestion more out of courtesy than interest, and randomly picked a book from its holder without regard for the title. It was about the origins and history of the Shawangunks, the mountain range where the Montgomery Resort was situated. She closed it to study the front and recognized the impressive building on the cover.

"It's a fascinating place, isn't it?"

Maya turned to address the librarian, who pointed at Montgomery Resort on the cover. "This is one of the main reasons why people come here," she said with a smile. Then she held out a thin booklet to Maya. It had a simple green cover and looked like a self-published book of sorts. "You strike me as someone who appreciates good books."

Maya took the book: *The Spirit of Montgomery.* The thick layer of dust on the cover told Maya it hadn't been dug out for a long time.

"It's a historical guide." The librarian sounded chipper now. "It's much better than the others, a good one to read in front of the fire place at Montgomery. You can borrow it and bring it back before you leave if you'd like."

"Thank you." Maya accepted it and dropped it in her bag. Maybe it was written by someone close to the librarian, family or a friend, and she didn't want to offend her by declining the offer.

"Come with me up front; I'll draw you the map."

Maya followed her to the circulation desk.

"Now, it is quite easy to find your way from here, when you leave the driveway you turn right, on to Route 209, then turn left, on to Route 213, that takes you over a bridge into High Falls, and you turn right after you'll see a café called The Kitchenette on your right. Then follow this road all the way up the mountain, and you'll see the entry on your right." Her hands were shaking as she sketched the map.

Maya accepted the map, and the librarian led her back to the entrance.

Maya was about to exit when the librarian held her back by the arm.

"My name is Paula. If you need any help I'm here."

Maya followed the map and turned right at a sign that proclaimed *MONTGOMERY RESORT AND PRESERVE, 12 MILES.* The woods along the steadily ascending road became denser but suddenly opened up when the road curved hairpin-style. A kingdom of colors unfolded before her, with the Catskill Mountains and their rolling hills in the background, stretching as far as the eye could see.

She almost missed the next sign, a wooden one pointing

to Montgomery Resort and Preserve. Maya made a sharp right turn, immediately coming to a gate. She rolled down her window. Someone who looked like a park ranger opened the window of his little booth.

"What brings you to Montgomery Preserve, ma'am?"

"I'm staying at the resort."

It was only a split second but she saw it: he quickly checked the type of rental car.

"If you just want to hike here, it's gonna cost you twenty-one dollars for the day, which also gives you entrance to the other parts of the national preserve."

"I thought this was the entrance to the hotel?"

"Ma'am, this is also a national preserve, and yes, the hotel is in it. But I'd need to see some kind of proof that you indeed are staying at the hotel." She produced her reservation. When he handed the paper back to her, he gave her an apologetic look.

"Sorry, ma'am. Many people try to enter the premises under the pretext of being guests. I'm sure you'll have a great stay. Have a nice day."

She couldn't really blame the ranger for his initial reaction. What she paid for five nights would have easily covered a month of rent for her bookstore—and she couldn't afford it. But she had decided that she needed to stay close to where Grandmother was found. And she had to admit that this place had made her curious. The more she had read up about it the more intrigued she had become. It was not only at the center of the national preserve, it was its heart. Every single hiking trail originated behind the hotel. Grandmother, too, must have passed it. Or maybe even stayed here, although Maya found it hard to imagine that Grandmother would have spent that much on a hotel.

A dirt road zigzagged its way up through a dark forest, the green of the trees muted to black by the dense canopy. Maya followed more signs to the hotel. *Had Grandmother driven up this same road?* Maya thought as she made another right turn after a good half a mile past the entrance to the preserve. Or had she walked up? One last curve and there it was: the Montgomery Resort, standing tall above the dark forest she had just traversed. Maya caught her breath: seeing this place for real almost felt surreal. The building itself was much bigger than she had expected, in every sense. It loomed high above her as she slowed down the car, as if expecting her arrival. A zealous bellboy came running over to her car at the generous entrance, two oaken doors framing colorful glass, and pushed a number into her hand.

"Welcome to the Montgomery!"

Maya got out of the car and entered the hotel. She lined up behind a couple of guests at the check-in counter, studying the lobby as she was waiting for her turn. The floor, the walls, and the ceiling—everything in the lobby—was covered in expensive mahogany wood, lending it a cozy, but also dark feel.

Maya stepped forward when her turn arrived, handing her passport to the receptionist. "Miss Wiesberg." The friendly girl at the reception desk beamed at Maya. "It's an honor to have you as our guest here at Montgomery. I've reserved you an especially nice room, one of our best! All our rooms come with a fireplace, which at night can come in handy here. But of course, you don't *have* to use it—just if you want to. You can always call us any time if you need help with kindling the fire. We serve dinner starting at six over there." She pointed to an elegant hall behind Maya. "And if you need any tips for hikes, please don't hesitate to ask us."

Maya followed another bellboy through the hallways. The place was teeming with history and character. Photos of prominent guests, along with paintings from different eras, lined the walls left and right. The hotel must have had more than two hundred rooms, the hallways' seemingly infinite, dark wood stretching like the bowels of a cruise ship.

The receptionist had not exaggerated: the room they entered was gorgeous; the furniture and decor was all Victorian. To her right stood a four-poster bed. The fireplace was closer to the bedhead, the wood in the fireplace neatly arranged for immediate use. In front of the huge window two armchairs and a table offered a rest with an incredible view of the lake beneath. The wallpaper matched the curtains, sporting a tasteful design reflecting the era from which the furniture originated. Framed pictures featured black-and-white photos of the view throughout different seasons of the year, and colorful ones of the view in autumn. She pressed a five-dollar bill into the bellboy's hands and approached the window, soaking in the view of the sun setting over the lake, the magic hour intensifying the colorful splendor of the landscape. She could see guests coming back from hikes, a couple walking hand in hand, blissful smiles on their faces, taking pictures of the autumn leaves. She pictured herself with Michael here, had she accepted his offer. Would they have been as happy as these hikers?

After showering and changing, Maya approached the front desk in the lobby. The same receptionist stood guard and smiled when she saw her.

"Everything to your liking, Ms. Wiesberg?"

"Yes, the room is beautiful. Thank you. Can I get those hiking tips you mentioned?"

"Of course! These woods are amazing! Let me grab you a map."

She unfolded a map of the hiking trails. "This one here is especially beautiful for a start." She drew a line with her pen. "And this one is..."

"I heard there was a landslide here in the spring?" Maya interrupted her.

The receptionist stopped and looked up. "Oh, yes, we had terrible rains here."

"Where did it happen?" Maya nodded at the map, hoping she would point it out.

"Deep in the woods."

"Was anyone hurt?" Maya asked cautiously, frustrated that the receptionist hadn't taken her bait.

"It happened far away from any of our hiking trails, thank God." Then she hesitated and lowered her voice: "But they did find the remains of a body in the landslide."

"Wow," Maya said, pretending to be awed.

"I still wonder what a hiker was doing that far off the beaten tracks." She shook her head, as if to reinforce her words, and reverted to the map. But before continuing to draw, she looked up at Maya again. "Why are you asking about it?"

Maya hesitated. She could tell her the truth, just like she had told the librarian, but decided against it. "I'm a writer."

"Oh, wow! Fantastic! What kind of books do you write?"

Maya felt self-confidence consume her when she realized that the receptionist had so easily bought her lie.

"Murder mysteries," Maya heard herself say.

"Ooh, I love murder mysteries; they're my favorite! But promise me not to go to that landslide for inspiration! It's too dangerous!"

"Oh, I wouldn't! I promise," Maya said.

She smiled at the receptionist and stood aside to make way for other guests. Not sure as to her next step, she looked around the room and recognized the dining hall that the receptionist had pointed out to her earlier. The greedy growl in her stomach reminded her that she had not touched her food on the plane—she had been too anxious. Maya entered the dining hall and felt like she had just experienced a time warp. The furniture here, too, was all Victorian, with expensive-looking antiques and oil paintings lining the wall. But it was the limited use of electronic light that loaned the room the sensation of a time long past. The space was lit almost entirely by candles on tables covered in immaculately white cloth. Waves of conversation reached her from outside, where many guests had decided to enjoy one of the last warm nights on the terrace.

A waiter hurried over to her, offering her choice of seating. Nearly all the tables inside were empty. Maya was tired; all she wanted was to get food in her belly and go to bed, so she motioned to one of the tables.

"Certainly," the waiter murmured and guided her to a seat by the window. He presented her with a menu, of which she was invited to select any three-course meal. At least the steep hotel rate included full board. She made her decision quickly and sat back with a glass of Malbec.

A bulky man, clearly not a waiter, guided a couple to a table two away from hers. She overheard them discussing Dubai; they were expats from the United Arab Emirates, and this was their second time at the hotel. The husband said that it was only good working in Dubai if you avoided dealing with the locals. The man laughed, replying that it was exactly the same here.

Maya zoned out, concentrating on the appetizer that had just been set in front of her. Suddenly the bulky man appeared next to her.

"Good evening. Is everything to your liking?"

She looked up, startled. The man had almost no neck, and she noticed him angling his head ever so slightly as to glimpse her décolletage. She hoped it was just her jet-lagged imagination; the idea of that man eying her filled her with disgust.

She nodded. "Yes. It's delicious. Thank you."

"That accent. Are you from Scandinavia?"

"Germany."

He flashed a big smile and extended his thick hand to her. "My family is originally from Germany. My name is Edgar Montgomery. It's a pleasure to have you here."

"Thank you."

"So what brings you here?"

She decided to stick to her lie. "I'm a writer."

"Oh, how delightful. We've hosted very famous writers here, like Stephen King and..."

"Yes, I read about all of that before coming here. Very impressive."

"Are you a published writer?"

She hesitated only for a second, then nodded her head. She had the impression he noticed.

"So, you must be here for the writers' conference then?"

She felt her next answer would seal her fate. She shook her head. He looked at her, bemused, and came closer, lowering his voice as if to spare her a certain shame from allowing his next words to be overheard by others.

"Look, I saw you sitting here, and you look real good. We get a lot of German guests, some of them really struggle with the language, and we're a little short on staff right now. You could try it for a week, expenses on me, of course, and we can see how we are getting along. And if you like it, I could also help with the visa."

She raised her eyebrows. "I just told you I am a published writer. I am not looking for a job."

"Well, should you change your mind, you know where to find me." He gave her a flirtatious look and motioned to the waiter for another glass of wine before he bid her good night.

Maya entered her room, slightly tipsy, and curled up on the bed with her laptop. Maybe the internet would hold some clues as to where the landslide had occurred. She was surprised at herself that she hadn't thought about researching this before, but the terrible news and preparing with aviophobia for the trip had kept her more than distracted. She arrived online at the Daily Freeman, the local newspaper, and their online archive. After a while, she found what she was looking for—an article from March 28:

***BODY OF HIKER FOUND IN MONTGOMERY PRESERVE***
*The recent landslide in the area around Montgomery Preserve revealed the remains of an approximately seventy-year-old woman. The hiker is said to have had an accident about twenty-five years ago. She was found deep in the woods, far away from any hiking trail. "We caution all our guests against leaving these trails, which we keep in immaculate condition,"*

*commented Edgar Montgomery, the hotel's manager, whose family has owned the hotel for over one hundred years. "Please, for anyone hiking here, no matter whether a guest of ours or a visitor for the day, do not leave the designated hiking trails. It is for your own safety.*

*We feel for the family of the deceased." The identity of the deceased woman has not been determined.*

She could hear Edgar Montgomery's sleazy tone as she read his quotes. She shuddered as she remembered their conversation, the arrogance in his voice, his lingering gaze on her cleavage.

Beneath the article were links to related stories. She scrolled down and found the next one of interest, dated September 15:

### IDENTITY OF DECEASED HIKER REVEALED

*The identity of the body that was uncovered in Montgomery Park after the massive landslide caused by unseasonal heavy rains in early spring has finally been revealed. The woman was a tourist from Germany who was hiking off-trail in the mountains. The cause of death was suffocation when an earlier minor landslide common to the area surprised her on the hike. "Here is a lesson for every hiker about staying on the designated paths," Mr. Edgar Montgomery said. "We feel for the family."*

*The cause of death was suffocation.* Maya's eyes wandered back to the date the article had been published: September 15, one week after her father and Maya had met with the police in Munich, who had informed them that the cause of death was not yet known. She wondered if her father had been informed by the police and had decided again not to tell her. *Listen, Maya, I just try not to think too much about the past, that's all.* That's what he had told her in Munich.

Seething with anger, she plugged the charger for her cell

phone into the wall, and started dialing as soon as it had come to life. But halfway through she dropped the phone. She had no desire to speak to her father right now anyway. Her thoughts returned to the article. How had Grandmother felt when she was caught among the masses of earth? Had she been afraid? Grandmother had been the most fearless person Maya had ever known, and for some reason she had trouble imagining Grandmother afraid in that moment. Instead, Maya imagined her determined. Ready to face death. What were her last thoughts? Had she thought of Maya? Maya's eyes filled with tears. How much she wished she could turn back time, be with Grandmother again, even for one more moment.

# Day 2

Maya's mouth felt like cotton candy when she woke up, terribly jet-lagged. She checked her watch; it was 4:30 A.M. She dozed in a restless half-sleep. When dawn finally announced itself with a pinkish hue on the horizon, Maya rose, too. She opened the window and was greeted with a gush of warm air that promised another beautiful Indian-summer day. She got dressed and left the hotel.

She was the only one out at that time of day and was rewarded with a breathtaking sunrise. Maya rounded the lake toward the hiking trails on the opposite shore, inhaling the scent of the early morning. Dew was glistening on the leaves, and the birds had just woken up to serenade her. She felt invigorated—and strangely relieved the farther she moved away from the hotel. This part of the high plateau, with its unusual rock formations, wildflowers, and thick woods had a soothing effect on her, and she almost felt at peace up here, far away from Germany for the first time in decades.

"One day, you have to see the world, *mein Engel*," Grandmother had said to her in the clearing in Perlach, where they had allowed their yearning to take over and fantasized about faraway places. "You must climb Machu Picchu, explore Angkor Wat; you must travel to Australia, be dazzled by Ayers Rock, and you must see Bali, be in awe of the volcanoes. And to the Chinese Wall, and by all means to India, you must stay at an ashram, and meditate. And I want postcards from all of these places, *mein Engel*."

Grandmother had seemingly dreamed of every destination *but* the United States.

Maya had asked Grandmother once why she wouldn't go on all those trips. But Grandmother had shrugged her shoulders. "I am old," she had said, "and I don't get the pension that would allow me to do all of this." Maya had thought that one day she would invite Grandmother to travel with her. Instead, it seemed neither of them had fulfilled that dream.

Maya arrived at another hiking trail, one that led deep into the woods. Maya paused and studied the facade of the hotel from this angle: from here, its architecture was even more astonishing. The color of the lake appeared black in the early daylight and its perfectly still surface reflected, yes, even doubled, the uniqueness of the structure, making it look as if its darker twin was observing her from the bottom of the lake. She entered the trail, and already after a few feet, the dense canopy swallowed the young daylight. As she walked in near darkness, Maya was reminded of the Black Forest, the forest that had brought the Brothers Grimm to the world. A branch broke somewhere behind her and Maya jumped. But when she turned around, nobody was there. She had read the warnings in the hotel that bears, especially mother bears and their cubs, walk these woods early in the morning. When confronted with a bear, the warning sign suggested for the hiker to make him or herself as tall as possible and make a lot of noise. Running away was not recommended. Maya doubted she would remember that if faced with a bear.

After she had been walking for half an hour, she heard other hikers behind her. She had enjoyed her solitude and suddenly felt unnerved by the prospect that soon she would need to share her trail and the woods with others. Maya spotted a sign on her right, forbidding the hiker to leave the designated trails. A deer trail behind the sign led farther up the mountain. She wanted to escape the hikers; she longed to be alone. Maya entered the trail and soon found herself engaged in a steep climb. There were large boulders ahead of her, mounted atop each other, as if they had suddenly been frozen on their hurried way down from the top of the mountain. When she looked closer, however, she realized that some of the bigger boulders were actually solid mounds of dirt. Could these formations be the result of a landslide? She had never seen one, so she wasn't sure. She carefully climbed the biggest boulder for an expanded view of what lay ahead and noticed a sign farther up, but too far away to be legible. She scrambled onto the next rock, alternating between rocks and the large mounds of dirt; the hard surface made it easier than expected, and she gained distance quickly at first, but it became harder and harder as the mountain grew steeper with every hundred feet. After another five minutes of arduous climbing she had finally come close enough to read the sign: *WARNING: DANGEROUS SWAMP AHEAD. LIFE DANGER*. The fairly new looking sign failed to have the intended effect on Maya. On the contrary, she felt even more driven to get up that mound, fueled by the thought that she might have stumbled across the landslide that had proven fatal. In the last stretch, Maya had to use her whole body to heave herself over the last rocks. After what felt like an eternity, she jumped over the last one, bracing herself for a wet landing in a swamp, but instead she landed hard on the soil of a clearing.

Maya looked up and inhaled sharply.

The clearing resembled the one in Perlach. Their happy spot. It was the same oval shape. Just like the clearing in Perlach, this one, too, had a big oak tree toward one side, with a stump next to it, and two birch trees on the opposite side. Was it possible? Or was she imagining the resemblance? After all, it was just a clearing in the woods.

She glanced around and caught sight of a turquoise lake off the other side of the mountain, further in the distance. Had Grandmother also beheld this breathtaking view? Had she been up here? Wasn't the resemblance too striking to be a coincidence?

It took her a while to realize that not all the drops on her cheeks were tears, but the first raindrops of a storm, thunder echoing in the distance. It was a fine rain at first, then gradually began to soak Maya to the bones. She started to shiver and tried to move, but her ankles were sinking into the softening earth, which the rain was now turning into a dark, gluey mass. She thought she heard a twig snap somewhere in the woods. She squinted, trying to make out a shape in the darkness of the pine forest, but the more she struggled, the deeper her shoes got stuck in the sludge. A gust of wind rattled the leaves on the maple trees, seeming to come from all directions, quietly whispering her name, enveloping her. The woods started to spin, but the dark mass held her firmly in its grip. Suddenly, a rasping breathing. Something—or someone—was right behind her. The breath felt wet, musky. Maya shut her eyes tightly and stayed as still as possible. After a while the breathing stopped. Maya opened her eyes again—and that is when she saw it: a tall, gaunt figure off in the distance, staring back at her; it had no eyes, no mouth, no nothing; it was a faceless being, almost like her fellow passengers from the past whose faces had been blurred out to protect their identity. Maya let out a scream. She could hear her heart hammering in her chest and her breathing coming in short gasps. The dark forest that stretched into the horizon behind the clearing seemed like a black hole, swallowing every noise around her. She tried not to panic, tried not to move too fast. She knew the mud would not let her go unless she was as still as possible. But all she wanted to do was run. She managed to wiggle her feet closer to freedom, an inch at a time, fearful. But whenever she stopped to listen into the darkness around her, all she heard was her own heartbeat and the sound the rain made when landing on the leaves on the trees. When the mud finally gave way for both feet, Maya lunged away, careful not to dig herself back into it. Though the rain made it difficult to see, she quickened her pace, not sure if the rasping breathing were all in her head or just her shoes flopping against the wet soil.

Suddenly, the black figure filled her field of vision, jumping from behind a tree in front of her. Too close to run away. Maya screamed as it firmly held her by the arms, and she struggled to free herself, kicking with her legs as she was lifted off the ground.

And then everything went black around her.

"What are you doing here?" She heard a raspy voice somewhere above her. She sensed dampness around her, her wet clothes. She had never fainted before. And she didn't want to return to the cold and rain and mud; it had been nicer where she was.

She squinted up at the blurry, dark spot hovering over her. Slowly the figure became clearer. A man in his seventies stared down at her, a scowl on his face. As she sat up, holding her head, she noticed an emblem on his black shirt: *MONTGOMERY PRESERVE*. A park ranger, she thought with relief.

The ranger didn't meet her eyes. Instead he looked at the spot next to her, tugging nervously at the black scarf around his neck. He wiped the snot off his nose with his right hand, and then, reluctantly, extended that same hand to help her up. Equally reluctantly, she took the wet palm and rose from the ground. The rain had become a light drizzle.

"What are you doing here?" he repeated his question.

"I got lost."

"Yes, by leaving the main trail!"

"Really, I'm so sorry."

"A hiker died in these woods! She, like you, had wandered off the track...," he said. "I was the one who found her remains after a landslide. A terrible, terrible sight!" He shook his head as if trying to shake away the horrible memory.

"Was it this landslide where she was found?" He slowly nodded, affirming Maya's suspicions.

"It was... I mean... the skull, the way it was bashed in, the way she..."

"How long have you worked for the Montgomery?" she interrupted quickly, trying desperately to erase the image of Grandmother's bloody head that had just materialized in her mind.

"I started under Hans Montgomery." His right eye began to twitch. "*The* Hans Montgomery," he added in reaction to Maya's blank look.

"Edgar Montgomery's father?"

"No."

Maya waited for him to continue, but he didn't volunteer any additional information.

"I bet the place has changed a lot since you started working here," Maya said to end the silence.

He now looked straight at Maya, almost as if he was noticing her for the first time since he'd found her. "Everything changed after Hans Montgomery," she heard him whisper, so low that at first she wasn't sure he had said anything at all.

Maya waited for him to continue, but the only sounds were the blowing of the wind and the dripping of the raindrops from the foliage.

"This way," he said and started walking.

Maya knew she had no choice but to follow him. After several minutes they landed on a narrow path, almost as if the forest had decided to spit them out. He was walking fast, as a trained and experienced mountaineer might. After less than a mile, she noticed a sign pointing to the Lemon Quench. The ranger turned right, and she again followed until they reached one solid rock formation that marked the end of the path. At further inspection, Maya noted a split in the middle, with hooks on each side for the hiker to climb down into a sheer crevice. A sign warned that appropriate gear was recommended, even for the most experienced of hikers.

She paused. "Do you think this is safe?"

"Safer than using the landslide," he said without turning around.

Maya craved a warm shower, dry clothes—but more than anything else, she wanted to get out of here. She wanted to escape the image the ranger had painted for her. *The skull, the way it was bashed in.* As she descended after him, she lost her grip on the wet, slippery rocks more than once. Ironically, it was the mental image of Grandmother's skull that kept her holding on to the rocks. When she landed hard on the last rock, the ranger was already waiting for her. She recognized the main hiking trail behind him.

"I know the way from here," Maya said.

"Stay out of these woods," the ranger warned, and without further comment, he turned around and walked back into the woods.

She followed the trail for several hundred feet; birds chirped merrily in the aftermath of the rain, and everything appeared harmless and peaceful again. And then she stopped dead in her tracks. She had felt that something hadn't been quite right. Now, on even ground and with the hotel in sight, she knew what detail it was that didn't add up: the newspaper article had reported death by suffocation.

Maya entered the impeccable lobby with her muddy shoes, eager to get up to her room and find the officer's card. The person manning the reception, a man about the same age as the park ranger, watched her critically as she hurried to the elevator, leaving spots of caked dirt on the shiny oaken floor.

Her room had been tidied up. The mess around her suitcase was the only area untouched, and she rummaged through the piles of clothes, vaguely remembering to have dropped the officer's card in there last-minute. And her memory served her well.

Her fingers trembled as she dialed his number.

"Brentlmayer. Please leave a message after the tone."

Her first impulse was to hang up, but then she changed her mind.

"This is Maya Wiesberg calling. I wanted to find out if there's news about my grandmother, Martha Wiesberg." She left him both her cell number and the hotel number with her extension. It was past 5:00 P.M. in Germany. Maybe he had gone home for the day and wasn't taking any more calls.

She waited around for half an hour, pacing up and down the room, phone in her hand, hoping he would call her back. When the voice mail came on again a second time, she hung up without leaving another message and dropped the phone in her pocket, overcome with a sudden urge for fresh air.

More light than usual flooded the lobby, thanks to an open wooden door farther back in the lobby between the dining room and reception. She caught a glimpse of a massive ballroom, with huge floor-to-ceiling windows that almost seemed to touch the shores of the lake. Inside people were scurrying about, setting up chairs, moving centerpieces, and hanging artwork.

"Who told you to put this up here?" a male voice yelled hysterically. The older male receptionist appeared in the doorframe, his face bright red. "Take it down, now!" he demanded to his colleague, a short, mousy woman trailing him.

The receptionist turned toward Maya, and his face froze.

Maya felt a cool gush of wind and shivered. Following his gaze, she caught sight of a slightly hunched over, short old woman, and turned her head to observe her path to the ballroom. She was wearing high heels despite her age walking gracefully with the aid of a golden cane. Her other hand clutched a Hermès bag against a bespoke expensive-looking black dress.

"Mrs. Montgomery." The receptionist came back to life and waved.

The woman didn't return his greeting, instead brushed by him and into the ballroom. She stopped a few feet inside.

"Who dared to...?" was all Maya could make out before Mrs. Montgomery slammed the door shut with a power extraordinary for her size and age. The bang echoed throughout the lobby.

Mrs. Montgomery. Maya had read about her on the resort's website. She was the second generation of the Montgomery family, still manning the whole place together with her grandson, Edgar.

The lobby was charged with negative energy, and Maya was in even more of a hurry to get out. When she turned toward the main door, she saw Edgar striding up the driveway and decided to head down a hallway to her right. Knowing only that she wanted to avoid an encounter with Edgar, she went right again, into another hallway and a part of the hotel she had not entered before.

She almost ran into him—a man larger-than-life, looking down at her, an exhorting expression on his face, from a huge portrait prominently featured at this end of the hallway. She would need to go to bed early tonight. She was beginning to feel paranoid, imagining admonishing looks everywhere. But still, his intense stare made Maya linger. He was an astonishing man, very tall, intimidating posture. His eyes were piercing blue and intelligent. Was this Hans Montgomery, the one the park ranger had mentioned earlier? She came closer and read a small sign next to the painting: *FRANZ MONTGOMERY, FOUNDER*. There was plenty of information about him on Montgomery's website. He had been a fellow countryman of Maya's, who had fled Germany before the start of World War I with no means and had built this place from scratch, just as Edgar had referenced the previous night. Maya stood very still, gazing into his eyes. What must it have been like to leave your home with no means and then end up building this place?

Maya ventured farther down the hallway and studied the other frames. Most of them featured Franz Montgomery with famous guests, including several vice presidents and even Teddy Roosevelt himself. One, of Franz and John D. Rockefeller, hung alongside a testimonial by the billionaire claiming that *HE LEFT RICHER THAN UPON HIS ARRIVAL*. There was a portrait of Franz with John Burroughs, whose essay collection Maya had devoured with the utmost pleasure. Maya noticed there were only a few of Mr. Montgomery with his wife, Florence, and from a certain age onward, all of the photos showed Franz standing next to Elisa Montgomery. Whoever she was in relation to Franz, Maya could tell she was a stunning beauty once upon a time! There were also various photos of Edgar Montgomery at different ages, and of a man named William Montgomery who, judging from the posture and absence of a neck, must have been Edgar's father.

At the end of the hallway, Maya had arrived at a glass door that prevented her from advancing farther. She went back to the hallway entrance and once more viewed the photos on the walls, carefully, daring to be proven wrong. And she came to the same conclusion when she reached the glass door again: she had not come across a single photo of Hans Montgomery, the *Hans Montgomery,* as the ranger had stressed earlier. Who was Hans Montgomery? Maybe she would find more pictures in the other hallways? She was surprised at her own sudden interest in the family. She, who had banished any thought of the past for the major part of her life, found it extremely gratifying to wander in someone else's. The ranger's words came back to her, *Everything changed after Hans Montgomery*. What had he meant? She shook her head. Why did she even care?

Her attention returned to the glass door in front of her. A gold-plated sign next to it read *PRIVATE*. She started heading back to the elevators, when she made out a familiar and unpleasant voice in the lobby. Edgar. The voice was coming closer, Maya remembered having passed the door to a stairwell halfway down the long corridor. Now she tiptoed back toward it, feeling childish for being so secretive. But talking to Edgar still was the last thing she wanted to do. She ascended the stairs to the next level and walked in the opposite direction, away from Edgar beneath her. Here, too, the walls were filled with frames. But this time she didn't stop to study them.

Soon she arrived at a junction where the hallway continued and where two other hallways split off to the sides. One, however, stood out. It was narrower, darker; the floral wallpaper and absence of frames lent it a different feel. A wooden frame adorned the hallway's entrance, where two angels at the top looked down on Maya, as if silently guiding her in. She couldn't help but feel drawn in by the hallway, which looked like a leftover from older times, as if had not been touched in decades. She advanced toward a light source farther down on the right. She reached a door, the sunlight behind it lending the hallway an ethereal glow. She felt like an intruder when she pushed the door open and found herself in a nursery, furnished in the style of the 1920s. She turned to her left, where she caught site of an army of dead, plastic eyes watching her from the faces of stuffed animals sitting on shelves. Adjacent to the shelves, she made out a large, roughly six-foot-by-six-foot spot where the floral wallpaper was less faded. In front of a huge window at the opposite end of the room stood a rocking chair next to a crib, with a dream catcher dangling over it, which seemed out of place in the room. The floor squeaked as she moved toward the crib. She half expected to find a baby in it when she peered over the rim of the antique. There had been a time when she had wished to have children of her own. Michael's children. His reluctance had always pained her. Michael shouldn't have been the father of her children. The thought struck her hard, but oddly enough the sudden insight filled her only with relief, not sadness. As Maya scanned the crib, she noticed a wooden sign on the edge. Delicate, thin lines were carved around the words, *MY FALLEN ANGEL, FOREVER*. She looked around again. Now she caught site of several other carved wooden objects in the room. Like the dream catcher, those all looked like Native art.

Maya heard voices approaching. Instinctively, she hid behind one of the long, thick window curtains; she still felt like she had entered a forbidden zone, a room that was usually closed to the public. The curtains smelled like the room looked—not unpleasant, but filled with history, memories. She looked out the window and observed gardeners buzzing about in a nearby garden. In the center stood the statue of an angel, its face angled in a way that made it appear to be looking over the room.

Several people entered, judging from the sounds of feet hurrying into the room.

"Put it back up! Immediately!" she heard Edgar say. "Who gave you a key to this room?"

"We were instructed to bring it to the ballroom," a man's voice said weakly.

"Who instructed you?"

The man mumbled something inaudible.

"You're all fired—unless you change your mind and come clean."

Maya winced at the forceful bang of the closing door. From behind the curtain, she heard the other men groan and the sound of a drill.

When there was silence at last, a voice close to her made her jump. "You can come out now."

She emerged from behind the curtain and found herself opposite a man about her age, tall, curly blond hair, blue eyes. She felt herself blush the brightest red.

"I'm sorry," she mumbled. "The door was open, and I..."

"...thought, *why not hide behind a curtain?* No need to apologize. We all do that sometimes." He laughed and gestured for her to leave the room with him.

On the way out she craned her neck to see what the men had been drilling. The spot on the wall had been covered by a huge frame. Inside was an ornately painted family tree that had been put back in its rightful place. She caught sight of the names Franz Montgomery and Florence O'Donald, prominently featured at the top of the tree, with pictures next to their names, and branches reaching out underneath, drawing the bloodline of their descendants. She was about to ask about the tree when she saw the blond man waiting impatiently, holding the door open for her. She hurried out.

The man locked the door behind them and led her down the hallway in the opposite direction from which she came. Maya noticed the same wooden frame and angels as at the other end as they stepped out of the hallway — and back into the present, back to the hotel hallways, back to the frames, the hotel's bright halogen lights. Here, the modern touches made the room she had just stumbled across feel surreal in comparison.

"Ben." He offered her his hand.

She took it with a damp palm, hoping he wouldn't notice. She knew she was still bright red in the face. She had turned into a sixteen-year-old girl again, painfully shy.

"And your name?"

Maya had to swallow before opening her dry mouth. "Wiesberg," she said — the German way to introduce yourself to other adults. By your family name.

"That's all?" He had raised his eyebrows in a mock gesture. Maya quickly added, "Maya, Maya Wiesberg."

He was still holding Maya's hand. And she was still staring at this handsome man in front of her, wishing on the one hand that he would let go of her increasingly sweaty hand, and on the other that he would keep looking at her with that smile. He lingered, and then his smile became even broader. "Oh, my gosh, that's amazing. I can't believe that nobody told me you're staying here! I would be delighted to host you at our upcoming writers' conference." He looked at her expectantly.

"Okay, I'll think about it," she heard herself say.

Ben smiled broadly. "Oh, fantastic. Thank you!" He waved his goodbyes and ran off.

Maya wanted to shout after him that she hadn't agreed to anything, that he was mistaken, but he had already turned a corner and was gone. What had just happened? Then it dawned on her: there was a Swedish mystery writer named Maya Viesberg. Though Maya's last name was spelled with a "w," it was pronounced with a "v" sound in German. She took out her phone and googled the other name. She recognized one of Viesberg's titles. Maya had read it, and not liked it. She wouldn't have expected for the writer to have a following in the United States. There was not a single photo of Maya Viesberg on the internet.

Maya started to walk in the direction that he had disappeared. She had to correct this misunderstanding immediately.

When she turned the corner, she heard Ben's voice again and almost ran into a sign that read *WRITERS' ROOM— PRE-CONFERENCE SEMINAR ON CREATIVE WRITING.*

"The day after tomorrow, I expect you to hand in your first writing exercise," she heard Ben say. He had a soft voice. "After that you will concentrate on your personal story. And then we will break for the conference. We will be hosting authors of all genres. The Swedish writer Maya Viesberg just confirmed her attendance." A murmur of acknowledgment filled the room.

"Ma'am—" She heard a female voice behind her. "I'm sorry, but could you let me pass, please?"

Maya turned around. It was a woman from housekeeping whose cart wouldn't fit between Maya and the sign in the hallway. Maya was forced to step in front of the sign and into full view of the writers' room. Ben noticed her immediately.

"And speaking of the devil, there she is!"

Maya stood frozen in the doorway of the boardroom. Ben again showered her with his delightful smile. Maya couldn't help but smile back at the eager faces of the students. Most were young and seemed to be in their twenties or thirties. She waved her hand shyly, blushing again to the bones, then nodded toward Ben and continued on her way.

The moment she knew she was out of sight, she nearly ran back to her room, weirdly excited. She stood at the window, looking out onto the lake and the setting sun.

The ring of the phone made her jump.

"Hello?"

"Miss Wiesberg. Brentlmayer here."

She plunged down on the bed. This had been the first time, since the terrible news, that not every single thought of hers had been consumed by Grandmother. And she felt guilt about that. She was here for Grandmother, not to feel flattered by a group of aspiring writers.

"What on earth are you doing there? I thought you couldn't fly?"

"I know, so did I."

"For Christ sake, I cannot believe you're there! You mustn't tell the local police, you hear me? Strictly speaking I wasn't authorized to tell you where..."

Maya sat upright, a horrible feeling was creeping up to her. "How did my grandmother die?"

There was a heavy pause. "She was murdered."

It seemed as if the world around her had come to a standstill. All she heard was water dripping from the tap in the bathroom. She noticed a chipped nail on her finger. Paint peeling off on one of the window frames. And then the police officer's voice came back as if from very far away.

"...You there, Frau Wiesberg?"

"That isn't possible. My grandmother wasn't murdered." Maya had found her voice again.

"I'm afraid she was, Frau Wiesberg. I know this is hard to accept..."

"But everybody here says it was an accident!"

"What are you doing over there, anyway?"

Her mind was racing as she summarized, more for herself

111

than him, the discoveries she had made in only a couple of days. "The newspaper mentioned death by suffocation in an article dated September fifteen, one week after we met in Munich. I met the park ranger this morning, and he mentioned a broken skull, so I called you earlier to ask for an update. Everybody here, the staff at the hotel, the townspeople — everyone says it was an accident. There are no local police investigating anything!"

He was quiet for a while. Then she heard him sigh.

"Please email me the article, and I will call the state police. If I get through I'll pass this case on to them. Listen, I can't promise you anything, Frau Wiesberg. You have to understand: this is out of our hands now. This is international law. Your grandmother was found on their turf. The police over there need to investigate the murder, not us. But we can always go one level higher up, and the state police can overrule the local police. But only if they want to."

"Thank you, officer."

"Now listen, we are dealing with a murderer here. A murderer that hasn't been found yet. And if he or she is still alive, then that person most likely doesn't want to be found — and would most likely do anything not to be found out! The hole in your grandmother's skull indicates that your grandmother was hit on the head twice — once by something long, but the second blow, probably a rock, is the one that killed her. It could have been manslaughter, but it could have also been a premeditated murder. You should stay out of this. I'm serious. People sometimes think they can live out their own crime novels; this is never the case. I'm not happy to hear you're over there. Not at all."

His tone had grown softer toward the end. She realized that he was genuinely worried about her.

"Take a breather. Enjoy your vacation. Use the time for that. *Don't* investigate on your own, you hear me?"

She grabbed her laptop and half-heartedly set off on a search for an earlier flight back, but the thought of having to board another plane so soon again filled her with despair—and made way only too easily for other, far-darker thoughts: the image the park ranger had painted for her back in the woods. *The skull, the way it was bashed in. The way her skull was bashed in. The way her skull was bashed in.* Why would someone do this to Grandmother? She was almost seventy years old when she was killed. Grandmother had been a quiet person; she had never had any enemies. Maya felt cold even though the setting sun was shining right into her room. She lay down on the bed, the framed photo of Grandmother pressed against her chest. She started crying, first quietly, and then the tears came in waves.

# Day 3

When she woke up the next morning her laptop was still open next to her, showing her latest results for the earliest affordable possibility to fly back home—a flight with an endless stop-over, leaving in a little less than twenty-four hours. And then slowly, as her conscience woke up, it came back to her: Grandmother had been murdered. Her eyes wandered back to the screen and the flight times. She had enough time to say goodbye.

The full moon was waning but still shed enough light for Maya to find the hiking trail. The police officer's warning to stay out of it echoed in her mind. But she had to see the clearing one last time. This time, however, she was going back with the knowledge that Grandmother was murdered.

She had reached the turnoff to the landslide. The dense canopy ahead of her let in only a little light, so Maya took out her cell phone and switched on the flashlight. She heard a sound right behind her and quickly lowered her cell phone, standing as still as possible. Her trembling hands created dancing shadows in front of her when she lifted her phone again to illuminate the way ahead. She felt vulnerable as she walked on, an easy target.

As soon as early signs of dawn arrived, she switched off the light and advanced in semidarkness. She found herself unable to ascend as fast as she had the first time.

The early morning light was breaking through the dense canopy by the time she arrived at the clearing, adding an otherworldly aura to the place. This time she went straight for the oak tree and let her hand glide between the thicket and the tree, feeling for the ultimate proof. Her heart beat faster when her hands found it. Here, too, someone had eternalized his or her initials into the tree trunk. She squeezed herself into the undergrowth behind the tree, half expecting to find Grandmother's initials. She hadn't paid attention to the actual letters back in Perlach. She had been too preoccupied with other things. This time, here, she shone the light of her cell on the carvings: H. M. the initials read. Not M. W. And still, Maya could feel Grandmother, stronger than she had back in Perlach.

"I'm sorry!" she screamed into the woods, and this time the flood of tears hit her with such a force that it pulled her down. She would never find out why Grandmother came here. Never learn what had ailed her in the last moments of her life. Maya buried her face in the wet leaves, muffling her cries, sinking her hands into the earth around her. She let go, more so than ever before, and let herself feel the pain. Grandmother had been her mother when Maya's own had rejected her. Grandmother had been her friend when the other kids had bullied her. Grandmother had meant life to her.

She was so sorry. Sorry for how she had behaved at the airport, for her ingratitude, but most of all sorry for having shut her out.

She rolled onto her back and stared up at the sky, her vision blurred but her heart clear.

As her tears slowly ebbed, she concentrated on the absolute silence around her. Even the leaves in the trees had stopped brushing against each other. She listened carefully and shivered when she heard rasping breathing. She held her own breath to make out the direction it was coming from, but the wind picked up again and leaves were falling down in hordes onto the forest floor, blocking her view. Was it the park ranger again? She wasn't keen for him to sneak up on her like that again.

She quickly got up and jogged through the clearing, farther into the woods behind it. She heard the heavy breathing again, much closer this time—and she crouched down, watching from behind the branches of a tree. A man entered the clearing, huffing and puffing from the effort of the climb. He seemed to be around her age, and loafers and slacks definitely not dressed appropriately for a hike. He looked around, examining the clearing. That was no ordinary hiker. Nobody undertook the strenuous climb simply because they were lost. They came with a purpose. And whoever he was, she didn't want to be spotted. She slowly retreated backward, moving like a spider on all four legs farther into the thicket of the underbrush behind her, when all of a sudden, her hands reached into nothingness, and she quickly had to hold on to a branch. When she turned around she realized that she had reached the edge of a plateau. A sign to her left repeated what the other sign had warned against: *DANGEROUS SWAMP AHEAD. LIFE DANGER.* She looked down. An extremely steep descent lead into a dense carpet of vines below. You definitely wouldn't want to get lost in there, but she had a different image in her head when she had read about the "dangerous swamp." That spot down there looked like an untamed forest to her, not like a swamp. She decided to wait a couple of minutes longer before she would slowly return to the clearing. He was still there, examining the oak tree. By now almost half an hour had passed. Maya listened to his feet crunch leaves as he paced around the clearing again—and then he left. Maya returned when she was sure she was out of sight and sat down on the trunk in front of the oak tree.

But the moment was gone. The man had destroyed the magic. There was nothing more to say.

"Goodbye," she whispered one last time, wiping away one last tear from her face, and started to descend.

By the time Maya arrived back at the hotel she had lost all sense of time. It had taken her hours to return.

"Can I please get something to eat?" Maya asked in the dining room.

She ordered a hamburger. When it came, Maya shoveled it down as if she hadn't eaten in days.

A hand landed softly on her shoulder. "Hello Maya!"

Ben. Maya kept her head down. She was embarrassed. She didn't have on any makeup; she hadn't brushed her hair. She was wearing the same clothes as yesterday. She wiped her mouth and turned around.

"Oh, my God. What happened?"

She didn't look *that* bad, did she?

He extended a hand and stroked her face and then hair. Maya trembled at the touch. He dangled a dry leaf in front of her eyes. He studied her face intently, looking momentarily puzzled, and Maya guessed what thoughts had to fill his head when looking at her: that she probably didn't fit the image he had in his head of the Maya Viesberg she had just read up about. She flinched, having been reminded of the misunderstanding, but he didn't seem to notice and smiled again.

"There are several more where this came from. Is this how you Swedes go on hikes?" he chortled. And then he paused briefly, looking pensive. "Maya Viesberg, you are very different from what I had in mind. I always suspected there was a reason there are no photos of you anywhere." He laughed. "I thought maybe you're ugly, with a hunchback, or warts. But quite the contrary."

Maya felt a sensation in her stomach that she hadn't felt in a long while. It felt good to bask in that feeling, a welcome distraction from her grief.

"Listen, my students and I will finish early today. So I thought I could show you around and we can grab dinner somewhere?"

Maya thought she should come clean with him now about who she really was.

"Fantastic idea," she heard herself say instead.

He beamed, then he checked his watch. "Wonderful. I'll pick you up at five."

The knock on the door surprised her. She had started to pack and hadn't even noticed time had gone by so fast.

She took a side glance into the mirror as she walked over to the door, remorsefully noticing that she should have done some damage control, instead of getting ready for tomorrow's departure. She opened the door, and there it was again, that smile. And that sensation in her belly.

"Ready?" He offered his arm. She took it, brushing against the muscles under the sleeve of his shirt.

They had left the resort and were driving down a different road, opposite the direction Maya had come from on her arrival. A mix of all sorts of feelings were washing over her. There was shame. Shame about the excitement she felt. Guilt that she hadn't told Ben who she truly was. And sadness. For he had only invited her because he thought her to be someone else. A successful writer. Not the owner of an insignificant little bookstore on the brink of closing. And sadness that Grandmother was no longer here. She would have chuckled, listening to Maya go on about her date with a man who took her to be someone else.

Grandmother winked at her from a different place.

"Thinking about your next novel?" He glanced at her. She shook her head.

"Well, Miss Viesberg, it is an honor to be spending the evening with you. Thank you for regaling me with the precious time of a critically acclaimed and best-selling author!"

Again, that sensation in her belly.

*Just enjoy it, Maya*, she told herself, feeling like the princess who had until midnight for a dance — before she had to go back to her old self and her old life. *Just for this one evening*.

They drove around for a while, over the Shawangunks, into New Paltz through Rosendale into High Falls, the village she had passed through on the day of her arrival. He was telling her the history of the area. Paleo-Indians had been the first people to settle there, and for centuries Native Americans had hunted there, long before the first Europeans came over. "This is why so many names are of Indian origin," he explained, "like Shawangunk, which actually means 'smoky air.' "

With every mile they traveled, Maya felt more comfortable in the car, more at ease with her surroundings, more like herself. For the first time she allowed herself some peace. She had found what she had come for: feeling close to Grandmother again, letting her back into her life.

She smiled at Ben. "Thank you for taking me out," she said with gratitude. This time Ben's smile lingered a little longer. She looked away before he could see her blush.

They stopped at a cozy place called the Egg's Nest. There were artifacts, statues, masks, and little knickknacks from places the owner had traveled. The owner, Richard, gave Ben a bear hug and led him to a table in the corner. Ben explained that Richard was an artist who once a month would lock himself in the restaurant overnight and redesign it.

They ordered the Egg's Nest's "infamous" martinis, as Ben insisted, and other patrons continuously stopped by to greet Ben. To Maya's great relief, Ben never asked her about Maya Viesberg, her books, her activities. She hadn't looked her up again. Instead she learned that they liked and hated the same novels, and agreed on favorite characters, quoting favorite lines throughout their meal. Ben was very different from Michael, and Maya enjoyed every second.

"So what do you do for a living?" she asked when the conversation about books petered out.

"I teach writing, mostly, and I'm also a travel writer."

"Are you from around here?"

She could sense him tense up at her question. He looked at her for a moment, then shook his head no. "I try to go home as much as possible."

He started to talk about a recent trip he took. She wished they were still discussing books, a field she felt confident in, but soon realized that her "virtraveling" on Google Earth had educated her more than she would have thought. This way of traveling, combined with her reading, had given her much knowledge about different cultures.

"So what is the most fascinating country you've been to?" Ben asked her after a while.

Maya swallowed the martini the wrong way and coughed. She wouldn't lie to him this time. "I've never been to any of these places."

He raised his eyebrows in surprise. "How do you know about them then?"

"Reading."

He shook his head, frowning. "You talked about them as if you'd actually been there."

She hesitated, feeling ashamed to share her hobby with him, because of how Michael had always made fun of it.

"I have a rather weird hobby."

Ben studied Maya's face, waiting for more.

"I look up all the places on Google Earth. On satellite. Then I zoom in and study them. I've fantasized about visiting so many places. This is my way of getting as close to them as I can."

She realized how naive she must have sounded. For a second she was afraid he would laugh at her as Michael had.

"So why do you never travel?" he asked instead.

"I suffer from aviophobia. Most of my life I haven't been able to board planes."

He sat upright, and for a second Maya was afraid that she had just betrayed herself. Had Maya Viesberg been to many writers' conferences around the world?

"How did you get here then?"

"I..." Maya needed to find the right words. "I beat it, my fear of flying."

"How?"

"It was my grandmother who helped me." The sudden sadness consumed her without warning. Thinking about Grandmother was no less painful. Her will, however, not to let down her guard in front of him was stronger. She suddenly felt nauseous; she should have never agreed to this dinner. It had been silly. This whole charade was childish, immature. As immature as that hobby of hers that Michael had so belittled.

"I'm so sorry. I don't feel well." She got up from her seat, but Ben took her hand, squeezing it softly. The look of concern and compassion told her that he had seen the sting in her eyes. She sank back into her chair.

"Do you want me to drive you home?" he asked her in a low voice.

Maya looked around. There was only one other couple still enjoying their dinner, and the night was nearing its end. But she didn't want this to end. She didn't want to return to the gloomy hotel room.

"We don't have to leave, if you don't want to." Ben's look lingered. "I'm a good listener."

She looked into his eyes and decided to follow her instincts.

"My grandmother disappeared in 1990, and they've just found her remains."

"What happened to her?"

Maya paused. "She was murdered."

Ben sat back, frowning. "Hang on here. Are you pitching me your new novel?"

"No, unfortunately I'm not. So once I received the confirmation that she hadn't intentionally abandoned me, I noticed that my fear of flying wasn't as strong anymore. It wasn't gone. And I still had a hard time. I panicked on the runway. But it was my grandmother who helped me. I transported myself to a place in the woods that I loved—a clearing where my grandmother always took me when I was little."

Ben shifted on his chair, and she stopped. But he squeezed her hand again, encouraging her to continue.

"So I imagined this beautiful stretch of forest before me. And I imagined what I would feel, having my fingers glide through the brush of the leaves on the ground. And I heard the birds chirp, and then I felt and smelled her next to me, holding my hand, brushing my hair. Telling me that everything would be all right." She looked up. Ben was nodding his head in sympathy. "And so the next time I opened my eyes I had missed both breakfast and lunch and had only three hours left to my destination."

He squeezed her hand one more time. He hadn't let go of it the entire time. Now, self-conscious of his warm hand in hers, she wanted to change the subject.

"That room I met you in the other day — what is it?"

He released her hand as if it were a piece of hot coal, and a shadow came over his face. She regretted her question instantly.

"They usually keep that part shut," he said, and then raised his arm for the check.

The clock had struck midnight.

They didn't talk on the drive back to the hotel. The closer they got, the gloomier Maya felt. Only this one last night, she told herself, and it would be over. She would go back to Germany and get on with her life.

She observed Ben's profile. This had been her first date since Michael. Michael, who had taught her everything she knew about love; she had never been with another man. His feelings for her had always assured her. He was reliable, steady in the way he had loved her. She had never felt vulnerable. But she did now.

They arrived at the hotel, and he turned toward her with a genuine smile. She noticed he left the motor running.

"You don't live at the hotel?"

He chuckled. "No way. I spend enough time here." He

became more serious. "Listen, I had meant to ask you earlier, during dinner. Tomorrow there's a big celebration here at the hotel. The hundredth birthday of Elisa Montgomery. Would you want to accompany me?"

He looked at her again with boyish adoration. He was nervous, and that fact alone was enough to give her butterflies.

How she wished he knew who she really was. Couldn't she just tell him now? But she was leaving tomorrow anyway. Why overshadow a beautiful evening by admitting to a stupid lie?

Instead, Maya leaned forward and did something she would have never done in a million years. She wasn't Maya Wiesberg. She was acclaimed author Maya Viesberg. So she grabbed his face with her hands and planted a kiss on his lips.

His lips were soft. She thought she felt him open them to hers, ever so slightly, but maybe it was she who had opened his lips. How would she know? She had only ever kissed one man, it struck her again. She pulled away.

"Ben, I'm leaving tomorrow. I'm sorry."

He winced, and the disappointment that spread over his face pained Maya more than she would have thought. She slipped into the hotel before he could say another word.

Maya noticed it immediately upon entering the room—a letter on the side table next to the armchair. Her name, Maya Dorothy, was handwritten in script on the envelope. She sat down on the bed and unfolded the clipped-together pages inside.

She gasped as she read, each word, each syllable flowing through her mind. She saw it written out for the first time: "The War Fairy," her fairy tale.

She couldn't remember how long she sat on the bed, motionless, the papers still in her hands. Someone out there knew *her* fairy tale. Someone nearby. Someone who knew she was staying at the hotel. That person had to have known

Grandmother. How else would they have known the fairy tale?

She reached for the phone, almost automatically.

"Miss Wiesberg, how may I help you?" It was the friendly receptionist that had checked her in.

"I won't be checking out tomorrow after all," Maya said as she reached for her bag on the floor. She would need to change her flight as well.

"Certainly. No problem, Miss Wiesberg. By how many days would you like to extend?"

She was feeling for her laptop inside the bag when her hand brushed the rough surface of linen. She pulled out the booklet Paula, the librarian, had given to her: *The Spirit of Montgomery*. She had completely forgotten about it. Paula's imaginary face hovered in front of Maya. *You strike me as someone who appreciates good books*. Paula had given her more than just a history book, Maya began to suspect. She had mentioned Grandmother to the librarian. Only then the woman had passed this booklet to her. Would it bring Maya closer to the truth?

"Four, please," she heard herself say, already reading the first sentence.

# The Spirit of Montgomery

*The following is a true account of the Montgomery dynasty, passed down from generation to generation by staff members who worked closely (and some of them still do) with the family and gained insights that the family tried to keep secret.*

*All conversations you' ll find in this book have been overheard by those who had to suffer under their employment and lived to tell the tales of greed, adultery, injustice, and unrequited love.*

*Names have been changed to protect those brave enough to contribute to the truth.*

—Anonymous January 12, 1992, Stone Ridge, New York

It was the year 1914 when a man named Franz Mönchinger arrived on Ellis Island. He would tell everyone in the decades to come that he had fled Germany after the shot in Sarajevo—where a Serbian nationalist killed the Archduke Franz Ferdinand, heir to the Austro-Hungarian Empire—that he had been smart to anticipate World War I, and that he had arrived a poor man who had worked his way to the top.

The truth was that he ticked all the boxes for an immigrant who would help foster the prosperity of this country: he brought a lot of cash, he was in good health, well-educated, and young. The problem was that most of his money had not been earned legally: he was a notorious gambler and still owed money to some thugs back in Berlin. So upon arrival in New York, months before World War I even broke out, he decided against staying in the city, boarded the next boat, and headed up the Hudson River to Poughkeepsie, about eighty miles north of the city.

When he disembarked at the dock in "Po'keepsie," a horse carriage and a finely dressed coachman caught Franz's attention: he thought that the horse carriage was a thing of the past, even in the countryside outside of New York City. As he followed the gaze of a group of wealthy people from the city approaching the carriage with their suitcases, he spotted *MONTGOMERY RESORT* written on its side. Franz realized that this was part of a hotel's smart marketing. Franz knew a thing or two about the hospitality business—and he had a fine nose for money, and good instincts. He decided without further ado that this would be the first address he would head to in his new home country. He paid the coachman the steep $2.75 for the ride to the resort, not without making sure he'd seen the fat stash of bills in Franz's wallet.

The coach passed through several small villages and farmland and finally entered the ornate gateway to the resort. They drove through an oak-lined alley for half a mile before the coach was swallowed by a dense wood. As it began its ascent up a steep windy road, Franz grew impatient, aggravated by the sudden darkness around him. But when they reached the top, it felt as if the forest had spat them out straight into paradise. Franz's earlier frustration became awe—and Franz was not a man to be impressed easily. The resort stood at a lake the color reminiscent of a black opal. Its surface revealed minimal shades of brighter colors underneath, which changed with every second, as the beholder's point of view shifted. It brooded as if harboring something beneath it—something magical. It almost had a hypnotizing effect on Franz. The building itself seemed something like a European chalet or a castle, and Franz understood why this resort hadn't embraced the American automobile industry yet: this hotel swept its guests back in time.

Franz knew that once again his instincts had proven reliable: this was a gold mine.

And Franz was determined to make it his.

He noticed, with delight, that some parts of the hotel were in serious need of renovation. That could mean that the owner was short on cash — and cash was what Franz had plenty of. He negotiated a deal for a month's stay with full board, which could be renewed at a similar or better rate should he decide to extend his stay. But Franz knew he wouldn't have to.

When Franz made a plan, he would see it through, no matter the obstacles in his way. Even before unpacking, he approached the coachman with a nice sum of money and the request to drive him around so that Franz could explore the land surrounding the Montgomery estate. The coachman readily agreed and offered to take him to a very "special" lake on the other side on the high plateau, called Coxing Pond. Land for sale. What unfolded before Franz's eyes was even more breathtaking than he'd imagined: a turquoise lake larger in size than the lake of Montgomery. With its transparent water, it lacked the mysterious aura of Shadow Lake at the resort, but it made up for that with its crystal beauty; its effect on Franz was no less hypnotizing than the other lake. A closer look at the geography, and Franz realized that the two properties could be joined. And he could create an even bigger paradise situated within easy reach of wealthy New Yorkers. Franz never thought small; he was already a step ahead.

That night, as Franz sat down for the exquisite dinner, he singled out the founder and owner of the place, Montgomery Stockwell. The man's puffy face revealed his vice: there was a man who liked his booze. His hands were shaking ever so slightly, and the sides of his mouth were twitching. Franz never drank. Alcohol clouded the mind.

Later that night, after the guests had gone to bed, Franz approached Mr. Stockwell at the hotel bar and asked him for a game of cards. He wasn't the least bit surprised to see Stockwell's bloodshot eyes light up.

And from then on they would shine brightly every night when Franz shuffled the deck.

During the day, Franz investigated further: he found out that Stockwell harvested hemlock bark for additional income. Three years before, however, he had lost a huge sum of money after a forest fire burned over three hundred acres of his land. One year later, his wife, who had a more astute business sense than he did, died suddenly. Since then Stockwell's debt had grown consistently, as he no longer was able to keep up with the growing costs and demands of the hotel.

It took Franz less than three weeks to force Stockwell into even worse debt. He took his money to Stockwell's bank and made sure at lunch to let the bank manager know about his old client's precarious situation—right in time for the pending credit that Stockwell had asked for. Stockwell had also started borrowing money from local people. Franz hired some local thugs to pay Stockwell a visit, to threaten him should he not pay back the money he owed. And to make matters worse, one small side of the hotel that Stockwell had failed to repair finally collapsed. So Franz knew when his moment had arrived: he offered the weeping Stockwell a less-than-generous offer for three thousand acres of land, the Montgomery lake, and the hotel building itself: one hundred thou- sand dollars, a sum that Stockwell couldn't refuse if he didn't want to end up in prison—or dead.

Stockwell and his children moved out and into a modest house in Stone Ridge; he needed the rest of the money to pay off his debt. Franz, the new king of the castle, was now the one greeting hotel guests upon arrival, cashing in on the steep fees after giving the coachman his meager salary. Even though automobiles were becoming popular, he kept the horse carriage.

Franz then put in his request to Americanize his last name, as nobody in the country could pronounce or spell it correctly. "What should it be?" the officer at the immigration office in

New York City asked Franz. "Make it Montgomery; that is what Mönchinger would translate to," he explained, which was, of course, total rubbish; Montgomery was derived from the French, but Franz was his convincing self and the officer changed Franz's last name forever.

Franz invested more money into urgent renovations, guests left more satisfied than before, and the reputation slowly grew. But Franz was full of plans for the remodeling of the hotel and didn't stop there. He wanted to add a porch with a steep roof at the side of the lake, built of dark wood, which would be a stark contrast to the gray stone of the original core building and the wooden extensions that had been painted in a stark green color. He also needed to repair the roads around the lake so people could stroll along it, and wanted to make the hotel easier to access, so it didn't put off those who feared the journey by horse and carriage from Poughkeepsie, after a long ferry ride. He would turn this place into an even more impressive getaway from New York City! But he also recognized that while he was a very wealthy man, it wouldn't be enough to realize all his plans. One late night, he did the math and realized that he had six more months before he would face a similar fate as his predecessor Stockwell. Franz had never much been tempted by the idea of marriage, but he knew it would be the only way to see through his vision: he needed to find a wife with a wealthy father.

It was early summer when Franz started to throw parties and balls at the hotel, to which he invited the most influential families of the area. He knew it was a risk to be spending the last of his money this way, but big risks reap big rewards. However, none of the families fit the profile: the people whose acquaintance he made were either childless or had only given birth to sons, or their daughters had already been married off.

One month later he received a letter from the Board of Indian Commissioners. The board had written to him because Montgomery Resort was built on sacred ground where once the Paleo-Indians had hunted. The letter asked if the resort could host the next conference for the Friends of the Indians at Montgomery. Franz investigated the members of the Friends of the Indians, as well as the board members of the Indian Commissioners, and concluded that the letter had arrived just in time: why not invite the board as well and have them hold their annual meeting there? This would not only allow Franz to appear in their annual reports, but it would also allow him to attract wealthy individuals with daughters in their prime.

It was the end of August when the day of the conference finally arrived, and with it, prominent women and men from all over the state. Franz was particularly interested in those who had come in search of causes in which to invest their fortunes. One such man was Thomas O'Donald, a real-estate investor turned multimillionaire from New York City. Franz understood O'Donald only minutes into their first conversation. There were two kinds of charity donors—those who really cared with heart and soul, and those who did everything for social standing. O'Donald clearly belonged to the latter. Franz could tell from the way O'Donald's eyes were dancing around the room, the way he held his body, tall and proud. He was all about "see and be seen."

Franz knew exactly how to play O'Donald. He stepped onto the podium of the boardroom to give the opening speech of the conference.

Franz started out by saying how immensely proud he was to be hosting not only this event but also the annual board meeting the following day. Further on, Franz stressed how important it was for a place like Montgomery to embrace the roots of the Americas, the Native Americans. He praised the States for having given him hope and prosperity, and told the typical rags-to-riches story that everyone wanted to hear when they came to the land of unlimited possibility, making it sound like he was a poor man who had worked hard to earn his golden ticket to the promised land. He stressed how much he wanted to thank all immigrants, but especially the Native Americans for having taken such good care of the area's natural beauty, and how he thought he had arrived in paradise when he saw the land. He was careful not to mention Stockwell.

Franz continued that it was wrong to isolate Native Americans on reservations—which earned him cheers all around the room. His speech was working well and as intended. Franz's eyes wandered over to O'Donald, and he could see that he was nodding, satisfied. Franz's moment had arrived. "Ladies and Gentlemen," he said, "let me be clear here, and honest, because I feel we are all among friends, family, like-minded people: we are indebted to the Indians, and conservation should rank highest on our agenda. The conservation of their indigenous arts and handicrafts." The room roared with applause. "We need to create a fund to help grant legal protection to the Pueblos, the Pimas, and the Alaskan natives, and I herewith reveal my plan to open foundations to support the arts in Oklahoma and New Mexico. And aside from cultural support, we need to provide them with direct medical benefits. I hope for everyone's financial support to make this possible." People started applauding again, but Franz's voice rose one more time: "Health," he shouted, "equal opportunity, and full civil rights—these, ladies and gentlemen, are the words I am leaving you with, to have a successful day here at the Montgomery Resort. And an equally successful board meeting tomorrow. I will see you for dinner." His exit from the podium was accompanied by cheers, as various attendees stepped forward to shake his hand.

After dinner, Thomas O'Donald asked if he could have a private word. Franz took his arm gently, and guided him into the cigar lounge, motioning to one of the waitresses for a bottle of port wine.

"Your words have touched me deeply, Mr. Montgomery," he said. "And I would love to be the first and biggest donor for your foundations."

Franz raised a glass. "I feel honored that you share my hope and belief in the cause." The glasses clinked.

There was, of course, an additional reason Franz had singled out Thomas O'Donald among all the others: he had only one daughter, who would be the sole heir of his fortune.

"Why don't you come back next weekend? I shall send a car down to New York City to pick you and your family up, and please be my guest for the weekend, and then you and I can discuss plans."

"Oh, that would only be my daughter and me, then."

Franz knew well that O'Donald was a widower. "Splendid. I'll see to it that the car picks you up next Friday?"

Franz and the resort enjoyed high status, and he knew the invitation would give O'Donald another topic to brag about in his social gatherings.

"I would be delighted," O'Donald said, and they returned to the dining hall.

Franz only approached the bar when he was sure everyone else had retired to the rooms—except the barkeep and a gorgeous woman he had noticed earlier during the conference who was awaiting him eagerly. Yes, Franz always made sure he got what he wanted.

When the car, the latest Ford model, drove up, Franz's face didn't betray any emotions, but inside he was nervous. His future bride would exit that car. He'd found out that O'Donald had been married to a French woman, and he hoped that his daughter had inherited the French genes and not her father's Irish ones; he wasn't fond of ginger women.

O'Donald climbed out the front and opened a back door for his daughter before the driver had the chance to walk around the car. Franz's face fell when he saw her. Not only was she a redhead, but she was a rather unfortunate blend of the worst genes of the Irish and French: she had the plump figure of Irish girls, and a French nose that was a bit too long. She had the white skin of the Irish, her face peppered with red freckles, and her lips were French, but way too small for her large face. She would prove a challenge—not one Franz Montgomery would not be able to overcome. He was very well aware that his financial situation didn't give him the luxury to wait any longer. So he straightened up and welcomed O'Donald like a long lost friend, and his daughter like the woman of his dreams.

That night Franz dined with the two by the lake, serving them the best items on the menu: oysters, foie gras, caviar. He noticed that Florence, O'Donald's daughter, was quite taken with him. That night he made an exception and drank, as there was no way he could pass a decent attempt at flirting convincingly with her without the sweet intoxication of alcohol. Half an hour after the coffee had been served, O'Donald got up from his seat and excused himself for bed. Franz was surprised when O'Donald indicated to Florence to stay; there was no reason to break up such a pleasant night. Then he threw Franz an ever so slightly encouraging look and left the two on their own. Florence seemed delighted but extremely nervous. Franz went to work. Inebriated from the alcohol, he took her out to the lake, to a spot where none of the other hotel guests could see them. Florence was about five years older than him, and he was sure there had been numerous suitors keen on her fortune. But O'Donald was a smart man, and he must have seen through all of them.

Franz extended his arm and softly caressed her back. She smiled shyly, leaning into him, and then offered her tiny mouth. Her empty stomach had left her with stale breath, and he remembered that she had hardly touched her food, probably too nervous to eat. Good God, he thought, and imagined the waitress he was having an affair with. Her perky breasts, luscious lips, her tongue. And then he placed a long kiss on Florence's mouth.

Only half a year later, Florence and Franz would marry, at Montgomery, of course. He invited politicians, the press, everyone within ninety miles with power and influence, hoping guests would talk the place up among their friends.

This, in turn, would bring the resort a new clientele of the utmost reputation and class.

After a lavish celebration that the region would talk about for months, the moment Franz had long dreaded arrived. Florence had been raised Catholic, and Franz had been more than happy to comply with her wish to wait to consummate their union. For the two weeks leading up to the wedding, Franz had only seen his mistress once, so that he might be able to stay aroused when he saw Florence naked for the first time. When they made love that night, it took all of three minutes.

O'Donald had already given Franz a more-than-generous donation for the Indian "foundations," and gifted a sizable sum for their wedding. Now that Franz had enough to execute his plans, he added the porch overlooking the cliffs opposite the hotel and the Paltz Point above. The latest addition looked as he had imagined: like a chalet from the Alps, with a long balustrade and numerous rocking chairs the color of mahogany. He had built the porch right where the breeze was guided between the cliffs, facilitating natural air-conditioning and relief from the heat for guests as they rocked away in their chairs and shed the stress of the city. Construction of a whole new hotel wing and a boat dock for the lake was also in full operation. He had added a beach to the lake, with palapas, so-called "Swiss Villages," on each side. He was in the process of deforesting a great part of the property to create a golf course for the coming year, and a lavish garden. He had listened to the hotel guests and knew what he needed to do to raise prices at Montgomery.

Over the next couple of years, Franz admitted to himself that he had grown fond of Florence. He still didn't find her any more attractive than on the day he had first met her, but he had come to learn that Florence had other qualities. Behind her dull facade was a woman who had surprised him with an astute business sense and exquisite taste and had proven herself to be an excellent sparring partner who understood Franz's vision. She was also a skilled woodcarver with an extraordinary eye for woodwork, which helped Franz execute his ideas for more extensions in the most adequate and cost-efficient ways. She contributed quality and creative ideas for how to make the business as self-sufficient as possible. She started to farm vegetables and fruits, and the leftovers from the hotel restaurants were fed to their livestock, which would be sold in town. The animal fat was used to produce soap, serving the hotel's kitchen and laundry needs. She had also suggested that the hotel produce its own power so they could be more self-reliant during the strong winters.

It was the year 1917 when Florence proudly announced that she was pregnant. Franz was delighted: this would mean another generous sum of money from O'Donald, which he could use after the spending of the past couple of years. O'Donald was upset with Florence for working so hard during her pregnancy, but Franz repeatedly assured him that he would make sure she got enough rest, before distracting him with photos from the "numerous" foundations O'Donald's money was supporting.

In November, Florence's labor had commenced. In preparation for the baby, Franz had turned a section of the first floor into their residential wing, which offered the best view of the lake and cliffs. The doctor and two female staff members were there preparing for birth. Franz retreated into the anteroom, plunged down into one of the armchairs, and listened to the cries of pain emanating from inside the room as he held Maria's hand; his mistress at that time was one of the very few people he regularly confided in.

After five hours of agonized screams, one of the servants brought out a bundle and placed it in Franz's arm.

"A boy," he whispered, tears forming in his eyes. "Can I see her, now?" But then a new wave of pain sent Florence into another frenzy.

"No, not yet, sir. You're lucky. You'll be having another one!"

The second birth wasn't as easy as the first; the baby was stuck. Franz was still holding Maria's hand as they overheard the doctor's instructions inside. At one point, everything went quiet, and Franz asked himself what the inheritance rule would be if Florence died, but he immediately stopped that thought. Of course, it would go to him, or his son. As he looked up, he saw Maria staring at him and wondered if he had said his thoughts out loud. Another scream cut through the night. But it was different. More horrifying. As Franz jumped up from his seat, one of the receptionists came rushing into the antechamber. "Mr. Montgomery!" she bellowed. "Mr. O'Donald is downstairs waiting to see you. He's a bit hysterical."

For those few privy to witness the spectacle that day, it was one of the most memorable occasions in Montgomery's history. A rare moment in which the Franz Montgomery had been completely taken off guard.

Franz collided with his red-faced father-in-law in the doorway to the antechamber.

"A 'friend'"—O'Donald made quotation marks with his fingers as Franz pushed him into the hallway—"just came back from a long trip to New Mexico."

Franz grew pale.

"Well, guess what? There is *no* foundation!"

Franz had hoped his father-in-law wouldn't live long enough to find out. He cast a nervous glance in the direction of the bedroom. "Let's go to the cigar lounge and talk there, Father."

"Father! FATHER!" he screamed. "What I have to say," and he looked to the servants and receptionist hovering in the door to the antechamber, "everyone should hear! You are what we call scum in America!"

Franz again tried to take O'Donald's arm, but his father-in-law brushed him off.

"Don't you dare touch me with your filthy fingers! You'll pay me back my money, you hear me? Every single cent. And I will make sure you're finished!"

"But," said Franz slowly, remaining calm, "You need to keep in mind your daughter's happiness."

"I'll make sure she finds someone she deserves."

Franz looked at him. "She just gave birth to a healthy baby boy."

O'Donald seemed to forget about his rage, and pushed past Franz back toward the antechamber.

A servant took O'Donald into the adjacent nursing room and pointed at a little cradle: there he was, the little fellow, dressed in fine light-blue clothes, looking up at his grandfather.

"Where is my daughter?" he demanded.

The servant threw him a sad look. "Has something happened to her?"

She shook her head and motioned for him to follow. He entered the bedroom, where Florence was lying in bed, sobbing uncontrollably.

"There, there, "O'Donald said, trying to console her. "I heard this can be quite normal after birth."

O'Donald motioned for the servant to leave.

"We've been punished, Father." Everyone in the ante-chamber could overhear what Florence said.

O'Donald now spoke tenderly. "You've been blessed with a healthy baby boy!"

She started crying again. "No, father, we pay for our sins."

"What are you talking about?" O'Donald asked.

Another series of heartbreaking sobs filled the room.

The door opened, and a very pale O'Donald entered the anteroom, coming face-to-face with Franz.

"You..." He closed his mouth, opened it again, but was unable to produce more words. He looked like a fish on land, gasping for air as he clutched his chest and collapsed onto the floor.

But what was it that killed O'Donald in the end? Was it "only" the horrible truth he had uncovered about his son-in-law? Or was there something else? What was the sin Florence had spoken about? And what had he seen in the room that made him look like he had seen the devil himself when he exited the room? Whatever it was, O'Donald took the knowledge to his grave.

It wasn't rare to see Franz meander through the hallways late at night: either after a long session at the cigar lounge with an important guest, on his way to or from one of his lovers, or simply looking at the photos in the hallways, always with a self-assured smile on his face.

That night, however, Franz was seen with a deeply worried expression on his face, as he exited the basement and wandered the long hallways, all night, until he returned to the bedroom before dawn.

Florence's wailing that followed shortly afterward reverberated throughout the entire building, piercing the hearts of everyone in the hotel and beyond.

One week later, Franz took Florence to a new garden beneath the large window of the nursery. There, he presented his wife a white statue, with a smiling angel atop that looked up to Hans's nursery.

"This is where it is buried, Florence." He whispered to his wife.

Florence's stare was ice-cold as she looked at him. "Don't you dare call him that. His name is Nicolas."

Franz nodded patiently. "A beautiful name. Nicolas will always look up to his brother and you in the nursery." He had come closer to her, supporting her in her fragile state. She had just buried her father as well, and the woman was overcome with grief. But Florence pushed Franz away and fell down on her knees, patting the soil in front of the statue, shaking as she wept.

"So you didn't even put up a cross?" she said after a

while, her voice raised to a dangerous shrill. Franz looked nervously over at the gardeners around them. "Like I told you, only the two of us will know," he pressed through clenched teeth, and before she could say anything more, he pulled her up and opened his arms wide. But she didn't allow him the embrace. Instead she made a step back. "Franz, that nursery will remain Nicolas's. We will move out of there as soon as possible. I won't be able to forget him, ever, but I don't need more reminders of what we—or you—did." That would be the last time Florence would ever mention the mysterious sin again, wrapping it in yet another shroud of riddles and suspicion.

The next morning, Franz fired the two servants who had helped with the birthing, the receptionist, and his mistress Maria— the latter with a heavy heart. He paid them each a sizable severance package; he was sure they'd understand they were a constant reminder to his wife of that fatal day and loss. In reality, however, they left with the clear "understanding" that no stories about O'Donald's visit would leave Montgomery. And one would never cross Franz Montgomery.

Franz did what his wife had asked and built a separate house adjacent to the main building, providing the family more privacy. In fact, he had been happy about her demand: this would also make space in the former residential wings for more guest rooms. Little Hans was an absolute delight and gave Florence the distraction she needed to cope with the tragedy. She threw herself back into the business with an unprecedented energy whenever Hans slept. One day Hans would be able to enjoy and take over the fruits of their hard labor.

Still, Franz was sometimes seen, late at night, walking along the lake, his shoulders slumped, his head down. Then he would straighten up and would look around nervously, scanning the dark forest around Shadow Lake, looking as if someone—or something—was haunting him. Most people attributed it to the increased stress of business, now that he had a child to provide for.

The reason why Franz had supposedly left Germany had turned into reality: the same year that Hans was born, America entered the Great War, "the war to end all wars." There were fewer guests now that the whole nation was in turmoil. He and Florence tried to maintain a faithful clientele that would help with the high costs of maintaining the estate, and they were seen spending more time with each other, smiling through inexpensive events launched for their most loyal guests. And one could have suspected that the recent losses had helped to heal their sad marriage. But the opposite was the case: Florence had moved out of their bedroom and shared the nursery with little Hans, and other than for business matters, she barely glanced at her husband. All of which gave Franz the carte blanche to build a healthy sex life once again within the walls of Montgomery. Some nights, however, Florence would spend in the former residential wing, embellishing and decorating the old nursery in what some witnesses described as a "trancelike state."

Florence and Franz managed to pull the estate through the recession in 1920, but the postwar era posed new challenges. Franz had heard that many other resorts were closing down because they had lost their appeal; they were a thing of the past, a reflection on a period in history that many people didn't want to remember. Franz and Florence introduced additional sports activities in winter, when the hotel usually was closed for a couple of months, and guests kept coming, though not as abundantly as in the past.

Franz still followed the dream that had formed when he set foot in this country. If business continued like that he would not be able to ever make it come true. It kept them afloat for almost a decade, but then the Depression hit in 1929, and with it, economic uncertainties and financial failures. Many loyal guests stopped visiting, and it was difficult to attract a new and equally influential and wealthy clientele: a vacation in a resort hotel was not on top of the list for most Americans.

For Franz and Florence and the business, it was now all about mere survival. People no longer came in the winter, and Franz and Florence had to let go of many staff members, increasing their own already substantial workload. Florence focused on streamlining the farm and sale of produce from their land, increasing the additional albeit very meager income. And slowly but surely, both of them grew depressed. The Montgomery Resort they had known had died, and they didn't have the financial means to usher in a new era.

Their only joy was their son, Hans, who had grown into a fine adolescent. Luckily he had inherited his father's looks—tall, broad-shouldered, and blond. Since his birth, Florence and Franz had been doing something that many other Americans had chosen not to at that time, hoping to assimilate more quickly into American culture. Franz, however, taught Hans German songs and spoke to him in German—and Florence did the same in French, as she had been brought up bilingual. The boy was fluent in German, French, and English, which would come in handy one day when the resort built up its international clientele.

Hans, however, had not inherited his parents' business sense. Starting early on in childhood, it became clear that Hans's interest was in literature and nature, and not in the hospitality business. Whenever they held social events, Hans would either hide somewhere in the woods or in the hotel with a good book. Florence and Franz blamed themselves that he had turned out to be somewhat of a hermit. Being hoteliers meant working all the time, and they felt they had neglected the boy, had left him alone too often in the name of business.

It was the year 1936, when a man named Albert Goldberg

showed up at the hotel wanting to meet with Franz. It turned out that Mr. Goldberg—who had fled Nazi Germany with a fortune in his back pocket—had not only discovered Franz's turquoise lake, he had already bought it as part of a project to build a more modern hotel, one that would offer a different form of leisure and a more affordable stay to post-Depression citizens. Albert was interested in Franz's land. Albert had discovered what Franz had on his first day in the region: the lakes could be perfectly combined, as they both sat on the high plateau, which would make construction of a road along the ridge of the mountain fairly easy. This would help to turn the territory into an even bigger nature preserve that would offer activities like hiking, biking, and rock climbing.

What Albert was planning was to invade his neighbor's land.

Franz was devastated. Not only did this mean the death of the Montgomery; it also meant the death of his decades-long dream to own the turquoise lake. A lake that he now longed to own more than ever, yearning for the soothing effect of the crystal clear color of its water. He required the same degree of transparency in his life. Shadow Lake had once mesmerized him with its magic, allowing his mind to relax. Over the years, however, its magic had turned into something more sinister, and Franz couldn't help but feel a certain sense of foreboding whenever he stood at its shore, staring, as if asking the opaque water for a solution to his predicament.

To make matters worse, Goldberg was aware of Franz's precarious financial situation and offered a less-than-appropriate price. Franz felt cornered—much in the same way that he had cornered Stockwell after his arrival in America all those years ago.

But Franz wasn't ready to give up, and he looked into Goldberg's family. It turned out that Goldberg had a daughter, Elisa, the same age as Hans. So after a week he had a new proposal for Goldberg: let's combine forces and marry our children.

Franz invited Albert and his family over for dinner. Albert's daughter was gorgeous, Franz thought greedily. Both fathers realized that Elisa was absolutely taken with Franz's handsome boy. Hans, on the other hand, was more reserved, and Franz dismissed his attitude as shyness.

Franz started to plan the wedding nevertheless. Hans would come around, he was certain. "Where do you think the reception should be held?" he would ask his wife, hoping they'd find another topic to talk about aside from the stress of business.

But Florence simply shook her head. "I am not helping to lay the foundations of yet another loveless marriage."

"I learned to love you over the years."

A mocking laugh escaped Florence's mouth. "Love is not something you learn, Franz. And, well, now that we're talking about it, I will put it in your words: I have learned to fall out of love with you, Franz."

During the next two years, times became even tougher for Franz: people were buying farmland all around the estate, threatening to minimize the appeal of Montgomery's isolation. His greatest hope was still Hans, who was approaching his twenty-first birthday. Elisa's love for Hans seemed to have only grown over the years. His love, on the other hand, had not. He was working with his parents in the business, but only half-heartedly. He had become an introverted young man, quiet and kind. And all he wanted to do was study.

But Franz would have none of that.

And so Hans's and Franz's despair grew with every month that went by. None of them had ever been seen more depressed than during that time.

And then came Roosevelt and, along with him, change. Up to the present, people fail to understand what exactly it was that caused the change. What is known is that the president booked the biggest suite at Montgomery in spring of 1938, which lightened Franz's mood considerably: the president's visit and the media attention were invaluable to the reputation of the hotel. It is also known that on the first day of the president's visit Hans was called into the suite, where the president and Hans conversed for several hours. Those who saw Hans after that conversation that day saw a young, proud man, his eyes glowing. He looked more blissful than he had ever looked before. However, Franz's good spirit seemed to have evaporated during his own private meeting with Roosevelt, following Hans's, and Franz looked ashen as he came out of the suite. What he announced bitterly at the end of another tense week at the hotel surprised everyone, including Albert Goldberg and his daughter: His son would leave for California, where he would study science on a scholarship from the president himself. Franz was stunned but compliant; Florence looked as sad as a mother can look when a son leaves the house, but also very proud.

There was not a trace of pride in Franz's eyes.

Florence cried the most when the driver picked up Hans at the hotel. "You promise me you'll write?"

Their son nodded his head.

"And you promise me you'll take care of yourself?" He again nodded but looked away quickly.

While Florence hugged him tightly, Franz was more distant. He hadn't forgiven his son for accepting the scholarship, even though Hans had declared that he would indeed agree to the marriage after all, but that he needed those years away. But what Franz had especially not forgiven Hans for was denying him one favor: to stay at least over the summer and help in the hotel, until classes started. Franz had hoped that another summer in the woods of his beloved Montgomery would convince his son to stay behind after all, and marry Elisa already. But Hans had shaken his head and explained that he was acting upon the president's wishes. That shut Franz up.

"I hope you know what you're doing," Franz said simply next to a sobbing Florence, and turned around before the car left.

Shortly after Roosevelt's visit, a new law was passed that allowed for the state to "donate" certain land to the owner, granting the conservation of such land. The remaining land around Montgomery Resort that had not been bought up was donated to Franz Montgomery by the state as a trust, which enlarged his land by a considerable amount.

It was known that Roosevelt loved the Hudson Valley, in whose heart the resort sat, and hence the new law and donation seemed nothing unusual—and still, people couldn't shake the feeling that somehow there was a connection between Roosevelt's visit, the donation, and Hans's departure for California.

One of the unsolved mysteries in the family history...

Albert was more than disgruntled. How long was his daughter supposed to wait for Hans now that he left for California? Franz soothed him, telling him that Hans would be back for good after his studies and marry Elisa. "And," he said, with a jovial slap on Albert's back, "now my territory has just increased considerably!"

Hans didn't keep his promise to write regularly. In fact, he hardly wrote at all. He wrote his family one letter in which he informed them that he would not visit for Christmas. Elisa occasionally called on Franz and Florence. To Franz's relief, Elisa was waiting for Hans.

Hans did come home for Christmas after all. But he was different. He had always stuck to himself, but now he was more serious and closed off than before. Elisa came to see him as soon as she found out that he was back, but he brushed her off, this time with determination. Albert approached Franz and renewed his offer, as it was obvious the marriage wouldn't happen; still, Franz stalled him.

Hans had turned into a stranger, and it was increasingly hard to get through to him. People wondered what had happened to him back in California. The only one who got through to him was Florence. Franz ignored his son's obviously distraught state of mind and kept pushing him relentlessly to marry Elisa, from the minute Hans had set foot in the resort after his return from the West Coast. But Hans simply ignored his father's pleas.

When World War II broke out, a growing number of guests simply stayed away—and Franz grew desperate, and mad. He'd always had a temper, but nobody had ever seen him this furious. Staff members would stay out of his way as much as possible.

Franz knew he could achieve whatever he wanted, but he didn't know how to change Hans's mind. He could threaten to disinherit his son, but he knew Hans simply wouldn't care. And one night, after Franz had finished another round of bookkeeping, he ran into Hans, who had returned from the woods. There was an altercation, and Franz struck his son for the first time ever. Servants still swear that a murder would have happened if it hadn't been for Florence's intervention. After Franz was heard snoring drunkenly in his bed later that night, Florence and Hans left the hotel. Florence returned the next morning, without Hans, and with a much calmer expression on her face.

"Where is he?" Franz demanded to know from her, as he had been waiting for her in the main entrance of their house, mad with rage.

"He is in safety," she explained with a calm expression on her face. "Safe from you," she hissed as she brushed past him.

Nothing much changed in the next couple of years. Elisa continued waiting for Hans, who had begged Florence to keep his whereabouts a secret. And Florence kept her promise. Franz lied to Elisa—and everyone else for that matter—that Hans had gone back to California to finish his studies, even though he had no idea where Florence had taken him. But he didn't fail to repeat to her what Hans had said to his father before his first departure: that he would marry Elisa as soon as he had finished his studies.

Only his sadness at seeing Florence was greater than the anger at his son. She had changed over the past years; her soul had broken. And he blamed Hans and his refusal to undertake his responsibility, as their only son, to rescue Montgomery.

It was the evening of Florence's birthday in February of 1942 when Franz again complained loudly about their son's absence.

"It's not him, Franz."

"How can he leave us and the business hanging like this, year after year. We need him! You're the only one who knows where he is. Why don't you tell me where he is?" He shouted in desperation."

"I don't know where Hans is, Franz!" "What do you mean?"

She shook her head. "He is no longer in the place where I took him. He left a while ago. All I found from him was a letter, saying that he had to take care of something, that I'd understand. He promised he'd be back, and that from then on everything would be fine." She smiled through her tears. "*Mon petit Hans.*"

"And you believe that fool?" He got up from his seat, paced around. "You know what I think? He never went to California in the first place! Something else is going on!"

Florence slowly shook her head. "Stop blaming Hans for the errors we've made. This has nothing to do with Hans." She had summoned all her energy to raise her voice one more time, tears shimmering in her eyes. "I've never overcome that loss. We paid such a high price for what you did, Franz!"

"We could have..." Franz said.

Florence laughed bitterly. "A marriage like ours never carries more than one fruit. All I want is for Hans to be happy."

When Franz emerged from his bedroom early the next morning, he was pale as a ghost and sank down onto his knees in front of the first staff member he crossed paths with in the long hallway. "My Florence," he wept, over and over again, clutching the man's legs. "My beloved Florence!" The staff member carefully untangled Franz's arms around his knees and entered the bedroom. There he found Florence, lying dead in bed. Her heart had simply stopped beating, the doctor declared later. She had departed peacefully, he added. But everyone knew that she had died of a broken heart.

They buried her one week later. It surprised Franz himself how much he was mourning the loss of his wife—and how much he had come to love her over the years. And he noticed something else: he missed Hans. He still hadn't forgiven him. But Hans was all he had left now.

His son returned seven months later. Hans's already pain-stricken face worsened when he heard about his mother's death, and Franz hugged his long lost son. But he barely recognized Hans. He had already changed considerably during his first stay in California. But now he seemed a different person altogether. Empty eyes looked out from a bearded face. He answered mechanically and never spoke unless addressed. Some suspected that this time he had finally lost his mind out in California. He looked as if he had stared death in the face, it was rumored in town. How would Elisa feel about him now?

It turned out that Franz needn't worry about her. Elisa was the only one who didn't notice a change—or simply didn't want to notice it. She was charmed more than ever by his handsome looks; he was even leaner than before, and whatever it was that had broken his soul had lent his face a new depth and character that made him appear even more mysterious.

To everyone's surprise, the marriage to Elisa was announced only two days after Hans's return. Should the resort be named Turquoise Montgomery or Montgomery Turquoise? Or should they change the name altogether? Albert and Franz had a hard time agreeing on that matter, but what they did agree on was that this place would become the most unique on the East Coast. The wedding would take place at the small chapel on the premises of the Montgomery Resort, and then there would be a champagne reception at the Turquoise Lake Resort, followed by dinner at the Montgomery Resort, where everyone would be taken by horse carriage along the ridge.

Half a year later, Hans stood at the altar waiting for his future wife, who was led in by Albert in a stunning eggshell-colored dress and an ornately stitched veil. A woman in the choir loft sang "Ave Maria," and Hans's eyes glistened with tears. The guests were moved at this sight, hoping that his marriage to the wonderful Elisa, a woman who loved him so deeply, would change him.

During the ceremony everyone noticed that the groom had a hard time concentrating. When the pastor asked the question of all questions, Hans's mind seemed to be elsewhere. The embarrassing silence that spread through the church was interrupted only by Elisa's frantic words. "Hans? Hans? Say something!" The pastor repeated the question, "Do you, Hans Montgomery, take Elisa as your lawful wife...?" But the groom didn't even let him finish the sentence:

"Yes, I do." Hans slid the ring onto Elisa's finger, the way one would put a hoof on a horse, and ran out of the church without his bride. Total chaos erupted in the church as Elisa fainted at the altar.

Franz and Albert calmed down the guests and walked them over to the reception. "Nerves," they said. "They're so young."

But Franz was furious. This was a disaster. It had turned

into a Montgomery wedding that people would talk about forever, but for all the wrong reasons!

After half an hour, Hans marched into the reception, grabbed his father by the arm, and dragged him away from the guests' curious eyes and ears. They returned five minutes later, Franz pale as a sheet, and Hans trembling with rage.

The rest of the afternoon went by without any other uncomfortable interruptions. In the late afternoon the wedding party rode back to Montgomery, to an outside area by the lake, which also offered an adjacent dance floor by the water, and a band. Dinner was served and the mood was jolly again—until the first dance. The groom was a great dancer, swirling his bride around gracefully. But then, mid-dance, he stopped and stared out into the night, squinting hard at the opposite shore with those mad eyes. And once again he rushed out, leaving an embarrassed bride behind. Albert and Franz ran after him, followed by the once again sobbing bride, red with shame.

It was a full moon and they didn't have to scan the area for long to find Hans on the boat deck. Franz and Albert were furious, and Elisa looked devastated. Hans looked up at his wife, reached out for her hand, and squeezed it. "I am sorry."

The rest of the celebration went by uneventfully.

The next day, when Elisa woke up in the Roosevelt Suite (they had changed the name to honor their presidential guest), her husband was gone. When he finally emerged out of the woods after several days, he declared to his father publicly and for everyone to hear that he would never speak to him ever again, and he kept that promise.

Hans stopped talking after that, and only "conversed" with nature, as many claimed when they caught a glimpse of him in the woods, some fearful of this man that had become a recluse. He took over the nature trust, turned it into a preserve, and delivered invaluable research in botany over the years. But as successful as his research was, just as unsuccessful was his marriage. As Elisa's smile was replaced with sadness and resignation, people suspected that Hans mistreated her.

Elisa threw herself into the hotel business with the same passion and ferocity that Franz and Florence had so many decades before, and so Franz took Elisa under his wing (and, some suspected, into his bed).

Albert died of a heart attack shortly after World War II had ended, and Franz consoled Elisa day and night. She fell pregnant only a month after her father's death, which brought her the happiness that she had longed for. Her cheeks were rosy, her features joyful with the anticipation of her child.

It was in July of 1946 that she gave birth to a boy, William. Elisa's wounds seemed to have healed, and while Hans was mostly absent, it was Franz and Elisa who brought up the boy. He grew into an eager, ambitious boy who, to everyone's relief, hadn't inherited any of Hans's traits (most likely because he hadn't fathered the child), but had gained Elisa's astute business sense. William also inherited Franz's insatiable lust for women, and for years the resort was known for having good-looking staff members, almost all of them female. However, William turned out to be less careful than Franz had been, and so he impregnated two women over the course of ten years. The first pregnancy resulted in Edgar, born in 1964, and ten years later in Benjamin. Both mothers greedily gave their unwanted children up for adoption when they heard the sum Franz Montgomery himself was willing to pay to keep the children for himself.

Other than William's sexual escapades, those decades would register as rather uneventful in the Montgomery history books: Franz took to Edgar, who also took after Franz and his father, while Benjamin was Elisa's delight. The older he got, the more he resembled Hans, still Elisa's true love after all. Hans, like Elisa, took a delight in the boy and was always seen playing with him on those rare occasions he set foot in the hotel.

It was the first of March, 1985, Franz's hundredth birthday, when Franz left the hotel in the morning and headed for the woods, clearly equipped for a longer journey. Even at that age he was in great shape and had been blessed with good health, but something had started to ail him and he had developed certain traits not known to him before. He had become sentimental and melancholic, and was often seen with red-rimmed eyes. Everyone suspected that he suffered from the fact that his only son (or eldest son) wasn't talking to him, and that he hadn't been able to make peace. He would often repeat to staff members what Florence had said to him shortly before her death, a haunted expression on his face: "I am paying for my sins, late in life, but I am paying for them after all."

When Franz still hadn't returned three days later, a sobbing Elisa was seen racing off in her convertible, in a mad rush to find Franz and bring him back. But her drive ended badly: she slid off a dirt road and collided head-on with a tree. Back in the hospital they could only save one leg; the other one was so severely damaged that she would never walk properly again.

Hans was the one who carried Franz out of the woods days later and into the hotel. The town would gossip for months about that day: Elisa and William were outside greeting new guests when they saw Hans approach, Franz in his arms. Elisa limped over, sustained on her golden cane, which would soon become her trademark. She collapsed onto the ground as she cradled the dead Franz in her arms and kissed his cold face.

After a while she looked up and screamed at Hans that he was a murderer, cursing him for having killed his own father and the only man who had ever truly loved her.

For the first time in years, Hans spoke to Elisa, and his words became hotel lore. Quietly, but still loud enough for everyone to hear, he said, "I've committed many crimes, one of them marrying a woman I would never be able to love. But if you knew the crime my father committed, then you, too, as a mother, would have despised him as much as I did."

# Maya
# Day 4

Maya lay in her dark room for hours, staring at the ceiling, the booklet on her lap. Why did the librarian have it? Why had she given it to *Maya*? She turned her head toward the window; it was pitch black outside. She would need to wait until the morning to set out and find her, Paula. Maya closed her eyes to find sleep, but she was too agitated. In her mind she replayed the day she arrived. *The remains they found in the landslide were your grandmother's?* Paula had asked. She remembered the way Paula's eyes had lingered. She had been nervous, a bit strange. Or was it just playing out like that in Maya's imagination after an exhausting few days?

She tossed and turned in bed. The demanding cries of a baby next door were oddly comforting; she wasn't the only one having trouble sleeping. She heard the shushing sounds from one of the parents, which failed to have any effect.

Her thoughts wandered back to Paula. What else had Paula said when she gave her the booklet? She had said it was a *historical guide*.

*It's much better than the others*, Paula had said. Had Paula also slid the fairy tale under her door?

And then, suddenly, the baby was quiet. And its cries were replaced by different cries. Cries that came from the woods. They sounded like a group of women screaming, outside in the darkness of the night. And the screams got louder and more aggressive; they were coming closer, encircling the hotel. And the closer they came, the clearer the sounds became. Then Maya realized that the sounds came from a pack of coyotes. She sat up, giving up on sleep. The coyotes sounded famished for food, for helpless prey that would fill their empty stomachs. And then the baby began to cry again—but this time the cries sounded different. The child had changed its tune. While the baby's cries before had been the pleading cry for sleep that simply would not come, this time, it was a pleading for help, for company, a message from one mammal to the next. The baby cried for a bit and stopped as suddenly as it had begun, awaiting the coyotes' response. And when they did reply, they, too, had changed their tune: it now resembled a call that carried a promise, a promise that they would help the helpless mammal in the night. She remembered the tales about wolves who'd raised a baby found in the woods among themselves, instead of letting Darwinism rule over their animal kingdom. Now they had come to look for the infant, to rescue it. The baby started again, almost sending a melody out into the dark. And the wild beasts outside echoed its pleading, getting more and more desperate, getting closer and closer. Their screams were almost deafening, overriding the baby's cries.

And then there was utter silence.

Maya felt him in the room before she actually saw him— the faceless man from the woods. He hovered right next to her bed, the flat surface of his face turned in her direction. She pressed her eyes shut, hoping he'd go away. And when she opened them again, he was no longer standing there. She slowly scanned the room and found him facing the door, silently waiting for her. When she got up, he opened the door and turned left, soundlessly striding into the hallway. She followed. In the silence of the night, her own steps made too much noise, and she tried to tiptoe. The man had disappeared behind the corner of the hallway ahead of her, and she quickened her pace. She turned right, and caught sight of him at the other end. He was waiting for her at the entrance to the narrow hallway. When she entered she noticed that it had been lined with a thick carpet that made it difficult for her to move, its thickness threatening to swallow her, just like the gooey mush had in the forest. She advanced and stepped through the door—and straight into the woods.

The coyotes were there, watching her from behind the trees with their cold blue eyes. In the middle was the baby, attached to the nipple of one of the wolves, feeding. Maya started running, fell, picked herself up again. The coyotes were on her heels, close. Growling. And then they vanished as she stepped into the clearing. The faceless man was already there, hovering in front of her, waiting, his back turned toward her. Over his shoulder, she made out Grandmother sitting on the ground in the middle of it, with her back also turned toward Maya. She was surrounded by the characters from the fairy tale, who now turned around to stare at the faceless man and her as they stepped farther into the clearing. Still with his back toward her, the faceless man raised his arm and pointed with his index finger in the direction of the woods behind the clearing, the direction of the dangerous swamp. Grandmother turned around and broke into a smile when she spotted the faceless man. And then his head snapped around, only his faceless head, to look straight into Maya's eyes. She closed her eyes, not willing to face the horrible sight again. And when she finally dared to open them again, she saw Grandmother and the fairy-tale characters had gotten up and were now standing at the edge of an abyss. Maya tried in vain to open her mouth and warn them. Instead, she had to watch helplessly as they all jumped off the cliff and into the deadly swamp—and landed with a terrible, terminal thud.

Maya woke up with a jolt. It had begun to rain again, the heavy drops hammering against the windows. She felt the urge to get out of the room, the hotel, as quickly as possible.

Maya felt awful from her nightmare and the lack of sleep.

Her vision was still slightly blurred as she drove down the windy road in her rental car.

It was past 9:00 A.M. by the time she arrived at the library, and she had to wait for an hour in the car until a woman hurried through the rain across the parking lot toward the building, keys in hand.

"Is Paula working today?" Maya couldn't wait any longer, not even until they were dry and inside.

The woman gave her a puzzled look. "Hang on," she said, fumbling with the keys.

"I need to speak to her," Maya repeated, right on the heels of the woman.

The librarian now seemed irritated by her insistence.

"It's urgent," Maya quickly added. "Something personal."

"Paula doesn't work on Saturdays."

"Do you know where she lives?"

The woman assessed Maya, the deep shadows under her eyes. Her uncombed hair. She slowly shook her head. "I'll let her know you were looking for her."

Maya left her name and cell number.

She was about to back out of her space when she saw two men walk behind her car through the parking lot. Maya faced forward again, instinctively studying them in the rearview mirror. It was still raining, but she recognized Edgar and another man dressed in a uniform. They shook hands, and Edgar mounted a motorbike, his exaggerated posture treating the bike like a Harley—while in reality it was nothing more than a glorified scooter. His companion waited for Edgar to drive off.

Then the uniformed man headed for another car down the street.

A police car.

Maya drove around town in utter frustration. How else could she get in touch with Paula? She scanned the streets for her—maybe she was shopping at the small grocery store for the weekend—but there was no sign of her. Maya even contemplated the idea of asking a passerby—after all this was a small community—but due to the rain few were out and about. When she spotted a man walking his dog, she slowed the car and rolled down her window. He stopped, but as soon as Maya saw his facial expression—which was not dissimilar to how Paula's colleague had looked at her—she knew she wouldn't get lucky. And his brisk rejection when asked about Paula did not fill her with more optimism that others would react any differently. She turned the car around and drove back to the hotel with a heavy heart.

She kept her head down as she crossed the lobby, wanting to keep to herself, to avoid the sinister feeling she now associated with the Montgomery. And still, when she exited the elevator on her floor, her eyes were almost automatically drawn to the photos on the wall. This time, when she looked into the face of the "founder" Franz Montgomery, she saw a criminal, an abusive boss, an unfaithful husband, a devil. She studied Florence, Franz's wife. She was still no beauty, but Maya saw her differently, now that she was aware of the hardship that woman had faced, how strong she had been. This time Maya spotted a photo of the young Elisa; Maya came very close to study it: the young woman that was smiling at her from the oval-shaped frame looked naive, innocent, almost weak. A young girl with big dreams. Not that demanding woman she had encountered the other day.

When Maya took the last corner of the hallway leading to her room, she felt butterflies in her stomach: she saw Ben about to knock on her door. She remembered the kiss last night, his eyes on hers. The disappointment when she had told him she was leaving.

"Hi, there," she said, her voice shaky.

He turned around, and her earlier frustration evaporated instantly.

"I just came to say goodbye."

"Well, that's a good move. Because I changed my mind."

His smile became even broader. "You're not leaving?" He shuffled his feet. "So then will you join me for the party?"

The sensation in her stomach was too strong to ignore. The prospect of spending more time with this man filled her with joy. She didn't want to let him go, not quite yet. Plus she needed a way to kill time until she located Paula. "I would love to."

"I'll pick you up here in two hours." He walked backward down the hallway, then waved and was on his way. Maya watched him approach the corner, her heart beating fast, her legs weak. Shortly before he took the corner, he turned around one more time, catching her watching him. She blushed.

"I'm delighted I could change your mind," he called over to her.

Maya opened her mouth, but he waved his hands.

"Just let me believe it, even if it's not true."

All she had that was festive enough for the occasion were a black dress and sandals. The rain continued to pour outside, mocking her choice.

Ben knocked two hours later on the dot. He looked more handsome than ever in a suit and tie.

"Maya Viesberg, you look stunning."

Maya's legs felt wobbly as she followed him through the hallways.

Shortly before they rounded the last corner to the ballroom, he stopped.

Only now did she notice that he had grown extremely tense.

"Maya, I..." But then he shook his head. "Thank you, Maya, for coming with me." He offered his arm and together they entered.

As soon as they were inside, his nerves seemed to fade away. People lit up when they saw him. Men as much as women, of all ages. "Ben, how long has it been?" "Ben, you look fantastic." "Ben, how nice of you to join." "Not traveling at the moment?"

He hugged and smiled and nodded his head. Each time he introduced her as Maya, not as Maya Viesberg, or a novelist. Just Maya. And each time he kept the conversation very short, strategically moving on to the next group before they could ask more questions. Ben seemed in a hurry, dodging questions. When he'd introduced her, she noticed the same silent question in people's eyes. Who is she? And Ben would turn and smile at her, gently holding on to her arm, wordlessly giving his answer.

They were talking to a couple from the city when Edgar joined them. "Ah, I see the writers have singled each other out already."

This was the first time Ben released Maya's arm. He took a step back. "So I see you two already had the pleasure," Ben said, looking between Edgar and Maya.

"Yes, the writer from Germany," Edgar said.

"No, Maya is from Sweden," the woman she had just been introduced to chimed in.

"Sorry, I must have misunderstood; I could have sworn you said you were German." Edgar's eyes assessed her dress, her shoes.

"Well, no, I must have said European, isn't that all the same to you anyway?" she added quickly.

Edgar now examined her face, and she realized that he could always look up her passport copy in the records.

She addressed Edgar again: "But I am also a fellow countryman of your great-grandfather."

Edgar nodded proudly. "Yes, he fled Germany shortly before World War One, and our country made him rich. He had nothing when he came."

"Did he educate his children bilingually? Like Hans Montgomery?"

The opportunity was too good, her curiosity too overpowering.

Her question was followed by an embarrassing silence. Edgar looked at her in shock.

"We're all set for your speech, Mr. Montgomery." It was the male receptionist who had appeared behind Edgar.

Without another word, Edgar adjusted his bow tie and walked off.

"He seems to be a tricky subject," she whispered to Ben, angling her head. But when he didn't respond, she noticed he had paled, glancing nervously around as guests came closer to the stage, closing in around them for the speech.

One of the men she had been introduced to, Jamie, approached them from behind with champagne glasses. "This could take a while. Better have another one; you'll need it," he said.

She grabbed the flute he was offering. How many glasses had she had? She was starting to feel them.

The screeching sound of the microphone turned everyone's attention to the front. Edgar appeared on the stage, pausing theatrically before clearing his throat. "We have gathered here today to celebrate another milestone in the history of Montgomery. The birthday of the eldest member of the initial brain trust behind Montgomery."

Applause filled the room. She felt Ben's hand reach for hers.

"I've made an appearance. Let's go," he whispered into Maya's ear, his lips brushing against her neck.

Everything and everyone around her was starting to blur. She quickly put the champagne glass down on one of the trays flying by. She felt bubbly enough.

"I want to be alone with you." His hands touched her waist, only ever so slightly, but it made Maya shiver, a sensation that spread through her. She allowed him to pull her by the hand as they squeezed through the audience in the direction of the exit.

"She was the driving force in maintaining Montgomery, carrying it often single-handedly through difficult times, never losing sight of the prize. Esteemed family, and guests, please join me in welcoming our birthday girl onto the stage and giving her the applause she deserves: Elisa Montgomery!"

The round of applause was deafening, clapping hands preventing Ben from moving forward. He squeezed her hand reassuringly, his eyes trained on the exit that still seemed too far away.

When Elisa took the microphone the atmosphere in the room changed instantly. Ben looked utterly unhappy about the forced halt, but it gave Maya the opportunity to catch another glance at the stage. There she stood supported by her golden cane. And still, that woman up there was larger than life.

"Today, at my hundredth birthday, I will give a much shorter speech than the one a decade ago, so relax. I want to thank everyone here in the room for regaling me with your presence. I am grateful for my strong health, grateful to God and to all my friends and family who helped me through the ups and downs of being a hotelier. Today I would like to commemorate two men that have been crucial in my life, crucial to the success of Montgomery: my father, Albert Goldberg, and Franz Montgomery."

Maya saw two people in the crowd putting their heads together, shaking them dismissively.

"I learned everything there is to know about this trade from those two outstanding men, who left our world way too soon." Elisa paused.

Ben's hand had tensed up so much in hers that it hurt. He started to move again, pushing guests left and right, tugging her more forcefully.

"And then there is a third person I would like to single out today as a man who did not only help me carry our resort and all the values it represents firmly into the twenty-first century, but who supported me in making it stronger and more successful than ever before. My grandson, Edgar Montgomery, to whom I now return the stage to give you all an update on the hotel's latest awards and achievements." She concluded her short speech, scanning the crowd in front of her before exiting the podium.

Edgar took the microphone, beaming proudly as he started to list the prizes, droning on and on about them, not without making sure it was understood that he was the principle driver behind each achievement. Several guests started to peter out before Ben and Maya, forcing the couple to slow down again. Hopefully for the last time, Maya thought longingly. Ben turned to her, tingling her ear with his lips. "Quickly." He grinned, and Maya followed, enjoying the feeling of sweet anticipation, as he pushed through the crowd of hungry guests.

"The buffet is now open," they heard Edgar conclude, and now everyone had started to head for the buffet, forcing the couple to swim against the stream.

Then Ben stopped in his tracks. Maya nearly ran into him from behind.

"Ben, how nice of you to come."

Ben was blocking Maya's sight, but she recognized the voice: Elisa Montgomery.

"Happy birthday," Ben said, and then felt behind him for Maya, grabbing her by the waist this time and pushing her in front of him. "May I introduce you to Maya Viesberg?" he said, a satisfied smile on his face.

Maya extended her hand, but Elisa didn't move a finger. As Elisa's eyes met hers, Maya noticed the woman's near-waxen face as she stared at Maya in terror.

"No, no, no," Elisa Montgomery started to babble, little drops of spit drooling from her lips. "How is this...?" Her hands were trembling, the golden cane shaking dangerously. It appeared as if she had aged years in just those few seconds. Someone nearby offered her a chair, and she plunged down, not taking her eyes off Maya.

Guests had noticed the commotion and started to gather around them. Edgar came running over, a glass of water in his hand. "Grandma, what happened?" He squatted down next to her, deep concern showing on his face.

Maya looked around; more and more faces had now

turned in her direction, all eyes were on her. She wanted to get out of there as fast as possible.

She turned and pushed past the onlookers and then started to run out of the ballroom, through the lobby, blindly stumbling into the elevator, and down the hallway toward her room. Her mind was racing; she had drunk too much champagne.

It took her a while to open the door. Inside her room, she paced. Why did this woman have such a reaction to her? Maya remembered those photos of the innocent-looking girl at her wedding to Hans Montgomery.

She felt hands closing around her waist from behind. Ben's. He turned her around to face him and grabbed her, kissing her first gently, then more passionately, more urgently, as he softly pushed her backward toward the bed. He lifted her up and laid her down, not letting go of her for one second.

"Ben, I am not what you think I am," she managed to whisper between kisses.

He looked surprised. "I figured it out myself, Maya." He shook his head, chuckling. "It's pretty obvious." Had she not seen the warmth in his face, the way he looked deeply into her eyes, she might have felt offended. Instead, she had just been assured that his adoration was meant for her, Maya Wiesberg. She would no longer have to pretend to be someone else.

The intensity of his kisses increased, but then Elisa Montgomery's waxen face appeared in her mind.

Noticing Maya's stiffness, Ben silently told her that she was safe to let go. And the minute she did, he took her places she had never been before, touched her in ways she had never been touched. Their legs entangled as the passion consumed them with a force she had never experienced before. The last thought that crossed her mind before she fell asleep was that she hadn't felt like this in a long time, maybe ever.

# Day 5

Maya reached for Ben the next morning but found only the warm sheet next to her, and a note on the pillow.

*Last night was very special to me. Thank you.*

She smiled at the memory—and his choice of words.

*P.S. I am sorry I had to leave early this morning, but I didn't want to wake you—you looked so peaceful.*

When Maya entered the breakfast room, she noticed people eyeing her suspiciously. She sat down in the corner, her back to the room, feeling uncomfortable.

"May I?" She looked up and saw Jamie, pointing to the chair next to hers.

"Of course."

"Are you and Ben an item?" he asked straight away.

She blushed against her will.

"Okay, no need to say more." He giggled. "He's taken with you, as well."

She felt that weird sensation in her belly and smiled involuntarily. "I think he's very charming."

"Ever since he was a teenager none of the other male cousins ever stood a chance—even a lot of our female cousins were smitten with him..."

"So you're Ben's cousin?" she interrupted Jamie. He nodded his head.

"But Ben never mentioned..."

"...anything about his family? Ben hasn't made an appearance in ten years at any of these family celebrations. It must be your good influence that he came to this one!"

Maya tried everything to wipe the puzzled look that must have formed on her face. Why had it not come up yesterday? How could she have not made the connection, with all the people so glad to see Ben at the celebration? Edgar had pointed out the writer's conference. Paula's booklet had referred to William Montgomery's two sons: Edgar and Benjamin, which of course, she now understood, was long for "Ben." Who turned out to look like Hans, broad-shouldered, blue eyes, and blond curly hair. How could she have been so blind?

"How is Mrs. Montgomery?" she asked, to take her racing mind off this new revelation.

He shook his head. "Not too well, I heard. She's at the hospital in Kingston."

"Is Ben there?"

"I don't know. He might be."

"What about her husband? Hans Montgomery. He wasn't mentioned once in the speech yesterday."

Jamie's eyebrows raised in surprise. "You never heard?" Maya shook her head.

"He disappeared twenty-seven years ago."

Back in Stone Ridge, Maya recognized the woman from earlier, still manning the library desk, and decided to try a different route. She entered the bagel shop next door and joined the long line of hungry customers. Jamie's sentence played over and over in her head. H*e disappeared twenty-seven years ago*. Hans Montgomery disappeared the same year Grandmother disappeared. This couldn't be a coincidence, could it?

"Regular, pumpernickel. Blueberry?" the woman's harsh voice interrupted Maya's train of thoughts.

"I'm looking for the librarian, Paula."

"We're selling bagels here," the woman answered, clearly stressed.

"But do you know her?" Maya insisted.

"Would you like a bagel?" The woman's patience was wearing thin.

Maya shook her head, disappointed, and left.

She felt a tap on her shoulder as she walked over to her car.

"Hi. I saw you yesterday at Montgomery. You're Ben's girlfriend, right?"

A woman about Maya's age was standing behind her. "Why are you looking for Paula?"

"Oh, I just need to return something to her. A book."

The woman was eyeing her curiously. "Interesting." She paused. "In any case, Paula lives down Buck Road, that way." She pointed in the opposite direction Maya had come from. "Don't know the number, but look out for a ranch-style house."

She drove down a winding road off the main street and then deeper into the woods, with beautiful stone houses on both sides. After a mile she saw a house that fitted the lady's description: Paula's modest ranch seemed completely misplaced on this road, dwarfed between more-upscale structures.

She knocked at the door.

"Come to the back!" She heard Paula's anxious call from inside.

Maya did as instructed. She walked through a small but very well kept garden, with lovingly arranged flowers, a little pagoda in the middle.

Paula was standing in the doorframe. "Maya, I cannot help you anymore."

"The book. Did you write it?"

Paula shook her head. "The writer died about ten years ago. His family gave it to me. He left it to me."

"Why did you give it to me, then? There has to be a reason."

They heard the sound of a car door opening. Paula looked panicked. "He cannot know why you are here." She pushed her around the side of the house, toward the front.

A man emerged from behind a black pickup truck. He was about the same age as Paula, his shirt stained with oil. "Hey, honey. Finished earl—" He broke off when he saw Maya.

"This is Maya Wiesberg, Adam. She's a writer. I met her at the library." Paula smiled nervously.

"Nice to meet you," Maya said, and shook his outstretched hand.

"I'm taking my wife out to an early lunch!"

"Wonderful!" Paula exclaimed. Then she turned to Maya. "See you at the arts exhibition this afternoon?"

"Yes, absolutely. What's the name of the place again?" "Last Bite, at two?"

Maya nodded, pretending she knew exactly where Last Bite was located, or even what kind of establishment it was.

"Would you like to come, Adam?" "No. Thanks, hon."

She turned to Maya. "Okay, dear, see you then."

There were only two hours to kill until she would meet Paula. She had neither the desire nor time to return to the hotel, so she decided to drive over to the Egg's Nest for lunch. As she took a more scenic route along Leggett Road, her thoughts returned to Ben. She longed to hear his voice but she wanted to gather her thoughts before facing him again. She still couldn't comprehend why he had lied to her about not being from around here. Why had he not told her that he was a Montgomery despite the many opportunities to do so? She was approaching a narrow bend in the road when she noticed the car behind wasn't slowing. Another black pickup truck. Signs along the road alerted drivers to slow down to 10 mph, but the car behind her didn't. Instead, it overtook her where the road was narrowest, pushing her car into a field. Maya was in shock and, instead of braking, just let the car roll itself onto the field until it stopped.

She sat in the quiet car for a few minutes, trying to process what had just happened. Had there been any witnesses? Had this been a warning? She felt the pit in her stomach grow.

When she arrived at the Egg's Nest she was still shaking. She would order herself a martini; she didn't care what others might think. But one look at the bar told her she didn't have to worry. She wasn't the first one to nurse a drink at lunchtime.

A familiar voice wafted over to her—it was Ben, finishing lunch in another part of the restaurant. Jamie was with him. As if he'd felt her eyes on him, he looked her way, said something to Jamie, and got up from his seat.

Maya shuffled nervously on her barstool, the intimacy of the previous night suddenly weighing on her. He didn't smile when he approached. He had dark rings under his eyes.

"I tried calling you in your room this morning," he said.

"I went out. How is your grandmother?"

He didn't flinch at her choice of words. He was too worried to notice. "Not good, not good at all." He sighed, staring off into the distance, his face pained with sorrow—and something else Maya couldn't quite pin down. But then he turned his head and smiled at her, or at least attempted a smile. "I need to stop by the hospital one more time but wanted to ask you if you could take my mind off things later today? Five o'clock?"

Maya flushed but nodded.

The art exhibition was about Marc Chagall, who had lived in the area for many years. Paula was waiting in a corner of the adjacent café when Maya entered.

"You must never tell my husband that I gave you that book," Paula said.

"What is your history with the Montgomery? Are you using me for some sort of revenge?" Maya's voice was calm, but inside she was nervous.

"Listen, I'm not using you for anything. I'm helping you. What you do with it is your own business."

"What does all of this have to do with my grandmother? Are they involved in her murder?"

Paula's expression softened. "She was murdered? I didn't know that."

"What *do* you know, then?"

"I worked at the resort." She studied Maya's face before continuing. "In 1990."

Maya felt chills run down her spine.

Paula leaned back in her chair, her hands shaking as she took another sip of her coffee. "And I think I met your grandmother. You have her eyes, my dear." She smiled at Maya. "But I remember her because things changed with her arrival. And your grandmother... well, she wasn't the conventional guest you'd imagine."

"So she stayed at the resort?"

"Oh, yes. See, I worked there as a receptionist; I was doing the night shift when your grandmother arrived. Your grandmother paid for a week in advance, in cash. For identification papers she showed me a passport that had expired in the fifties. And when I started to protest, I remember her giving me this pleading yet determined look. 'I am almost seventy. There is something in my life that I left...'—she paused, I remember, searching for the right word—'unfinished. And I cannot leave this world without trying. You're still young, you don't understand. But you will.' I was still young, that's true. My heart was broken at that time. The man I loved only seemed to accept me, not to love me back. I looked at your grandmother; she seemed like such an extraordinary woman, strong-willed yet so genuine, so..." Paula was at a loss for words. Maya knew exactly what she meant. "Genuine" was definitely one word to describe

Grandmother. Her face couldn't hide anything. It had been one of the most honest faces Maya had ever seen.

"So I accepted it. Your grandmother was very grateful." Paula paused as she remembered something else. "I'm pretty sure it was an American or British passport, but I remember her English being weak."

Maya was baffled. *Why would Grandmother have owned a different passport than her German one?* "Do you think she came for a vacation?" She asked instead.

Paula shook her head. "I don't know. She came back several times in the next days, asked me about hikes and things to do in the area; we discussed books—I think we bonded over books, really—and she also asked me several things about the family. But I didn't make too much about it then. But one early morning, probably three days or so into her stay, she approached me in one of the hallways..." —Paula paused again—"and gave me a letter. It said '*Hans Montgomery*' on it in beautiful handwriting. She asked if I could give it to him. She was adamant that nobody else should be present when I handed it to him. I wasn't too happy about it: I didn't trust Montgomery Senior myself, to be honest; he was a strange man. But she'd probably heard that I..." Paula shook her head. "In any case, I wore a dress that day, so I had nowhere to store it but in my purse. I was on my way to the reception that morning, but I promised her to hand it him when I got a chance. Then, later that day, I was hurried away from reception, to fetch something in the village, which was bizarre, as the family always had so many handymen working for them, but I complied. And when I came back later that day, the letter had vanished from my purse.

"And then three days later I was called into the office by Elisa Montgomery; Edgar was there, too. Hans Montgomery had just suffered his stroke—the atmosphere was gloomy in the house—and they fired me on the spot, though they did offer a respectable severance package for the next months. I pleaded with them to not do it, but Elisa told me she would prefer not to see me in the vicinity of the hotel again. They never gave me an official reason."

"Do you know what was written in the letter?"

"No, I never opened it, of course. I looked for your grandmother to inform her of the loss, but your grandmother had vanished along with the letter. I pointed this out to William." She swallowed. "But he was already so cancer-stricken at that stage, I..."

"I thought he suffered a stroke?"

"No, I mean William Montgomery. William died of cancer." She swallowed, briefly averting her eyes." It was Hans who had a stroke. I never really spoke to him." She was looking for the right words. "He was kind of a weirdo, a hermit; most of the time he didn't even live in the house. He had no interest in the hotel business whatsoever. He headed up the nature trust that had been founded under Roosevelt. He spent most of his days studying the flora and fauna of the preserve around the hotel, and he stayed away at night. Probably in the woods. He frankly gave me the creeps. God knows, I hate all of them, but you've got to believe in karma."

"You mentioned things changed after my grandmother arrived. What else happened?"

"Elisa and Edgar had never been close, and it wasn't for lack of trying on his part. He followed her around like a little duckling. Elisa, she always despised Edgar openly. But suddenly, Edgar took over. Right after Montgomery Senior, Hans Montgomery, suffered the stroke. Up until then the senior been in good health — which of course doesn't mean much; even athletes can suffer a heart attack and die on the spot."

"Did that letter ever resurface?"

"Not that I'm aware of. All I heard is that your grandmother tried to blackmail Hans in her letter. Or at least that was the rumor in town."

Maya stared at Paula, trying to absorb what she had just

said. If all this was true, why would Grandmother have taken on such a powerful family? What could she have possibly held against them? And especially against Hans Montgomery, a guy who had kept to himself, a hermit?

A beeping sound from Paula's purse interrupted her thoughts.

Paula checked it quickly. "I've got to run." She got up. "I can't tell you more than I already have. You must do the rest of the legwork." She smiled sadly at Maya.

"One last question, please."

Paula shuffled her feet impatiently.

"Is it you who knows the fairy tale?"

She shook her head.

It wasn't until Paula had hurried out of the café that Maya realized that Paula's response indirectly acknowledged that she knew the fairy tale existed.

Maya felt as if she were swimming in a sea of information, with no sense of direction and only the risk of drowning the longer she swam. Who really was Hans Montgomery? Why did the family keep such a closed lid on him? What would Grandmother have blackmailed him about? Back at the hotel, Maya walked up and down the hallways one more time, confirming what she knew already: Hans Montgomery was in none of the photos, as if he had been wiped from the family's history.

She knew Ben was her only way to find out more.

Ben didn't seem any less concerned when he picked her up later that day.

"How is she?" This time she avoided the term "grand-mother."

"A little better," he said. Then he smiled at her. "Sorry I'm not in a better mood today."

They drove for a while in silence. Now would be a good moment to confront him about his lie, but something was holding Maya back. She could tell something else, beside Elisa, was bothering Ben. They drove through town and then off Main Street, and after several miles on a quiet country lane called Springtown Road, they turned onto a private gravel drive that led to a red barn.

"This was a farm once," Ben explained as he opened the car door for Maya.

The high plateau with the Montgomery Resort loomed over the barn from a distance, across a wide field. Maya hadn't noticed until now that the road had curved all the way around the high plateau, bringing her much closer again to the resort.

"Is this where you live?"

Ben nodded. "I thought I could cook us dinner here, if you don't mind?"

She entered the place first. It was cozy, stretching over two floors with a wraparound balcony inside that led to additional rooms on the upper floor. The day was nearing its end and the house was bathed in the warm light of the setting sun.

She was nervous, delaying the moment to confront him. "Are you hiding your wife and children up there?" she said instead.

"No, they're in the basement." He snickered. "I'll get the cooking started. Make yourself at home," he said, and walked off into the kitchen.

Maya took a look around, curious to find out more about him. The house was filled with books—novels, coffee-table books, travel guides. The walls were lined with memories of all the places he must have visited: Moroccan rugs, paintings, wooden masks. She felt envious.

She heard the pop of a cork, and Ben approached with two filled glasses. His eyes stayed on hers as he moved toward her. She wanted to relive the intimacy of the previous night. His lips came closer.

"Why didn't you tell me you're a Montgomery?" It was out, finally; she felt lighter already.

He winced at her question. A glint of resignation in his eyes.

"Why did you lie to me at the Egg's Nest?" She hated the nagging tone in her voice.

He put his glass down and sighed. Then he took her hands. "Listen, my family is... Being a Montgomery is... quite the burden to carry sometimes." He explored her face, looking for understanding. "I somehow feel"—to her surprise he blushed—"that we don't need to bore each other with the usual details; to me it feels like I know you already in a different way." And then he placed a long kiss on her lips.

"My mother received a 'severance package,'" he said after they ended the kiss. "Sort of. I never met her. I was raised by my grandmother. But a long time ago we had a falling out." He hesitated. "Over twenty-five years ago, now."

"Why?"

He shrugged his shoulders, "I still don't know."

Now was a good moment, Maya told herself. "What about her husband, your grandfather, Hans?" Maya kept her eyes focused on him. She felt guilty for pressing him. But right now her curiosity had the upper hand; she felt she was getting closer to answers. "Is he still alive?"

He looked puzzled, his eyebrows furrowed. "Why are you asking me this? Didn't Jamie tell you that he disappeared?" He sounded angry, but then his features softened. "I'm sorry. There's just so much going on right now. I can't talk about this."

When he dropped her off at the hotel a few hours later, he took her face in his hands. "Thank you for putting up with me." He smiled, sending her another silent apology. "And thank you for coming tomorrow. This conference... It means a lot to me."

The conference? Maya had totally forgotten about it. How had she managed to put the conference so far out of her mind? And why would he still want her to participate? She had come clean with him the previous night.

"Please tell me you're still coming, Maya? I need you."

So instead of asking him about it, she just nodded her head. She couldn't help it.

"What are you planning to talk about?"

"But I thought..." Maya started again, but he had let go of her face and sat upright. "I'm not an idiot," he said. "I can tell there's something bothering you, so I didn't want to add to your worries, but tomorrow is the big day and we need to add it to the program...."

"'The War Fairy,'" she said without thinking. "The program should just say, 'The War Fairy.'"

His eyes widened. "What a coincidence," he said to himself. Then he shook his head, and smiled at Maya. "I like the title."

He placed one more long kiss on her lips.

"Maya, please don't take it personally if I'm rather standoffish tomorrow. I don't like to mix my professional and personal lives.

Maya nodded her understanding. This would be their last moment of happiness; everything would change from now onward. She had made the decision to confront the murderer tomorrow at the conference. She would take advantage of Ben again. One time too many. She didn't know if the murderer would be there, or the person who knew her fairy tale, or if it would get her any answers at all. But she knew tomorrow would be the day that marked the end to their romance.

"What's the matter?" he asked, concerned.

"I never mean to hurt you, whatever happens tomorrow," Maya said, planting one last kiss on his lips and hurrying out of the car before he could ask more questions.

She heard the program for the conference being slid under her door one hour after she had arrived at the room. She grabbed it and found her name first, at nine o'clock.

*Maya Viesberg:*
*"The War Fairy"*

She didn't understand. Hadn't she come clean with Ben?
It must have been a mistake made by reception or whoever
typed up the program. *Don't make a big deal of it*, she
reprimanded herself. Focus. But the doubt accompanied her
into her sleep, plunging her into another nightmare as the
faceless man chased her through the dark forest.

# Day 6

Her first thought the next morning was of Ben. She felt incredibly sad. But hadn't she known all along that this day would come? That the truth would surface? When she'd received the fairy tale, she had made a decision, a decision not to let the past rest but to dig deeper into it.

Maya entered the lobby just before 9:00 A.M. and was sent to the side entrance of the ballroom. She walked over with newly invigorated determination and self-confidence—only to have both crushed instantly when she looked through the doors of the ballroom. There were at least one hundred people there. Ben was sitting in the front row with the professional writers; the seat next to him was empty.

The friendly receptionist placed the program in her hand. "Good luck!" she said warmly.

Maya entered and walked over to Ben on wobbly legs. The smile that spread over his face when he saw her was different from the one he usually gifted her with—professional, more distanced. "Maya," was all he said, and that was all took to fill her with intense emotion.

He introduced her to the other professional writers, again as Maya. And then, without further ado, he stepped onto the podium, grabbed the microphone, and delivered his introductory remarks for the tenth writer's conference at Montgomery.

Maya watched him in awe. He was an excellent public speaker, entertaining, charming, filled with pride about the conference, its history, the caliber of writers he had brought together. The longer she listened to him, the more nervous she got. She would be none of that, had always been anxious when she had to speak in front of crowds. And then she heard her name. "Maya Viesberg, the Swedish novelist!" He praised her latest title for the numerous awards for which it had been nominated. Her heart sank. There was no typo on the program; after all, the misunderstanding had never been lifted.

Everyone clapped as Maya got up from her seat and took the microphone from the beaming Ben. The podium she was now climbing onto was the same one where Edgar had stood with Elisa only two days before. Too much had transpired in those two days. She still hadn't really had the chance to process it all. She had fallen in love. With a Montgomery. The family who might somehow be involved in Grandmother's murder.

She looked into the eager faces of her audience and cleared her throat several times.

"First of all, I would like to correct a mistake here. I am not Maya *V*iesberg, I am Maya *W*iesberg, pronounced *V*iesberg in Germany, where I'm from. I'm not from Sweden and I'm not a published writer." She heard her own shaky, feeble voice, and despised herself for what she was about to do to Ben. She sensed his questioning eyes, but knew she wouldn't be able to continue with her speech if she processed what must be going through his mind right now. And it would only get worse.

"But, nevertheless, I have an interesting story to tell you all. A personal one. My grandmother disappeared without a trace when I was sixteen years old, in the year 1990. I was on a school exchange in Tarrytown, not too far from here, and when I returned to Germany I learned that my grandmother had disappeared a month after my departure. My world was shattered; my grandmother was also my surrogate mother, as my own mother left me and my father when I was only two years old."

She had to swallow again, but she could sense that the audience was hers. *I am so sorry*—she sent Ben a silent apology, but she had to continue. Someone in the crowd might know her fairy tale. Know Grandmother. Know what happened.

"There was recently a landslide near here that revealed the remains of a body. After some testing, the police concluded that it was the remains of my grandmother. But it gets better, or, rather, worse. She had been murdered. But the press here reported it as an accident. I had initially come here to find closure, to see the last place my grandmother had seen with my own eyes, to wander in her last steps, to understand why she had abandoned me. And when I heard she was murdered, I wanted to get away from this place as fast as possible. But then I received something that changed everything: When I was little, my grandmother told me a special fairy tale. She said that she was the only one left who knew the story and that the time had come to pass it on to me. But then only three days after I arrived here, I found several handwritten pages that had been slid under the door of my hotel room. It was *my* fairy tale."

The audience members gasped. She could feel the energy in the room change instantly.

There was silence; everyone was hanging on her words. "I have yet to find out who went through the trouble of writing down the fairy tale and leaving those pages under my door." She scanned the room one more time, reading the expressions on people's faces, hoping to find one that might betray nervousness, or guilt. "Today I will share the fairy tale with all of you."

*This is for you*, she told Grandmother silently.

The room waited patiently. And then she did exactly what she had done to overcome her fear on the plane: she became young Maya again and transported herself back to the clearing in Perlach, where her only audience member was Grandmother, to whom she would now tell her own story.

And she noticed that the longer she talked, the stronger her voice grew.

When she finished, the audience applauded and cheered, and she realized with relief and also surprise that she had managed to hold the audience in her thrall the same way Grandmother once had in the clearing.

When she finally dared to look at Ben, he was staring at her in shock. Once he snapped out of it, he walked up to the front and spoke into the microphone.

"We have fifteen minutes for questions." He nodded briefly at Maya, then fled down the aisle and out of the room.

During the next fifteen minutes she was bombarded with all sorts of questions from the passionate crowd—about the murder, the fairy tale itself, if she was planning to turn that into a fantasy novel. But instead of executing her plan, instead of scanning the crowd carefully, watching out for some suspicious behavior, of someone present knowing her fairy tale, she heard herself answering robotically, as her thoughts drifted off to Ben. She didn't care about the murderer in this instance. All she could think about was the look on Ben's face, a mixture of astonishment and anger, but worst of all, disappointment.

"Thank you all. I have to leave now," she eventually said to the crowd, and hurried away.

She locked herself in her hotel room, panting. She should have never agreed to this. She had never felt smaller than in this moment. Who was she after all? A nobody. The tears were coming.

A knock at the door made her sit up straight.

"Maya, open up!" It was Ben.

She was shaking as she opened the door. "I'm so sorry, Ben," she mumbled as he swept past her. She looked up slowly, cautiously daring to look into that face she had so naturally grown to adore. He looked more confused than angered.

"Who are you?"

"I'm Maya Wiesberg," she answered truthfully.

"But not the Swedish novelist?"

She nodded her head and swallowed in an attempt to steady her shaky voice. She felt confused. She had told him, twice now. "I told you that the night we made..." The word "love" was hanging in the air and felt so out of place with the tension in the room that she didn't dare say it out loud.

"We discussed your sexual orientation, *not* who you really are!"

Maya was puzzled.

"The writer you were pretending to be has lived in total reclusion from the world since she lost her *wife*. That's pretty much all you can find out about her on the Web!" His voice had risen in anger now. "Had you bothered doing some research about the role you were playing, you would have found that out yourself. And don't you think I would have cared a bit more had I understood you right? Do you think I would have invited you to speak knowing that you are *not* a published writer?"

"Ben, I am so sorry that I embarrassed you at the conference."

He angrily waved her off. "You don't need to worry about that. You fooled all of them as well as you've fooled me. Rest assured, the crowd was also eating out of your hands. They loved your story." He started pacing the room. Then he stopped to look at her. "You're really good at that, you know it?" He almost whispered now. The look of hurt on his face was almost unbearable. "Worming your way into the family. All your questions about my grandfather, about my family. You poking around. Spending so much time with me. Looking at me the way..." He broke off. "How could I have been so blind?"

"Will you be able to forgive me?"

"Forgive you? I don't even know you!" he averted his gaze to avoid facing her. Instead, he looked around the room, *the room they had made love in*, Maya thought sadly.

And then his eyes widened as they caught something behind her. She turned; Paula's booklet was lying on the table. Maya quickly moved toward it, but Ben got there first. The booklet securely in his hand, he stared at her with a puzzled expression.

He flipped through the pages, painful recognition showing on his face, and contempt in his eyes when he looked back up at her. He brushed past her and closed the door behind him, the loud bang echoing through the room.

She sat down on her bed. Exhausted. Defeated. She knew she would lose him. The room phone rang; she hoped so much it would be him.

"There's a Mr. Melbert on the phone for you. Can I put him through?" the receptionist said.

"Sure." A click followed.

"Is this Maya Wiesberg I am talking to?"

"Yes, speaking."

"Are you safe to talk? This is Detective Melbert."

She knew that this must be a detective calling her from the State Police, as the German police had warned might happen. Now, with the feelings she had developed for Ben, she hesitated to get the police involved in his family.

The detective must have sensed her hesitation. "Listen, you're not the only person that reacts that way when the police call back. Life moves on, we all move on. But always remember: justice should always come first."

She had lost sight of the big picture. Because of her feelings for Ben.

She was here for Grandmother.

They agreed to meet at a restaurant in New Paltz. "And until then stay out of trouble, Miss Wiesberg."

The place hadn't really opened yet for lunch, so there was only one waitress and one other person sitting inside. She immediately recognized the tall man who got up from his chair when she entered. He was the one she had seen up in the clearing. He introduced himself as Detective Melbert.

"I thank you for bringing this case to our attention," he said after both had sat down again. "But I must ask you to stay out of it." His look was admonishing. "Are you staying at the hotel?"

Maya nodded.

"I think you should move out of there. Today. How much longer do you plan to stay in town?"

"As long as it takes for you to find the murderer." She wouldn't leave before she got answers, but she also wasn't going to stay longer than that. She remembered the look of utter disappointment in Ben's face. Her lie. She had come here for Grandmother. When that chapter closed, she would be gone.

"First of all, I need your cell number. So I can reach you."

The way the officer was looking at her, the way he talked to her, made Maya feel increasingly nervous.

"Now tell me more about your grandmother." He checked the notes he had brought in a folder. "Why were you surprised when you heard she'd traveled to the United States?"

She explained it to him the same way she'd explained it to the German police officer, but he didn't seem satisfied with her explanation.

"So would you say she was almost opposed to the United States?"

Maya tried to remember, and then, slowly, she shook her head. "It wasn't so much opposition; it was more a lack of interest."

The police officer nodded his head. "We tend to do this sometimes, don't we? We have painful memories and try to suppress them by banning them from our interactions with others, as if not sharing them with others makes them less real. And still, we only do this on the surface; we still think about them all the time."

Maya sat still. It felt like he had summarized in three

sentences how she had coped with Grandmother's disappearance over the past decades. "So you're saying that it wasn't disinterest in the USA that made her not talk about it but an event in the past that..." Maya swallowed, not finishing her observation. She was disappointed that Grandmother had kept so many secrets from her.

The detective nodded his head. "Yes, I think your grandmother had some kind of past with someone from the Montgomery."

Maya nodded her head. "Yes, I think so, too." "What makes you think that?"

"Someone told me that she tried to blackmail Hans Montgomery. But I don't believe that."

"Did someone at the conference tell you that?"

She shook her head. "From people who worked there when my grandmother disappeared."

"So you've also asked around? Actively?" Maya nodded her head slowly.

"Are you aware of how dangerous all of this is? Talking to people, to the potential murderer? Exposing yourself like that at the conference?"

*Of course he knew. News traveled fast in this town.*

"Yes, but can you really blame me? I came here to find closure. Instead, I found out that my grandmother was *murdered* and that nobody was treating it like murder!"

His tone turned softer. "I understand; that's why we're here, looking into this. But I'm also concerned for you. Playing detective won't help anybody. You or me. Understand?"

"I think it was Hans Montgomery who killed her," she blurted instead. "But there are still people out there who try to cover it up for him, even though he's long gone! So who else is there, then? Edgar? He never got along with Hans. Elisa is..."

"What do you mean by 'he's long gone'?"

"I was told that he suffered a stroke—which he apparently survived, according to the family, and that he then

184

disappeared without a trace, just like my grandmother did. The same year! It's suspicious if you..."

"Ms. Wiesberg, Hans Montgomery never disappeared."

She hurried back to the hotel, fueled by the detective's order to get out of there as soon as possible. Where was Hans Montgomery?

When she returned to the hotel, it suddenly felt like a prison. She stormed into her room but stopped short when she noted a bundle of papers on the table, wrapped with a rubber band and a Post-it note that read *For Maya*.

Maya took the pages with shaky hands. The front page read Hans.

Then a letter addressed to her:

*Maya,*
*You should know the truth about my grandfather. I owe it to him. Please don' t contact me again.*
*Ben*

# Hans

# 1938

It was early summer when Hans arrived at the train station in Munich, after a four-day-long journey across the Atlantic. It was raining hard as he walked to the parking lot behind the station, scanning the cars to identify the green Adler Trumpf car that he had purchased from an American contact with money his mother had slipped him back home. "You'll need a car in California," she had whispered to him.

That is where his family believed him to be—in sunny California, not in gloomy Munich.

Hans had the keys to a simple, fully furnished studio in the Schellingstraße, also taken over from the same contact, which was situated right in the heart of Schwabing and within walking distance of Ludwig-Maximilians University, where he would study biology, starting in October.

He parked his new car and heaved his two suitcases up the stairs and onto the bed. As he opened one for the first time since his departure, he found a book on top of the piles of clothes. It was a copy of *The Great Gatsby*. He smiled for the first time since his arrival. The inscription read: *Profite bien de la Californie, profite de la liberté. Je t'aime, Maman—* "Enjoy California, enjoy your freedom. Love, Mom."

The guilt that he had tried to suppress while crossing the Atlantic came back to haunt him now in his tiny dark studio. He had escaped what was expected of him: to marry Elisa

Goldberg, combine Goldberg's land with his father's, and to take over the hotel, the life project of his parents.

It had been President Roosevelt's visit to Montgomery that had saved him at the last minute. And fate: the president had overheard Hans speak German fluently in the lobby one day. Five days later, Hans was on a walk in the woods when a man intercepted him off the official hiking trails. A stout man in his fifties, who introduced himself as Thomas Wagner, he had been sent by Roosevelt. He got straight to the point and offered Hans a scholarship at the university of his choice in Munich. In return he would undergo a month-long training in Washington and would then provide the United States with on-the-ground information. Wagner went on to explain that America's Achilles' heel was the lack of an espionage organization—an independent one. The U.S. government had been too slow organizing a proper secret agency.

"You want me to become a spy?" Hans had dared to interrupt the man, in total awe.

Wagner hadn't given a direct answer. "We want you to play the role of a German student and 'report' back to your country."

"Why can't I go as an American?"

Times had changed, Wagner had explained. There was not only an air of mistrust toward the Americans, toward the other, toward anyone not already a part of them, but even most of the U.S. diplomats in Germany had faltered under the pressure from the Nazi regime and had stopped sending objective accounts of what was really happening in Germany, the government had started to suspect.

"Germany is united now; that is our biggest threat," Wagner had concluded.

And then he had anticipated Hans's next concern: his father and the hotel.

"Your father has already agreed—to you studying in California. You'll leave in one week."

After Wagner had given Hans more instructions, one of them being not to disclose this to anyone, he had vanished as quickly as he had appeared to Hans in the woods.

He was now Siegfried Hofstätter, twenty-one years of age, from Hanover, Germany. He had come to study biology. He was proud to be in Munich, the city that gave birth to the German Reich.

He knew he had to find a way to ignore the concerns of Hans Montgomery.

Hans got up early the next morning and went down to a kiosk on one of the street corners. The owner was a stout man.

"Heil Hitler," Hans greeted him. "Heil Hitler."

Wagner had trained him so well that the salute came to him automatically. He picked up the Nazi party's newspaper, *Völkischer Beobachter,* "People's Observer," Goebbels's *Der Angriff,* "The Attack", and *Münchner Neueste Nachrichten*, "Munich's Latest Newest".

The owner studied Hans as he gathered the coins.

"Returning home or having an early morning?"

"No, I like to get up early."

"Ha," the man replied, "I knew it. You're not from here!"

Hans became nervous, but his training set in. "I'm from Hanover."

"Ah," replied the Bavarian, "a *Zuagroasda*. Are you enjoying Minga?" Hans didn't understand.

"Yes, Minga, Munich. That's what the locals call the city."

"I've only arrived recently." Hans quickly gathered his papers and bid farewell to the owner, avoiding a longer discussion.

In the month before Hans's departure, Wagner had taught Hans everything he knew about Munich, but wasn't as successful drilling the Bavarian dialect into Hans.

"Just stick to the dialect your father spoke to you." A dialect that betrayed him as a *Zuagroasda*, as the man had said, a *Zugereister*, not a local, born and bred in Munich.

But better that than something that would betray him as "un-German."

That morning the newspaper chronicled Hitler's achievements since seizing power. Hitler had fulfilled the promise that he had given during his victory speech in 1933: unemployment had gone down drastically. Back in Washington, Hans had attended a lecture by William E. Dodd, the U.S. ambassador in Berlin until the end of 1937, who spoke out about the threat of Nazi Germany to the rest of the world. Hans had learned from him that the employment figures were delusionary, as in many cases Hitler had assigned two people to the same post to have the numbers drop. Hitler's demand for the annexation of the Sudetenland, a bordering, German-speaking region of Czechoslovakia, was the hottest topic that day. However, Hans had been encouraged to especially seek out those details that wouldn't make it into the international newspapers. Such as scanning the page with job ads. What and how many gun companies were hiring?

Hans's had been assigned several tasks. First, to build a network of contacts for gathering intelligence: German dissidents, other spies, any anti-Fascist brave enough to help with the intel. He had also been encouraged to recruit new informants, or turn existing spies into double spies for the United States. The discrimination against Jews was known, but Hans was asked to seek out the degree of violence against them and report back, as Roosevelt had stopped relying fully on the reports from his consular in Munich.

In the first weeks, Hans reduced his activities to his daily morning routine: buy the newspapers, study them, and mail a report to a private address in Washington, coded the way he had been trained. He had been happy to be asked to depart months before the university would start in October to start this process. "Be active right away; mingle, make friends," Wagner had encouraged him. To overcome his introversion, however, was a far bigger challenge than he had anticipated, and the reality of the situation was hitting him. Hans had always stuck to himself and he didn't mind being alone. On the contrary, he could only truly be himself when he was alone, and a childhood in the woods had taught him to be at ease with himself.

As a result, Hans left the studio as little as necessary, other than when visiting the newspaper stand. At home, he practiced coding and burnt the results immediately afterward over the stove; he familiarized himself with the radio transmitter. He reread both volumes of Hitler's *Mein Kampf*. He cooked at home, practicing eating the "continental" way: the fork never changed hands. "You must eat like them, talk like them, urinate like them. Violating those details could blow your cover," Wagner had said.

It was after those early morning walks back from the newspaper stand that he crossed paths with the neighbors who lived upstairs from him: a mother with her son and daughter, and a family of four opposite them, all of them Jews, all of them branded with the yellow star. None of them spoke much, or not at all. A stark contrast to the neighbors below him: an extremely loud family of five who occupied the entire first floor and largest flat in the building. The father's uniform proudly flashed the party label. From him Hans learned that the Gestapo, the Geheime Staatspolizei, the "Secret State Police," had already taken away the husband of "the Jewish cow" and that the clock was also ticking for the other family. That they had owned the grocery store downstairs before it had become a victim of the Aryanization. And that the mother with the son and daughter had not given up their store farther down the road yet, the man said with utter contempt in his voice.

"You never know when they'll show up!" his Nazi neighbor barked, loud enough for anyone in the house to hear.

And such was the atmosphere in his house: the Gestapo could show up unannounced, at any time of the day or night, and take them—or anyone else for that matter, if denounced "by a colleague, friend, or neighbor," the neighbor bellowed again, loud enough to echo through the staircase.

Hans was happy when the door to his studio clicked shut behind him.

The atmosphere wasn't any different outside the house on the streets of Schwabing, and Hans felt nervous when he was on his way to Ludwig-Maximilians University to enroll himself at the university. *What if someone grew suspicious?* As he walked around the city, he thought of his father. He had sometimes spoken about Munich and the Alps, and Hans had imagined the city to be literally at the foot of the mountain range. But everything looked flat around the city. Men in uniforms were roaming the streets, the swastika present on every corner, the city's colors reduced to black, red, and white.

He began to incorporate a walk into his daily routine, so that by the start of the school year, he'd be well acquainted with his surroundings — and accustomed to being around others.

It was July 4, 1938, and Hans felt homesick. He had always looked forward to the fireworks over the lake at Montgomery; he yearned for the mild summer nights surrounded by nature. That day was also sunny in Munich, and Hans felt the sudden need to get out of the city. He drove along the Isar River and then across it, southbound, in the direction of the Alps, but only ten minutes later he came across a stretch of forest called Perlacher Wald. He stopped the car. He hadn't expected to find a forest so close to a major German city. He entered the woods and hungrily breathed in a smell so familiar to him. He chose the path that led farther into the forest, running into only a few other people along the way. After several hundred feet he had the entire forest to himself, it seemed. He left the path and walked farther into the woods — just like he would have done back home. After about fifteen minutes he reached a clearing. A hidden piece of land, cut off from the rest of the world, surrounded only by birds and the rustling of leaves. It reminded him of his refuge in the forests around Montgomery, a secret clearing he had discovered in his childhood. The clearing sat on an elevation overlooking the neighboring turquoise lake. Albert Goldberg's land. He missed those woods, his safe haven from the madness at the hotel, from his father. As a child, he would create his own imaginary friends in the forest, while his parents were busy working around the clock. How much he had yearned for a sibling when he was a boy, but that sibling had never arrived, and he had spent a childhood in solitude.

Hans sat down and leaned against an oak tree, relaxing for the first time in months. The flora here was slightly different from back home, with more conifers and birches; those were rare around Montgomery. As his thoughts returned to the home he had left behind, he recognized that the only person he truly missed was his mother. He knew she would have understood his decision. However, Hans had received clear instructions to never reveal to anyone where he truly was, what he was truly doing. He had not minded lying to his father; lying to his own mother, on the other hand, he found harder to bear—and yet more bearable than the thought of marriage with Elisa.

He reached for his pocketknife. His mother had taught him wood carving. As he started to sink the knife into the bark of the tree, he felt like a boy again, young, free—happy. He carved the initials of his real name: *H.M.*

This act alone made him feel real, inviting him to cherish the illusion that there was peace out in the world.

In the coming days he often returned to the clearing in Perlach, running away from his other responsibilities. Reading the newspapers alone would not be sufficient to fulfill his mission. The lectures at university were still three months away. He was too idle.

His predecessor had left him a couple of names worth contacting, among them a professor at the university, several other German dissidents, and a couple of spies from other anti-Fascist countries. But as he began to seek them out, he soon learned that most of them had left, all for the same reasons: the German Reich had become too dangerous. At first, as anticipated, he had battled with his introverted nature, but eventually he realized with relief that it was much easier for him to socialize with others when in disguise. His meeting with a French spy proved promising, the one with the remaining German contact disappointing: when Hans went to see him at his home in the Prinzregentenstraße, the man's eyes widened as Hans mentioned the purpose of his visit; that German dissident had succumbed to the fear under the regime and would be of no help anymore. He complied, however, with Hans's friendly request that Hans could mention the man's address as his residing address should it ever come up in conversations with others.

He sought out jazz and swing clubs, another thorn in the Nazi's side, and met several like-minded people. He also met a Soviet spy from the NKVD, the Soviet secret police, a surprisingly pleasant fellow. The Soviet Union and the United States had been far from fostering a close contact, but both men outside their respective countries immediately bonded over their shared fight against Fascism.

He looked at groups or organizations to join, to team up with other infiltrators. He was too old to join the Hitler Youth, and it was almost impossible to become a member of the Nazi Party those days due to their recently imposed restrictions. He attended several gatherings and political speeches in beer halls, which, aside from an occasional hangover the next morning, didn't bring him any new insights and only confirmed what he knew already: that this regime was vile and Germany was heading full speed into its next war. Originally he was afraid to drink, as he didn't want to lose control of the situation, but not drinking proved to be the greater risk. To become one with them and not stick out, he had to drink just as much as the people he was pretending to be.

And then one evening in July he got lucky. He was driving through Perlach on his way back from his spot in the forest and thought he might stop at a beer garden. He bought a beer and looked for a place to sit. It was customary for patrons in Bavaria to join strangers at a table, but Hans passed the half-full tables and walked to an empty one in the corner of the garden. He thought he felt eyes on him, but when he looked up, everyone else seemed engrossed in their Hendl, the roasted chicken, their beers, and the music from the live band. As Hans looked over to his right he caught sight of a young man, around his age, who was also nursing a beer at an otherwise empty table. The man quickly averted his eyes, blushing a deep red. Hans thought this odd. The men he'd normally come across in beer gardens and beer halls were fueled with self-confidence, strong in the tribe they were moving in. This one wasn't. When Hans caught the blond man staring again, he got up from his table and walked over to the stranger.

"Heil Hitler," he saluted, and motioned to the table with his beer. "May I join you?"

The man nodded. "Wolfgang Wiesberg," he introduced himself.

"I'm Siegfried Hofstätter."

"Nice name. Where are you from?"

Hans gave his story.

"Ah, this is why I've never seen you here before." Wolfgang paused, his eyes lingering on Hans's as if wanting to say more.

"What about you, then?"

"I'm from the north, but my family moved here when we were young."

"Are you studying?" Hans asked.

"Yes. I have a scholarship to study engineering, at LMU."

"Me, too!" Hans said, and a wide smile spread across Wolfgang's face.

The band had played itself into a frenzy, swallowing Wolfgang's next words.

"How about a different place where we don't have to shout at each other over the music?" Wolfgang suggested timidly.

Wolfgang was impressed that Hans had a car.

"Where do you live?" Wolfgang asked.

"In Lehel" Hans answered.

"Where in Lehel?" Wolfgang probed.

"Prinzregentenstraße."

Wolfgang's eyebrows shot up. "Have you seen him? Our Führer?"

"No, I haven't." Hans shook his head, not knowing what to make of the question.

"What street number do you live at?"

"Forty-two." Hans gave the number of the man he had met there.

"Yes, not too far away. Our Führer stays in the Prinz-regentenplatz sixteen when he is in town."

Should Hans have been aware of that? He felt that familiar nervousness tiptoe up to him whenever he didn't know something he ought to know.

"I know a nice bar around there," Wolfgang suggested as Hans packed Wolfgang's bike into the back of his car.

They drove to a much quieter place. Hans felt the renewed self-confidence of his disguise surge through him. This blond man in front of him seemed to be just as blinded by the regime as the others Hans had met, and he certainly wasn't on the list of people he was supposed to target—and still, there was something else about Wolfgang that made him stand out.

As the evening drew to a close, Hans exclaimed that he'd leave his car behind and walk home, hoping Wolfgang would join him. He wanted to gauge a bit further if this guy was worth paying special attention to. Wolfgang agreed, a shy smile on his face, and pushed his bike as the two headed in the direction of Prinzregentenstraße. After less than a mile they reached a crossroad that would lead them straight to Hans's supposed home. To Hans's surprise, he noticed reluctance on Wolfgang's part to walk down the street. Hans pushed him on, pretending not to realize.

"Let's change sides," Wolfgang said, suddenly nervous.

It was unnecessary to cross, but Hans followed, and they continued walking on the opposite side, in silence. After about five hundred feet they passed a restaurant on the other side of the narrow street. French music blared from within, and several males sat at the outside tables, smoking and drinking. These men were different from the customers in the beer halls: some were dressed in brighter colors, wearing shawls; two males walked in, greeting another male couple. Someone called Wolfgang's name, but he ignored it and walked faster, keeping his eyes straight ahead, his face turned away from the place. Hans recognized the clientele. Montgomery had hosted similar men, who had come to enjoy the reclusive nature of the resort. It had been his father, in fact, who had taught Hans that they were the best-paying guests and to treat with utmost respect.

The atmosphere was tense as they continued.

When they reached the apartment, Wolfgang lingered.

"Same bar tomorrow if you'd like?"

Wolfgang smiled and nodded, then climbed on his bike and drove off into the night.

Hans walked back to his car and headed to Schwabing deep in thought.

It turned out that Hans's suspicions about Wolfgang being a valuable target were right after all. As Hans's new acquaintance warmed up to him, Wolfgang revealed that he was working for the Gestapo, under a boss who was in charge of seeking out enemies of the regime—Communists, liberals, and reactionaries—and who investigated cases of counterespionage and sabotage. Wolfgang's eyes glowed as he told Hans about their activities, how his success in the Hitler Youth had led to his current role. He also briefly explained how much happier people were now, since the Führer had saved them. From how Wolfgang described the organization, from how he talked about his years at school, it became clear to Hans that instead of fostering the development of an adolescent's individual mind, the Nazi regime molded it into what they needed. From the tender age of ten onward, and with the entrance to the Hitler Youth, Wolfgang had been subjected to the *Führerprinzip*, and had never been given the chance to question any of the Nazi propaganda. What followed then was total subordination. *Führer befiehl, wir folgen.* "Führer gives orders, we follow!" Independent thinking had been stifled from the outset. Wolfgang, in addition, was a shy man with weak self-confidence, who had lost his father too early and was in strong need of guidance. A perfect candidate.

Hans grew increasingly aware that Wolfgang's interest in him was beyond that of friendship, and he felt it growing each time they were together. And that vulnerability exposed Hans to classified information, Wolfgang feeling the constant need to impress Hans with stories of his work at the Gestapo.

Hans knew that he had to play his role well and make Wolfgang believe that their feelings were mutual. And he was more than relieved that Wolfgang was aware—and afraid—of the harsh punishments for that type of activity, not in small thanks to his boss at the Gestapo, whom Hans knew was actively after people like Wolfgang.

One warm evening in late July, Wolfgang again accompanied Hans "home" in Prinzregentenstraße, a custom that Hans tried to avoid whenever possible. He lingered, searching Hans's eyes for an offer that wouldn't come.

"Can I come up?" he finally asked, nervously looking around.

Hans slowly shook his head. "That wouldn't be wise," he whispered. "The building has too many eyes and ears."

Wolfgang nodded in disappointed understanding. "Do you want to come to my house for dinner tomorrow night?"

Hans couldn't find a good reason to decline, and accepted the offer with a smile he hoped didn't look forced.

They met at the beer garden where they had first connected a couple of weeks before and drove together through the suburb of Perlach. After a couple of miles, Wolfgang directed Hans onto an unpaved road, not too far from Hans's secret spot, and Wolfgang placed his hand tenderly on Hans's leg, smiling at him from the side.

Hans grew nervous but tried not to show it. "Pretty spot you got here!" Relief washed over him when he saw a house at the end of the road.

Wolfgang nodded. "My father was offered a job here, and thank God we were able to purchase the house before 1929."

It was a small house, set among tall pine trees that allowed for only a little sunlight to get through the small windows. Hans thought of his home, how sitting on a high plateau brought you closer to the sky and a generous amount of light.

"Muttchen!" Wolfgang bellowed as soon as they entered.

Hans heard the rattling of dishes, and then a woman appeared. She must have been pretty once upon a time, but she looked like a woman who had been branded by too many blows of fate. The tear sacs under her eyes harbored her grief for all eternity; the deep wrinkles were not laugh lines but had furrowed the face in those places where sorrow had constantly contorted it. The way she watched him made him feel like an intruder, the eyebrows deeply furrowed, a glint of suspicion in her eyes. She was quick to dry her hands on her apron.

"Heil Hitler," she said, peering at the two men.

Wolfgang made introductions, and they followed his mother into the kitchen.

"Would you like a beer?" Wolfgang asked him.

Hans sat down and allowed Wolfgang's mother to pour him a glass. They started discussing the current political situation in Germany, and Hans, as always, faked contentment to encourage Wolfgang to talk about his work at the Gestapo. The Sudeten crisis had grown over the summer; headlines read statements like *DIE TSCHECHEN ERZIEHEN ZU, VÖLKERHASS*—"The Czechs breed ethnic hatred." Hans asked himself how much of these headlines were entirely true. He suspected that Hitler had spread those to be able to make his claim the previous month: that the unstable Czechoslovakia was threatening the peace in Europe. Hans also learned from Wolfgang that Hitler had executed a heavy buildup of arms on the front in the west, all of which was very valuable information for Washington.

"In May our Führer announced already to our army that he would eventually annihilate the entire Czechoslovakia. But like Hänschel says: Germany isn't ready for war... yet." Wolfgang stated for what felt like the fifth time since Hans had picked him up that evening.

"I agree." Hans nodded enthusiastically.

"But he thinks that we'll be ready sooner than later," Wolfgang added. "We could not start early enough!" As Hans raised his glass to toast Wolfgang he heard the clunking of glass bottles outside, and the kitchen door opened to reveal a girl Wolfgang's age, with long red hair. She wasn't a beauty in the classical sense like Elisa. However, her posture, her body language, everything about her, struck him. She had green eyes of a shade he had never seen before, and there was something beneath them that made him linger. A fire, a curiosity. When Hans sensed Wolfgang's eyes on him, he quickly returned his attention to his new friend and didn't allow himself to look at her again all night.

Two days later, Wolfgang took Hans to see and hear one of Hitler's speeches in the Hofbräuhaus. Hans was absolutely stunned to witness how Hitler whipped the crowd into a frenzy. Wolfgang, next to him, was trembling with excitement, and if Hans had had any before, he now had no doubt that Europe was heading fast into the next world war. After the speech,

Wolfgang suggested they go back to his place for dinner. A smile crossed Hans's face—to Wolfgang's delight. Yet that smile wasn't for Wolfgang, but at the thought that he might see her again.

When Hans greeted Martha he felt drawn in again, but he pushed the sensation away.

When the conversation shifted to the speech Wolfgang and Hans had just attended, he saw a glimpse into what was brewing beneath her surface: she was different—and also dangerously generous with her opinion of the Führer. Judging from Wolfgang's and his mother's reaction to her antiregime outburst, it was obvious that she hadn't acted out like that before. Hans hoped she never would again.

After the incident, Wolfgang was quick to suggest having another beer elsewhere. The second they stepped outside and the door closed shut, Wolfgang stopped in his tracks and held Hans back by his arm.

"I ought to report her," Wolfgang said, his hand trembling. "What would you do, Siegfried?"

Hans didn't know how to react. What if Wolfgang was just testing him?

Wolfgang's sister would have been reported if a neighbor had overheard. But how could Hans possibly agree with him, or worse, encourage him to report her? He knew from Wolfgang firsthand what happened to those people: they were taken into Schutzhaft, into protective custody, which was as far removed from protection as Hitler was from democratic ideals. Many were never seen again and instead sent to the concentration camp in Dachau, without any judicial hearing or chance to prove their innocence. But he also had to maintain the pretense of his feelings toward Wolfgang, for the sake of his own cover, for his country. "Stay away from women!" Wagner had croaked more than once. "They are the worst distractions!" Would Wolfgang read into Hans's response and see right through him? Hans remembered her eyes, how they had lit up when she had raised her voice...

"She is your sister, your twin sister. I am sure she is smart enough not to say anything in public," he finally remarked.

Wolfgang frowned, nervously shuffling his feet. Hans broke into a sweat and turned his head toward the forest, trying to suppress the panic that was slowly rising in him. But then he felt Wolfgang stroking his arm lightly. "You're right, Siegfried. Thank you."

Wolfgang was visibly shaken by his sister's behavior at home and drank more than usual. Hans took advantage of Wolfgang's intoxication to grill him more intensely and was rewarded with more specifics. Wolfgang gave several names: of the latest deportations to Dachau, of the victims of murder, names and locations of the opposition the Gestapo was plotting to crush around Munich and Bavaria. Among the names were several Americans, some of them Jews. Hans had been trained to memorize information in the absence of pen and paper or a recording device. Every time his thoughts reverted back to Martha, he had to work hard to push them away so he could focus on the intel.

Back in his studio he made use of a shortwave radio for the first time in his life.

Wagner was right. He didn't have the luxury to be distracted. His country came first.

In the next weeks, Hans kept busy: he identified some of the members of the opposition Wolfgang had mentioned and warned them of raids, sometimes locating them only a short time before the Gestapo arrived. He made contact with a French woman and a Russian spy in Munich. As Wolfgang's longing for Hans grew, Hans's net of information expanded. Hans just hoped there would not be another attempt to take the friendship further.

It was the beginning of September and they were about to leave for Hänschel's birthday party. Wolfgang had invited Hans along but insisted that they needed to bring dates. Wolfgang was taking Martha's friend, Else, and Hans was paired with Martha. He had never seen Martha in anything but the typical Hitler fashion: modest and matronly. But in her blue ball gown, she took his breath away. The dress reminded him of the gowns the women wore at the balls at Montgomery, not only accentuating her figure but making her appear as a woman he could have met outside of this terrible regime, in a different time and a different place. And when he looked into her eyes, he noticed something that hadn't been there before: happiness. She was smiling.

He quickly took her by the arm and guided her out of the house, but then he heard Wolfgang's voice behind him: "I want you to change before we go. Wear that brown dress of yours. Hänschel will not appreciate a daring dress like that."

Hans felt helpless in that moment. He could feel her deep disappointment, but what could he say that wouldn't seem suspicious to Wolfgang? All he dared do was squeeze her arm, ever so slightly, the tiniest of gestures that could still be too much, that could seed questions and doubts if noticed by the wrong person.

In the car to the Odeonsplatz, Hans held an animated conversation with Wolfgang, pointedly leaving Martha out to appease Wolfgang. And to his huge relief, Wolfgang relaxed next to him in the car. Hans glanced at Martha briefly in the rearview mirror a couple of times. All he saw were those green eyes, void of the happiness that he had noted before, replaced with clear disdain. He knew how he appeared to her: another one of them, and it felt increasingly painful to accept.

Hänschel was exactly how Hans had imagined: obese, borderline alcoholic.

After Wolfgang and Hans followed him around for a while, Wolfgang scanned the room for his sister. "Would you mind dancing with her?"

Hans could tell Wolfgang felt sorry for the incident at home.

His heart filled with warmth as he addressed her. "Would you allow me this dance?"

Martha shook her head. "Thank you. I cannot dance."

He had anticipated that reaction, but he would have carried her over to the dance floor if he had to. When would he ever be presented with this chance again? To hold her in his arms even if only for one modest waltz? He held his hand out to her and she hesitated, but the expression on her face was less decisive than her verbal rejection. She nodded her head ever so slightly and allowed him to guide her onto the dance floor. He hoped she wouldn't notice his trembling hands as he took her waist and moved to the rhythm, respecting the distance required by the dance—and the regime. The smell of her rose soap entered his nose as they circled around the dance floor in perfect harmony. She was a good dancer, and he never wanted the dance to end, painfully aware that this was the closest he would ever get to her. He told her she looked beautiful, and for a split second she smiled up at him, genuinely. He hadn't been with a woman in a long time, and holding the one and only he desired so close made him dizzy. He wanted her to know that he was like her, that they could be friends, that they should be lovers. That...

He broke away before losing control. He couldn't let this happen. It was too dangerous.

He walked over to Wolfgang, who was listening intensely to Hänschel.

"Wolfgang told me a lot about you," Hänschel said. He assessed Hans and offered him a beer.

"We should..." Hänschel's eyes wandered behind Hans, who turned as Martha's friend Else approached the group.

Hänschel reached out for Else's hand with his meaty arm and planted a kiss on it.

"Fräulein Schwarzkopf, what a pleasure to see you again. I had the pleasure to meet Fräulein in Berlin already," he explained, his eyes lingering greedily on her bosom. "Are you and your girls performing at the party day in Nuremberg?"

Her smile fell. "No, not everyone performed their best

the day Frau Zu Castell came." She gave Wolfgang a reprimanding look. He frowned.

Else blushed as she then extended her arm to Hans. "A dance?"

He found it easiest to plaster a fake smile on his face to cope with his feelings as he started to dance with Else. Probably something his father had taught him. She didn't let him out of her fangs for a couple of dances. But as soon as he could, he excused himself. He was bathed in sweat, not from the dancing alone. He simply wanted to get away from it all.

It was difficult to hide in the room. He noticed a small bar at the entrance to the ballroom and walked over to grab the first beer that was offered to him and drowned it in one go.

And suddenly she was back, Martha.

"I saw you the other day," she whispered. Her words hit him hard. "Where?"

"In that pub, in Berg am Laim."

He felt the beer. The room seemed to start spinning as he looked around, trying to gather his thoughts. He had met his French contact there. But she? She had no business in Berg am Laim. And then a terrible thought suddenly crossed his mind. Was he being played? Had she followed him? He caught Wolfgang looking at him, creepily observing his every move, and he forced a smile back on his face as he grabbed her arm, needing to hold on to her, to steady himself. He came closer, studying her face, but her contemptuous expression was even more intense. No, she wasn't testing him, wasn't one of them. He noticed her squint and realized that he had squeezed her arm harder than intended.

He quickly let go and took big strides until he reached Wolfgang and Hänschel, laughing at Hänschel's cheap jokes without listening to a word, his thoughts still racing. He had to get out of there. When Hänschel finally moved on, he came as close to Wolfgang as he could without arousing any suspicion.

"Enough Hänschel. I'd like to be alone with you."

Wolfgang stood tall at the promise in Hans's words, and Hans felt him right behind him as they returned to Hänschel to say goodbye and then make their exit.

He drove the two home but pretended to fall ill in the car so he could get back to Schwabing immediately.

Wagner had said that many spies underestimate the effect of loneliness. Hans, however, was used to it. But now, on this side of the ocean, loneliness had become his enemy. And he never felt lonelier than when the door to his tiny studio closed behind him that night.

He pictured himself with her in there. She was the only person he knew who felt like him, who was like him. The person who made him almost lose control of himself. And he knew with sadness in his heart that the only person he longed to be with was the one person whose path he should never cross again.

In less than a month, the lectures would start, and he hoped that they would bring him the necessary distraction and distance he needed.

He also saw less of Wolfgang in the weeks to come. Wolfgang was busy developing a new code with a team of specialists, which he wasn't tired of telling Hans about the few times they saw each other. But Hans received fewer opportunities to gather intel before the start of his classes. An invite to Hänschel's flat to watch from his generous balcony and celebrate Mussolini's arrival on September 29 promised the next chance for Hans, even though he despised the prospect of coming face-to-face with Hänschel again.

Mussolini's arrival in Munich was a much-celebrated event. Italy's dictator had come to sign the Munich Agreement, along with Neville Chamberlain and Édouard Daladier, Britain's and France's leaders, to finally grant Hitler the annexation of the Sudetenland. Hans recognized some of the faces from Hänschel's birthday; others were new to him. He noticed the SS Totenkopf emblem, the "death's head," on the collar of a couple of them. He had not seen those before: the death's head marked them as being in charge of the camps.

Hitler had declared to Chamberlain that his demand for the Sudetenland was the last one he would make to Europe; and Hans had gathered from the international press and his network of spies that some people considered the agreement an appeasement to a war-hungry Hitler. Few considered it a lasting guarantee for peace.

When the first sign of commotion wafted from the outside into the Hänschel's living room, Hans got up and stepped out onto the balcony, fleeing the nasty smell of the Reemtsma cigarettes everyone else was smoking inside. But only moments later he was joined by Wolfgang, Hänschel, and one other *Volksgenosse* and was yet again enfolded in the unpleasant cloud he had just fled. The commotion outside was caused by a group of audacious French tourists who were bellowing protests about Mussolini, as Hitler and Italy's dictator were approaching in the distance. The puzzled look of those present outside told Hans they didn't speak French, so Hans translated for them. By the time they understood and turned back to look at the protestors, the instigators had disappeared into the growing crowd.

A couple of hours after midnight an SS officer busted into the room to proudly announce the signing of the Munich Agreement. Numerous champagne bottles were opened to celebrate. The guests' faces carried the smug expression of those that knew they had just successfully fooled their European neighbors—the ultimate proof to Hans, in addition to what Wolfgang had already told him, that there had been nothing appeasing in this agreement to Hitler; on the contrary, he had just come a lot closer to his ultimate goal: waging war. War instead of expansion.

When Hans was back at his studio, he sent out his reports, reviewing the evening. Volunteering to translate had been a calculated decision; Hans needed to reveal a skill that might not be entirely unique to himself, but with a bit of luck might give him more access to intel, such as the translation of code grabs that Wolfgang was working on. Now, however, he wasn't sure if it had been a wise move after all. How much did he want to be on Hänschel's radar?

His first biology lecture the following week proved to be a disappointment. It was all about infiltrating sciences with the notion that the Aryan race was the leading one. He realized that many important subjects were omitted from the syllabus. Hitler had left his imprint even here.

So he decided to skip the next one and attend a literature lecture instead—even though there was not a single title on the reading list that he was keen to revisit. Still, he wanted to dwell in the illusion that this could be a literature lecture in a healthy world.

As he descended the center staircase of the hall that morning, he was surprised, almost shocked, to spot Wolfgang in the first row. He stopped in his tracks, the person behind him cursing him for stopping so suddenly. He turned to apologize and was surprised again. There she sat in the last row of the hall: Martha! The sight of her sent a mixture of joy and shock through him. She was disguised as a male student, staring at him, raw terror in her eyes. The eyes that haunted him the minute he closed his own to sleep, the eyes that kept him awake instead.

He quickly looked away and turned around, his thoughts returning to Wolfgang. The lectures for Wolfgang's studies were held in a different wing of the faculty, he remembered as he stumbled forward down the stairs. "What are you doing in this class?" Wolfgang asked suspiciously as Hans arrived in his row, still shaken.

"My biology class was canceled. And you?"

"I am here with the Gestapo." He looked at him, not without his usual air of importance when he brought up the Gestapo. "We suspect there are a couple of students that are forming an opposition here. Hänschel is upstairs." He turned around, nodding at someone in the back. To Hans's relief, he didn't seem to spot his sister.

Hans had trouble following the lecturer's words. Why had Martha come? She was putting herself in danger. Schinkenhuber was an influential party member, and Hans knew that he was working closely with Hänschel on a secret operation that even Wolfgang had not been let in on. Why would she risk this?

Only two days later, Wolfgang intercepted Hans on his way to a biology lecture.

"Hänschel is taking us to lunch today," he said matter-of-factly.

Hans was filled with unease but nodded his head, faking enthusiasm. At the Schelling-Salon, Hänschel ordered *Schweinsbraten* with dumplings, drowning the masses of greasy food with two beers, while talking tirelessly about the *Judenpolitick*, a term introduced by the party in late 1937. Wolfgang nodded his head in agreement; Hänschel's contempt toward the Jews found a mirror in Wolfgang's eyes.

"We've been too negligent. They have nothing left to do here, no economic power, no nothing! And still, some wouldn't get out of our country," he bellowed, his fork raised high, fat dripping off his mouth. "Now we will take tougher measures! This is a matter of life or death!" He paused dramatically, looking between Hans and Wolfgang. "The next on the list will be the Polish Jews," he exclaimed, triumphantly.

Hans sat upright and was glad that it was Wolfgang who dug deeper. "What are the plans?"

Hänschel sat back, and lifted his hand to order an *Apfelstrudel* and another beer without offering anything to them. "Dachau is filling up. We'll just deport them, all of them."

This time Wolfgang didn't ask further, instead he banged his hand on the table. "Yes!" He called out. "All" could mean all Polish Jews, all men—or all, as in all men, women, and children, which was something that hadn't happened yet.

His thoughts returned to his Polish Jewish neighbors. Hans would need to warn them.

The beers in Munich came in half-liter mugs, and the one-and-a half liters of beer were more than noticeable on Hänschel's breath as they left. He was an aggressive drunk, talking loudly while they walked back in the direction of Gestapo headquarters. On their way they passed a restaurant that Hans had usually seen filled with people for lunch, but now it was closed, barred with wooden boards, marked with swastikas.

"I just had this one closed," Hänschel blared proudly. "Next one on my list is the one around the corner from Prinzregentenstraße"—the place that Wolfgang had given a wide berth to before, the night Hans and Wolfgang had met. "But that time I'll go myself. And you, Wolfgang, come along and help me," he bellowed under a nasty laugh. "Those fairies are a disgrace to the Aryan race. In my experience you can only drill it out of them; arresting them doesn't do any good!"

Hans looked over at Wolfgang.

"Did you find the members of the opposition you were looking for two days ago?" Hans asked Hänschel quickly to end the horrible conversation, knowing the answer already from Wolfgang.

"No. Not yet. But we are close, *very* close. We've found their filthy pamphlets all over Schwabing. They had printed them on a makeshift printer in the copy room right next to the lecture hall! Can you imagine? Right in sight of everyone!" His meaty hand made a fist. "Making us look like fools!" He was bright red in his face.

"What happens when they get caught?" Hans asked.

Hänschel stopped in his tracks and turned his head toward Hans, who shuddered. Hänschel's face was contorted into an ugly grimace, and then, very slowly, it gave way to a smile. "*Everyone* talks under torture."

A shiver ran down Hans's spine. That was exactly what Wagner had explained to Hans when he had handed him a small white pill. "Should they catch you, take this. It kills you instantaneously."

Hänschel held out his meaty hand to Hans. "What other languages do you speak?" His eyes were barely visible under the heavy lids.

"English. Learned both languages from my grandparents."

"Great," was all Hänschel said before he turned around and left with Wolfgang for the Gestapo offices.

That evening, Hans waited for silence to descend over the house in the Schellingstraße. He knew from experience that about half an hour after bedtime he heard the mother from above on the stairs on her way out. He waited until he heard the door close downstairs and made his way up. His hands trembled slightly as he knocked on the door of the Polish family. It was the father who opened the door, his face contorted in fear at the late visitor.

"You need to leave," Hans whispered. "They are coming for you, to deport you. Leave as soon as you can." Then he turned around, and walked back to his studio.

That night he used his radio transmitter for the second time since his arrival.

The next morning he managed to meet with his French spy again—the woman he had met in Laim am Berg. She was married to a Polish Jew. He delivered the latest news. She was desperately grateful.

"I owe you," she said.

Wolfgang was already waiting for Hans when he arrived at the university.

"You missed your first lecture," he said, greeting Hans, a deep furrow between his brows. What was it in his look, suspicion or jealousy, or both? Hans thought, the pit in his stomach growing. He shrugged his shoulders, trying to appear unaffected as he held Wolfgang's gaze.

"I overslept."

"What did you do last night?"

"I stayed at home. The *Schweinsbraten* with Hänschel weighed heavy on me. I slept horribly." He smiled at Wolfgang. Slowly, Wolfgang's face relaxed.

"I decoded them," Wolfgang whispered proudly, as he held out a couple of papers to Hans. "Hänschel needs you to translate them."

Then he turned around and disappeared among students hurrying to their next lecture.

Back at home Hans studied the papers in detail: they were code grabs, some in French, some in English. His plan had worked out: he had found a way to tap into a network of new spies. He spent the entire night decoding the intel.

From then on Hans was more careful to meet his contacts outside his hours at the university—which Wolfgang seemed to know by heart. It deeply worried him that he wasn't able to discern the reason for Wolfgang's occasional suspicion. Was it jealousy—or worse? As he entered the university in the second week of the term, he caught sight of Hänschel and Wolfgang disappearing into the building's basement— followed shortly by Martha. He followed them, witnessed them capture the students of the opposition—and almost Martha, too. But worst of all, he saw a new side of Wolfgang; he had become a dangerous man, one who wouldn't stop at murdering those that posed a threat to the only thing he believed in—the Führer—even if it meant killing those he loved: him, but even worse, his own sister.

Again, Hans couldn't sleep that night, thinking about Martha. He stood right behind her in the pitch-black basement after Wolfgang and Hänschel had dragged the students out. He had smelled her rose scent, he had wanted to hold her trembling body, tell her she wasn't alone in her fear. But he didn't announce himself to her. How was it possible that he felt that much for this girl? A girl who was heading fast toward her own destruction, he knew. What had she been doing down there in the basement? She was either part of the opposition or had followed them, like he had done himself. He was smoking at the half-open window, one of his Gold Dollar cigarette brand, which to his pleasant surprise upon arrival were also sold in Germany. He inhaled, enjoying the familiar taste and smell of the Virginia blend, when he heard a commotion outside: opposite his window, he saw a couple of drunk SS officers calling over someone on his side of the street. "Hey, you, what are you doing out here this late at night?" His heart stood still when he saw who the girl was: Martha. And then the SS officers began to cross the street.

Hans ran down the stairs at top speed, driven by an impulse that he had been trained to avoid at any cost. He opened the door ever so slightly and pulled her inside as fast as he could, before they could get to her, pressing his hand firmly over her mouth to muffle her scream. And then she fell, and he wasn't quick enough to hold her. He saw in terror as she fell headfirst onto the stony pavement, the blood spurting out instantly from a head wound. His face contorted in pain as he saw it: the look she gave him before passing out was a mixture of fear and hatred.

Fortunately, the SS officers had been too drunk to pursue her and had left. Two hours had gone by since the incident, and she was lying on his bed — he had nothing else to lay her on. He had examined the head injury; it didn't need immediate attention. He sat next to her and allowed himself an intimate moment with this woman. He watched her in her sleep, which had taken away her look of fierce determination. He eventually got up and walked over to her bag. He felt like he was snooping around, and had to remind himself that he was a spy and only doing his job. And there, at the bottom of the bag, he found them: two pamphlets that she must have taken with her from the university's basement.

"Where am I?"

He turned around. She sat up in bed and was now feeling her head.

"You're in my place."

She slowly seemed to regain her memory.

"Why?"

"Because I'm not like your brother."

She let out a bitter laugh.

"No, you're probably worse. Judging from how he's changed since he met you."

She threw him a scrutinizing look, filled with contempt.

"I'm sorry, Martha, but it wasn't me who changed him."

She opened her mouth, words of defense on her lips. But she changed her mind and remained silent. Her face softened ever so slightly.

He held up the two pamphlets he had found in her bag. "Why?"

"When are they picking me up? Or when are you taking me?"

"Nobody is going to pick you up."

He pulled up a chair and sat opposite her. He felt nervous. He knew he had this one opportunity to somehow prove to her that he was different, without betraying who he was.

"Why?" he asked again, instead.

"Because I couldn't live with myself anymore if I didn't at least try. I don't know how you and my brother can do this, how you can be so blind, but I..." She swallowed and her eyes filled with tears. "I am afraid of what will happen to me now, and worst of all, that this was for nothing. I didn't even get a chance to distribute them anywhere because of you!" She stared at him, then looked out the window.

"Martha, I'm not one of them."

She slowly turned toward him.

"I find that hard to believe. Why did you befriend my brother then?"

"I didn't."

"Who are you then?"

"I believe in democracy, like you do."

He could sense that she hadn't quite yet trusted his revelation, that she was scared.

"You're the only friend my brother ever had," she said after a while.

Even now, she considered her brother's emotions over her own.

"I don't think I'll ever be your brother's friend."

"Then why do you pretend you agree with his insane ideals?" she practically spat out. "What's this all about?"

Instead of answering her question, he stood up with the two pamphlets and threw them into the hot stove, destroying them.

"If you're not one of them, why did you not let me distribute those?"

"I helped you stay out of trouble!"

"Are you with the opposition?"

"No, I'm not."

She got up to leave, but he came over and gently pressed her back down onto the bed. "Don't go just yet."

She gave him a puzzled look. "What is it to you, anyway?"

"Please, promise me not to do anything for the moment, will you?"

"Why? Why should I promise *you* of all people?"

"Believe me, it's too dangerous. The opposition isn't organized well enough. A couple of people are not going to achieve anything. You need someone bigger among your opposition. How long have you worked with those students?"

Her eyes became narrow slits. "How would you know about that?"

"I was in the basement right behind you, after everyone had left," he admitted.

"That was you?" she paused, confused. And then her voice started to rise. "You terrified me! I thought I was next!"

He looked at her more intensely. "Reporting you is the last thing on my agenda. Martha, answer my question: How long have you worked with those students?"

She shook her head. "I don't even know them. I wanted to see where they were going. I had made up my mind last week to become more proactive, now that I am with that family, and... I know it was naive. How could I have known that my brother was on to them?" She buried her face in her hands. "Oh, God, what has happened to him? I don't recognize my own brother!" she nearly shouted.

"I never had a sibling, but I can only imagine what it must be like to see your brother transform like that before your eyes."

She suddenly jumped up, panicking, "Oh, my God, the twins—they must have woken up by now. What will I tell them, where I've been all this time?"

"I'll help you. Let me take you back."

He went over to his tiny wardrobe and quickly put on his jacket, then turned to the fridge, taking out a milk bottle and some food. His plan was to tell the family that Martha had been attacked on her way back from grocery shopping, and had passed out in one of the house entrances where he had found her. He was too tired to come up with a better excuse.

When he turned around to his bed, she was no longer there. She must have tiptoed out.

He stepped into the crisp air, and scanned the street—it was empty as far as the eye could see. He walked along the street, searching the house entrances along the road, hoping she was hiding in one of them. But after a while he gave up. There were several roads leading to the Schinkenhubers from his street. He selected one and headed for Agnesstraße. When he got there, he saw that the flat was brightly lit—she hadn't been able to return unnoticed.

"We caught them," Wolfgang gloated the next morning. "In the basement of the university."

"Congratulations."

"It was only a question of time," Wolfgang answered, with

arrogance in his voice. Hans's thoughts constantly revolved around Martha: What had happened to her? What had Schinkenhuber done to her? He longed for news about her, but Wolfgang didn't volunteer any, and Hans couldn't ask, remembering Wolfgang's look only too well the two times he had found Hans looking at his sister.

Hans passed by the Schinkenhubers' home several times, hoping to run into Martha on one of her errands. But she never showed. And he thought, with his heart heavy, that he wouldn't have been able to talk openly to her in the streets anyway. He would need to see her alone.

He left Schwabing in his car before dawn and reached the forest twenty minutes later. He knew Martha rose early on Mondays to get back to the Schinkenhubers. Hans parked and then walked to the road leading to the Wiesbergs' house, cowering in the bushes nearby. At six she made an appearance, and he stepped out of his hiding place, right in front of her bike.

"How is your head?"

She startled. "I doubt you came all the way out here to ask me about that," she said, motioning for him to get out of her way so she could continue.

"I want to show you something, and then I'll drive you to the Schinkenhubers," he said.

"I cannot be late," she said, but allowed him to hide her bike in the bushes.

He walked with her deeper into the forest. He had brought a flashlight that he only switched on once he was sure the light couldn't be seen from the path. Even though he hadn't been back in weeks, he still knew this path almost in his sleep, even in darkness, a valuable skill he had learned in the woods around Montgomery. But he didn't want her to panic, and as he was guiding her by the arm through the dense foliage he could already sense that Martha was becoming increasingly nervous—and afraid.

"Where are you taking me?"

He just kept going. She didn't resist as he guided her deeper and deeper into the woods. And then he stopped. In front of him was the clearing. Dawn had just set in, bathing the place in a dim yet ethereal light.

"I thought I knew this forest by heart," She said, and shook her head in awe. "This is a wonderful piece of earth."

"I wanted to share this place with you." He looked at her, hopeful.

"It's so peaceful here."

He nodded. "That's why I come here often. It's hard to find places without ears and eyes these days."

"I know I shouldn't have spoken like that."

"Like what?"

"That openly, the second time you came around."

He shook his head. "No, you shouldn't have. I kept telling you, you need to be much more careful."

"Do you think my brother could really betray me like that?"

"Even in summer, I would have said no—but now he might not even have a choice, given his involvement with the Gestapo. Down there in the basement, what do you think he would have done if he had found you?"

"I'm afraid to find out," she said in a shaky voice. She looked up at him. "Why did you bring me here?"

"I would love to meet you here once in a while."

"But why?"

"I think we have more in common than you know."

"I need to go," she said suddenly, light from the early morning sun starting to break through the branches.

He didn't want her to leave, and grabbed her hand. "And because ever since we danced, I've barely been able to think of anything else."

She paused, thinking hard before she responded. "I'm off work Wednesday afternoons for a couple of hours. And on Sundays I'm at home." She looked up at him and smiled.

Hans couldn't help but feel giddy inside as he drove her to

the Schinkenhubers. He let her out at a nearby park that she always cycled through on her way to work.

"Thank you," she said before she got out.

"For what?"

"For letting me know that I'm not that alone in this world."

Wednesday turned out to be a sunny day. He basked in the warm rays of the sun as he waited for her in the same park where he had let her out two days earlier.

She gave a small, shy smile when she saw him.

"Should we go to the class?" he asked.

She shook her head. "Let's go back to the clearing."

Hans removed his jacket when they arrived at the clearing and spread it on the ground, inviting Martha to sit down next to him. The whiff of her rose scent filling the air when she sat down next to him made him want to come closer, but he resisted his urge. He needed to be careful, move slowly. In his head, he was frantically searching for what to say next. He produced a pack of cigarettes from his pocket and offered one to Martha. She declined.

"'I don't understand how someone can not be a smoker— why, it's like robbing oneself of the best part of life... if a man has a good cigar, then he is home safe, nothing, literally nothing, can happen to him,'" Hans said.

Martha was quick to answer. "*Magic Mountain*, Thomas Mann."

He smiled. "You're good!"

She smiled back at him. Less shy this time. "Okay, my turn," she said. "'There is no point in trying to sabotage fate.'"

"Same novel." He paused before continuing. "You know you have to be—"

"...careful with these books, I know," she interrupted him.

"Do you still own any of them?" His concern for her overshadowed the joy he had just felt when discussing one of his favorite novels, the joy about feeling one with her against the rest of the world out there.

She nodded.

"At the Schinkenhuber's place or at home?"

"At home," Martha admitted grudgingly.

"Martha, you have to be—"

"Yes, Siegfried," she interrupted him again. "I was there when most of those titles were burned on the Königsplatz."

He reached for her hand and squeezed it softly.

"Those books—they're my only chance at journeying to faraway places." She smiled sadly.

"Some journeys are too dangerous," he said.

She released his hand and looked away, as if his words were too hard to face.

Still, knowing her pain, he reached for her hand again and gently pulled her into his lap. He tenderly took her face and looked into her eyes, hesitating only a couple of seconds before drawing her in for a kiss.

The prospect of seeing Martha helped him keep his head above water, made him see clearly when fear threatened to take over. Each time they parted ways, his heart sank with the knowledge that so many hours would go by until he'd see her again. They both knew that they were treading on thin ice. Yet all the more reason to fully enjoy those hours, which they both knew could end at any moment.

She never asked Hans what he was doing, or why he had been so upset when she had spotted him entering that bar in Schleißheimer Straße.

She had only asked once about the woman that she had seen him with in the bar. He had assured her that she was someone he worked with. And she seemed content with the answer.

Instead, they escaped into the world of literature. They liked the same type of stories, the same authors. And that wasn't all: between stealing kisses from each other, they shared stories they made up for each other in the days between their visits.

They were cuddled together, staring up into the sky. He

was just finishing his latest tale: "...and when he left the house the brother saw..."—he paused theatrically—"...his dead sister."

"The one he buried alive in the basement?"

"Yes, her exactly. She came to take revenge! And while the house was collapsing, she took the brother with her to the other side." He looked at her expectantly.

She laughed heartily.

"Edgar Allan Poe."

"You've know that the entire time and didn't say anything?"

She laughed, then became pensive. "I've always asked myself why our German literature almost always lacks the fantastic or the supernatural, some sort of fantastic realism! After all, we gave birth to the Brothers Grimm, but even my favorite authors, like Brecht, Mann, or Hesse—they never weave those elements into their stories!"

He used the moment to produce a wrapped gift for her. "Open it." Thanks to a contact in Berlin, he had been able to purchase for her a copy of *The Wizard of Oz*, even though most American literature had been banned.

"It's one of my favorite books." Hans explained.

Martha's eyes sparkled as she held the book in her hand.

"Thank you." She opened the book and started reading. Seeing the joy and excitement in her eyes was the best reward he could wish for.

When they separated, she continued to occupy his mind, but without the pain he had felt earlier in summer whenever he had thought about her. Now that she knew he wasn't one of them, the contempt had left her eyes when she looked at him. Now she looked happy.

It was another night in which he couldn't find sleep. He had just seen Martha the previous day and found it almost unbearable to have to wait more than two days to return to the clearing that had become their shelter of utter bliss. He got up and lit a cigarette. Smoking at night at the half-open window had become a routine for him, his only way to fight insomnia. He was on his second cigarette when a car stopped opposite his house. Out came several police officers, all from the SiPo. Hans quickly ducked behind the curtain, and felt the fear rise in him. Had they found out? And if they had, wouldn't he or Wolfgang show up? But then he heard other cars farther off in the distance, and he craned his neck to look outside, where he saw similar vehicles, down the streets, and people being dragged out of their homes. They hadn't come for him, he realized with relief. But the relief vanished only a second later. Hänschel had announced it: they had come to deport the Polish Jews.

They knocked on his door first. He opened it wide, as if he had nothing to hide, and they quickly assessed that he wasn't the target. Then they climbed up. They wouldn't find the Polish family, Hans thought with satisfaction; they had heeded his warnings and had moved out one night, about a week ago.

As the echoes of the heavy boots ebbed away, there was a shy knock on the door and he opened it, this time to the Jewish mother from upstairs. "You're a good man," she whispered. "They'll be forever grateful to you." Then she turned around and hurried up the stairs.

Hans was on his way to the Osteria Bavaria, Hitler's most frequented restaurant, where he would meet Wolfgang for a beer. It was definitely one step up from the more-economic beer halls they usually met at. It seemed as if not only Wolfgang's arrogance had become more abundant, so had his income. Hans noticed the change on the streets since the regime had deported some seventeen thousand Jews all over the Reich, and this time they hadn't spared women and children. Hans felt sick thinking what else they would be willing to do to chase them out of the country.

Wolfgang spotted Hans immediately when he entered. Hans was relieved at the absence of suspicion or disgruntlement in his face.

"Have you heard?" Wolfgang asked. "Heard what?" Hans shook his head.

"A Polish Jew shot Ernst vom Rath today in the French embassy." Wolfgang became outraged. "A German diplomat. We cannot tolerate that!"

Hans realized that this would kindle a much bigger fire. "Do you know what our Führer is planning to do about it?"

"No, but Hänschel's boss will see him the day after tomorrow! Everyone is going to be here. It's the fifteenth anniversary of his Beer Hall Putsch." That was Hitler's failed coup that led him to write Mein Kampf. "Maybe he'll take me." Wolfgang added hopefully.

At the end of the evening, Wolfgang passed Hans a thick folder. "Translate those, as well. As fast as possible."

Hans nodded his head, eager to get back home and dive into new intel.

The front pages of every newspaper covered the latest news the next day, and the air was tense in the city, the rage against the Jews more palpable than ever before. He noticed brownshirts—state troopers—on the streets of the city. Since Hitler's purge against them in 1934 on the Night of the Long Knives, the brownshirts now only played a marginal role, and weren't seen very often.

Hans met with several of his contacts, and they exchanged the intel they had gathered collectively: several Jews in possession of a gun had been disarmed, mostly in Berlin, and residences were broken into. More attacks were expected; foreign Jews were to be spared. Hans rushed home, shared his intel, and ran up the stairs to the Jewish family in his house. They didn't open. He slid a paper under their door, with one word—"leave"—the least he could do, and hurried back down and out of the house. It was time to meet Martha.

This clearing had become a world of its own, separate from the one they had to face outside this forest. When he looked at her now, the way she smiled at him, it seemed as if Martha had always been a part of this spot, and that only the two of them held the key to this sacred place, that they could only enter it together. It wasn't complete without the other.

"Do you like him at all—my brother?" Martha asked. The Föhn from the Alps had brought a warm wind to the clearing, warming their faces as they held each other.

He could tell she was keen on knowing the truth. He thought about it for a while before offering an answer. "I don't think he is a bad person. But he is weak. He is very different from you."

She took a deep breath. "May I ever tell him then that I really like his new best friend?"

"No. It must remain our secret." He tried to remain calm on the outside, twirling her hair with his finger. It wasn't his place to tell her. She needed to find out by herself.

"Why? I think he might be less ruthless with me if he thought I had befriended his friend, a friend of the regime, of 'our Führer.'" Contempt was in her voice as she mentioned Hitler. "Every day I have to pretend to believe in a system that is so wrong and so evil; why can't I at least show openly whom I love?"

He noticed it was the first time the word "love" had come up between them. He kissed her in response.

"I hardly know anything about you," she added sadly, after they ended the kiss.

He tenderly stroked her cheek as a quiet tear came loose from her eye. "I need to show you something," he said seriously, guiding her toward the back of the oak tree where he had carved his initials.

"This is so beautiful" she remarked when she saw the carvings in the woods. "Did you do that?" she remarked.

Hans nodded his head.

"*H. M.*—What does it mean?" she asked.

"They're initials. My real initials." He gazed at her intently, trusting her, giving her as much of his soul as he could.

She didn't ask for more. Not yet.

Hans was still in high spirit when he approached Schwabing in the evening. He could still taste Martha's soft lips on his, the word "love" was still hanging in the air, still ringing in his ear with her sweet voice—but once he crossed the city lines, his mood changed suddenly. A mad rage had descended over the city. The rage Hans had felt among the civilians earlier that day was released through the most violent actions: brownshirts and civilians threw stones into Jewish property. The storm troopers acted with a newly assigned power; the civilians appeared to be an organic part of the evening.

Schwabing wasn't any different. Hans parked his car farther away from his street and the density of the houses. He couldn't believe his eyes when he saw the violence unfold. Brownshirts were yelling at him, encouraging him to join them; others were shouting at him, reprimanding him for not participating. He hurried on, his head held low. When he turned the corner onto his street, he immediately recognized the shop the brownshirts and civilians were bombarding with stones: it belonged to his Jewish neighbor, the woman, with her son and daughter. Out of the corner of his eyes he saw a black car enter the street after him. He hurried on.

"Siegfried!" He heard Wolfgang's voice behind him. Almost instinctively Hans bent down to pick up a stone. As he turned around, he saw Wolfgang and Hänschel exit the car, this time Wolfgang, too, wore a long black leather coat. They were a frightful sight. He spotted the stone in Hans's hand.

"So you've heard, I see. Unbelievable. They truly killed him!"

"Who?"

"Vom Rath died at five thirty today!" Wolfgang bellowed.

"Help Hofstätter," Hänschel bellowed to Wolfgang from

behind him and headed for Hans's house. Hans had a hard time concentrating on both men at the same time. His eyes were drawn to Hänschel disappearing in Hans's apartment block, when he heard Wolfgang whisper to him: "I am so relieved to find you here! You weren't at your class at the university, nor at home, either. But now I see what you've been up to." Wolfgang bent down and picked up a stone. He threw it with a force that surprised Hans. Then he looked at Hans, waiting for him to throw the one he was holding. Hans felt the panic rise in him; his impulse was to run, run away from this violence, this world; he felt nauseous. But the rational side of him knew he couldn't. This was the moment when he could easily blow his cover with one wrong move. As he raised the stone in his hand, he caught sight of the Jewish mother, standing next to her shop, crying. As she spotted Hans, she stopped crying, too shocked and puzzled by the sight that had unfolded in front of her. Hans would never forget her face, the way she looked at him, in absolute puzzlement, as Hans hurled the stone full force into her shop. Wolfgang chuckled with pleasure, as he picked up more, in total ecstasy. "Let's finish them off, Hofstätter," he bellowed at him, mimicking Hänschel's ugly tone, watching Hans in delight as they hurled one stone after the other into the woman's property. With every stone Wolfgang threw, the picture became clearer for Hans: tonight was a night for Wolfgang to unburden his frustration at being considered the same as the Jews: a disgrace to the Aryan race. Hans was not only forced to execute acts of violence against innocent helpless people, their property, their religious sites, but was pushed to perform them with vigor, passion, and conviction, the growing bile churning in his stomach with each stone he threw. They stopped when they heard the commotion coming from Hans's house, and he and the mother turned their heads to watch the mother's son being dragged out of the house by Hänschel, who looked like the reaper in his black cloak. Taken away to Dachau—Hans knew what she didn't.

As the tears streamed down her face, she mouthed only

one word to Hans: Why? Hans stood paralyzed. Wolfgang seemed completely oblivious to the torture Hans was undergoing and grabbed him by the arm. "Come with me."

Hans followed. They turned into Türkenstraße, where the violence continued. Here, too, civilians had joined the brownshirts, while the police stood back and watched. And after a few blocks, Hans realized with shock which direction they were walking: Toward Brienner Straße 22, the Gestapo's headquarters. Had he made a mistake? Had Wolfgang seen the exchange of looks between the Jewish woman and him? Had he just pretended to be oblivious? Had Hans blown his cover? His mind conjured up the image of Wolfgang kicking the male student from the opposition, and he considered making a run for it. If he was panicking for no reason, then making a run for it would blow his cover for sure. Several times he called out Wolfgang's name, but he just motioned to Hans to carry on. Hans couldn't tell. So he kept following on shaky legs. When Wolfgang finally turned to Hans, he looked as if he had awoken from a state of total ecstasy. "Here we are," he said with reverence in his voice. "I was so nervous the first time I set foot in here. That I wouldn't be good enough," he whispered to Hans, the tone conspiratorial. Hans was flooded with relief, and still, the door that was being held open for him led to no other place but the Gestapo headquarters—and their infamous torture cells underneath.

Hänschel was already there and greeted them. "Let's have a drink to celebrate," he shouted. They walked into the adjacent room. More than once during the night, Hans wasn't sure if he had imagined it or if he heard screams wafting up to him from down there, but it was overpowered by the laughter, cheers, and occasional bellowed orders in the room. His beautiful afternoon with Martha seemed ages away, surreal in light of what he had just seen and what he was about to witness that tragic night. Hans was introduced to several crucial Nazi figures who had all come to Munich to attend the anniversary of the Beer Hall Putsch, which conveniently coincided with the death of Ernst vom Rath, giving them all the excuse they needed for what would follow that night. Hans was introduced to Hänschel's boss, Criminal Police Chief Inspector Heinrich Müller, whom everyone else called Gestapo Müller, and Müller's superior, Reinhard Heydrich, whom Hitler, Wolfgang had told him, called the Man with the Iron Heart. Looking into that man's face sent a shiver down Hans's spine. Over the course of the next hours, through midnight, Müller sent orders to all Gestapo offices throughout the German Reich, which were then followed by more orders from the Man with the Iron Heart, who was concerned there wasn't enough space for all the Jews in Dachau, and Hans realized to his even greater terror that the night was far from being over yet. He overheard some of the atrocious orders that were bellowed through the room at the secretaries who were eagerly typing away on their typewriters Among them were the order to arrest twenty thousand to thirty thousand Jews throughout Germany; plundering, looting, and larceny were strictly prohibited, German property to be spared; only healthy male (not too old) Jews were to be arrested and taken to the concentration camps. The violent acts were to be executed by the storm troopers; civilians, however, were expected to participate—the police were not to intervene. Exactly what Hans had just witnessed—except that now it had become official.

Hans returned home as soon as he could without arousing suspicion. Wolfgang was so starstruck that he only nodded his head when Hans said goodbye, his eyes glowing like a little boy's from the excitement of being among all his heroes. Hänschel, however, had noticed him leaving, and Hans hadn't liked the scrutinizing look on Hänschel's fat face. Hans ran at top speed through the violence of the night, which had increased since the orders had been sent out. He held his head low, trying to avoid the sights around him, but the noises alone left a deep mark; the cries of men, women, and children alike echoed through the night—and in his head, a long time after he had used his radio to send off his latest reports and had gone to bed, lying awake for the next days to come.

He didn't leave the house for forty-eight hours, and only the prospect of seeing Martha in just a couple of days helped him not to lose his mind. But the next day Wolfgang intercepted Hans at university and invited him to his house for the following Sunday, of all days, to "celebrate," first with *Kaffee und Kuchen*, "coffee and cake," a popular Sunday-afternoon meal shared among Germans, followed by dinner—an obligation that would cut right into his cherished hours with Martha. He hadn't seen, hadn't held or kissed her for a week. But he knew very well that he couldn't decline. As always, Wolfgang's mother threw Hans a weary look as he entered the home but greeted him properly, her hand held out in the Hitler salute. Hans knew Martha was waiting at the clearing for him while Hans had to listen to Wolfgang discuss the Reichskristallnacht in light of the major turning point for the Aryanization for Germany.

Half an hour later, Martha hurried in.

"Where have you been?" her mother reprimanded her the second she set foot in there. The relief in her eyes upon seeing Hans warmed his heart. Her cheeks were rosy from the cold outside, her eyes were glowing, she held her body tall and proud. She had never looked more beautiful to him, and yet he couldn't hold her, couldn't kiss her. He knew that he played his spy role well, that he had become a good actor, but when it came to Martha he didn't know how long he could keep up his facade. He got up from his seat to greet her. "Heil Hitler. Fräulein Wiesberg."

"Heil Hitler. Herr Hofstätter, I haven't seen you in a while," Martha exclaimed, with a glance at her brother.

As usual, Wolfgang seemed annoyed at the interruption. "'Cause we've been busy weeding out the Jewish cockroaches." He grinned at Hans. "We were a good team,

Siegfried, weren't we? Even though I have to admit you're better at hauling rocks than me." His laugh was triumphant. Hans felt Martha's questioning eyes on him, but he didn't dare look at her. He felt ashamed.

Unfortunately, the topic arose again several times during dinner, Wolfgang gloating about how "they had shown those filthy Jews."

At one point, Wolfgang stopped himself in his flow and looked at Hans. "Siegfried, I think I am very close; Hänschel only needs some more convincing, but I have him almost there." He made a theatrical pause. "How would you feel about joining us?"

Hans tried his best to keep a straight face and fake enthusiasm. He had hoped this offer would never come up. "Come on, you don't need to ask me; you know how I feel!" He said instead, with a proud smile on his face.

"How are the Schinkenhubers treating you?" He addressed Martha, trying to stir the conversation in a different direction, as he felt his face falling slowly.

"Fine, just fine. All thanks to my brother." She gave Wolfgang a bright smile, but his face seemed frozen. "I just have to work a bit more these days, as Frau Schinkenhuber is pregnant with her seventh child."

"Herr Schinkenhuber certainly knows how to please our Führer," Wolfgang said before addressing Hans again.

"Come on now, Siegfried, we have reasons to celebrate some more, don't we?" Wolfgang got up from the table.

"It was very nice to see you again, and thank you for the meals." Hans looked from their mother to Martha, his look lingering on her face a few seconds longer, his heart heavy, as they had just missed another opportunity to meet at the clearing.

The next morning, Hans drove out to Perlach at dawn, waiting for her to emerge out of the forest. But she didn't appear, nor on Wednesday. Hans was almost mad with despair and his longing to see her. Finally, the following Sunday, she waited for him at the clearing. This time, Hans sank into Martha's arms, asking her to hold him tight. They sat like that for a long time. It took him some courage and time to tell Martha what had happened during the fateful night, and why he had been involved. When they ended the embrace, Martha looked up at him. He at first was afraid to meet her eyes, afraid that he would see repulsion in them, but she looked at him with adoration and respect.

"You've been very courageous, Siegfried."

Hans laughed bitterly, shaking his head.

"You warned that family! You couldn't have prevented what happened."

"Throwing stones with them just felt so..." He shook his head, at a loss for words about how it had felt. "Evil" was not strong enough to describe what he had witnessed.

"Siegfried, I've been approached by a member of the opposition. I knew him from a book club. He asked me to distribute flyers around the Glockenbachviertel. She swallowed. "I've decided I will join them." She threw him a desperate look. "I want you to be proud of me, Siegfried! As proud as I am of you."

"I was worried you'd come back to that thought sooner or later."

"How can you love me? How could you be disappointed if I did things like you? We could become real partners. Like you and that woman in the bar," she pled with him.

He looked at her long and hard, wincing. His French contact. Her husband was in safety, thanks to his warnings; she wasn't, though. "They arrested her last week. Hänschel himself did; he found out she was sending messages to France." He swallowed. In fact he had translated a coded message that was from her, unbeknownst to him.

Hans took her by the arm. "Promise me you will not do this."

He could see her eyes fill with tears of rage before she

spoke, her tone growing stronger, but colder. "I want to make a difference."

"Martha, I know, and I understand. But believe me, nobody thanks you for being a martyr!"

"So why do you do it, then? One day I'll lose you to a brave, interesting woman, who will usher in the fall of the Führer."

"No, you won't. But you will lose your life if you join the opposition!"

Martha turned away, but he took hold of her face and pulled it toward his, forcing her to look into his eyes.

"Promise!"

She sat up, a determined look on her face. "I will. If you tell me who you are in return."

Hans shook his head. 'I can't, Martha. It's for your own good."

Martha grew impatient. "Why don't you trust me?"

Hans sighed heavily. "Martha, I trust you with my life." He laughed bitterly. "Literally. All I live for right now are these precious moments with you. Let's hold on to them."

He could tell that the urgency with which he was pleading had an effect on her.

"Will I ever get to meet *H.M.*?" Her look wouldn't allow for another evasive answer.

"I'm trying, Martha. To make plans for us. But times are... difficult, as you know. For now we need to lay low and trust only each other."

"I cannot meet you on Wednesdays anymore," Martha said sadly.

Hans nodded. "I feared that when you didn't show up last week. We cannot afford to have your brother become suspicious of us, either."

"My God, why does he act like a scorned lover some-times?" He still didn't have the heart to tell her.

"Believe me, I'm in full control of your brother." But he was starting to doubt that.

He reached for an envelope underneath his jacket. He looked around one more time before giving it to her.

"Listen, take this."

"What is it?"

"It's a fake passport and a fake birth certificate that will enable you to adopt a different identity. But you must promise me to hide them well, each in a different place, and promise me not tell anyone about them. Use them at the right moment." He had received some of the documents from the French contact. The favor she had owed him.

Martha just looked at him in silence. "You're asking me for a lot of promises, without telling me anything I want to know," she said between clenched teeth.

"Because I know what is best for you." Martha rolled her eyes.

"I know how this sounds. Martha, I want to go with you when the time is right. But I need to arrange for that."

She looked at him, astonished. "Go? Where?"

"England, America, France. There are several possibilities."

Martha seemed at a loss for words. "I couldn't, Siegfried. I can't leave my mother and brother and..."

"There is no question that we would try to get your mother out at a later stage."

"What about Wolfgang?"

"Him, too, if he wanted. But I doubt he would be willing anytime soon."

Martha became restless. He could tell she was battling with herself.

"Would you want to do this? And fight this regime from the outside?" he asked.

She was staring, not saying anything.

Hans motioned to the envelope. "Hide it under your skirt for now."

Without taking her eyes off Hans, she lifted her skirt and slowly slipped the package in her underwear, a provocative gesture. He was overcome with lust. It was cold out here; it would need to be quick, and the ground was almost frozen. He was surprised he was still able to think so clearly, as so many nights he had dreamed of just this.

Instead, he pushed her away gently. "Not here."

"Don't wait too long," she teased him. And with that she hopped up and tore away. He ran after her, caught her by the waist, and twirled her around. With the setting sun came the force of imagination. As he kissed her hard in the forests of Montgomery, for once he was able to forget where he really was.

Two days later he received his first official assignment from an American contact in Berlin, ordering him to check out Dachau immediately, to check the condition of the prison.

This time the anti-Semitic actions of the Nazi regime had made huge international waves, much to the chagrin of the Nazis, who so far had managed somewhat successfully to hide the degree of violence against the Jews. This latest development, however, was impossible to hide to the outside world: it was said that about eleven thousand Jews had been deported to Dachau and that ninety-one people had been killed.

But Hans had already made other plans for the next day: it was his birthday, which he didn't want to spend in Dachau but with his love.

Some few remaining shards of glass shattered under his feet the next morning as he made his way to the university at dawn. The day promised to be rainy and ugly, fitting the gloomy atmosphere in the city that the atrocious riot had left behind. The few people he passed looked as ashamed as he felt. They looked as if they had woken up from a bad nightmare, as if the fervor of the previous night had worn off and all there was left was shame and guilt.

He was already waiting for her outside the entrance to the university when she arrived. They hugged.

"What if my brother sees us?"

"Believe me, I made sure he won't be a problem this morning. But that's why I couldn't pick you up." Hans had gone with him to a beer hall the previous night and had made sure that Wolfgang's glass remained perpetually full.

He took her cold hands in his and guided her toward another oak door leading into the building.

"Do you trust me, Martha?"

"Yes."

"Then close your eyes."

He took her by the arm, guiding her down the stairs leading into the basement. From his conversations with Wolfgang, he knew that the Gestapo considered the basement of the university "cleaned." Still, his hands shook uncontrollably as he tried to pry open the stubborn lock of one of the rooms. The heavy door opened with a loud moan.

"You can open them, now."

They were standing in a theater, a movie theater. A professor—another contact of his—had helped him organize the film and setting up the projector, had explained him how it operated.

He produced a bottle of champagne and ushered her to a seat.

"What will we watch?"

"It's a surprise."

With shaking hands, he locked the heavy door from inside. Then the lights went off, and it went pitch black in the room. In gigantic white letters, the film title appeared on the screen in front of them: *It Happened One Night*, starring Clark Gable and Claudette Colbert. He sat down next to Martha and pulled her into his arms. He thought how ironic it was that he had never been happier in his entire life than at this moment, in a room near where students had been arrested for holding different opinions, in a country run by a mad dictator, in a world that had opened its doors wide for extremism, violence, and death. He wanted to preserve this happiness for the future.

They watched the film, laughed loudly together. This was

their own universe, free of the impending war, free of Elisa, free of his despotic father, of Wolfgang, of Hans's responsibilities toward his father and "fatherland." Free of Siegfried Hofstätter. It was a bubble that nobody would be able to destroy in that moment. And so they used the darkness, a long time after the movie had ended.

It was the first time for Martha, and an act for both that sealed the moment of perfect happiness, and also the most tragic turning point in both of their lives.

Afterward, Hans took Martha out to lunch. Their elated mood had made them feel invincible—and carefree. For them, at that particular moment, the world consisted of nothing else.

They ordered trout, with potatoes and butter sauce. Hans looked longingly into her clear green eyes. Those honest eyes.

"I've made up my mind. I'll go with you," she said.

"You just made me the nicest present. Today is my birthday," he said.

Both their eyes filled with tears. He was overjoyed by the happiness that life had finally revealed.

"Bon appetit," she said, raising her cutlery.

Hans smiled at her, elated, nervous, feeling silly with love. He now also took his knife and fork with his hands. With the knife in his right hand, he cut the soft skin of the trout. Then he put the knife down, and the fork changed hands. With his right hand he lifted the succulent piece of fish toward his mouth. He closed his eyes in anticipation of the taste. And then he opened them wide. He had done it. He had not eaten "continental."

But it was too late. In the moment that Hans realized his faux pas, he also realized that Hänschel was eating at a table nearby and had been observing them closely.

Martha reacted the fastest of them all.

"It happened one night," she whispered harshly and pulled him up from the chair. "Run!"

"I can't. I won't leave you here alone."

"If you don't, I swear, I will betray you!"

He began to run.

He didn't know what to do next. Nobody had ever provided him with the address of a safe house or a contact who could hide him in dire circumstances. In that instant he cursed Wagner, even Roosevelt. The United States, unlike others, had no proper intelligence agency. That is why he had never been a proper spy. That was why he didn't have a proper fallback plan. He was alone.

He sprinted down the street, which was almost empty at this time of day, over to his car and drove off, still not sure where to go. Martha's words echoed in his head: *It Happened One Night*. The film they had just watched. She had cleverly hinted at the basement, which was probably the worst hideout for him at the moment, but it would be better than... than what? He had nowhere else to go. He was a traitor. To his own family, to his country. To himself.

He didn't want to become a traitor to Martha, too.

He returned to the theater, only this time, he felt trapped there. He waited for her, hour after hour, wondering if she would make it as he paced the room. He had cursed himself again and again for having blindfolded her, but he hoped she would find him anyway. When he heard a knock at the door, his name on her lips, he had lost all sense of time. He could only guess by how cold her skin felt, when she ran into his arms, that night had descended on the city.

"Thank God!" he whispered into her ears, again and again. Then he held her at arm's length from him, taking a closer look. There were some bloody spots and swelling in her face.

The rage inside of him began to build. "What did they do to you?"

"It wasn't that bad," she said, trying out a smile.

"Who did this to you?"

She looked at him, and the brave face crumbled. "It was terrible," she said, sobbing.

"My brother, he was wild, Siegfried." She clenched her teeth. "Why did you never tell me?"

"I told you everything."

"No," she said, and there was disappointment in her eyes. "You never told me that my brother and I have something in common after all." She paused, breathing in, hard. Her eyes filled with tears again. "Our love for you."

Hans looked down at the floor, embarrassed.

"Why have you never told me? How could I have never noticed it?"

"Between your brother and me, nothing ever happened."

Martha nodded her head. "I know. I could tell, when we realized we were in love with the same man..."

"What happened next?"

"They let me go."

"Were you followed?"

Martha shook her head. "No, he's with Mother. She had a crying fit when Wolfgang told her what happened. They locked me in my room, but obviously I managed to escape."

She had brought him water and food, and he only let her out of his arms so he could gulp it down.

"I'm so sorry, Martha." His words sounded hollow even to himself.

"There's nothing to apologize for."

"I'll never forgive myself for the danger that I brought to you and your family. I've been a fool! If I had only stayed away from you, if I only tried harder, none of this would have ever happened." His voice had risen.

Martha squeezed his hand.

He took her into his arms, the woman whose love he couldn't even begin to understand.

"I was afraid you wouldn't make it," Martha said.

His mind was racing; he didn't know how to put it, how to tell her goodbye without giving her the impression that he was letting her down. He wanted her to know how he felt. To his surprise, it was Martha who spoke first.

"I couldn't have let you go without a last goodbye."

Hans opened his mouth to protest, but she put a finger to his lips.

"When you told me that we could escape together, when you said that to me for the first time, I saw a light at the end of the tunnel. And I know that this cannot go on forever. As far as I can tell right now, your country will not necessarily have to join our fight." She smiled up at him, knowingly. He stared at her incredulous.

"I know more about you than you think. Most I know from reading your face. The country you're from—the way you held your fork and knife in the restaurant." She stroked his face lovingly. "I can meet you in your country. Follow you with the documents you gave me!"

"Not now, Martha! And not without me! It would be too dangerous! Now that they have me—and you—on their radar! We need to wait!" His fear for her was unbearable. "I will come. Get you out of here safely." He took her face into the palms of his hands. "I swear I will come for you, Martha!"

She nodded. "I know. That's the only reason I'm here." He let go of her face, and she reached for her bag. "Here, I also brought you some warm clothes. And extra food."

"I should go."

"The sun only sank a couple of hours ago. Stay for a little while longer?" He put his hands in his pocket and produced a pill. "Take this and always have it handy."

"What is it?"

"Everyone talks under torture."

"But I have nothing to tell. All I know of you are the initials of your real name."

"And that might just be enough. Please. Take it for in case. It will kill you almost instantly."

She quickly slipped it into the pocket of her brown dress.

They made love one last time.

As she was lying on his lap afterward, she murmured, "I

have a new story, one that I created just for us. For you. In the clearing, when I was waiting for you that day."

And she told him the most beautiful fairy tale he had ever heard. It was a story about peace. As her soft voice vibrated through the room, she infiltrated the space with the innocence of her story, and their bubble formed again. The room became their haven of oblivion from the outside world again. When she finished, he took her lovely face in his hands, looking at it one last time.

"Thank you," he said, with tears in his eyes. "I will treasure it—and you—forever." And he knew he would. His photographic memory was the true apex of his spy training. It had helped him memorize the names Wolfgang had given him, invaluable information. But right at this moment nothing seemed more invaluable to him than the fairy tale, a piece of Martha, a part of her beautiful mind.

"Don't leave yet," she murmured. He reached out and caressed her face. And then, finally, sleep came over her. She was holding him tight. And he, too, gave in to the fatigue that consumed him.

He was woken by a tap on his shoulder. Martha was still lying in his arms. He looked up—and into the eyes of Wolfgang. Wolfgang's wooden face motioned for him to be quiet. Very gently, Hans unwound out of Martha's embrace, under the watchful eyes of Wolfgang. The earlier shame hit him again. He was nothing but a cheater, cheating on his country, on his family, and on this man. This man might have been brainwashed by the regime, but so were millions of others. He now understood that, after all, he never really had to doubt that the love this man felt for him was as genuine as the love he felt for this man's sister. He looked over at Martha, feeling again reassured that he at least was truthful to the one person he loved the most in this world. He noticed that the pill he had given her had rolled out of her dress, he hoped unnoticed by Wolfgang. He hesitated, tempted to take it back. The one thing that would grant him a sudden and painless death. But his hesitation only lasted a second. Long enough for Wolfgang to notice. But then, Hans shook his head. No, she had been worth everything, including enduring all the pain that he would now have to.

Love was stronger than fear. An important life lesson.

He looked up at Wolfgang, finding it hard to look him straight in the eyes. "I'm sorry, Wolfgang."

Wolfgang's nostrils were now flaring with rage. Hans was trembling. Wolfgang grabbed Hans by the arm and pulled him up from the floor, as silently as he could. He looked away when Hans put on his pants. Hans turned his head one more time to have the image of the sleeping woman burned into his memory.

"Don't dare wake her," Wolfgang said between clenched teeth. Then he dragged Hans toward the door.

Hans realized with surprise that Wolfgang had come alone. Wolfgang gave him several pushes as they walked through the dark hallway. Both men were of a similar build, yet Wolfgang's strength surprised Hans—but he remembered the force with which Wolfgang had kicked the student from the opposition in the basement, and he shivered. Wolfgang's hand had sunk deep into Hans's flesh, making even the mere thought of fleeing impossible.

"Who do you work for?"

"You'd need to torture me to find out."

Wolfgang laughed; it sounded hollow.

"I'm sorry, Wolfgang. I acted under clear instructions. I had no choice!"

Wolfgang's hand tightened around Hans's arm even more. "Neither do I."

Hans stopped in his track. He turned around, confronting Wolfgang directly for the first time. He was shaking, but he had nothing to lose. Martha and he had witnessed the transformation of this man into a cruel man; but after all, he was Martha's twin.

"Yes, you do. Don't you see what is going on here?"

Wolfgang's eyes became tiny little slits.

"I pretended to be someone else, but so do you," Hans added.

"Shut up!" Wolfgang yelled at him, and then looked away.

Hans wanted to try again. In hindsight, he would not be able to say what exactly his reasons were for bringing up his homosexuality; he felt he was treading on very thin ice. Part of him wanted a better future for Martha, and he hoped that by talking to him, Wolfgang might change; even only a tiny bit would already help Martha. His reasons for it were also selfish: he hoped that by talking to him, he might change Wolfgang's plan to take him to the torture cell... but he knew that his chances were almost zero. He looked at this man that he had betrayed in the worst way possible—Martha's flesh and blood. At that moment he could see the old Wolfgang, the twin Martha once had. "And there is nothing wrong with who you are!"

Wolfgang let Hans's arm go. This would have been his chance to escape—but Hans didn't take it.

"Of course there is," Wolfgang screamed desperately. "Do you know what they do to people like me?" Wolfgang looked at Hans, pained. "I witnessed it last week. One of my friends." He shuddered at the memories: "They tied him to posts and put raw meat all around him, and then the dogs..." He couldn't continue and broke into tears.

"I'm sorry," Hans said again, in a second attempt.

"For what happened to my friend?"

"No, I'm sorry for having misled you."

Wolfgang just stood there, looking down, his arms dangling at his sides like a marionette. And that is what they all were, really—Hitler's marionettes.

Hans decided to make a run for it.

# Maya
## 2017

The world had been turned upside down. Maya had just glimpsed a side of Grandmother that she had never been privy to before. Grandmother had always been a special person to her, but Maya had never respected her, never loved her, never missed her more than now. Grandmother had been a fighter! A fighter for a cause. A fighter for love. How courageous she had been. She must have loved Hans Montgomery with such devotion, such certainty, that she remained alone for the rest of her life, knowing that she would never love like that again. Maya's father was the result of one night, fathered after the war, by a man three times Grandmother's age, who was married with children of his own and moved away after the end of the war. Grandmother hadn't come back to the United States to blackmail Hans; she came back because she had somehow found him all those years later! She had fought for her love until the bitter end—until her death. Maya was ashamed for suspecting that Hans Montgomery might be involved in the murder. He had been as brave as Grandmother.

Maya was grateful to Ben for having shared this journal with her. Ben. Her heart became heavy again. She wanted to try to forget, but whenever she closed her eyes, there he was, smiling at her. And then his facial expression had changed to disappointment at the conference, and then even worse, contempt, when he had discovered Paula's booklet.

Maya sank down against a pillow. Ben's smell still lingered. Grandmother paid a price, and so would she. After all, Grandmother had never given up. How could she give up on Grandmother now? She would continue, find out the truth about her murder.

She was driving way too fast as she made her way down the windy road from the resort in complete darkness. It had taken her all afternoon to read the pages; she had read them over and over again. So many questions were spinning in her head. Why had Edgar reacted the way he had when she mentioned Hans at the birthday celebration? She had assumed then that it was related to the stress of the party, but in hindsight she realized that Ben, too, had reacted similarly to the mention of Hans's name. Why did he refuse to talk about Hans when she asked? Why did that book paint Hans Montgomery as a weirdo, a hermit, a social misfit? And why did everyone claim that Hans disappeared in 1990? The ranger's words came back to her: *Everything changed after Hans Montgomery.*

Only Paula's car was parked in front of the house when Maya arrived. The waning moon was covered by clouds, so it was pitch black when she ran around to the back, Ben's pages firmly clutched in her hands. Maya had expected Paula to chase her away, but Paula said nothing after opening the door; instead she simply took a step toward Maya, opened her arms wide, and invited her into a tight embrace as she finally released her tears.

When they entered the house, Paula made strong tea. Maya was sipping at her cup when Paula brought out a cushion and a blanket.

"Don't go back there," she said, concern showing on her face.

"I've been advised that already. But what will your husband...?"

"We had a fight." She sat down next to Maya. "He won't

243

be back tonight. Adam, he..." Paula sighed, "he doesn't like it when I bring up the past."

"What is your past with the Montgomery?"

"I told you..."

Maya shook her head. "No, you didn't."

Paula sank back into the sofa. "Ben's father and I, we... we were lovers a long time ago."

"William?" Paula nodded. "Are you—?"

"Ben's mother? No, I'm not. But I love the boy like a mother." Paula's eyes filled with tears. "I never could have children of my own, and when I... when I was with William, I grew very close to the boy. William never loved me, at least not the way I loved him." She laughed bitterly. "The men of Montgomery! But Ben, he was very fond of me. When Elisa Montgomery fired me, she made sure I would never be able to come back. William was already cancer-stricken at that time and had no energy to fight for me. And I wonder if he even would have in good health. But I didn't give up that easily. I came back for Ben. She even got a restraining order on me!"

"But you stayed."

"Yes, I still hope he will come around one day. Accept me back. I don't know what Elisa told him, but he turned against me as much as the rest." She sighed. "He, too, is damaged goods." Paula's words hit Maya hard. Paula's eyes had shifted to the pages in Maya's hands.

"Who gave you those?"

"Ben."

Paula jumped up from the sofa. "Did you tell Ben that I gave you that book?" Her voice was panicked.

"No. Of course not"

"You must not tell him!" Fear showed in her face. "It... you must be careful with the Montgomerys, Maya!"

"These pages are about Hans Montgomery."

"And what do they say about him?"

"That he was in love with my grandmother."

Paula's eyes fluttered. "So she came here to reunite with

Hans Montgomery," she mumbled to herself as she put the pieces together. "So the fairy tale—" Paula broke off as she realized what she had just revealed.

Maya rose from the couch and came closer to Paula.

"You know this fairy tale, don't you?" She grabbed Paula by the arm, more forcefully than she had intended.

Paula looked at Maya, her lips pressed together. "I can't tell you, Maya. That's not up to me," she whispered. "I should have stayed out of all this. All these years!"

"Who can tell me, then?" Maya insisted.

"Listen, Maya, I honestly don't know who murdered your grandmother. Up until you came I only had my suspicions about what might have happened when she disappeared. Please, don't press me for more. I've said too much already. He'd be so upset."

"Who is *he*?" Maya noticed her voice sounded shrill now.

Paula hesitated. And then her shoulders sank as if in defeat. "Ben." She whispered.

Maya looked outside, wishing it were daytime, that the clouds would part and unleash light to guide her back to the clearing. Paula's revelations had not brought her closer to the truth, and she was certain, now more than ever, that the answer to all her questions—and Grandmother's murder—still could only be found out there. Deep in the woods.

"I think you should take a rest now, Maya. It's been a stressful couple of days for you."

Maya smiled at Paula. "You're right."

"Please make yourself at home. If you need anything to eat, to drink, please don't hesitate to take what you need. Tomorrow will be another day."

She waved good night to Maya. Maya couldn't help but feel pity for Paula, who looked defeated.

In the guest bathroom, Maya caught sight of her reflection in the mirror. All her life she had cowered, she had always run away—from Munich, from her father, from Michael. And her life had stagnated. Coming here had been the first time to face her past. No matter how painful. And she should feel victorious: Grandmother's case had been reopened because of her. But she didn't feel that way, at all. She still wanted the truth, a truth that was much bigger than she'd ever imagined.

She heard Paula close the door to her bedroom and waited long enough until she heard the woman snoring softly.

She tiptoed to the front of the house and had just opened and closed the door of her rental car as quietly as possible when her phone rang.

"Hello, Miss Wiesberg, this is Detective Melbert. I know it's late, but I just wanted to let you know that we've identified a circle of possible suspects. The State Police..."

She looked up into the sky as the dense blanket of clouds opened for a couple of seconds, but long enough to reveal the peaks of the highest towers of the resort—Paula's view from her house reminded her of her past, her own unrequited love.

"Thank you again for bringing this to our attention. We..." She heard the detective speak as if from far away.

A pickup truck turned into Paula's driveway, its headlight blinding Maya. Paula's husband.

Maya opened her car door.

"...what you must feel right now, Miss Wiesberg, but I..."

She should explain to Paula's husband why his wife had become involved in this, that it was about Maya, that Paula was just helping her; she felt she owed Paula that much.

"Miss Wiesberg?" she heard the detective call out to her on the phone.

"Yes, yes." Maya walked over to the truck.

"Did you hear what I said?"

Her heart missed a beat when she spotted Ben's silhouette in the window.

"I need to go," Maya mumbled into the phone and hung up. She was moving as if in slow-motion. She knew in this moment that he had forgiven her, and nothing else mattered anymore.

She came around the black pickup, and he leaned over

from inside to push open the door for her. She climbed in and looked up at Ben in eager anticipation—and then froze at his ice-cold stare.

He hardly waited for Maya to close the door when he reversed the car and drove out onto the road, in the direction of the resort.

"Why did you have to do this to my family?" His voice sounded different, harsher.

It is all about doing justice, she wanted to explain; she was certain, he wouldn't have acted any differently in her place. But she wasn't able to speak; she hardly recognized this person next to her.

"This won't bring her back! But my grandfather, he—"

Her cell phone rang. Maya silenced it without looking at the caller. "And you lied to me, Maya. How could you lie to me like that?"

"I didn't! It was a misunderstanding."

"You had plenty of opportunities to come clean!"

"So did your grandfather. With your family, Elisa, and last but not least, my grandmother. He never came back for her!"

He stopped the car short. Cold air swept in through the window as he pulled over. Then he faced her for the first time since they had left Paula's driveway, his tone even icier. "I gave you those pages so you'd understand that my grandfather was no madman! He was a noble man!"

"And what if *he* had been murdered, Ben? My grandmother was taken away from me! I didn't plan to involve—"

He laughed bitterly. "You smuggled yourself into this family under false pretext. You know what I think? That you knew very well who I was from the beginning, and you faked interest in me just so you could stick your nose where it doesn't belong. What makes you think we could be involved in the murder? Did you want to harm us simply because she died on our land? Send the police after us, harm us and our reputation?"

Goose bumps spread over her arms. She peered out into

the dark woods around her. Something in the back of her mind had bothered her when she saw Ben's silhouette in the window, and now she knew what it was. Ben had always driven her in a different car, never a pickup truck. Now Ben was driving a similar vehicle to the one that had driven her off the road, a black pickup truck... Or was it the same one?

"Whose car is this?" she noticed her voice sounding shrill. Maya's heart started to beat faster. The ringing cell phone made her jump as it cut into the silence.

"Who keeps calling you?" Ben threw her a cold side glance.

She looked at the screen. It was Detective Melbert. She pressed "ignore." "So you think there's no connection between my grandmother and your family? The pages you gave me... How can you be so blind? Or are you just pretending? I don't recognize you, Ben! I think you're all hiding something. I was out there," she pointed to the woods. "There is no deadly swamp back there, beyond the clearing."

"Did Richard tell you?"

"Who is Richard?'

He shook his head angrily. "Did you tell the police about that as well?" His whisper had assumed a threatening tone, sending a shiver down Maya's spine.

"Not yet!" She had been testing him—and had not been prepared for his reaction. As fast as he had brought the car to a standstill, he now veered the car back onto the road.

Her phone rang again. This time she answered.

"Finally," the detective said. "Where are you now?"

"I am at a bed-and-breakfast," she lied.

"Good, stay away from everyone else, you hear me? *All* of them. And that includes Ben Montgomery, Miss Wiesberg! He, too, is a suspect!"

She hung up in shock. Had Ben overheard the detective? His look didn't betray anything: he was staring straight ahead in deep concentration as he took the curves at a neck-breaking speed. Maya held on to the hook above the door.

Now she truly was afraid—afraid that they would drive off the cliff. They drove by the outlook point that he had showed her the first time, when he had taken her on a leisurely tour of the area. She swore both tires on her side lost touch with the asphalt for a couple of seconds, before the car came down with a thump and continued on into complete darkness. But she was also afraid of this man sitting next to her. Afraid for her life.

Her phone rang again. Ben glared at her, waiting for her next move. She chose to ignore it, all the while asking herself if this was a wise decision.

"Ben, please slow down, please?"

"Go on, answer the phone. Tell him you're with me. So they at least know who to go to after they find you."

Maya couldn't help it. She started to cry. How could she have been so intimate with this man just days ago? Warm, loving, passionate, honest—the man next to her had no semblance of that distant memory. They passed the entrance to the hotel, but he didn't turn off.

"Where are we going?" she said, panicked.

"Sit tight."

He turned right straight into the woods. And at that moment, Maya, or that part of her brain that gave in to her paranoia and lively imagination, the same part that had made her dream of the faceless man, convinced her that she was in the car with a murderer and that her life would end here. She noticed after a couple of feet that they were now driving on a dirt road. She would have never noticed the turnoff. Ben continued driving fast into the darkness. Pebbles were hitting the windshield, and twice the car almost hit a tree. She thought about texting the detective but noticed that she no longer had reception where they were now.

After what seemed like miles, Ben slowed and stopped the car. Without looking at her, he got out, grabbed a flashlight, and slammed the door behind him. Maya watched him walk off into the woods. Maybe now was the moment to escape?

Ben looked back over his shoulder. "Please come. I want to show you something," he called, more gently than expected.

Maya hesitated.

"Maya. We're miles away from anywhere, in the middle of the woods. You'd never make it back."

Then he continued on swiftly into the dense forest, and Maya watched motionless as both he and the light from the flashlight were swallowed by the dense woods, making it seem as if Ben had dissolved into thin air right in front of her.

"Ben?" The only answer was the sounds of the forest. She heard Ben somewhere in front of her, and she followed the distant sounds of branches giving way under his weight. She had a hard time keeping up. The dim light from her cell phone didn't help at all.

"Ben?" She started to run now, toward what she thought were the echoing sounds of Ben's footsteps. It became lighter in the forest ahead of her, and she ran faster.

A twig snapped behind her. She turned around. It was Ben.

"Was it you who sent me the fairy tale?" she asked. But she knew the answer already—if he had, he would have known all along who she was.

"I would have never shared the fairy tale with anyone," Ben whispered. "It was holy to my grandfather."

With his hands he gestured for her to continue. Maya hesitated but then ventured farther. She heard the rasping breathing, the same as she had heard in the clearing.

It was the faceless man.

His face resembled a plain sheet of paper, with slits for eyes, two tiny holes as nostrils, and another slit serving as a mouth. He had no lips, no eyelids, no nose. His ears had no earlobes.

"It's okay. She's a friend," she heard Ben say behind her.

The faceless man lingered on the spot, trembling, then he brushed by Maya. Ben motioned at Maya to follow, and she obeyed.

Her mind had not tricked her. The faceless man was real.

The three walked for a few minutes until they reached a cottage. The pine trees had grown very close to the house, almost camouflaging it. A wraparound porch filled with meticulously carved wooden animal statues was the only thing that separated the structure from the woods.

Ben walked past Maya and into the cottage. As Maya followed him inside, Ben tapped the shoulder of the faceless man, who now stood staring out one of the side windows.

"This, Uncle," he motioned to Maya, "is Maya Wiesberg, and this, Maya, is my granduncle, Nicolas."

"Hans's twin brother?" Maya asked, incredulous. Nicolas turned around and looked at Maya.

"So you didn't die?" she asked the faceless man in front of her. She caught Ben studying her. "Your father just made it look like you did?"

Nicolas nodded, a pained expression on his face.

"But why?"

"Oh, that history booklet provides no answer to that?" Ben asked sarcastically. But then he paused and briefly exchanged looks with Nicolas. "My grandfather asked him the same question when he found out about Nicolas, at his wedding. Apparently my grandmother had become obsessed with Native American folklore from this region during her pregnancy, and she kept saying that they had been punished by the Indians for their sins. She was about to go crazy. Franz couldn't afford to lose her, and he believed that he would have if he didn't move Nicolas out of her sight." He shook his head in disgust. "I think that's a lie. I believe he thought the sight of Nicolas would drive guests away."

"So you lived here all that time?" Maya addressed Nicolas again.

"He grew up elsewhere, but he came back when his surrogate mother died." Ben answered in Nicolas's stead.

A deep crease showed on Uncle Nicolas's forehead.

"I told her about Hans and Martha, Uncle Nicolas."

Hearing Ben talk in such a familiar tone about Grandmother to a complete stranger made Maya feel like an outsider. Ben and Nicolas had known about Martha all this time. Whereas Hans Montgomery had invited these two to share his life story, Grandmother had kept it to herself. Maya had known nothing.

Nicolas came over and studied Maya closely through his tiny slits. And then he turned around to whisper something into Ben's ear.

Ben looked at her: "He is happy you finally came."

Before she could react, Nicolas stepped closer and embraced her in a firm hug. Under Ben's watchful eyes, she answered the gesture of affection by putting her arms around his fragile shoulders.

"Was it you who sent me the fairy tale?" she asked him.

He let go of her hand, gently, and looked over to Ben as he nodded again.

"Why would you do that, Uncle Nicolas?" Ben demanded.

He ignored Ben's question and instead waved him over, so all three of them stood very close to each other. She could smell Ben. She yearned for the man he had been before.

"He wants to know if you want something to drink. He has water or vodka."

"I'll take both, please," Maya said, smiling.

"And he said you should sit down," Ben commanded her.

Nicolas went to a cabinet and produced glasses and a bottle. He moved very slowly. One of his legs was shorter than the other, which caused him to make a step, then stop and drag the other leg behind, and each time his body made an unusual movement, as if he were hovering. At some point, Maya wanted to get up and help him, but Ben motioned for her to stay seated. After he poured everyone a drink, Nicolas sat down himself and addressed Ben. Again, inaudible to Maya.

"He said he immediately knew who you were when he first saw you at the clearing," Ben said.

"How?"

He again said something, and Ben spoke: "A photo."

"Hans showed you a photo of my grandmother?"

Nicolas nodded his head.

"How did you get the fairy tale to my hotel room?"

Ben intervened. "He had help. There are two of us helping Uncle Nicolas out here."

"But it wasn't you who brought me the fairy tale?"

"No!" Ben practically spat the words out.

"Uncle Nicolas, did Paula help you?" Maya asked.

Ben seemed angered at hearing her name. "Yes, she must have. I wouldn't have helped him if he had asked me."

"Why?"

"Because all of this is sacred to me. This is my real family. I don't want this fairy tale and my grandfather to get mixed up in the murder, in all that's wrong about Montgomery."

"But my grandmother, she was the love of his life!"

"And we still don't know why she came back. People change over time!" He was defensive. "My grandfather was always vague about your grandmother's death. He always just said he 'heard' about her death a couple of years into the war. And I think he kept it vague for a reason. I think his pride didn't allow him to tell me what really happened. That he was rejected, that he came back and your grandmother had found someone else. What do we know about what happened in the past? It's over, done. Leave it in peace, Maya. The only reason I brought you here is so that you would leave Uncle Nicolas out of all of this! Because you would have—"

"Stop it!" Nicolas had pressed out these words so forcefully that even Maya had been able to understand him.

Ben looked up, shocked, as if not used to hearing Nicolas's voice.

"Why did you give me the fairy tale?" Maya asked Nicolas gently. The faceless man paused, then motioned with his hand for Ben to join Maya on the couch. Reluctantly, Ben complied but sat far enough so their legs wouldn't touch.

Nicolas moved over to a shelf and removed a book. For

a couple of minutes that stretched like hours he just stared at it, his shoulders rising and falling. Then he slowly turned around. He hesitated another couple of seconds before he walked over and placed an envelope between them on the sofa.

At first, neither Ben nor Maya made a move. And after a moment they both did at once, quickly withdrawing when their hands accidentally touched.

"You go," she said to Ben.

He hesitated at first and then reached for it.

There was a thin layer of dust coating the envelope. She could feel Ben tense up as he took the thick letter out of the pouch.

"Did Grandpa write this?" Ben asked.

Uncle Nicolas nodded.

"You want us to read it. The whole thing?"

He nodded again.

And Maya traveled again into the past as Ben and she started reading.

# TO NICOLAS

*To Nicolas, the only person that I will share my last chapter with—so you know that I suffered as much as you suffered—and that life is unfair to many of us. But it was fair to me when I learned—however late—that I have a twin brother, whom I admire above anyone.*

*The first one I went to see in Washington was Wagner. He did not ask further questions as to why I had returned so suddenly, and he didn't ask why when I told him that I'd like to go back to Germany as fast as possible.*

*"You need a recommendation from Roosevelt," Wagner explained. "To shorten Donovan's extensive recruitment process." I knew, and I also knew that Wagner was my direct line to the president. Wagner told me that Roosevelt didn't like Donovan, that they had actually gone to college together, and I found out later that they had already hated each other's guts back then. Now Donovan was working directly for Roosevelt, who paid for his services with his emergency fund. Roosevelt had told Wagner that he couldn't not employ him. "I still don't understand why he keeps defending his decision." Wagner said, laughing. Then he looked at me, long. I had grown to become a good liar and convinced him silently that I was one of the most devoted spies he had ever trained. "If you come recommended by Roosevelt, it's almost impossible for Donovan to turn you down."*

*It was December 1941 and I was standing in front of*

*the building that housed the Office of the Coordination of Information, a name that brought to mind only bureaucracy and moldy folders. Bill Donovan, Wild Bill, as they called him, was running the place. He was known for his heroism with the "Fighting Sixty-Ninth" during World War I. Father had told me this story of bravery and courage again and again. To our father, Wild Bill epitomized everything that America stood for. And in hindsight, I came to understand why he secretly adored this man so much—because he himself was the polar opposite: our father was a coward.*

*See, my timing was kind of ideal, and I smelled a golden opportunity to be able to return to Germany—to Martha. The three years back here had been pure torture for me. I had abandoned her. And even though I knew I had no other choice, I felt so guilty, Nicolas. As guilty as our father must have felt for having abandoned you. Pearl Harbor had just happened, and now they needed people, desperately. God knows if I'd have stood a chance before that, but I would not have left any option unexplored. I needed to get back to Martha, and I need to take her home with me this time.*

*When I entered the building, the letter of recommendation from Roosevelt in hand, I was told that the interview would be personally handled by Wild Bill himself. I instantly became nervous. I suspected that somehow Wild Bill might not be as easily fooled as Wagner. Don't get me wrong, Wagner was an impressive person and a veteran and highly experienced spy, but he had first come to know me at a different moment in time; I had been a different age, a different man in many ways, and the world had not been plunged into complete turmoil yet. Now, there was no space for error.*

*As I stepped into the elevator, I noticed this dapper, middle-aged gentleman who was eyeing me curiously. His suit had wide lapels and lifted shoulders; there was cream in his hair and a strong "scent"—he simply was too groomed to be an American. Yet when he spoke, he didn't reveal the slightest trace of an accent.*

"We're here for the same reasons, I suspect?" I simply nodded, too shocked to speak.

We entered the floor together, but while he was sent to an office at the back, I was taken elsewhere. I was surprised to find a reddish-haired individual waiting for me in a room not unlike an interrogation room at a police station. The man explained to me that I would now undergo a series of interviews—just a simple screening process, I was assured. "We usually have people fill out a form, we ask for their background, then we send them home—most don't get this far into this building when they first set foot here. A group looks through those papers and filters out the good ones. Those of interest are sifted out, and the FBI makes a spot-check on them. But as you come recommended by our president, we've skipped the first two steps."

He leaned back in his chair, carrying an aura of importance that seemed too carefully crafted. "So, we of course know that you were in Germany in 1938, providing the United States with valuable information until your cover was blown." I nodded. "And you did impressive work. But now, of course, there is a different situation at hand, and the requirements have changed."

I remember I was getting impatient with this guy. "Yes, because back then an independent agency hadn't existed!" The ONI, the naval intelligence, and G2, the intelligence branch of the Army, were the only two existing espionage organizations in the United States at that time, neither of the two were independent but service-oriented.

"Correct, correct! Roosevelt should have agreed much earlier to Bill's requests"—he held his nose up high—"but it's not too late. Why do you want to return to Germany?" He asked then, a stern expression on his face.

"Because I want to finish what I started."

He smiled at me. "Okay, good answer." He paused. When he spoke again he seemed somewhat more amicable.

"You need to understand the procedure as well; we get

*a lot of applications for the purpose of infiltration. There are Russian sympathizers, Nazi agents, Fascist agents, Jap agents, Communist agents; we just need to make sure you haven't been corrupted between 1938 and now."*

*The only thing I had been corrupted by was despair and, well, love, as goofball as that might sound to you, Nicolas. But I was still able to declare to that ginger man, without the slightest hesitation, that I was anti-Nazi and pro-democracy.*

*A week went by and I didn't hear a word. I considered going to see Wagner again but was afraid that I would seem too desperate to him to get back into the trenches. I almost went crazy in my hotel room while waiting every day for that phone call that simply wouldn't come. At night I walked the Parisian streets of the city, always accompanied by an imaginary Martha.*

*Then one night the red-haired agent called me at my hotel in Washington.*

*"Bill Donovan wants to see you tomorrow at eleven," he simply said, and hung up.*

*So I returned to the same building. I was so nervous. See, Nicolas, I was driven by blind despair. I would have done literally anything to get back to her, but I had somehow assumed that everything would go smoothly, as I had come highly recommended by the president himself. But that obviously wasn't the case. There was hesitation on Donovan's side; I felt it even before I entered the building.*

*The same man who had been in the elevator with me the week before passed me on my way in, with a gorgeous woman by his side, both handcuffed, and I began to get an idea of how hard Bill Donovan's—and for that matter the redhead's job must be, even though I couldn't stand him. It seemed too big a challenge to be in charge of picking the right individual for the job, to know who is fit and who is truthful. And I could very well end up being led out in handcuffs one day— because even though my true motives had nothing to do with counterespionage, my reasons were even worse. At least those double spies Donovan had handcuffed were actual spies, passionate, political, fighting for a cause. My cause was Martha. It was that simple. And I was not ashamed that I didn't feel as much love for my country. But when I told you, during one of my first visits, that I had worked as a spy in Europe, when your eyes lit up, when you eyed me like I was some goddamned hero, doing heroic things, that was the moment I felt ashamed. No, I couldn't have cared less about having deceived Donovan and all of them, but I never wanted to deceive you.*

*I went to the reception area, and this time Donovan's personal assistant was already waiting for me. I didn't even have to say my name. We went deeper into the building this time. Donovan's office was at the far end of a long hallway. Farthest from the main entrance. To make it harder for people to escape if they tried?*

*He was standing at his desk when I was shown in, his back to the door.*

*Donovan wasn't very tall—he was heavyset, with thinning gray hair. He turned around, suspicion glistening in his sharp, blue-gray eyes, very intense, very intelligent. He held out a thick hand, which felt surprisingly soft. He motioned for me to sit down.*

*"Bob,"—that was the name of the red head—"and the FBI have spot-checked you, and you come out clean. But I wanted to see you, 'cause I have doubts you're the right man for us." His voice was soft, almost a whisper, yet dynamic.*

*I frowned. "I've served this country even before there was a proper organization. What type of doubt could you possibly have?"*

*Donovan smiled. "I know. It doesn't make sense. But in my job, our job, as you can possibly attest to, we need to go by instinct, too, sometimes.*

*And my instincts tell me that you might have ulterior motives."*

*I refused to give up easily.*

*"I was all alone, not working for the ONI, nor the G2, but the president.*

*It was an extremely difficult task."*

Donovan nodded, understanding. Then he looked at me, determined. *"And you've shown guts coming back here and reapplying. That's flattering, I have to admit."*

I relaxed a bit, but Donovan wasn't finished with me yet.

*"But this time things will be different. This time we will exploit every economic and political opportunity; nothing will seem impossible. We're working in espionage and sabotage, and this time you'll have to undergo proper training. You'll be dealing with life-or-death situations."*

I felt slightly insulted, and Donovan could tell.

*"What does self-sacrifice mean to you?"*

*"I will sacrifice my life if a coworker needs protection, or to ensure the successful outcome of a mission."* I meant absolutely none of this. I would sacrifice my life for only one person.

Donovan nodded. *"Yes. But what concerns me is that a lot of agents sometimes are incapable of determining when the act of self-sacrifice is necessary. Especially if other motives interfere."*

I swallowed hard. *"The well-being and victory of the United States of America comes first, no matter what. It is more important than your father, your mother, your siblings, your wife, your lover—or all of them together,"* I answered, hating myself for it. But my love for this woman was bigger than my self-respect.

*"If we say yes to you, there are a couple of rules: this time you work for us, with the currency agents. I trust you've been raised by your father with an astute business sense—for numbers especially."*

I nodded, lying again.

*"We'll send you to France next week."*

My heart sank. France? *"Why France, sir? I'm familiar with the German culture far more than the French."*

*Wild Bill looked down at his papers. "Your mother never took you there?"*

*I shook my head. "Whenever I would ask them for a holiday away, they smiled and pointed out the irony of my question, as that question was asked at one of the most popular holiday resorts in the United States."*

*Bill laughed. "Well, true, I have to give them that. So you truly want to get back to Germany?"*

*I nodded, trying to keep calm.*

*"I still can't help but think there is something more in this for you." This time Donovan didn't smile. He looked down at his papers again, pretending to study them, probably to make me even more nervous. He acted as if he'd found what he had been searching for.*

*"Why did you have fake passports made for this woman?"*

*I looked at the page that was held in front of me: a fake American and British passport. On both of them, Martha was smiling out at me, teasing me: When are you coming, Siegfried?*

*"She's a pretty lady, judging from her photos," Bill decided.*

*Bill looked at me, waiting for an answer, possibly counting the number of seconds that it took me to respond. The longer the hesitation, the longer the possibility that I was lying. "She was French with great connections to Russia, and I recruited her as a double spy. She helped me at one point with information, so this was my way to return the favor."*

*"Are you in love with that woman?"*

*"If I was, sir, I wouldn't have rejected France before."*

*"Listen, spies have no right to reject anyway, but you have a point there.*

*Did you have a personal relationship with that woman in 1938?"*

*No, I never had an affair with a female French spy, and so I felt honest when answering: "No, sir, I didn't."*

*"Well, I strongly suggest for you not to be so generous with passports; we live in more difficult times now."*

He gave me a long, hard stare, and then he sank back into his chair, drawing out a sigh. It was only seconds, but it felt like hours to me.

And then, finally, he exclaimed: "Okay, let's ditch France then, for now."

I had trouble concealing the joy I felt.

"You'll operate with our guy in Berlin, and Washington will be your base for now."

My heart sank again; I had hoped for a different assignment. Donovan's skill and training showed in that moment. He picked up on my inner turmoil, turning on me as if he had been electrically shocked, that quick, piercing glare of blue-gray eyes that I would become so familiar with.

"I knew there was something else."

"No, this is fine. Everything will be fine, if it means fighting against the Nazis."

Donovan got up from his seat and took my hand, shaking it.

"Welcome. I'm happy to have you with us. Bob is waiting for you outside to go through the next steps."

I felt relief wash over me. Even though I would not be sent to Germany at first, I was in! And a big step closer to getting Martha out of there.

Donovan was still holding my hand. Slightly squeezing it. His blue eyes went cold: "I must ask you not to return to Munich at all, you understand me?"

"Yes, sir." I quickly headed for the door so that he couldn't read the disappointment in my eyes. I'm coming for you, Martha, I said to myself as I closed the door silently.

This time I underwent extensive training: a far more detailed and professional training than what Roosevelt had me undergo with Wagner before I left for Germany the first time. Donovan had his agents trained in unorthodox methods— in planning, mounting, and implementing missions. Nothing was impossible, anything was allowed, as long as one was able to do it effectively and with the clear goal in sight. As *an agent you had to have nerve that wouldn't break when you found yourself among enemies, and a degree of patriotism and loyalty that wouldn't falter under torture.*

*This time, I was given a different biography, and I was drilled and redrilled until my real life seemed to exist no longer.*

*As an agent trainee, you were mentally tortured, and they would always try to find your weakness. They would deprive you of so much sleep that you would nearly start hallucinating from fatigue. Then they would let you nod off, only to wake you before you arrived in the deep sleep phase and ask you questions. My weakness was Martha, and there were times when I was afraid I would give it away. I always dreamed of her, leaning against the wall, smiling at me, silently beckoning me to come back. There were a couple of trainees in my group who had sought to become a spy for similar reasons, and they were found out only three weeks into the training. But I had the advantage that I had been a quasi spy before, a fact that I had been asked to keep secret from the others. I had grown stronger, more courageous, but my biggest motivation was still my love for that woman.*

*After that we were held in isolation, and I had yet another advantage: all those lonely hours from my childhood in the forest surrounding your cabin, Nicolas, when I had longed so badly for a sibling, someone to share all of it with. But back then, I hadn't known. So all that kept me sane was the thought of Martha. And, likewise, when they threw us into a challenge that demanded the maximum of physical strength, I excelled, driven by those luminous green eyes.*

*I had been instructed in code before, obviously, but those codes had been cracked by the enemy, so this time I learned more-complex ones. I had already learned the use of all types of weapons, but this time I was taught how to dismantle and repair them. The trainers always made sure that we were trained under the most realistic conditions. We were trained in U.S. companies, and only one key person at that company,* and Donovan, would know about the arrangement. And toward the end, Donovan would confront the CEO that his security department had failed to pick up on the fact that their most valued data had been microfilmed and was already in his hands.

I was impressed that Donovan personally kept in touch with all training groups, even after they had opened training bases throughout the world. It was exhausting to work for that man, but I respected and appreciated the calm, controlled manner in which he would put plans into effect. He would demand the ultimate sacrifice from you, yet at the same he was very personable and took time out to make a sacrifice of himself, to see that a package or letter would be delivered to your loved ones back home.

In mid-1942 Washington figured out that having the FBI and an independent secret war-intelligence organization under the same roof might not have been the most ingenious idea. The desks were reshuffled, the agency renamed: the Office of Strategic Services, the OSS was born The precursor of today's CIA. I was sent to the new OSS headquarters in London, where I would often see Donovan on his regular visits to the British offices.

In the beginning, Donovan, who by that time had earned himself the nickname of the Wizard of OSS among the spies, would barely let me out of his sight; I could sense a tiny trace of doubt every time he looked at me.

We had all moved into a hotel in the vicinity of the London office. Prime Minister Churchill lived in the penthouse; King George II of Greece took up residence there in exile. Then there was King Peter of Yugoslavia, with his wife and mother-in-law forming a royal court within the hotel premises.

Even though I had often asked myself why on earth someone would become a spy, I especially could understand the fascination.

Weeks went by, and I was getting more and more impatient.

One of my fellow agents went off to be trained for a mission: he would be sent into occupied France to identify resistance fighters who were lacking organization and means. I, on the other hand, was wasting my time in London, decoding messages from my counterpart in Berlin while a war was going on around me. I prayed every night that my Martha was still alive and well.

It was a rainy day in London, nothing unusual. I was sitting at my desk in the London headquarters, feeling more like a file pusher than a spy, when someone tapped me on the shoulder. I whirled around to look up into that intense stare of Wild Bill.

"Hans, I think" —and with that he looked around the piles of files on my desk— "you've proven your loyalty by doing this for so long. Must have driven you crazy." He laughed. I realized this had all been a part of a test. "Schneider," who was my counterpart in Berlin, "has just been killed in Berlin, and we need you to go over there and pick up from where he left off."

Schneider had a fiancée back in the United States, who would never learn how her future husband really died.

"You leave tomorrow. We prepared your passport. Schneider hid his decoded material. You need to retrieve it when you're on the ground there."

I nodded, relieved: my moment had come. I was about to turn back to the desk, when he touched me on the shoulder again.

"One more thing, Hans. Should I catch you leaving Berlin, I swear I'll make sure you're finished."

I'm not going to tell you much about what happened in Berlin. I will, briefly, but I am no Ian Fleming. What I experienced in Berlin would certainly be worthy of a James Bond novel, though Fleming was still a decade away from publishing the first book.

I went to Berlin, hooked up with the circle of secret agents with whom Schneider had been collaborating. I managed to retrieve the secret documents that Schneider had hidden but failed to decode before he'd been killed by the Gestapo. He had stored the material with his lover, unbeknownst to her. I managed to sneak into her heavily guarded flat at Unter den Linden, almost crossed paths with Hänschel himself, of all people, while she was being tortured in the cells under the Berlin Gestapo headquarters in the infamous Prinz-Albrecht-Straße 8. I had never felt more fear than at that moment. But it was the image of Martha that kept me going. I knew she still loved me. I felt it deep within me. But at times the doubt would creep in: I didn't even know if she was still alive.

In our team in Berlin was a Russian double spy, a woman tougher than all of us guys put together. Irina was her name. When she was sent to Munich by the Red Army to find out about one of their own, I gave her Martha's address. She asked if I seriously wanted her to waste her time distributing love letters, but I would have never put her in that kind of danger. All I asked her to do was to confirm if Martha was alive.

"Do you want me to tell her anything?"

I shook my head.

"What if she's with someone else?" she asked with raised eyebrows.

And I simply said, "She won't be."

Irina laughed, God bless her. "For that much arrogance alone, you would be hanged in Russia."

But when she came back, she told me that she had indeed seen Martha, and that despite what I had told her, she wanted to pass some news on to her. "After all, I had put my ass on the line anyway, so I thought I might as well complete the job for you," she said, grinning. "I followed her when she left the house, and she went in the woods, then sat down in a clearing, way off the beaten track. And, forgive me, but the spot was so far away I was afraid she might be meeting someone, and I might get tangled up in something. So I didn't get the chance to tell her anything after all."

Now it was my turn to grin. "No, now I just received confirmation from you that she is not only alive and well, but that she's still waiting for me."

"Ha," Irina said. "So you weren't that self-assured when you sent me, eh? You are a good spy after all."

I befriended someone on the enemy side, who took me to witness one of my own being tortured, a moment that still haunts me to this day. It was Irina. But her news kept me going through with that dangerous endeavor. And when I delivered the papers in London, I left immediately, for Munich. Not caring what Donovan would say or do. I had made plans for how we would escape through France. I had it all laid out.

So when I got off the train in Munich, I was ready to escape with her. I had bandaged my face, making myself look like one of the soldiers who had been injured badly and was now on leave. Some Germans' self-assurance had faded, I realized on the train to Munich. An old lady approached me shortly before she got off at her stop: "Young man, you lost your face for nothing."

I walked up the road toward the Wiesberg house in the heavy boots, sweating beneath the bandages, growing increasingly nervous the closer I got. I didn't want to see Wolfgang or his mother. Well, in fact, I couldn't afford to. I suspected that Wolfgang was still working closely with the Gestapo.

I thought I caught a whiff of her sweet rose scent just before I turned that last corner. And then I saw Wolfgang close the door, and I knew immediately that something was wrong. He was dressed in all black.

Through the window, I saw Frau Wiesberg upstairs, seemingly lost in thought, wrapped in blackness.

I was too late. I lost it, crying silently. I could not have been more broken than at that moment, Nicolas. And before I knew it, he was standing there, gazing down at me.

"She's gone" he said in greeting.

"How did she die?" I asked.

"That tablet of yours. She wasn't able to wait any longer."

It was too much. I went into a state of shock. "She committed suicide?"

Wolfgang looked at me, nodding. There was great sadness in his eyes, but also love, after all that had happened. I knew at that moment that I didn't have to fear him, and I realized that it had never been Wolfgang's intention to take me to Hänschel when he found out my hiding place. That he had actually come to help me escape.

He didn't betray me then. He wouldn't betray me now.

Nicolas, I will never tell this part of the story to anyone but you for the aforementioned reasons. I am no hero. I am your older brother, by twenty-five minutes, and that's it.

I often feel disillusioned, then ashamed, but most of all, I am just so sad. She was the love of my life. But fate often has something different in store for you. Had she not died, I would not have come back, and I wouldn't have learned about your existence. Or maybe I would have, with her, and if I had then learned about you, I would have taken you far away, on all those trips that I'd planned with Martha. Stop looking at me like I'm better than you. It hurts me. You are a person of pure heart and soul. YOU are courageous, not me. It took more than bravery to appear to me on the day of my wedding to a woman I knew I'd never love, to give in to the wish of a father I despised. Learning about our father's atrocious sin that day made me finally understand. Learning about you made me survive that day, that marriage, and give me hope.

I will be forever grateful to you.

Your twin brother, Hans

# Day 7

Ben had moved ever so slightly closer as they read Hans's letter silently. She couldn't tell if it was only her trembling, or if he was shaken, too. While Maya and Ben had traveled into the past, dawn had broken. She scanned the cabin for Nicolas and found him standing at the window, staring out into the dark forest that was blocking out most of the early daylight.

"But her brother lied to Hans," Maya said.

Nicholas turned around to face them.

"My grandmother was still alive when Hans came..." Her voice broke off. Had she seen him? Had the lovers reunited? What had happened that—

"Why have you never shown me this before?" Ben said, interrupting Maya's thoughts. He sounded disappointed, hurt.

"So you knew my grandmother was here!" Maya said. "Did you see her when she came in 1990? Did you meet her?"

Now Nicolas looked nervous.

"Nicolas, do you know who murdered her?" she said sternly.

Nicolas's tiny mouth opened in shock. He staggered, his face drained of blood. Ben quickly rushed over to him and helped him sit down on a chair. He turned around to look at Maya, silently scolding her. Nicolas stammered behind him as he gathered his thoughts.

"I had meant to tell you, Uncle Nicolas," Ben said softly to him, touching his arm. Then he turned to Maya again. "We didn't know it was your grandmother, or murder, until—" He broke off, and anger showed on his face. "Until the police started to bother my poor grandfather! He can't even speak anymore, has been bedridden for decades! He, of all people, doesn't deserve this! He's a good man. But someone planted this idea in the police's head that it was my grandfather who murdered Martha."

"I'm so sorry, Ben. If you hadn't given me those pages, I still wouldn't know what kind of man your grandfather was!"

Nicolas's voice sounded soft when he spoke. "My brother never stopped loving her." Ben translated what he said for her.

Maya looked into Nicolas's flat face. "My grandmother never told me anything about your brother, but she told me that fairy tale—in a clearing that looks very much like the one out there in the woods." She took another step toward Nicolas. "Did they see each other, when she came?" she finally dared to ask out loud, afraid of the answer.

Nicolas shrugged his shoulders in response.

"Why did she come here after all these years? How did she know he was still alive?" Ben chimed in.

This time it was Maya's turn to shrug her shoulders. "I don't know, Ben."

"So your grandmother never mentioned my grandfather?"

She shook her head. Nicolas got up from his chair with a great effort, mumbling something under his breath, but Ben didn't rush over to help him this time, his full attention on Maya.

"So we still don't know why she came then!"

"Why else would she have come, Ben? Would she have told me that fairy tale over and over again? The fairy tale that always reminded her of your grandfather? Would she have taken me to the clearing in Perlach, a place where she said she had spent the happiest hours of her life, with your grandfather, Ben, if she didn't love him?"

Nicolas had returned to the bookshelf, waving something

in his hand. He spoke again. Louder this time. Ben didn't even seem to notice him.

"So why did she let all those years go by? If her love for my grandfather was as strong, why didn't she come back earlier, Maya? Why? Because she didn't come for him. She came for something else!" His voice had risen another notch. Ben still wanted to see her grandmother as the enemy, someone who had ulterior motives for coming here.

Because of how she had hurt him, it crossed Maya's mind.

"I'm telling you once and for all: leave my grandfather and my family out of this! We have nothing to do with her!" He grabbed his jacket and walked toward the door.

Nicolas stomped his foot on the floor, so hard that the windows in the cabins shook. He was bright red in his face as he stared at Ben, who stood in the doorway, frozen. Maya noticed what Nicolas was holding in his hand. A letter. Without taking his eyes off Ben, he passed the piece of paper to Maya. The letter was in poor condition, some parts slightly smudged by water. But even then, Maya would have always recognized Grandmother's handwriting. Maya took the letter with trembling hands and unfolded it carefully. Nicolas put his hand on her arm, pointing at her mouth.

"You want me to translate?"

Nicolas nodded his head.

"This letter is from my grandmother." Maya noticed another piece of paper inside; Nicolas had tried a clumsy translation, seemingly with the help of a German dictionary.

"You never knew who this letter was from, did you?" Nicolas shook his head.

Ben had released the door handle and was coming closer, curiously eyeing the letter. Maya sank down onto the sofa again, feeling the weight of the truth in her hand. Her voice broke off as she started to translate the letter into English, filling with sense the gaps that the rainwater had left.

*October 10, 1990*

*Dear Mr. Montgomery,*

*I am writing to you today, as I believe you know someone I have been longing to hear from for a long time. His name is Siegfried Hoftstätter, whom you know as Hans. I had been told that he was dead, but learned a week ago that he is still alive. I know that he has a wife and a child, as people tend to have over the years, but I want to find out from you where he stands in life, and whether I am still welcome in his life.*

*I've been at your hotel for several days now, and one morning I saw him and followed him from a safe distance into the woods. To a clearing in the woods, a spot that resembles the one I often went to with Siegfried, in a faraway place, from a time long gone. Seeing the clearing showed me that he has not forgotten about me, either. And I was filled with joy. I wanted to run into his arms. But he disappeared, as if swallowed by the earth, and I have not been able to locate him since. This is why I am writing to you today. Please let Siegfried know that from today, the date on this letter, for as long as it takes, I will wait for him in the clearing, from dawn onward.*

*Martha Wiesberg*

*P.S. Please also let him know that I can understand if he doesn't have the energy or place in his heart to rekindle what we once had, but I would like for him to say it to my face.*

Maya felt as if Grandmother was sitting right next to her, as if she had been holding Maya's hand as she read out loud these words that Grandmother had written twenty-seven years ago, probably only days before she was murdered. This was the letter that had disappeared from Paula's purse. A letter that had never found its rightful recipient.

She felt someone next to her. Ben! This letter was proof that his grandfather's love had been reciprocated by

Grandmother until the day she died. But it was Nicolas who put his fragile arms around her, producing shushing sounds through his thin line of a mouth, in an attempt to console her. She nodded at Nicolas, thanking him for his compassion, then lifted her eyes, scanning the room for Ben, hoping to find the same in Ben's.

"Ben, my grandmother never blackmailed your grandfather. She came back to him. But someone intercepted this letter," Maya whispered.

Ben lingered in the entrance. "I need some fresh air," he said, and quickly hurried outside.

The loud bang of the door left Maya alone with Nicolas in the dark cabin. She returned to the date on the letter: October 10, 1990. Maya had just left for the States not even two months before. Had Grandmother sent her away so that she could follow Hans? And how had Martha even figured out that Hans was still alive? She was consumed with such a wave of love for Grandmother that the tears returned again. Maya, too, had been very much loved by her. And only now did she realize how relentlessly Grandmother had loved all her life. Maya looked at the letter again, read it one more time.

And then a horrible thought crept into Maya's mind.

"Where did you find this letter?" She slowly turned toward Nicolas. "Why do *you* have it?"

Nicolas stared at her.

With the letter still clutched in her fist, she jumped up from the couch. She was already at the door when he grabbed her by the wrist, trying to voice a word over and over again. Maya managed to wiggle free of his grip and stormed out of the cabin.

"Careful"—that was what he had tried to say to her, Maya realized as she was running at top speed through the forest, away from the cabin, away from Uncle Nicolas, Ben, Paula, the Montgomery, the truth. In the dim light of the early morning she crossed woods that seemed even denser than the one around the clearing, branches scratching her cheeks. But Maya couldn't stop. She ran and ran, trying to clear her mind. But instead she lost all sense of time—and place. And panic rose in her. *A murderer that... doesn't want to be found.* The police officer's warning came back to her, echoing in her head and through the dense forest around her. She felt eyes on her, everywhere. She looked around, imagining the murderer hiding behind trees, staring at her, waiting for her. She took out her cell—still no reception. She squinted into the trees around her. Nothing. North, south, west, east. She had no idea where she was.

She was growing dizzy, frantic, and was about to let herself sink onto the frozen ground when she made out something that looked like an arch several feet away. An entrance to something. She advanced, cautiously—and gasped when she realized what was in front of her. Grandmother's fairy tale! Someone had carved her fairy tale into the woods, stretching as far as the eye could see. Maya momentarily forgot her fear. She stood in the entrance to the realm of the Past. Farther down she spotted the other two realms, Present and Future, with their inhabitants, all sprung to life, every realm given form by someone's skill. The sight took her breath away, her pulse increased, and her eyes filled with tears, in shock about what had just happened, in awe of the beauty in front of her, and in grief about the loss of Grandmother. Had she seen her own fairy tale sprung to life? Had she seen these trees that had been carved to look like fairies, the branches that had been woven together decades ago, so that they would grow to become a dense canopy that would form a seemingly endless tunnel stretching out into the dark forest, connecting the realms with one another? With her fingers she traced the detailed carving work on the angelic faces of the Imaginations, with wings that had been carved so thinly that they did look like wings. They guarded the entrance to this universe, her universe. And then she looked up: the arch above read *TO HANS AND MARTHA*.

Nicolas. She remembered all the carved figures on the porch of his hut. It was Nicolas who had built this. He had treasured the fairy tale as much as Grandmother had, as much as Hans had. Nicolas hadn't murdered his twin brother's love. Instead, he had built this forest for his brother, for the lovers. Nicolas had provided her with the last piece of the puzzle— Grandmother's letter. She realized that only now. The letter was the key to who the murderer was.

She was so close to the truth, so close to the murderer. Only now she had understood who it was.

She stepped into the fairy tale, crossed through Past, Present, and Future, never feeling more driven that at this moment. She exited the fairy-tale forest through an equally beautiful arch on the other end of the tunnel. In front of her was a steep hill. Her heart sank again as she looked up: the hill was too steep for her to climb. She was about to turn around again when her eyes caught a spot with darker and less colorful leaves than the rest. She advanced and realized it was a camouflage tarp in the midst of the foliage. She lifted it—it gave way to a hidden staircase, leading up the hill. Maya breathed a sigh of relief and began to ascend.

When she reached the top she immediately realized where she was—the place where she had hidden from Detective Melbert, near the clearing. The fairy-tale forest wasn't visible from up here, carefully hidden underneath the vines that had formed the tunnel. Up on this end, the stairs leading down were camouflaged the same way. This must have been where Hans had "disappeared" to, as Grandmother had written in her letter. Gone down to visit his twin brother.

When she turned around, she realized she wasn't alone: a figure stood in the middle of the clearing. Hunched over. Supported by a cane.

Maya quickly hid behind a tree. Her breath accelerated in the cold autumn morning, producing misty puffs like the steam of an old locomotive. Maya knew whom she had just seen; she could feel her presence even from a distance:

Elisa Montgomery. Then she saw her shoulders heaving uncontrollably.

Elisa was crying.

Maya stared at her as slowly Elisa's golden cane gave way, as if it had carried more than just her body weight, and Elisa crashed down onto the half-frozen ground. As the gold on the cane caught and reflected a ray of the rising sunlight that had begun to creep into the clearing, blinding Maya for a second, a line from Paula's book came back to her: *Back in the hospital they could only save one leg; the other one was so severely damaged that she would never walk properly again.*

She had a horrible accident, in 1985, five years before Grandmother came here. Hadn't the German police officer told her that Grandmother's skull was beaten with a long object? But that most likely wasn't what killed her, he had said.

A dark figure appeared on the opposite side of the clearing. At first Maya thought it was Edgar, but she recognized the park ranger.

"Mrs. Montgomery!" he yelled as he squatted down to help her up.

"No, no, no!" she screamed at him. "I am not finished yet. Leave me!"

He let go, but then she grabbed him for support, and once she was back on her feet, she dragged him toward her and sank into his arms. And sobbed. They stood there like that for several minutes. And as suddenly as she had sunk into his arms, she pushed him away.

"Richard, what would you do in my stead? You've worked with us for so long. You know everything about us. What would you do?" she pleaded with him. Richard. The Richard Ben had mentioned in the car?

The ranger looked like a trapped animal. "I don't understand, ma'am..."

"If you knew that a family member, your own flesh and

blood, was involved in something. Something horrible. Would you—" She broke off to catch her breath. "Would you let justice prevail? And betray your own?"

He was shuffling his feet on the spot in hesitation, looking at the ground. When he looked back at Elisa, something had changed in his face. He had been invited to speak openly, probably for the first time ever. "I do believe we should pay for our sins," he said, nodding his head as if reassuring himself that it was okay to go on. "Franz paid for what he did; you should, too."

"Leave Franz out of this! He never—"

But she stopped herself, squinting at him with indignation, as if she had realized only now that he was out of line, that he had overstepped his boundaries as an employee to the family. She averted her eyes and covered her face with her hands, her diamonds glittering sadly in the morning sun. After what seemed an eternity she dropped her hands and looked at the ranger again.

"I know you've always liked my husband best, Richard, didn't you?"

"Would you like me to carry you down, ma'am?" He ignored her comment, but the "ma'am" this time sounded slightly condescending to Maya's ears.

Elisa nodded, defeated.

Before it was too late, Maya stepped out of her hiding place.

Elisa's eyes became tiny slits when she recognized Maya. "You!" she hissed. The way she looked at her, she wasn't seeing Maya, but Grandmother.

"You read this, didn't you?" she asked Elisa, waving the letter in her hand. The woman was so close now, Maya smelled her expensive perfume. Elisa raised her cane. It came crashing down right in front of Maya, barely missing her. The ranger rushed over to help Maya—but would have been too late if Elisa hadn't lost her aim. She fell down on her knees right in front of Maya.

"Leave me be!" And then, slowly, she looked up at Maya. The fanatic glare had been replaced with a look of defeat. "I am sorry for what I did," she wailed. "If he hadn't blackmailed me, I could have saved her!" she cried out loud.

There it was, the truth. The woman managed to stand up again with the help of her cane, and steadied herself. Through the curtain of Maya's tears, Elisa looked wrinkleless, as if the young Elisa stood in front of her. "Day after day since, I have been haunted by that question, that doubt." Then Elisa Montgomery opened her arms and came closer to Maya. "Please forgive me, Martha," the old woman whispered as she tried to invite her into an embrace.

All Maya could see was Grandmother opposite Elisa, waiting at the clearing for Hans, filled with love for him, hope for a new start, another chance. But instead, Elisa had intercepted the letter at the resort, had confronted Hans, had caused his stroke. She saw the horrific scene play out again in her inner eye: Elisa hitting Grandmother with her cane. The police officer's voice came back to her: *...but the second blow, probably a rock, is the one that killed her.* Maya suddenly saw them clearly in front of her: Elisa and Grandmother. Elisa's rage and frustration. The pain of unrequited love all funneled down to Grandmother in front of her. Elisa's cane came crashing down on her. And as darkness descended over the unconscious Grandmother, Elisa went for help, to hush up her horrible deed. Paula's words echoed in her mind: up until then *Edgar and Elisa had never been close.* Yes, up until he finished what his grandmother had started.

Maya pushed Elisa away and watched her coolly as she landed on the hard ground. Only one question bore itself into Maya's conscience, and she spoke it aloud. "Did my grandmother know that Hans never stopped loving her?"

Elisa stared at her, slowly nodding her head. "Yes, I told her, before—." Her voice broke off.

A certain satisfaction consumed Maya. Grandmother had died with the knowledge that she had been loved in return, all those years. Maya brushed past Elisa, crossed the clearing, and started to walk in direction of the hotel, leaving the sobbing old woman and her servant behind.

As she sipped a hot tea in the hotel lobby, waiting for Detective Melbert, Maya watched the ebb and flow of people in and out of the lobby. After everything, she felt removed from this scene, as if she wasn't here, wasn't breathing in the same air, wasn't touching the same ground. A chapter of her life had been closed. But her heart became heavy as she imagined Ben in the hotel, the way he had looked at her when she mentioned she'd stay, the way his hand had felt in hers when he had gently pushed her through the crowd into the intimacy of the hotel room, the way he had made love to her.

The friendly receptionist spotted her and was now walking over to her, her usual genuine smile on her face.

"How have you been? We've missed you!" She took in the leaves in Maya's hair, her scratched cheeks, but chose not to comment.

"Have you seen Ben, I mean, Mr. Montgomery?" Maya asked, not even trying to conceal the hope in her voice.

The receptionist smiled knowingly, not without pity. "He was here a little while ago."

The detective appeared behind the receptionist.

"Detective Melbert," she greeted him, then retreated back to the desk to give them privacy.

The detective raised his eyebrows upon noticing the state Maya was in. "I have something for you," Maya said, cutting straight to the point, holding out the letter to the detective. "I bumped into Elisa Montgomery in the woods, the same place you hiked up to a couple of days ago. I think
she is ready for a confession."

With that last statement, she walked away and out of the hotel. For the last time in her life.

The Montgomery offered her a complimentary stay, but Maya moved into a small bed-and-breakfast instead. She could have flown back home—as the door of the lobby closed behind her, so did that chapter of her life—but another chapter had begun and she wouldn't leave until she successfully closed the next one.

She started calling any nursing home within a hundred miles of Montgomery and had just ended another unsuccessful call when her cell rang. She felt excited, hoping it would be Ben, but deep down she knew that he wouldn't call.

"You're still here," Detective Melbert observed. "I wanted to thank you for the letter. The mere sight of it broke her. She confessed. And she had an accomplice. Edgar Montgomery."

His words failed to have much of an effect on her. She knew already.

"Thank you," she said.

"I hope you've found some closure. I want to thank you in the name of the State Police and my team for your help."

Maya's mind was elsewhere. "Could you do something for me?"

"What else?" he sounded crabby, as if he was disappointed that she hadn't reciprocated the gratitude.

"Can you give me the address of the nursing home?"

He sighed. "Don't you want the past to rest now? We solved the crime. Justice has been served."

"I need to pay him a visit. Tell him that my grandmother"— she had to swallow—"that she never stopped loving him."

There was silence on the line.

"Detective, I beg you. Please, can you give me the address?"

He sighed. "It's on the other side of the Hudson, close to Rhinebeck. It's called Bellevie, "Beautiful Life"; an ironic name for a nursing home, isn't it?"

Bellevie was one of the nursing homes that she had called first. They had denied that Hans was staying there.

Maya got into her car and drove over the Hudson River to

Rhinebeck. She pressed the button on the ornate gate. "This is Maya Wiesberg. I'm here to see Mr. Montgomery."

There was silence on the other line. "Nobody with that name lives here."

"Detective Melbert from the State Police gave me your address."

That helped. A buzzer went off, and she followed a long drive, lined left and right with old oak trees.

Bellevie was a beautiful building constructed in the Gilded Age by a wealthy captain of industry, then turned into a nursing home for the well-off some fifty years ago. Someone was waiting for her at the entrance.

As Maya got out of her car, the woman introduced herself as Tildy Greyser, the manager.

"You've come outside visiting hours," she said flatly.

Maya's eyes were still red from crying. "Please, I've come a very long way," Maya said.

Tildy Greyser paused for a moment and then nodded before guiding Maya through the entrance hall and up the stairs.

"We only have twenty residents here," she explained.

"It's beautiful."

"Hans Montgomery has been with us now for twenty-seven years. He's our oldest resident."

They arrived at a door, and Tildy knocked gently but didn't wait for an answer. She opened the door.

"You have fifteen minutes. Please be very gentle with him. He's not doing so well these days." She ushered Maya into the room. "I'll call the nurse who takes care of him. She'll help you communicate with him."

The bed had been moved against the window on the opposite side of the room. The man lying in the bed looked outside, into the surrounding trees.

"Mr. Montgomery?" Maya asked. She felt nervous, afraid to startle him and of how he might react.

Very slowly, the man followed the sound of her voice and

turned his head. The stroke had paralyzed one side entirely. But still, there they were: Ben's blue eyes, looking out at her from a wizened face.

Maya slowly drew closer. "Hans," she said, feeling like she knew him. His eyes opened wider, and when she was barely three feet away from his bed, he squinted. Maya stood still, holding his stare. Then his face slowly changed, contorting into a grimace as his breath accelerated. His chest started to move up and down, faster and faster, his lips started to tremble.

Maya rushed to his bed. "I am so sorry," she said.

He opened his eyes again, and she saw them, the tears, running down his cheek. He tried to smile through them, ever so slightly. Maya sat down at the side of his bed and reached for his hand. She was surprised about how natural his skin, his touch felt. As if she had known him for years.

He squeezed her hand tenderly, mumbling something over and over again.

"How lovely, Hans, you have a female visitor for once," Maya heard from behind her. "And such a pretty one!"

Maya quickly rose as a nurse approached the bed. Hans motioned for the nurse to come closer. She bent down, close to Hans's lips, only inches away as he spoke.

After a while, the nurse turned to Maya. "He calls you Martha. And he says he knew you'd come back to him one day."

Maya looked at him, her own eyes filling with tears. "No, Mr. Montgomery, I'm, I'm Maya. But I am someone who loved Martha as much as you did."

He mumbled again. He pointed at the nightstand.

"I don't understand exactly what he's telling me right now," the nurse said. Then she opened the bottom drawer of the nightstand and turned to Hans. "There's your medicine, and some of your books..."

He shook his head, vehemently pointing at the drawer.

"Okay, okay." The nurse looked at Maya. "I think your visit is upsetting him, Miss..."

"Wiesberg," she said.

Hans started to cry more, squeezing Maya's hand even more urgently. "Voddo. Voddo."

Now Maya understood. "Photo?" she said hopefully.

Yes, he nodded his head fast.

The nurse and Maya rummaged through the drawer. At first they couldn't find anything of note, but then Maya saw a corner of an old photo sticking out from behind the lining that had come lose in one corner in the back of the drawer. Maya took it out carefully and turned it over. Her grandmother's green eyes looked at her from an old photo, lovingly, longingly.

The nurse glanced between the photo and Maya, turning it over. The caption on the back read *1938, Martha Wiesberg*.

"You have a striking resemblance," the nurse said, smiling at Maya.

"I'm her granddaughter." Maya's face was lined with gentle tears. "Hans and my grandmother were lovers a long time ago."

They both looked at Hans, who only had eyes for Maya. Then he mumbled something again. The nurse leaned over again to hear him better.

She looked at Hans, then at Maya. "He's never looked happier than today." Tears shimmered in her eyes, too.

There was a knock at the door. When Maya turned, she saw Ben standing in the doorway.

"Hi, Ben." The nurse came over to him, and they kissed each other on the cheeks. Then she peeked out into the hallway. "You didn't bring Nicolas along today?"

Ben shook his head, and looked over at Maya. She quickly averted her gaze, unable to bear his disappointment again.

"Do you know this angel who came to see Hans?" She heard the nurse ask Ben. "I've never seen your grandfather happier."

"Yes, I do," he said quietly.

Maya's focused returned to Hans. He was the sole reason

for her visit, and she wanted to make the most of this moment, before Ben sent her away. Maya squeezed the old man's hand. "I just wanted to assure you that my grandmother never loved again." Hans's face didn't move an inch as she said it, but she could see the reaction in his incredible eyes. Then she bent down and kissed Hans's hand.

As she got up, she felt a soft push on her shoulders. When she turned around she saw Ben standing behind her.

"Stay, please," he said shyly.

He rounded the bed and sat down on the other side. "Grandfather, I..." he started to say, but Hans gathered the strength to lift one of his hands to interrupt Ben. Hans studied his grandson's face for what seemed minutes, then slowly turned toward Maya, as if searching for an answer to a question only he knew. And then slowly, his facial features relaxed even more, and for an instant Maya became Grandmother, seeing 'Siegfried' through her loving eyes. She watched Hans as he mustered all his strength and spoke, and Ben leaned closer to listen. For a while Maya stood there in a daze, not wanting to interfere. And then she felt Hans's hand on hers, as he took it with his right one and Ben's hand with his other and united them over his chest, as tears trickled down the sides of his face.

She felt eyes on hers. Ben's. And this time she dared to look at him. Ben's eyes were no longer filled with resentment. He looked at her the same way he had before, at the birthday party, and especially afterward.

"He..." Then Ben choked up tears. "He said that now he knows his life wasn't in vain, and that you and I are the proof that love endures, for he and Martha will live on in us."

They were standing outside, nervously shuffling their feet.

"Maya, will you be able to forgive me?" Ben finally asked.

"Now it is you asking me?" She smiled.

Ben took her hand and guided her over to one of the benches on the front porch of the nursing home.

He reached into his pocket and pulled out a letter. "This arrived at the hotel for you."

To her surprise, it was from her father.

*Dear Maya,*

*The police informed me about the murder and about what you did. I am proud of you, Maya. I looked through Grandma's old things for clues—sometimes a neurosis can be very helpful. And I found this letter. It helped me understand a lot, to find closure. Maybe it will help you, too.*

She smiled.

"Will you read it with me?" she asked Ben.

He moved closer and put his arms around her, squeezing her shoulders softly. And she knew in that instant that whatever she had come here for, she was leaving stronger. She no longer feared the memories of the past. Her fear had been replaced with hope for the future. She could start again, leave the anxiety behind. Live in the present, with the unique gift she had just received, the chance to continue Grandmother's journey. She had helped her overcome her worst fears, long after her death. She was still there for her.

Now she would see the world like Grandmother never could, love like Grandmother never could.

Grandmother's last words echoed in Maya's head: "Do for me what I couldn't." It had taken her many years to understand Grandmother's plea. And now she finally did.

*I will Grandmother,* she promised. *I will.*

# Martha
# 1990

Wolfgang's handwriting was burning in front of Martha's tear-filled eyes. He had never written a letter to her, not during their childhood, not from the front during the war. She had made peace with the past.

But now she was afraid to welcome her twin brother's words back into her life, after so much time.

She couldn't recall how long she'd been sitting in the dark room when she finally summoned the courage to read the words that had been locked away in a letter, guarded by a dead tyrant, frozen in time for forty-six years.

*Beloved sister!*

*The war is ending and it has to, as none of us can go on much longer. But it was not the war itself that corrupted us—it was the years before.*

*Martha, I am not the same person that I was when we parted. I've grown to admire you beyond words. You are the only one in our little family that truly understood, that truly saw. You were a step ahead of me, of all of us.*

*I've betrayed and deceived you.*

*As your twin, I felt your love for that man with every fiber of my being. And I couldn't bear it, for what you had was honest and pure.*

*I blamed my actions on false premises, in hindsight*

ludicrous pretexts, the regime, the honor of the family, my career, instead of being strong and truthful to myself and above all to you. I let my personal feelings cloud my judgment and, even worse, my soul.

I am aware that you will never be able to forgive me for what I did. Nor do I ask it of you. I cannot forgive myself.

I am writing to you because I feel that I will not make it to the end of the war. Part of me feels that I don't deserve to survive—not after what I've done. I want to say farewell, but not without sharing something with you first.

I know this man loves you. Have no doubt that he ever betrayed you! I betrayed the bond that you and I had.

I've only comprehended the true meaning of love through this war. Love is the key to everything. Last time I was home I hid a stash of money in the house, underneath that special bookshelf of yours. (Yes, I eventually discovered it. Go and find it, and get on a boat that will take you to him.)

You must promise me to forget the war, forget the past, and create a better present and an even better future. You must make the world make sense again after all of this madness ends.

Martha, be who you want to be. Put that beautiful mind of yours to use. Become a writer; use the money to get by. You owe it to the people. Become a traveler. Become a lover again. And find him.

I've relived that tragic moment many times. I could have helped you two get out. I have never wished more to be able to turn back time. It was a split second, a silent understanding between Mother and me, not to invite intruders, not to tell the truth, to keep you for us, and especially for Mother.

I will tell you something for which you will hate me even more, and it pains me so much when measured against how we used to be. He came back for you. When I saw him, his head was covered in bandages, but I would have recognized his blue eyes among a million men. He was brave enough to come back during the war and face me, of all people.

*Man knows no greater courage, no greater love. He, unlike me, kept his promise to you. I was home on a brief leave. You had gone to bring flowers to Father's grave—it was the anniversary of his death—and you had asked to be left alone with Father and your memories. We were all dressed in black. You had missed him by a minute.*

*So he had no doubt that what I was telling him was the truth: that you had committed suicide by taking the pill he had given you.*

*My hands are trembling as I write this, because I can only start to imagine how you must feel—and how much you must despise me right now. But this letter will still reach you in time! I betrayed my own country to make sure of that. I will tell you how one day, should you ever find it in your heart to face me again.*

*It is too late for me to undo what happened, but not too late for you!*

*His real name is Hans Montgomery. His father owns a hotel in New York.*

*If I make it out of here alive, I will help you, Martha, as God is my witness, to give you back the happiness you deserve.*

*Love always, Wolfgang*

Martha got up from her seat and walked over to the mirror. There had not been a single day that she hadn't thought of Siegfried. She came closer to the woman who was staring back at her, studying the lines and wrinkles in her face.

"Hans, Hans, Hans," she repeated, whispering his name into the dark room. He had never stopped existing. *What would you think of me if you saw me now? My fire, as you called it, died, my energy evaporated, my curiosity stilled— the minute Mother told me—lied to me about your death. But my love for you kept me alive.*

The past had just opened its door, and Hans was standing behind it, waiting for her.

# Acknowledgments

First of all, I would like to thank you, dear reader: I thought about you quite a bit while writing my first novel, and I am very grateful that you allowed me to share this story with you, a story that is very close to my heart.

I would like to thank my editor at Thomas Dunne Books, Melanie Fried, for everything: for believing in me, for keeping me on track, for helping me trim the fat of my story, for your decisive yet open mind, for sending me rays of light in the occasional darkness.

Thank you also for passing me on to Cameron Jones when moving on in your career. Cam, thank you for bringing me through to the finish line, safe and sound, your passion and positive energy.

Thank you, Janine Barlow, and all the team members at Thomas Dunne Books who I didn't get to meet directly: your work and dedication to my novel are very much appreciated.

My gratitude goes out to my incredibly talented agent and an extraordinary woman, Anna Soler Pontas. Anna, you were one of the first people who persuaded me to write my novel and who kept encouraging me throughout a process that is so easy to give up on without a strong support network around you. You have always been one of the strongest links in this network.

And another big thank you goes out to Maria Cardona, Marina Penalva, Ricard Domingo and the entire team at Pontas! Thank you for being the amazing agency that you are!

Thank you, Paul Tully. Your decades of work at the NYPD and with the FBI fueled me with bulletproof plot points during an unforgettable afternoon underneath the gable that seems to touch the sky, watching the thunderclouds rolling in over the Catskills. A spot that without a doubt provides the best views of a landscape that helped shape my plot as much you and your incredible life story with the police did.

Thank you, Dr. Gregor Kowal, for your thoughtful and occasionally hilarious insights into the human psyche, and the positive vibes you've always sent my way. Your positive spirit always kept me going!

Thank you, Grandmother Martha; may you rest in peace. It was your life story that inspired me to write this book. And thank you also for keeping this treasure of endless historical material—all the books, journals, and magazines that my parents have stored in our basement all those years... as well as that box of letters written during the war by your twin brother, Wolfgang.

Thank you to my parents-in-law, Jeannine and Martin Tully, for introducing me to the magical place that Upstate New York has become for me, and for providing me with the calm and peace I always find at your amazing home, the best writer's retreat any writer could wish for.

Also thank you to the Stone Ridge Library, for your treasure trove of books about the region, and for providing me with a place of serenity and calm to write several pages of my novel. My same gratitude goes out to the library in Bielefeld, the Stadtbibliothek Bielefeld.

Also thank you to my friends Annie Meikle, Florence Baret, and Peter Stueck for reading the draft at an early stage. To you, Annie, for traveling with me while I wrote the biggest chunk of the novel and zoned out into a different world. Thank you, Vera; I only remember your first name, but you know who you are: the lovely lady at lost and found in the Frankfurt Airport, where I'd lost my laptop on my way to a holiday in solitude to finish my novel.

Last but not least, my greatest gratitude goes out to the people whom I dedicated the novel to:

My parents, Renate and Norbert Astroth. Thank you, Mama and Papa, for your loving home, your support, for always giving me enough freedom to see the world and find what truly makes me happy (and for storing Grandmother's historical treasures, of course).

My husband, David, for who you are, for your love, faith, and pride in me. I know with certainty that without you, I wouldn't have made it past the first ten pages. You kept propelling me onward, relentlessly and unselfishly.

And thank you, dear Mae: your toothless smile always showed me — after hours of dwelling in the atrocities of the Third Reich — that everything is all right in the world. That love conquers fear.

COME VISIT US AT
WWW.LEGENDPRESS.CO.UK

FOLLOW US
@LEGEND_PRESS